The
TREASURES
of
Venice

LOUCINDA McGARY

SOURCEBOOKS CASABLANCA™
AN IMPRINT OF SOURCEBOOKS, INC.®
NAPERVILLE, ILLINOIS

Published by Sourcebooks Casablanca, an imprint of Sourcebooks, Inc.
P.O. Box 4410, Naperville, Illinois 60567-4410
(630) 961-3900
FAX: (630) 961-2168
www.sourcebooks.com

Printed and bound in the United States of America
QW 10 9 8 7 6 5 4 3 2 1

With love, I dedicate this book to the memory of:
My grandmother, Irene L. Hignite,
who told me stories and taught me to read,
and my mother, Anna M. McGary,
who took me to the library every other week and
let me bring home as many books as I could carry.
I still miss both of you every day.

Chapter 1

SAMANTHA LEWIS GAZED OVER THE NEARLY DESERTED square at the bulbous crown atop St. Mark's Cathedral. She blew across the surface of her hot caffè latte. The dull, dreary February morning matched her mood. Here she was in Venice on what should have been her honeymoon, but she was alone.

She took a sip of creamy beverage and tried to wash down the bitter taste of her failure. She still had a hard time accepting what had happened. Everything in her life had gone so well for the past ten years, just the way she'd planned and dreamed. She'd been so careful to make sure Michael Atcheson was the right guy, that he met her criteria for a stable, long-term commitment.

How could she have been so wrong?

Ending their engagement three weeks before their scheduled wedding was so unpredictable, so irresponsible, so unlike the Michael she thought she knew. He'd given her some lame excuse about not wanting to spend the rest of his life in a relationship that lacked spontaneous fun and excitement. Turned out what he had really meant was he wanted a fling with his twenty-one-year-old teaching assistant.

How had she not seen that one coming?

Determined to prove this was Michael's loss, not hers, Sam had highlighted her hair and started a new workout routine that included yoga. At least that had helped her relax, even if sleeping remained hit-and-miss, and her crying jags soon gave way to good old-fashioned indignation.

The ten-day tour of Italy had been purchased at discount and was non-refundable. At the urging of her psychologist and friend, Dr. Sandra Goldfarb, Sam went by herself.

Now here she was halfway through the tour. Even if she did feel like the odd-woman out and didn't really relate to the rest of the group, she was finally sleeping soundly. Though her dreams had become unusually vivid and seemed to take place during the Middle Ages—undoubtedly a side effect of jet lag and too many museums.

Wonderful museums and incredible sights! Dr. Goldfarb's advice had been right.

Michael was wrong.

She *was* capable of spontaneous fun and excitement. She hadn't really thought he would change his mind and join her when he found out, had she? He'd made it abundantly clear that he didn't need her and the new-and-improved Sam Lewis certainly didn't need him.

She'd repeated this litany to herself every day for the past three weeks. Maybe today she might start to believe it.

As she took another sip of the steaming brew, a flurry of movement in the corner of her vision made Sam turn her head. A dark-haired man in a black leather jacket strode purposefully across the damp, gray cobbles in her direction.

A dozen startled pigeons flapped into the air as he traversed the wide courtyard between St. Mark's and the outdoor restaurant where she sat. He wasn't exceptionally tall, maybe slightly over six feet, but his broad shoulders and narrow hips gave his stride an athlete's grace and self-assurance.

When he came closer, she could see that his hair, though cut away from his ears, spilled over the back of his collar with just enough curl to make him appear charming rather than unkempt. Then he made eye contact, and she almost dropped her cup. Such incredible blue belonged on the della Robbia Madonnas back in Florence, not on a mortal man.

She couldn't stop staring, and to her surprise, neither did he. He walked right up to her table as if they knew each other. In fact, Sam experienced this sudden eerie feeling in a far corner of her mind that she did know him.

"Hello, luv, sorry I'm late." The handsome stranger spoke with an unmistakably Irish lilt.

No way had she ever met him before; she'd definitely remember those eyes, that accent. Then he bent and kissed the air next to her right cheek in greeting, but as he moved to her left, instead of kissing, he whispered, "Play along with me, please."

His urgency surprised her even more than his bold actions. Sam pulled back and stared again into the clear sapphire depths of his eyes.

All the oxygen flew out of her lungs.

She gasped in a noisy breath. "I-I'd almost given up hope."

She had no idea where that inane statement sprang from, but she was rewarded with a wide smile as dazzling as the stranger's eyes.

"Ah, never do that, luv," he admonished, then signaled the waiter.

Feeling like she was observing the scene from outside her body, Sam watched him pull his wallet from inside his jacket and slap down a bill to pay for her half-finished drink. She'd seen plenty of men like him. He practically sported a neon sign flashing over his head: "Mr. Wrong."

His mesmerizing gaze locked on her again, and he extended his hand. "Ready to go to the Doge's Palace then?"

Dr. Goldfarb would probably tell her to go ahead. Her own mother certainly would. In almost fifty years of perpetually rash behavior with regard to men, the worst consequence Mom had ever suffered was a broken heart.

Well, Sam already had one of those, so what did she have to lose? The Doge's Palace was one of Venice's most crowded tourist attractions and all of a hundred yards away.

Throwing twenty-eight years of caution and predictability into the damp Venetian air, she grabbed his offered hand. "Sure, let's go."

That his touch was so warm in spite of the chilly temperature astonished her, but not half as much as the way the warmth seemed to seep right into her fingers and course up her arm. He felt it too. She saw the spark of bewilderment flare in the depths of his eyes in the moment it took her to rise from her chair.

Then he pulled her along, and she hurried to keep pace. They crossed the square in the direction of the Palace, which stood between the cathedral and the lagoon.

"The Wedding Cake," one guidebook called the famous structure. When she'd visited yesterday, Sam had pictured the ultramodern cake separated by translucent plastic columns Michael had convinced her to order. The pink, ornately carved Doge's Palace with stone curlicued windows bore no resemblance to that three-layered confection.

Today, all she could think about was the strange, though not unpleasant, heat sizzling up her arm. Something she never felt with Michael.

More pigeons flew up in front of them as they approached the wide swath of marble steps leading to the Palace entrance.

"You Americans are such good sports," the Irish rogue murmured as they mounted the stairs.

His unexpected comment left Sam's wits as scattered as the pigeons. Her mouth opened in surprise, but no sound came out. He dropped her hand, held the door for her, then proceeded to the cashier's window where he asked for *due biglietti, per piacere*, "two tickets, please," in what sounded like a perfect Italian accent. She continued to gape at him when he turned to hand her a ticket.

"This way." He placed his hand on the small of her back to guide her to the front staircase.

Even through her heavy coat and three layers of other clothes, Sam could feel the heat emanating from him and seeping into her. *Sexual attraction?* She stumbled on a carpeted step. *Surely not.*

He gave her a quick, questioning glance from the corner of his eye, and she suddenly realized where she'd seen him before. He'd been in her dream last night. She stumbled again on the top step.

"All right then?" he asked, his head cocked slightly to one side in a boyish gesture.

"How—" Sam took a steadying breath and changed the question. "How did you know I'm American?"

Yes, that sounded much saner than asking, "*How did you get into my dream about Renaissance Italy?*"

His head was still cocked, his grin lopsided. "Your sneakers, luv, they're a dead giveaway."

He dropped his hand and unsnapped his jacket. Sam caught a glimpse of a heavy fisherman's knit sweater before she stared self-consciously at her shoes.

"First time in Venice?"

"First time anywhere."

Maybe she was still dreaming. Hunky strangers just did not swoop into her real life. Or if they did, she'd learned better than to trust them. They were never around for long. When she looked up, he probably wouldn't be there at all.

"Came for Carnevale last week, did you?"

Okay, she had to peek.

He was still there, movie star handsome with his mussed hair and knowing azure gaze. He held open a gallery door, and she stepped inside.

"No, we only arrived yesterday. From Florence, I mean. We were there for three days."

She sounded like a flustered fourteen-year-old. Apparently her scanty knowledge of how to act with an attractive man had abandoned her along with her philandering fiancé. She could feel a blush creeping up her cheeks as they crossed the polished wooden floor.

"So, you're not traveling alone."

Was that an undertone of disappointment in his voice? No, she must be mistaken.

"I'm with a tour group. There are fourteen of them— fifteen counting me."

Sam's blush deepened as the Irish hunk's perceptive eyes made a slow trip from the toes of her shoes to the top of her head. She took one of those deep, cleansing breaths she'd learned in yoga then extended her hand.

"I'm Samantha Lewis. Most people call me Sam."

"Sam?" He frowned in a playful way. "That's no name for a pretty girl."

Rather than shaking her hand, he placed it in the crook of his arm and escorted her to a side door. The leather of his jacket felt smooth and supple under her fingers, the muscle in his forearm solid and substantial. Definitely not a dream.

"I'm Keirnan Fitzgerald from County Kildare." He opened the door and scanned the room beyond. "Though for the past nine years I've resided in your city of brotherly love."

"Philadelphia?"

"The same."

He led her to another door, and when he opened this one, Sam heard voices speaking what sounded like French. Keirnan held the door for her.

"Let's join this group, shall we?"

Together they sidled up to a cluster of elderly ladies and three men. A fiftyish man with a hawk nose gestured at a painting and spoke in rapid-fire French, then moved to the next painting and said something else. No one seemed aware of their presence.

Unfastening her coat, Sam pretended to listen carefully though she couldn't understand a word. Resting her hand on Keirnan Fitzgerald's arm felt like the most natural thing in the world. They shuffled from painting to painting, then moved into the next gallery.

How could she feel this comfortable with someone she'd only just met? *Heaven forbid! What if dear old Mom's propensity for attracting the wrong man was genetic?*

She studied him out of the corner of her eye and was struck again by a confusing sense of familiarity that raised more questions and no answers.

Slowly and unobtrusively, they traversed the second gallery. A subtle tightening of Keirnan's biceps registered inside her snarled brain. She could sense his suppressed energy gathering like coiled springs about to bounce.

Sam sneaked another peek at his profile. He looked impassive, his bright blue eyes focused straight ahead, betraying nothing. However, as they moved into a third gallery, he pressed his hand against her back.

"I've had enough of this bloody bore," he murmured close to her ear. The warmth and pressure of his hand urged her in the opposite direction of the group.

"You speak French, too?" she asked as he steered her to a roped-off staircase.

"Enough to know that guy is full of himself." He ducked under the thick velvet rope and held it up for her.

Sam glanced furtively behind them at the French tourists. Their departure seemed as unnoticed as their arrival had been. Then she looked at the coil of black velvet in his hand.

"I don't think we're supposed to go this way."

"Nah, I've been here dozens of times. It's a shortcut to the Bridge of Sighs on the exclusive Fitzgerald tour." He smiled in that endearing, lopsided way again.

A ribbon of warmth unfurled within the deep reaches of her stomach. Sam bit her lower lip for a second then ducked under and followed him up the narrow stone steps.

This was far and away the most exciting—not to mention illicit—thing she'd ever done. Now if she could just shut off that insistent voice whispering from the back of her mind about charming rapists and handsome axe murderers, it might be fun, too.

Well, they were in a public place with dozens of other people just a scream away if she needed them. A scream translated the same in any language.

A closed door blocked the top of the stairs, but it must not have been locked because Keirnan opened it after only a moment's hesitation. They emerged into another corridor right on the heels of a Japanese family—mother, father, and two bored teens. While one parent snapped photos, the other ran a camcorder to capture every millimeter.

Within moments, they all reached the Bridge of Sighs. Keirnan stepped forward and offered to take a picture of all four family members. Sam was not the least bit surprised to hear him utter some phrases in Japanese.

"Shall I take your picture, too?" he asked after the family moved on.

She gestured at the fanny pack beneath her coat. "No camera. Besides, I was just here yesterday."

He tilted his head and studied her for a long silent moment. The blue of his eyes gleamed, iridescent in the dimness of the narrow, enclosed bridge.

"You don't seem to fancy this romantic Venetian landmark."

His open scrutiny made funny flutters kick up along the nerve endings in her spine. She wished some other tourists would show up.

"I hardly think a bridge built to secretly imprison your political enemies is romantic."

His dark brows lifted in a sardonic salute. "You had an excellent tour guide yesterday."

"Actually, I'm a librarian, so I read several books before the trip."

Sam turned aside to escape the probing of his too-perceptive gaze and stared out the small square opening cut into the stone. Urban legend said during the Middle Ages prisoners got their last look at Venice through this window, and their sighs of longing gave the bridge its name. Wintry gray walls rose up on either side, and the cold, green-black water of the canal loomed far below. Nothing romantic here at all.

"He's a fool."

"Excuse me?" His sudden pronouncement caught Sam completely off guard. She turned to find the charming Irish rogue standing uncomfortably close. She took a step backward.

"Whoever 'twas that let you come to Venice alone. He's a bloody fool."

Was she that transparent? A mixture of humiliation and annoyance washed over Sam.

"Obviously." Annoyance won this round. "The trip was nonrefundable." She turned to look in the direction the Japanese tourists had disappeared. *End of story.* "Can we skip the prison section on this exclusive Fitzgerald tour?"

"Most surely. That's not exactly my favorite spot either." *Message received.* He extended his hand in what might be a peace offering. "Did you see the armory?"

The images of long pointed pikes and iron battle-axes hanging on the walls in easy grabbing distance sprang into the forefront of Sam's mind. "Uh, yes, and it's not high on my hit parade either."

Keirnan chuckled low in his throat as if he knew exactly what prompted her comment. "All right then, no prisons and no weapons. How about if I show you my favorite painting in the entire palace?" He raised his hand again, eyebrows lifted with feigned innocence.

That certainly sounded safe enough, not that she was afraid of him. Just the opposite in fact. That inexplicable feeling of familiarity continued to hover around him like an aura, if she believed in such things. And if she didn't, why did something in the depths of his sapphire eyes seem to cloud her judgment and paralyze her vocal cords?

"Okay," was all Sam could manage to say as she took his hand.

His favorite painting in the entire palace—that was the last place he needed to be taking her. Or himself, for that matter. Still, Keirnan knew better than to second-guess his seat-of-the-pants instincts. They seldom failed him in either personal or business pursuits, and the good Lord knew he could not afford to fail this time.

They walked through a large open gallery, and he slanted a sideways look at the girl beside him. Several inches shorter than he was, she was pretty in that wholesome American way he'd always found so appealing. But she wasn't empty-headed like so many others he'd been attracted to.

Oh yes, he most definitely felt attraction! The moment she'd taken his hand out in the piazza, in spite of this being the absolute worst time and place, a feeling akin to ten thousand volts of electricity pulsed into awareness inside him. Not merely sexual chemistry, something more was going on. Something Samantha sensed too.

Keirnan had watched the flickers of recognition swirl with the uncertainty and vulnerability in her lovely golden green eyes. He wasn't sure which surprised him the most, this unnatural compunction he felt to trust her when he had no business trusting anyone, or the fact that she'd gone along with him.

The painting in question was on the way out anyway. It couldn't hurt to be certain it was still there. He led the way across two smaller rooms to a flight of stairs.

His mind might be muddled, but his stirring libido knew exactly what it wanted. Without realizing what had happened, Keirnan found his hand pressed low against her back. Even in the chilly, unheated air, a warm prickly sensation flowed through him.

Down boyo! No time for tempting Americans! But his hand refused to budge as they descended the stairs.

A crowd at the foot of the second staircase finally forced him to break contact. He wove his way through the tourists with Samantha on his heels.

After a quick glance over his shoulder, Keirnan opened the door into another gallery. Deserted like he'd hoped. The rest of the palace had canvases attached firmly to the walls and ceilings. Frescoes didn't stand a chance in wet, humid Venice. The few paintings in this room were on easels. He ducked behind a rendering of Phaeton in his fiery chariot and carefully opened a door built directly into the wood paneling.

Despite the quizzical expression on her face, Samantha responded to his beckoning hand movement and slipped through the open door. He shut it quietly and scanned the four framed portraits arranged inside the small room.

"There she is." He gestured to the one on the far end. "What do you think of her?"

Samantha brushed past him to study the painting of the young woman. He didn't need to look. The picture was as familiar to him as any likeness of a family member.

The girl was painted in profile; her golden brown hair hung in ringlets next to her pale cheek and was swept up into a net of pearls at the back of her head. A choker of twisted pearls adorned her slender neck, and more pearls decorated the ornate gold and black sleeve of her Renaissance gown.

"She's lovely," Samantha murmured. "Who's the artist? It looks too early for Tintoretto. Titian maybe?"

So the lady knows something about art. Now more than his libido was engaged.

"Actually this is earlier than Titian too, around 1485."

Keirnan moved to stand behind her. Glancing down at the familiar portrait made him realize that Samantha's hair was the same shade of burnished gold. Maybe that had triggered the unusual feelings he experienced whenever he looked at her: unexplained twinges like the ones currently bouncing across his nervous system.

He cleared his throat and his thoughts. "The artist is unknown, but the girl's name was Serafina Lombardo."

"From a rich Venetian family, obviously."

Samantha turned, and her golden green gaze collided with his. His pulse stuttered unexpectedly.

He nodded. *Couldn't hurt to tell her a piece of trivia. Wasn't like he'd ever see her again.* His pulsed stumbled a second time.

Ignoring it, he asked, "Ever hear of *The Jewels of the Madonna*?"

"It's an opera isn't it?"

"A music buff, too. I'm quite impressed." Surprisingly so. "Did you know the plot of *The Jewels of the Madonna* was inspired by a real story?"

Samantha's expressive eyes told him she was interested. That gave him a nudge of self-satisfaction.

In for a penny, in for a pound, his sister always said. More than his pulse reacted to that inadvertent recollection.

Keirnan reined himself in sharply. Making sure his tone was light, he gestured at the painting. "Some people believe the opera was based on her life."

"Well, I hate to disappoint you, but I've never seen the opera, and I don't know the story." Samantha surveyed the portrait once again. "But considering most operas end tragically, that must be why she's not smiling."

Venice, 1485

The side door of the church opened, and an angel stepped inside. Nino Andriotto dropped his trowel in awe.

The clank of the hardwood on the marble floor of the chapel made the beautiful vision jerk her head in his direction. No angel after all, but no mere mortal either. She was the girl in Fredo's sketches.

Her wealthy family had commissioned his roommate and best friend to paint her portrait. Her beauty, even in simple line drawings, had stirred Nino's mind to flights of fancy such as he'd never experienced in all his twenty years.

The object of his most secret desires now hesitated in the side vestibule, her pale brows drawn in anxiety. "Forgive me. I didn't mean to intrude." Her voice sounded soft and delicate, the same way she looked.

Pulse hammering, Nino jumped from his waisthigh perch and stooped to retrieve his trowel. "Oh no, milady."

He doffed his dusty cap and did a quick half-bow, his gaze catching on the smears of plaster and glaze on his apron and shirtsleeves. Between the workday grime and the badly sewn patches on his hose, he presented a shabby contrast to the lady's elegant green damask gown and the matching lace-edged shawl draped lightly over her golden brown hair.

"'Tis I who should apologize for disturbing you. I came to work here this morning because few visit the cemetery isle so early." After taking a deep breath, Nino dared to raise his head and motioned to the large ceramic medallions behind him. "The Holy Fathers commissioned me to decorate this chapel of the church before Easter."

As she gazed at his work, he saw admiration then recognition chase across her porcelain features. "Oh, you must be the Florentine who studied under della Robbia."

Nino blushed a bit with pride. "Yes, Luca della Robbia was my old master." The admission emboldened him enough to add, "I'm Nino—I mean Antonino Andriotto. And you are the Signorina Lombardo."

She looked startled by his unexpected declaration and blushed prettily in her turn. "I didn't know we had met."

"We haven't." He dropped his eyes in embarrassment. "Forgive me for being bold. My fellow artist Alfredo Rosso is painting your portrait, and I recognize you from his sketches."

He could see her fingers toying with the folds of her gown.

"Oh, the portrait…"

Her tone made Nino lift his head. A cloud seemed to have settled over her velvety brown eyes.

"Fredo has much skill." He rushed to reassure her. "I'm sure you will be most pleased with the result, milady."

Obviously lost in her own thoughts, she looked away toward the main altar of the church. "It's a gift for the man who intends to marry me, the Viscount Treviso."

The idea of her married and him with nothing but his fanciful imaginings made Nino's heart plummet, though he could not honestly say he was surprised. He started to murmur an appropriate nicety, but she spoke again very low, her head still turned away.

"My sister's husband."

"Your sister, milady?"

His inquiry made her turn back to face him. Her beautiful features looked as lifeless as a *Carnevale* mask.

"My sister died on Ash Wednesday. I came this morning to lay flowers on her tomb and pray for her soul."

Nino twisted his hat into a dusty knot, abashed. "My most sincere condolences."

From beneath her composed façade, he could feel her sorrow and wished to placate it. "Let me clear away my things so that you can pray here in the Chapel of St. Anne. I insist." Nor did he want to leave her alone with her grief, which somehow did not seem the right thing to do. "And if 'twould not be unseemly, may I pray with you?"

His request restored life to her face. "You are most kind, sir."

She laid a tenuous hand upon his arm, her touch burning through the rough wool of his sleeve like a live cinder.

"Call me Nino," he blurted.

She did not draw her hand away. "Only if you call me Serafina." His face must have betrayed his shock, for she hastened to add, "My family is not of noble birth. My father is an artisan, same as yourself."

"Hardly the same, milady. The city's finest architect should not be compared to a mere sculptor of clay."

"Not a mere sculptor." She reached up and touched the bright blue glaze on the medallion he'd just fastened to the wall. "One with della Robbia's secrets of color. None other in Venice possesses such knowledge, Nino."

His name on her lips was surely the most beautiful sound he had ever heard. His own voice abandoned him. Unable to argue or even express thanks for her compliment, Nino picked up his tool case and step stool and placed them at the chapel entrance. Heart still pounding loud in his ears, he dropped his soiled apron on top of his case and pulled his doublet on over his shirt.

When he turned around, she had passed him and held two slim white tapers in her hand. She extended one to him.

"Thank you…"

"Serafina," she prompted, her velvety gaze no longer sorrowful. In fact, a slight upturn played at the edges of her lips.

"Serafina." His voice was a whisper, proper for such a solemn benediction.

Nino lit his candle from the same illuminate then placed it next to hers before the bronze likeness of the saint. He bowed his head as she did, but after a brief moment, he glanced sidelong at her.

Dark blonde lashes rested atop her flawless cheeks, and her rosebud lips moved in soundless prayer. The polished rosary beads slipped through her dainty fingers. She rivaled any holy vision he had ever imagined, but the feelings swirling through his body were far removed from holy.

Even though he was supposed to be praying for the soul of her recently departed sister, the only thing that sprang to Nino's mind was a fervent hope that this was not a dream. Or if it was, that he might never awaken.

Serafina felt the smooth rosewood slide through her fingers as she soundlessly mouthed the words of the familiar prayer she had repeated countless times. Only this morning, the litany was not working. After a few soothing minutes, images jumped across her mind in a bizarre dance.

Her sister, Simonetta, laughing and happy, then doubled over in pain. Simonetta lying in bed, her face more white than the linen bedclothes. Father Giancarlo delivering the last rites as her sister's blood left dark crimson stains just below the spot where Serafina clutched her cold, lifeless hand. The pale marble sarcophagus with her sister's name and likeness carved on the lid.

A tear leaked from the corner of her eye, eased its way onto her cheek then slid onto the edge of her lip. Before she could stop it, a weak sob fluttered up her throat, and two more tears followed the path of the first.

Mortified, Serafina dabbed at her face with the edge of her shawl. The handsome young sculptor touched her arm, and she opened her eyes into his worried gaze—a gaze as wondrously blue as the background of his trumpeting angel medallions.

Her breath momentarily caught in her throat. His hand felt warm and comforting, and a sudden urge to throw herself into his arms and weep seized her.

No! She had already been far too familiar with this stranger. Her mother would be beside herself if she found out. Serafina could hear her scolding voice sternly reminding that no matter his talent, this young man was far below her social station. Such things were of the utmost importance to her mother and father. As their only surviving daughter, she could not disgrace herself further.

"Please don't cry, milady, for surely your sister rests in a better place now."

The concern in his soft voice sounded genuine, caring. Her intentions wavered like the flickering candle flames.

"Oh, Nino, I don't deserve your sympathy," she admitted, dropping her rosary back into the pocket of her gown. "I weep for myself, not my poor sister. I'm a selfish monster who fears ending up like her."

"You are hardly selfish and far from a monster."

His rough thumb rubbed away yet another tear trailing down her cheek. His touch was surprisingly gentle and made a ribbon of warmth wind through her.

"Few of us seek death, even though he always finds us."

"'Tis marriage I do not seek, to the Viscount, nor any other man." She turned away from the warmth of his touch, unwilling to look any longer into the confusing depths of his beautiful eyes. "I-I want to enter a holy order."

She had believed that to be the best alternative to her dilemma, the only one open to her.

"Does your family know of your wish?"

They knew and had even been mildly supportive once. That now seemed a lifetime ago. Her marriage was merely another lucrative business arrangement for her father, especially since the Viscount was of noble birth.

Serafina pulled her feelings into submission and tried to sound as matter-of-fact as her father when he had told her the news.

"My wishes do not matter. An agreement was made between the Viscount and my father. The Viscount needs an heir. Since my sister did not fulfill her part of the bargain, the responsibility falls to me."

Nino had no reply, nor did she expect him to. She envied him for his more simple life. He didn't have to suffer under the social restrictions and expectations of her father's wealth and status. But she did.

"Please forgive me." She bit her bottom lip in frustration. "I should not have spoken and acted so rashly to you. It's just that I… I don't know why, but I feel as if I can trust you."

As unlikely as it sounded, that was the truth. From

the moment she had spoken and he answered so courte-ously, when she looked into the depths of his sea-blue eyes, Serafina knew she could trust him—with her very life if need be. Such strange thoughts were unsettling.

"I need to go… to let you finish your work."

"I've plenty of time. Easter is almost a fortnight still."

He blocked her path, standing tall and straight-limbed in the chapel entrance. The sight of his muscular body and handsome face caused her breath to catch in her suddenly dry throat.

"Can I take you back to the city? I've a skiff at the dock."

She licked her parched lips and forced words out. "No, thank you…" But he looked so crestfallen she gulped in a large draught of air and rushed to explain. "I've a boatman waiting for me."

"Then at least let me walk with you to the dock."

Unable to deny the entreaty in his beautiful eyes, Serafina nodded.

Silently, they walked out the front doors of the church and quickly covered the short distance to the shore where a half-dozen wooden docks fanned out into the lagoon. Mist still hung low over the water, refusing to be banished by the weak winter sun. Across the way, Venice looked not at all serene, but inhospi-tably cold, and far less inviting than the tomb-encrusted cemetery isle.

Serafina hugged her shawl more closely around her and wished she could stay here with the engaging young sculptor who stirred such a confusing mix of unknown emotions within her. But she saw her father's trusted old servant huddled in the stern of the gondola, the collar of his coat turned up against the damp chill. He took a sip from the leather flask he wasn't supposed to carry, then seeing her, started to stand.

"No, Umberto, I'll be right there," she called, and he sat back down and took another nip, knowing his secret was safe with her.

Beside her, Nino pulled off his cap and sketched a slight bow of farewell. Tiny droplets of mist clung to the unruly dark curls that lay scattered across his forehead, while his blue eyes shone with compassion, kindness, and something more.

Impulsively, she grasped his arm. "I shall be posing for your friend Signor Rosso tomorrow afternoon. Say you will accompany him to my house." She felt almost as startled by her sudden request as he looked.

"I don't think your father would—"

"My father will not be at home, and my mother won't mind since the dressmaker will be there at the same time."

Now that she had spoken, Serafina realized how very much she did want to see him again. She gave his arm a slight squeeze. "Please?"

"I…" He still looked and sounded surprised, but not unpleasantly so. A hint of a blush stained his finely chiseled cheekbones. "All right, if that is your wish… Serafina."

She found his hesitation over her name endearing. So much so that she smiled, a rarity for her these days.

"I wish it very much." She gave his arm another squeeze then turned to climb the three plank steps onto the dock. "Until the morrow, Nino."

Chapter 2

A RUSTLING SOUND STARTLED SAM, AND SHE SNAPPED her gaze from the strangely compelling portrait of the young woman to Keirnan. He raised a silencing finger to his lips then moved between her and the door.

After a long, tense moment, she chanced a whisper. "We're not supposed to be in here, are we?"

"Technically, no." His voice was a whisper too.

He moved quietly to the door and opened it a crack. After another long moment, he motioned for her to exit.

"But we can always pretend to be dumb American tourists who got lost."

Sam's spine stiffened, both her old and new self taking umbrage. "Is that why you came up to me in the square, because I looked like a dumb American tourist?"

"No, don't be silly." Keirnan ran his hand across the front of his dark hair, then closed the door behind them. "I mean, I could see you were American…"

He turned and crossed to the door that led to the outer corridor. Sam scowled her most imperious librarian glare. He shrugged with one shoulder.

"I went with my gut instinct."

She refused to let him skate by with a nonexplanation. "Enough with this cloak-and-dagger stuff. I've played along with you for an hour, and even though you seem to speak multiple languages, I can't quite believe you're a spy."

Apparently he was immune to authoritative scowls because he ushered her into the hall, grinning. "Nothing as glamorous as that. I sell and lease commercial real estate. Helps to know some key phrases."

Sam felt a twinge of disappointment at his admission to being a mortal man after all. She needed to stop watching so many movies. However, when the door shut behind them, she remembered the urgency in his voice back in the square.

Determined to get some answers, she crossed her arms over her chest. "Okay, but I don't believe all you wanted was to drag someone into the Doge's Palace to talk about paintings."

He scanned the empty corridor and sighed. "All right, I understand your curiosity. I really do. The thing is…" He shifted from foot to foot as if weighing his options. "I was being followed, and I figured the easiest way to dodge them was to make them think they had the wrong guy."

Wrong guy, indeed. No matter what kinds of strange and exciting feelings he elicited inside her, Sam knew beyond a doubt Keirnan Fitzgerald would meet none of her long-term commitment criteria. Not that she would even consider looking again so soon.

"So meeting a woman in St. Mark's Square and taking her into the Doge's Palace was a way to lose your tail?" She definitely watched way too many movies, and worse yet, she blurted out the next thought that leaped across her mind. "Please don't tell me you're a thief who's coming back later to steal these paintings."

Keirnan clutched at his chest in mock horror. "Samantha, you wound me with such aspersions! I assure you, I am not a thief."

Sam felt a little embarrassed, yet recognized the diversion. "Then who was following you?"

He pressed his lips together into a tight line and guided her toward the stairs before he finally admitted, "I'm not exactly sure."

She wasn't buying that line either. "But you have a pretty good idea, don't you?"

When he didn't answer, Sam paused at the foot of the staircase. He darn well owed her a few answers!

"So if you're not a spy or a thief, why are you being followed, and how do you know your way around this place so well?"

Perhaps gauging her resolve, his bright blue gaze made another of those disturbing sweeps from her head to her toes.

When he spoke, his tone was casual. "As for that last bit, I spent more than one summer holiday here when I was a student." His hand pressed against her back again and urged her up the stairs. "I even led a few real English language tours one year."

His touch made that strange heat spiral through her even more strongly, like her body was mocking her good sense.

"As for why I'm being followed…" He paused, and the lightness in his voice suddenly sounded forced. "Suffice it to say that likely involves a delicate situation with a lady."

Duh! He was handsome and charming—of course a woman was involved. Sam wanted to smack herself for being so dense. Or smack him. That had merit.

Some woman's husband was probably following him, or maybe his own wife had hired someone. Just because he didn't wear a wedding ring meant nothing. With his heart-stopping smile and incredible baby-blues, it must be easy for him to make women forget about their husbands.

They reached the top of the staircase, and Sam saw they were very near the exit. She glanced at her watch, and Keirnan cleared his throat to break the uncomfortable silence.

"I hope I haven't caused you to miss anything with your tour group."

"No, we're catching the two o'clock ferry to Murano after we have lunch at the hotel."

Oops! Too much information!

That heat emanating from his hand really did impair her brain function. She sidestepped to break contact.

"Ah, the isle of the glass blowers." He captured her hand, tucked it into the crook of his arm, then strolled toward the exit. "That stuff is terribly overpriced, you know."

"So I've read."

Sam noticed they would reach the door with a large group of people, and she didn't believe for a moment that was a coincidence. *Just in case he hadn't shaken whomever.* She tried to pull her hand away, but he pressed it back.

"At least let me walk you to your hotel."

No way, Jose!

"Okay."

Good grief! Had all this spontaneous excitement also severed the link between her brain and her vocal chords? Or had she truly inherited a defective gene from her mother?

Sam tried to calm her panic with the rationale that she

would not, under any circumstances, tell him her room number. Fortunately, her group was leaving tomorrow evening on the night train for Rome.

"It's the Albergo Bello Giardino, not far from the Rialto Bridge."

Her distrust was palpable, and worse, actually bothered him. What else could account for that funny little stab at his conscience? The one that had accompanied the look of disappointment in her golden green eyes when she assumed this was all about an illicit affair.

Well, far better if she did think that. Only his blasted conscience continued to sting like a sliver in a fingertip. Next thing he'd be going to confession.

Keirnan forced himself to amble at a leisurely pace in the midst of the large group of people for several minutes. The undercurrent of unease twisted deep in his gut, making him feel like he should rush. But to where, and to do what?

Ah, there's the rub, boyo.

Patience had never been his long suit.

The shops along the Mercerie were closing for their midday break, the sun shone weakly through the high fog, and a gull cried out overhead. "La Serenissima," Venice's longtime nickname, seemed bitterly ironic to him today, though the damp, salt-tinged air and the gleaming marble facades of the buildings appeared serene enough.

He glanced sidelong at Samantha and felt the tug of attraction followed immediately by another annoying prickle of conscience. He usually suffered no such qualms when it came to pretty girls. But then he'd never been in such an untenable situation.

Keirnan willed himself to relax, go with the flow. Maybe some small talk would ease her uncertainty. "Been to the Academia yet?"

Samantha nodded, still looking preoccupied. "Yesterday. My favorite paintings were the Venetian street scenes."

"Mine too." This strange, ever-increasing feeling of connection to her was quite uncanny. "All those saints and angels get rather repetitious after a while, enough to put a person on fat cherub overload."

She rewarded his flippant remark with a throaty chuckle, and the first real smile he'd seen. Her features lit up, and she looked even more appealing. Too bad this pleasant little interlude was almost over.

"I know what you mean," she said. Then regrettably, the smile was gone.

"What about the Guggenheim?"

The crowd had thinned to just a few people. Keirnan steered her off the main thoroughfare onto a side street. "Not a fat cherub in sight there."

"I don't really like modern art all that much," Samantha admitted as they crossed a piazzetta with its fifteenth-century carved stone wellhead still in the center. A pair of pigeons courted on top of it, oblivious to their passing.

"You should go there anyway just to see the building. It's one of the prettiest palazzos on the Grand Canal."

When they climbed a small iron bridge over a narrow canal, the sounds of outboard motors cut through the quiet surroundings. Keirnan could just make out the peaked white top of the Rialto Bridge ahead on the left.

"I'll try to get there if I have time."

She stopped abruptly and pulled her hand away. Keirnan followed her gaze across the street where white letters on a green cloth awning proclaimed "*Bello Giardino*." Window boxes filled with pink and yellow primroses decorated the front of the four-story hotel.

"Looks like we're here."

His libido suddenly overrode his conscience and urged him to do more than walk away. *Impossibly bad timing!* He fought back the urge.

"Thank you again for being such a good sport, Samantha."

When had he raised his hand? But he must have because it was poised next to her face. Of their own volition, his fingers cupped her cheek. Her smooth skin felt overheated in the cool air. Those ten thousand volts sizzled up his arm and made his pulse hammer.

"And I meant what I said back there on the Bridge of Sighs. He's a fool. You're better off without him." *And me.*

Though shock flickered across her expressive eyes, she said nothing, the tip of her tongue moistening her bottom lip. His hand moved from her cheek to cradle the back of her head, the silky strands of her hair flowing over and through his fingers. He lowered his head and slanted his mouth across hers, his own tongue lightly following the path of hers.

She tasted warm and sweet. But without warning, the painted image of Serafina Lombardo flashed behind his closed eyes.

Saints in heaven, he was losing it! Keirnan pulled back and dropped his hand, but instead of releasing her as he'd intended, he grasped her hand and raised it toward his mouth.

"Take care, Samantha, luv," he murmured and pressed his lips lightly against her palm.

Blood roared in his ears, but somehow he managed to let go before he made an even bigger and far stupider blunder. He forced himself to take a step away.

"Keirnan."

He froze in mid-stride. Slowly he turned and saw she hadn't moved. In fact she looked rooted to the spot.

...then move not, while my prayer's effect I take...

Keirnan didn't see her bright, down-filled parka, her jeans, and sneakers. Instead the image of Serafina Lombardo, lovely as any Renaissance Madonna, superimposed itself over Samantha's features. He dashed the back of his hand across his eyes, and the image disappeared.

Once again it was Samantha who regarded him. Sorrow clouded her eyes as her lips parted. "I hope she's worth it."

Her words snapped him fully back to reality, brought a small wry grin. "Oh, she is."

He spun on his heel and strode away in the direction of the Rialto Bridge.

Sam stared at his retreating figure for a full minute, too dumbfounded by both his and her own audacity to move. Her heart, which was supposed to be broken, threatened to pound out of her chest. Her lips and hand tingled from his touch.

Had she actually let him kiss her?

What in the world had possessed her to act so

recklessly? Only being kissed by Keirnan Fitzgerald hadn't felt the least bit reckless. It had felt oddly familiar, as if they were somehow destined to be together.

She bit her lip and shook her head in disbelief. How many times had she heard her mother impulsively gush about her newest boyfriend and how they were just meant to be?

Wrong! Wrong! Wrong!

Charming Mr. Fitzgerald already had someone. Someone he felt was worth the risks and hassles she was obviously putting him through.

Well, that was his problem, not hers. So why was a niggling worm of regret burrowing in the far corner of her mind? She took a deep yoga breath, blew it noisily out through her mouth, then turned and went inside the hotel.

Twenty minutes later, with a warm foccacia bread sandwich in front of her, the whole episode took on an unreal quality, like her weird dreams about the Italian Renaissance. This would be a great story to recount someday. Dr. Goldfarb would love to hear how she'd nearly had a fling with an Irish gigolo-spy-art thief.

Someday, when picturing his sapphire eyes and gleaming smile didn't kick up that funny little flutter in her stomach.

At a quarter before two, Sam met with the other members of her group and their Venetian guide, Paolo. Presently, their square tugboat-looking vessel lurched and sputtered across the lagoon to Murano, where they toured a glassblowing factory.

Most of the trinkets looked alike, except for one glass paperweight, a clear dome the size of Sam's fist that sported a border in the traditional colorful millefiori pattern. However, the center contained a single blue flower the exact shade of Keirnan Fitzgerald's eyes. Though it cost twice what she would have paid at home in Bloomington, she bought it anyway.

Back in Venice, Paolo offered to take the group on a pub crawl after dinner to celebrate their last night in his city. Sam had been so jet lagged in Florence that she hadn't done anything after hours, but since this was a chance for more spontaneous fun and adventure, she decided to go along, determined to have a good time. Finally, just before midnight, feeling slightly tipsy if not exactly cheery, she left the group and made her way back to the hotel.

Perhaps she wasn't entirely over jet lag yet because she clutched the handrail all the way up both flights of stairs. Elevators were a rarity in Italian hotels, it seemed.

The moment she pushed open her room's door she knew something wasn't right. It was the warm air—too warm. She hadn't left the radiator on, she was sure.

She hit the light switch, and that's when she saw someone sitting in the armchair opposite the bed. Before she could think, she sucked her breath in sharply.

"Samantha, luv?" The blanket-swathed figure rose slowly. "Please don't scream or carry on. 'Tis only me."

"Keirnan?"

The door clicked shut behind her. The package with the glass paperweight slipped from her suddenly numb grasp.

"Yes, and I—" He flinched at the thunk of the bag hitting the floor, then seemed to sway as if in a strong wind. "I'm afraid I need your help again."

"How did you get in here?" Her tone bordered on shrill.

Oh my God, maybe he really was a maniac!

Except why was he leaning and clutching the arm of the chair?

"I'm terribly sorry…" His voice sounded weak, but his knees must have been weaker for he slid back into the chair, hard.

Fear momentarily forgotten, Sam spoke and moved automatically. "Keirnan, what's wrong?"

She found herself bending over him. Surprisingly, the smell of alcohol was absent, but a repugnant musty odor with a metallic edge hung in the air.

"If I could just stay here awhile." His voice shook and seemed oddly strained. His face looked deathly pale under the dark stubble of five o'clock shadow, and his imploring eyes were dull, almost opaque. "Until my clothes dry out."

Sam glanced at the steaming, malodorous heap on the radiator. "What happened?"

"Fell into the canal." He attempted to sound light, but when she reached for the dripping clothes he gasped. "No! Don't—"

Too late.

She'd already picked up the heavy fisherman's knit sweater. Her eyes widened in horror at the gaping hole with the rusty red stain.

"My God, Keirnan, you're hurt!"

Her own knees threatened to buckle as new fear came roaring to life. Head spinning, Sam edged her way over to sit on the bed.

"Just a scratch." He held up one hand to ward her off,

while he clutched the blanket tight around him with the other. "'Tis nothing."

She seriously doubted his claim.

Taking several deep breaths to calm her quaking nerves, she leaned toward him. "Let me see. Are you still bleeding?"

Her old childhood habit of wanting to fix things surged to the forefront. Besides her beloved books, Sam's favorite toys had been a plastic doctor bag and a miniature tool kit. Only this wasn't a broken doll or an injured bird.

"Do you need a doctor?"

"No! No doctor!"

The sudden force of his words made her jump. His expression became visibly contrite. He swallowed with difficulty.

"I'll be fine." Before she could protest, he rushed to add, "No, really, I've stopped bleeding. I bandaged it with one of those oversized napkins the Italians call a towel."

Sam still wasn't convinced, but his voice sounded more normal and some color seemed to have leaked back into his face.

She would take a different tack then. "Tell me what happened."

He hesitated, obviously not liking this line of questioning either. Shoving aside her concern, she gave him the imperious librarian glare, and he shifted uncomfortably. "I, uh, had a disagreement with a couple of fellows over my wallet. Didn't realize one had a knife 'til it was too late. I jumped out of the way and went right into the drink. Guess I didn't jump quite fast enough."

"Guess not." She didn't believe him for a minute. Arms crossed over her chest, she continued to glare. "So why didn't you go to the police?"

Keirnan shifted again, like a naughty schoolboy caught in the act. "Well, I do still have my wallet, and on a Saturday night, I'd probably sit in the police station for at least three hours freezing my wet arse off."

He sighed heavily and shivered. Maybe just for effect, Sam couldn't be sure.

"My hotel is clear out by the airport. I'll have to take the train or a taxi. So if I could just wait here until my clothes dry out a bit?"

His story had more holes than his sweater, which wouldn't dry for a week. Still, he looked a long way from the "fine" he purported. She doubted he could make it down the two flights of stairs to the lobby. Matter of fact, she wasn't sure he could walk at all.

Panic blossomed somewhere behind her sternum, the insidious tendrils creeping up toward her throat. Sam quashed it back down. The knife obviously hadn't punctured a lung or anything else vital, or he wouldn't be talking. Maybe the wound really wasn't all that bad, and she could send him on his way, wet clothes and all. Or if it was that bad, she would call a doctor.

Only one way to find out.

She took a deep fortifying breath and stood up. "Well, at least let me put some antiseptic on you. Heaven knows what you'll catch from that filthy canal water."

He didn't look happy; however, he also didn't protest when she walked toward the bathroom. She picked up the bag with the paperweight and deposited it on top of the bureau on the way.

Inside the bathroom, Keirnan's wet leather jacket hung over the shower curtain pole, a gaping hole in the side just like his sweater.

That pesky bloom of panic reappeared. *What kind of knife sliced right through leather, knitted wool, and flesh?* Sam didn't want to know. This was way more excitement and adventure than she ever wanted to have.

Suppressing apprehension, she fished around in her cosmetic bag until she found the only first aid supplies she carried, a tube of antibiotic cream and a half-dozen adhesive bandages. Judging from the size of the hole in his jacket, she had the sinking feeling they were going to be woefully inadequate to treat his so-called scratch.

Squaring her shoulders for battle, she marched out and turned on the bedside lamp so she could see more clearly.

Did every hotel room in Italy have ten-watt light bulbs?

Clutching the tube and bandages in her left hand, Sam knelt in front of the chair. Keirnan watched her warily, his breathing shallow and fast like a cornered animal. Suddenly, she realized he probably had nothing on under the blanket. All at once, her breathing became shallow and fast too.

"Are you—I mean, do you—"

Come on, Sam, you've seen a naked man before.

He twitched the blanket open just enough for her to see the white cotton of the towel. They really were ridiculously small—the towels!

She squeezed her eyes shut for a moment then slowly forced them back open.

Concentrate! You can do this.

He had ripped the material lengthwise and tied

it around his upper ribs. From the little she could see, reddish blotches stained the thickest part. *Not a good sign.*

Sam rocked back on her heels, not meeting his gaze.

"I can't reach it like this. You need to get on the bed."

She rose quickly and turned aside. Staring at the heavy brown drapes covering the window, she dug the fingernails of her right hand into her palm and summoned her haughtiest librarian voice.

"Now. Go on."

Consciously relaxing her fist, Sam tried unsuccessfully to focus on that "happy place" her yoga instructor was always touting. She heard Keirnan groan, make some rustling noises, and groan again.

Pressing her lips together, she hesitantly turned around. He'd stretched himself into a reclining position, his head and shoulders resting against the wooden headboard. The blanket was discretely adjusted so that his shoulders and half his chest were uncovered.

"Will this do, then?" His tone held a sharp edge, and tight lines bracketed his mouth. His eyes were squeezed shut.

Sam's gaze moved away from his face, and the air slammed out of her lungs. So much for "seen one, seen 'em all."

More than Keirnan Fitzgerald's eyes were heavenly. Not an ounce of fat was visible anywhere, and the thick cord of muscle between his shoulders and neck reminded Sam of Michelangelo's *David* that she'd seen in Florence's Academia Museum two days ago.

"Yes, fine," she squeaked, thankful his eyes were closed.

Her disdainful librarian had vanished right along with
that yoga happy place.

Unable to trust her wobbly legs another moment, she
sat gingerly on the bed beside him and reached for the
makeshift bandage.

It was stuck. He sucked in his breath sharply when
she tried to jiggle it loose.

"Saints in heaven, woman," he hissed, eyes still
tightly shut. "Be quick about it!"

Obediently, she gave a swift tug, whimpering in
sympathy at the same time. The fabric came away,
revealing a four-inch slash. About half of the crusty,
still-forming scab leaked blood. Fortunately she'd never
been squeamish; nonetheless, Sam quickly pressed the
towel back into place.

Keirnan sucked in more breath. Long tense moments
ticked by before he slowly eased the air out.

She cast about for the remnants of her courage,
finally finding enough to speak. "This probably
needs stitches."

He slit open one eye just enough to glower at her.
"Not if you leave it alone."

Her leave him alone?

"Oh, right! You sneak into my hotel room in the
middle of the night, and I'm supposed to let you sit in
the armchair wet, cold, and bleeding."

He flinched like she'd struck him.

"Sorry, I…" He opened his eyes, and Sam saw both
pain and regret swirling in their depths. "I just couldn't
think what to do."

"I guess being stabbed does that."

She carefully moved the towel. The bleeding appeared

to have stopped. Though ugly, the gash wasn't as bad as she had feared. Not as good as she'd hoped either. She had no idea how much blood he might have lost. But he didn't appear to need a doctor's immediate attention, and he certainly didn't want it.

With grim resolve, she opened the tube of antiseptic.

"How did you find me anyway?"

"Wasn't hard."

Keirnan stiffened and caught his breath when she rubbed cream around the edges of the wound. The feel of his bare skin under her fingertips made Sam's mouth go abruptly dry. They were both breathing quick and shallow again.

He was in pain. What was her excuse?

She chewed her bottom lip and tried to think about something else. Nothing came to mind.

He stifled a groan.

Maybe if she kept him talking, it would take his mind off the injury.

"Really? Enlighten me." Okay, not just his mind. And maybe not just his knife wound either. "And try telling the truth this time."

She rubbed on more of the antiseptic, while he closed his eyes and held his breath. She held hers too.

Just when she thought he wasn't going to tell her, he spoke. "After I crawled out of the water, I must have wandered a bit. Shock, I suppose."

He opened his eyes and took another unsteady breath. "When I realized where I was, I came over the back wall into the courtyard. Where a couple of tables and flowerpots are?" She nodded, and he continued. "A boy around ten, American, was playing by himself.

I asked if he knew you, and he said he did—Ow! Have a care!"

"Sorry." Sam put down the empty tube and peeled the paper off a bandage. "Then what?"

"I gave him a clump of primroses I'd picked from one of the pots." Keirnan's voice wavered a little, and he swallowed convulsively when she stuck on another bandage. "Told him I'd fallen into the canal and couldn't wait for you. Would he leave the flowers at your door?"

He paused and so did she, giving him a "go on" look.

"'Twas a simple matter to follow him up then find the flowers."

"Very clever." Maybe she needed to reconsider her original conclusion that he was a thief. Carefully, she placed the last adhesive strip across the gash. "Only my door was locked."

"Well…"

Sam felt his diaphragm muscles stiffen just before she pulled her hands away. He broke eye contact for a moment.

When he looked at her again, he'd transformed back into his charming rogue persona. "I've always had a way with doors."

More than doors, mister. He could probably sell an ice floe to a Tlinget—a female tribe member, anyway.

She picked up the remnants of the bloody, ripped towel, the empty antiseptic tube, and the pieces of paper from the bandages, then stood up.

Keirnan glanced down and surveyed her handiwork, tried to shift his position, and stifled another groan. "Bugger hurts like the devil himself. Have any aspirin?"

"No. No aspirin until we're sure you've stopped bleeding."

She walked into the bathroom, dumped everything into the trash can, and washed her hands. Glancing into the mirror, she saw him struggling to sit up.

"Stop that moving around, or you'll start bleeding for sure!"

Now what?

If he knew anyone else in Venice, he certainly wouldn't have turned up in her room, would he? So what about the lady who was worth it? And whoever was following him? Had they stabbed him? Was the lady involved? Was that why he wouldn't go to the police or a doctor?

Sam's temples throbbed with the swirling questions. Questions she felt sure Keirnan Fitzgerald would not answer. At least not truthfully. Still, she knew she couldn't turn him out in the wee hours of a chilly winter morning in soaking wet clothes. *If* he could even get to the front door without collapsing...

All right, that settled that.

She switched off the bathroom light, walked back into the bedroom, and hit the overhead switch. Keirnan had pulled the blanket up around his neck and watched her like a contrite child.

Sam looked into his dark sapphire eyes, and a sliver of warmth tingled down her spine. Not fear, suspicion, or anything scary, the feeling was more like longing.

"Try to get some rest."

She pulled the edge of the comforter from the far side of the bed and placed it over him also. Then she reached for the bedside lamp.

"What about you? You must be tired too, what with sightseeing all day and playing doctor half the night." His eyes flicked to the empty space next to him. "There's room enough for us both."

No way, Jose! No, no, no, no, no!

No matter how weak and helpless he looked, she would not get into bed with him.

Her face must have clearly reflected her thoughts, for his expression suddenly melted into a pitiful, forlorn puppy look. "Samantha, I give you my word as a gentleman that even were I capable, I wouldn't lay a finger on you."

"A gentleman who has a way with doors and who knows what else? Thanks, but I'll take the chair."

She switched off the lamp so she wouldn't be able to see his eyes, his expression, or anything else.

"Be reasonable, woman. I happen to know that chair is deucedly uncomfortable."

"If I were reasonable, I would have already called the authorities." She heard his mouth snap shut. "Go to sleep."

Removing her heavy jacket and shoes, she crawled into the chair, tucked her feet under her, then pulled the jacket over her for a cover.

Thank goodness he had no idea that the command was not just for him.

What in heaven's name was wrong with her?

She was in a hotel room in Venice, Italy, with a naked man she didn't know. But it wasn't him she didn't trust.

❖ ❖ ❖

Venice, 1485

Fredo maneuvered the skiff around to the side of the landing in front of the enormous stone palazzo. Even dressed in the very best clothes he owned, Nino felt like a shabby beggar. The Lombardos were richer than he had imagined, and he suffered from no lack of imagination.

Despair washed over him. He had let his fanciful musings run too far afield this time. He had no business even dreaming of Serafina Lombardo. Might as well dream one of his ceramic angels had sprung to life.

"I said fasten your end." Fredo's impatient tone jolted him back to the present. "Don't let this place intimidate you, Nino," his friend chided. "For all their wealth, the Lombardos are only human after all."

"I'm not so sure."

Nino stood and secured the rope under the metal ring that protruded from the top of a marble column.

"They don't even live on the Grand Canal."

Wishing he possessed his friend's cavalier attitude, Nino picked up his leather portfolio of sketching materials. He followed Fredo out of the rocking boat and up the half-dozen wide stone steps.

Nothing much seemed to faze his friend, who wore a paint-spattered smock and carried his rickety easel under one arm. But then, he wasn't hopelessly smitten with his model like Nino was. And just how hopeless those feelings were slapped him rudely when Fredo clanked the heavy brass knocker against one of the carved wooden doors.

"Ah, the portrait painter." The servant who opened the door appeared to be better dressed than either of them, but greeted them warmly nevertheless. "*Buon giorno*, Signor Rosso. You have an assistant today? Please follow me, the Signorina is expecting you."

The enormity of his foolishness dragged oppressively at Nino, making him trail behind the servant and Fredo. Like most wealthy families in Venetian society, the first floor of the Lombardo palazzo contained offices and warehouse space, while the family resided on the floors above.

Wishing he'd had the sense to stay back at the room he shared with Fredo, Nino moved slower and slower up the staircase to the second floor. Fredo and the servant were ten steps ahead of him when they reached the top.

Nino heard the tread of slippers and the rustle of silk, then the servant said, "Ah, Signorina, here is the portrait painter."

Fredo bowed, and Nino glimpsed Serafina. A vision in gold and black, her angelic features were marred by a pensive frown.

"And his assistant." The servant stepped aside, and Nino mounted the top step.

A wave of bright sunlight passed over Serafina's face, and the oppressive weight around Nino's heart transformed into sheer joy.

While he sketched a bow, the lady said breathlessly, "Nino, I'm so glad to see you."

The servant remained silent. However, Fredo cleared his throat and cast Nino a sideways glance that spoke volumes.

"I brought sketching materials also." His voice sounded shaky even to himself and was scarcely above a whisper.

"You want to sculpt me in clay?" She sounded even more pleased.

His heart galloped with happiness. "If… if you have no objections."

"Objections?" She gave a little giggle that sounded to Nino like the tinkling of a pure silver bell. "Of course I don't, and since I must pose for Signor Rosso—"

"Fredo," his lanky friend interrupted with a twinkle in his eye. "Surely we need not be so formal."

The servant looked indulgently toward the ceiling while a rosy glow warmed Serafina's smiling face. "Not at all. Shall we go into the garden where the light is better?"

After two hours of what was, for Nino, utter bliss, staring at the object of all his desires, Serafina grew tired of posing and went to summon a servant to bring them some refreshments. Nino carefully laid aside his charcoal sketches while Fredo cleaned his palette and set his brushes to soak in a jar of mineral spirits. The two of them then walked to the cistern in the center of the garden to wash up.

"Quite a conquest, my friend."

While Nino pumped water into the wooden bucket, Fredo gave him a playful shove.

"But I am the one who is conquered, I'm afraid," Nino replied, not returning his grin.

Fredo snorted derisively. "Don't be modest. The lady cannot keep her eyes off you." While he talked, he scrubbed at the paint embedded under his nails with a rag. "And such smiles! She never smiled when she posed for me the other times. I'm sure she could make you smile too."

His friend's salacious meaning rankled Nino's suddenly acute sense of propriety. "The lady is promised elsewhere." No matter how much that pained him. "I could never toy with her affections or impugn her honor."

"Don't be so serious." Fredo rolled his eyes in mocking annoyance and ladled a dipper of cold water over Nino's outstretched hands. "Besides, her betrothed is twice her age, and I have heard he possesses an ample girth. Small wonder she wants a bit of harmless dalliance with a handsome young stranger. I told you the Lombardos are only human."

"Serafina is as pious as she is beautiful," Nino answered sharply. He dumped the dipper of water over Fredo's hands, splashing it on his hose. "She would never stoop to a dalliance."

Fredo laughed aloud. "You have it bad, my friend. Come, your most virtuous paragon is waiting."

Next to the stone bench where Serafina sat, the cook's helper hovered with a pewter platter of bread, cheese, and dried fruit.

"Set it here," she instructed, indicating the empty place beside her. The girl complied, then shifted from foot to foot at Fredo and Nino's approach.

Serafina understood the servant's nervousness. Seeing Nino again made her own nerves feel like lute strings stretched to the point of snapping. Though younger and not as tall as his painter friend, Nino's limbs and body were in perfect proportion, neither thin like Fredo, nor heavy, like the Viscount Treviso. His dark, curly hair framed his handsome features and his eyes seemed even more impossibly blue than they had yesterday.

The serving girl obviously shared her opinion

for she gave a little gasp when Nino's gaze moved across them.

"You may go back inside, Bianca." Serafina dismissed the awestruck girl, who glanced back over her shoulder several times on her way to the house.

Fredo wasted no time helping himself to everything. Nino, however, waited until she took a piece of bread off the platter before taking one himself. Only after some good-natured teasing by his friend did he partake in anything more.

Serafina had no appetite for the food. She could not tear her gaze away from Nino's mouth. His perfect, white teeth bit into a second slice of bread, and she wondered if his lips felt as soft as they looked. His clear blue eyes locked with hers and seemed to know her impure thoughts. Blood rushing to her cheeks, she looked away quickly.

"I meant no disrespect, but Doge's niece or not, Luciana Paltrano is homely." Fredo's words interrupted her shameful musings. "'Twould be better to paint her wearing her Carnevale mask."

Serafina carefully avoided looking at Nino. "You would not accept the commission then?"

Fredo snorted and took the last remaining slice of bread. "Of course I would accept it. I just doubt I would be paid if I painted her too realistically."

"'Tis not a problem with you for a subject." Nino's tone sounded husky, and the heat in his eyes made Serafina's heart beat faster.

"No indeed," Fredo agreed with a wide grin. "Your portrait will be fine. I need only leave off that wart on your nose."

He laughed when Serafina automatically touched her nose. She found herself giggling too.

"Oh, look." Fredo grabbed the last two slices of dried apple. "The tray is empty. Allow me to take it inside for you."

Before she could protest, he popped the apple slices into his mouth, shoved the tray under his arm, and loped off in the direction of the kitchen. She was alone with Nino.

"Fredo is very amusing," she said to fill the sudden silence.

"Sometimes he goes too far."

Nino paced the open space in front of the bench. His graceful movements made her think of dancing. Who had he danced with during Carnevale?

"Well, he was right about the Doge's niece."

Serafina shifted her voluminous skirts so that he could sit next to her on the bench. He hesitated for a moment before he sat down.

"Maybe so, but he should not have poked fun at you."

"I… don't mind." As at the cemetery isle, warmth seemed to radiate from him to her. "Besides, I may not have a wart on my nose, but my jaw is too square and my mouth is too small."

She repeated the faults her mother so frequently pointed out, except she never should have mentioned mouth. The instant she spoke the word, her eyes immediately went to his.

She watched in fascination as his lips parted and he spoke. "Your mouth looks perfect to me."

Her hand moved of its own accord. "Not so perfect as yours." Her fingers lightly brushed across his cheek and traced the edge of his lower lip. "Yours feels so soft."

Serafina lifted her face, and his warm smooth lips touched hers. The unexpected contact jolted them apart.

"Forgive me!" Nino leaped to his feet.

"Kiss me again," she whispered, pulling him back down beside her.

She felt his breath fan across her cheek, making her blood hum in her ears. Not loud enough to mask the sound of someone's approach, however.

Nino heard too, and jumped to his feet again. Serafina looked in the direction of the house. Fredo and the cook's helper, Bianca, ambled toward them. The former laughed overly loud as if he wanted to be sure they heard.

"Lady Serafina," the servant called out. "Your mother needs your assistance within."

Awash in guilt, Nino stared at the windows in the upper stories of the palazzo, which overlooked the garden. He fervently hoped that the Signora Lombardo had not seen them together on the bench.

Serafina rose, the look in her velvety brown eyes expressing the same fear. Wordlessly, she turned in a rustle of silk skirts and hurried away.

"We'll take our leave also," Fredo told the servant.

Nino helped him pack up his brushes and fold his easel, all the while silently cursing himself for acting so rashly.

"Sorry I couldn't give you more time alone," Fredo muttered as the girl escorted them to the entrance on the canal.

"I acted inexcusably bold," Nino answered in a hoarse whisper.

He doubted he would ever see Serafina again, and the knowledge hurt like a pike raked across his chest.

"Well, the lady did not seem all that pious to me," Fredo commented after they had expressed their thanks and the servant had left them at the top of the marble steps leading to the water.

They had almost reached their waiting boat when the front doors of the palazzo swung open and Serafina rushed out.

"Nino, you forgot this."

She flew down the stairs and pressed a sketchbook that obviously was not his into his hand. Then, before he could protest, she added, "Tomorrow afternoon, I will be at the fish market with the cook."

Her fingers curled around his and squeezed, causing a hot arrow of desire to flame up his arm.

His mouth was too dry to speak, so he gave a small nod of acknowledgement, and was rewarded with a dazzling smile that stopped his breath in his throat.

"Goodbye then, Nino." Her voice was low, then she added in a normal tone, "…and Fredo."

Blushing, she turned and bolted back up the stairs.

"Not very pious at all." Fredo chuckled.

Chapter 3

THE CHAIR WOKE SAM UP, OR MORE PRECISELY, THE pretzel shape the chair had forced her to assume. Pain in her neck, shoulders, and back had awakened her at frequent intervals the past few hours, but now all three ached in unison. Somewhere not far off, church bells rang out 6:00 a.m.

Stiff and bleary-eyed, Sam realized that more sleep was beyond the realm of her current capabilities and stumbled to her feet. Even when she had managed to doze off, troubling dreams of Renaissance Italy and marriage to the wrong man had kept her from resting.

Once in the bathroom, she splashed cold water on her face and groaned. The new and improved Sam Lewis didn't like early mornings any better than the old version. A long, hot shower was a definite necessity. She turned on the tap and tiptoed out to get clean clothes.

The Irish gigolo-spy-art thief still occupied the bed, which meant yesterday had not been a dream after all. Part of her couldn't quite believe such a thing, or maybe she didn't want to believe.

Though he was asleep, Keirnan didn't appear to be resting any better than she had. While Sam pulled clothes out of her nearby suitcase, he shifted fretfully and muttered some unintelligible phrases.

One of his arms lay atop the comforter. She was afraid to look more closely, in case anything else might be uncovered. When she closed the lid on her suitcase, he moaned and squirmed again.

Was he in pain? Before she could move closer, she distinctly heard him murmur the name, Kathleen.

Shock colder than the water had been slapped her in the face. *Just when she'd started to think he looked harmless.* Hugging her clean clothes against her like a shield, Sam hastily retreated into the bathroom, locking the door behind her.

Comforting steam rose from the flowing showerhead, and she took several deep breaths before hanging her clean clothes on the hook behind the door. She shucked off the clothes she'd slept in and kicked them into the corner. However, the plastic shower curtain didn't budge. Impatiently, she tugged down the ripped leather jacket, and without being aware of what she was doing, held an open wallet in her hands.

His Pennsylvania driver's license confirmed that his name was Keirnan Sean Fitzgerald. He lived in Philadelphia and was four years older than she was. Annoyingly, even his license picture looked charming. Sam also found an American Express card, a rather substantial wad of soggy paper Euros, and not much else.

Except, secreted into a tight compartment, she discovered a folded rectangle of paper, slightly damp around the edges. She could discern no address or phone number, but large, feminine-looking script covered one side of the unfolded sheet.

Even though the letters were Western, Sam couldn't make out any of the words or the language. The writing wasn't in a Romance language, but it didn't look Germanic either.

Some kind of love missive from the elusive Kathleen, no doubt. Not that she cared. His indiscretions were none of her business. And the sudden throb in her temples was lack of sleep.

Sam shoved the paper back into the wallet, placed the wallet back inside the jacket, then hung the sodden mess on the doorknob. Stepping into the shower stall, she jerked the curtain closed and let the hot water pound her into temporary oblivion.

Sometime later, she emerged from the bathroom and deposited her dirty clothes back into her suitcase. Keirnan still slept, but his breathing sounded shallow and raspy. Sam reached automatically for his forehead. To her dismay, his skin felt dry and too warm. Even worse, his eyes snapped open. She snatched her hand away.

"Kath—" he began. His glittery, unfocused gaze danced across her face for a brief moment, then he seemed to recognize her. "Samantha, luv?" He looked around the room in confusion and struggled to sit up.

She stopped him by pressing a firm hand against his bare shoulder. It felt too warm also, which didn't bode well for sending him on his way. Her thoughts remained a muddled mess. She needed to sort them out, which wouldn't happen if she stayed in the same room with him.

"Go back to sleep. I'm going down for some breakfast."

He licked his lips. "Need to get going." However, he sank back onto the pillow.

Her own mouth felt parched. The ache pounded harder in her temples.

"No, you don't. It's still early. Go back to sleep."

He really must have felt ill because he complied without another word. Sighing wearily, he closed his eyes and pulled his arm under the covers.

Trying not to run, Sam whirled and came face to face with the aromatic heap atop the radiator. Holding her breath, she examined the pieces. The sweater and T-shirt were bloody and ragged and went right into the trash can. The jeans, socks, and boxers were squelchy and reeked with smelly canal water.

Spying a plastic laundry bag, Sam shoved them inside. She squinted at the Italian words printed on the sack. Surely this system worked the same as back home. She would drop them off downstairs and have them back this afternoon. She was pretty sure *due del pomeriggio* meant "two in the afternoon," plenty of time for Keirnan to recuperate. She'd even buy him a new shirt between now and then.

Twenty minutes later, Sam unlocked the door and backed into the room, balancing a Styrofoam cup of hot tea and a plate with two slices of buttered toast. This was the closest to an American breakfast a person got in Italy. She hoped it would carry him through a couple of hours.

Easing the door closed, she heard muffled moaning and coughing behind the bathroom door.

Uh oh.

Judging from the sounds, eating was not going to be on Keirnan's agenda for awhile.

She set the food on top of the bureau and rapped on the door. "Are you all right?"

The only answer was another groan, then the toilet flushed, and more ominous sounds followed. Concern prompted Sam to try the door. Locked, of course.

"Keirnan?"

What if his ribs were bleeding again? Or what if he was bleeding internally? She took a step toward the phone.

"Afraid the canal water didn't agree with me." His voice sounded shaky in spite of his attempt at humor.

At least he was talking, which meant she didn't have to figure out the Italian phone system. Not just yet, anyway.

"Try the yellow pills in my cosmetic bag."

After several long moments, she heard the tap running. A minute later, the door opened just enough for her to see one accusing blue eye. "What have you done with my clothes?"

"I... I..."

The image of Keirnan naked on the other side of the bathroom door popped into her mind and rendered her momentarily incoherent. She covered her eyes with one hand in a futile attempt to block the tantalizing mental picture.

"I took them to the hotel laundry."

"What?" His tone wavered between accusatory and outrage. "Even my knickers?"

The enticing image swiftly dissolved. Sam rushed to defend her actions. "They'll be back this afternoon."

"No, they won't! This is Sunday. Everything in Italy is closed on Sunday."

"Oh my God!" Belatedly, she remembered reading about that in a guidebook. "I'm sorry, I didn't—"

The door thumped shut in the middle of her muddled apology. More indistinct sounds ensued, intermingled with what she guessed were curses. Never mind about that elusive "happy place," she'd settle for a nice deep hole to crawl into.

Since neither was available, she tried to apologize again. "I'm really sorry, Keirnan. Surely something is open."

His only reply was some hoarse coughing followed by another flush of the toilet, then dead silence.

Think, Sam! Think!

"I know! I'll go to your hotel and bring back your suitcase."

She heard the tap running again. Finally, he answered. "Let me ring them first."

She was standing too close to the door, and he nearly plowed into her. Gasping in alarm, Sam jumped aside and saw, to her immense relief, he was wrapped in a blanket from shoulders to knees. Still feeling decidedly uncomfortable, she looked in the other direction and listened to him sit on the bed and dial the phone.

That part of his story about spending summers in Italy must be true. He used the phone without hesitation and spoke Italian effortlessly, or so it seemed to her. She quite honestly couldn't understand more than a word or two, but she thought he asked someone to check his room. After a long pause, she heard excited babble coming out of the receiver. Startled, she whirled around.

"*Che cosa*?" Keirnan snapped, then interrupted the person on the other end by practically shouting, "No! No polizia!"

He swore under his breath in both Italian and English, then appeared to be mollifying the person on the other end. After a few more polite phrases, he hung up with a disgusted shake of his head. "Appears someone broke into my room."

Sam's stomach lurched. She willed it to stop and clutched her hands together behind her back so they wouldn't shake.

"Did they take anything? I can still go—"

"No! I—" He broke off with a gasp, seized his ribs, and spat out another epithet in what she guessed was Italian.

Her heart sprang up in the direction of her throat. "Are you bleeding again?"

"No." However, no color remained in his face. "Maybe." He moved his hand away. "Doesn't matter. I have to get out of here."

"You have to let me call a doctor!"

Thanks to his stubbornness, irritation was rapidly displacing her apprehension.

Keirnan shook his head emphatically. "No, Samantha, you don't understand. This is dangerous business, and I can't get you involved."

Well, he was half right. She didn't understand this sudden need for him to keep her in the dark. How dare he pull this on her now!

"Too late. I'm already involved, and I think I deserve an explanation."

He shut his eyes, and another spasm of pain appeared to pass through him. After a moment, he opened his eyes, and they had taken on a steely quality. His jaw was also set in a firm, determined clench. He stared at her and said nothing.

Sam edged her way over, slid into the uncomfortable armchair, and glared right back at him. Two could play at this game.

After exchanging silent stares for what felt like an eternity, Keirnan finally broke eye contact.

"All right, I suppose I do owe you something." His voice sounded strained again.

He readjusted the blanket around his chest, his knuckles white from the force of his grip.

"The thing is… someone's been kidnapped."

"Oh my God! Kathleen?" Sam shocked herself by gasping her first thought aloud.

The look he shot her was equally astonished. His dark brows drew warily together. "Yes, my sister Kathleen. How did you know?"

Sister?

Sam's stomach did an unexpected loop-de-loop. She was grateful to be sitting.

"You, uh, talked in your sleep."

To say he looked chagrined was an understatement. Flabbergasted wasn't too far off. "Bloody bad habit, that. What else did I say?"

"Nothing."

Her sudden elation at the news that Kathleen was his sister screeched to a crashing halt. "Keirnan, if she's been kidnapped, we have to call the authorities!"

"No!" Both his voice and his hand holding the blanket shook. A mixture of anger and anguish chased across his face. "Don't you know the track record Italian police have with kidnappers?"

Sam gulped and recalled several old news stories, none with happy endings.

"What about the consulate? Can you contact the Irish embassy in Rome?"

Keirnan shook his head and sighed. "My sister has dual citizenship. She was married to an Italian."

Sam opened her mouth, but he shook his head more firmly. "Please, Samantha, I can handle this."

His dismissal hurt, downright stung.

"Butt out, honey, is that it?" She blurted in sudden ire. "Well, I won't. Not while you're sitting here wrapped in a blanket with a seeping knife wound and no clothes…"

Her righteous indignation flew away with the realization of why he had no clothes. She leaped up from the chair and threw open her suitcase.

"I have to find you something to wear!"

"No!" Keirnan's command froze her in the middle of her frantic dig. "I am absolutely not wearing any of your—"

He stopped short, moaned, and staggered toward the bathroom. The blanket slipped dangerously askew just before he slammed the door.

Get a grip! Sam gave herself a mental slap.

Of course he couldn't wear her clothes. Gender issues aside, he was almost a head taller and at least forty pounds heavier. Still, she couldn't just sit around doing nothing to solve a problem she had created, even if inadvertently. She grabbed her heavy parka off the back of the chair.

"I'm going out," she called in the direction of the bathroom. "Some place must be open somewhere."

And she'd find it if she had to tramp through every piece of solid ground in this lagoon! She rushed out without waiting for his reply.

After an hour of wandering up and down damp, empty streets, Sam finally found a small shop with the red cross of a pharmacy over the door and an *aperto* sign in the window.

A quick cruise up and down the aisles confirmed her suspicion, nothing resembled clothing. However, Keirnan needed some other things, starting with disinfectant and butterfly bandages. She snagged a plastic shopping basket and collected those and some other items—a comb, a toothbrush, a plastic razor, and a travel-size cylinder of shaving cream.

Buying toiletries for a man she'd met less than twenty-four hours ago seemed embarrassingly personal. Michael was the only man she'd ever bought that kind of stuff for, so this was a strange new experience.

A bubble of hysterical laughter rose in Sam's throat. Back in her hotel room waited a wounded, naked man in desperate circumstances. A man she felt an immediate, intense attraction to, who had haunted her dreams before she'd ever laid waking eyes on him. Strange didn't even begin to cover the situation!

She threw in a package of anti-nausea pills and a bottle of aspirin, then approached the cashier.

Her phrase book was in her suitcase, and her limited Italian vocabulary deserted her completely.

"Is there another store open? A place that sells clothes?"

The clerk kept shaking his head and muttering, "No, *mi dispiache*, *mi dispiache*. I'm sorry, I'm sorry."

With a groan of frustration, Sam paid, grabbed the plastic bag, and left. She couldn't go back to Keirnan like this. Not when his sister's life might be at stake.

Back out on the street, the winter sun gleamed on the red tile roofs and turned the lingering wisps of mist to silver. Spying the top of the Rialto Bridge, she hurried in that direction.

A few minutes later, she almost shouted in triumph when her instincts proved correct at last. At the foot of one of the most famous landmarks in Venice, a swarthy woman stood behind a narrow table piled with T-shirts, sweatshirts, and sweatpants.

Sam dug through the garish colors in search of the largest sizes. Everything seemed to be emblazoned with "Venezia" in block letters or had a gold-winged lion, a symbol of ancient Venice. Keirnan would be making quite a fashion statement.

She'd taken his clothes! Well, everything but his shoes and coat, and he could hardly go parading down the street in just those. Never mind that he hurt absolutely everywhere and couldn't stay out of the loo for more than ten minutes running. He had to get to the train station. The kidnapper had left instructions in a locker at Ferrovia Santa Lucia.

Until the two guys had jumped him last night outside his sister's apartment, Keirnan thought he'd figured out who had taken Kathleen. The most likely in his estimation was Professor Roberto Spinelli.

Almost a decade ago, Kathleen had lived with the pompous old bag of wind, so he knew all about her obsession with the Jewels of the Madonna. Back then, Spinelli had expensive tastes that sometimes ran to high-stakes gambling. He must be in truly desperate straits to pull something like this, but Keirnan didn't doubt Spinelli was capable.

So then who the bloody hell were the two guys that had jumped him?

They'd worn white Carnevale masks to hide their faces. He had a strong hunch they'd broken into his hotel room as well. Were they friends of Spinelli? Or had someone else learned of Kathleen's recent research and believed, like Spinelli, that she'd already found the jewels?

They were wrong, of course. She hadn't found them yet. Her note said she was close—on the verge of forcing Venice to divulge the secret. If he could find her latest set of working papers, then he could find the jewels himself. That was his only hope.

Except now his pretty American had thrown a huge spanner into everything by taking his clothes!

His American?

Blessed Saints! Where had that come from?

That's what came of allowing his libido to get in the way. His libido must have been driving last night because he didn't remember much after he plunged into the murky water.

Next thing he remembered was seeing the green awning, the same place he'd been earlier in the day. Then he'd asked the lad about Samantha, staggered up the stairs, found the flowers, and he honestly didn't remember another thing until she'd entered the room.

He'd probably never know why she decided to save his worthless hide. He was just bloody thankful she had. What Keirnan had witnessed of her so far had left him impressed with her spirit and tenacity, not unlike a certain sibling of his. He most definitely would not repay Samantha's kindness by jeopardizing her safety. That much of the old Irish chivalry still flowed in his veins.

His stomach pitched then rolled, signaling another eminent bout in the loo. Keirnan stumbled into the bathroom, praying that whatever he'd swallowed with the canal water would finish working its way through his system soon.

The shower was running when Sam came back with her purchases. Surely that was a good sign. Also the toast was missing from the plate on top of the bureau—good sign number two. She rapped lightly on the bathroom door, and the water stopped.

"Keirnan? I found you some sweats."

"Thank bloody God!" The door cracked open just wide enough for his wet arm to snake out. "Give them to me."

Sam averted her eyes and thrust the plastic bags at him.

"I got you a few other things, too." The door thunked shut, and she turned around. "So you're feeling better?"

"Not much, but I expect I'll live." The bags rustled. "A razor and a toothbrush! You're an angel, Samantha, luv."

Relieved, she crossed the room and plopped onto the disheveled bed. She didn't feel the least bit angelic. Angels didn't have lustful images of naked, hunky Irishmen dancing through their brains. She massaged her aching temples with her fingertips and tried to think of something else. Like his kidnapped sister.

Why would someone take her?

Keirnan didn't appear to be wealthy. He said he sold and leased real estate, which was a regular job, wasn't it? Was his sister's husband rich? Then why wasn't he here trying to ransom her?

The opening of the bathroom door interrupted her

tangled thoughts. Keirnan emerged looking less than
pleased with his new outfit. Even though Sam had
tried to find the largest sizes, the pants appeared to
be a tight fit. To compensate, he had pulled the huge
green T-shirt on over the sweatshirt, and it hung at the
top of his thighs.

Most guys would have looked silly in that get up.
But even with wet hair plastered to his skull and dark
stubble on his jaw, Keirnan Fitzgerald still managed to
look charming.

He dropped into the armchair and reached for his
shoes. "I don't suppose you found any socks?"

"No, you can wear a pair of mine. Don't worry.
They're tube socks, gender neutral."

She got up, fished in her suitcase, and then tossed a
white bundle at him. "And I don't think anyone will be
looking at your socks."

Certainly no women would, herself included.

"I'm sure you're right." He slipped on his shoes and
sat back with a groan. "I'll shave when I get back. Toss
me my coat, will you?"

"Get back? You're leaving now?"

Sam seemed to have developed the bad habit of blurting
out her thoughts. She couldn't help herself. His complexion
looked ashen under his stubbly beard, she noticed, and
merely putting on shoes and socks had winded him.

"At least dry your hair. I'll get my blow-dryer."

"Sorry, can't. I figure I've only got strength enough to
get to the *stazione* and back." His look told her succinctly.

His sister, the kidnappers.

Her pulse pounded in her ears. "Will they be there?"

He shook his head. His face wore the same obstinate

look as earlier, right before she'd forced him to tell her about his sister.

She still harbored serious doubts about those two flights of stairs. An image of him lying in a twisted heap at the bottom flashed across Sam's brain.

"Then I'm going with you." He opened his mouth to protest, and she threw his ripped leather jacket at him. "No arguments!"

Even though he'd wisely conserved his energy and kept quiet, by the time they walked out the front door of the hotel, Keirnan looked near collapse.

"Isn't the train station this way?" Sam asked when he turned in seemingly the wrong direction. She reached for his arm, but he shrugged her hand away.

"Vaporetti stand is over here."

She heaved a silent sigh of relief. Five minutes later, they were seated on a wooden bench in the Venetian equivalent of the city bus, a motor-driven launch.

Keirnan breathed in rapid, raspy pants and said nothing when Sam impulsively reached to brush a wet lock of hair out of his eyes. His skin felt clammy in spite of the chilly salt-tinged air. A cold, greasy ball of worry congealed in the pit of her stomach. The boat pulled over and let off several passengers.

"Keirnan, if you'll just tell me what to do—"

"No!" The scowl he shot her told her not to mention it again.

Fine. She would just pull a joined-at-the-hip routine. Not like he had the strength to stop her. Then she remembered the stupid phrase book was still in her suitcase. Sam bit her lip and tried to recall how to say "doctor" and "hospital" in Italian.

Fifteen minutes later, the vaporetto sputtered to a halt in front of the wide concrete steps leading from the Grand Canal to the Santa Lucia train station. The other three remaining passengers disembarked, and Keirnan grabbed her proffered hand to lever himself to his feet. The look in his eyes told her he was less than pleased, but he also realized he was too unsteady to refuse her help.

Once they were out of the boat, he continued to grip her arm as they climbed the score of steep stairs. He was gasping for breath when they reached the top, and he sat down hard on a wooden bench just inside the station doors. Sam sat next to him. The large waiting room looked busy for a Sunday morning with people bustling around amid a swirling miasma of cigarette smoke.

Finally, Keirnan pushed himself to his feet. "Wait here. I'll be right back."

Jaw tightly clenched, he pressed a restraining hand against her shoulder. She stood anyway.

"You are the most pigheaded—"

He placed two fingers across her lips, stopping her words. "I know. Wait." Then he shuffled away.

Stifling the urge to scream, Sam watched him weave his way around the knots of people in the sizable lobby. Within moments, she lost sight of him. She sighed and plunked back onto the bench. She'd never had a sibling, but if she did, she would probably do most of the same things Keirnan was doing.

In the past twenty-four hours she'd said and done things she would have never believed herself capable of, but she'd also never felt more alive. That really scared her.

Just a few weeks ago she had believed her life was going so well, right according to plan. How had she ended up here in Venice with a man she hardly knew but felt compelled to help?

On some elemental level, she'd broken free, flown beyond the limits she'd imposed upon herself and, for the first time, let her feelings take over. Would Dr. Goldfarb say that was a good thing? Well, good or bad, she'd done it, and she wasn't going back now.

She rose, craning her neck. Keirnan stood in the middle of a line of pay phones, receiver to his ear. He did not look happy.

She crossed the room and heard him speaking in Italian as she approached. All she understood was his frequently repeated "no," however, his tone and body language shouted frustration. He frowned when he saw her and turned away to continue the conversation. After two more clipped sentences, he hung up and sagged heavily against the wall.

A bolt of fear made coherent speech refuse to emerge. "Is everything… your sister, is she…?"

Keirnan turned to face her. Pain and uncertainty swam in the depths of his eyes. "They assured me she's all right and gave me a twenty-four-hour reprieve."

Relief surged through her. "That's good!"

The impulsiveness, which seemed to have overtaken her senses, urged her to throw her arms around him. She rashly obeyed and instantly regretted it. A shock wave of physical awareness surged between them.

He jerked away, and she hastily took a step back. The momentary jolt dissolved.

"You need to go back to the hotel."

Keirnan rubbed his forehead and nodded wearily. "For an hour or two, then I'll leave."

She didn't think a couple of hours would suffice. He

looked ready to drop in his tracks, but she would wait until she got him back to argue. For the moment she kept a firm grip on his arm as they made their way out of the station.

Keirnan glanced over his shoulder when they started down the steps, then again after they descended halfway. Sam felt his arm muscles tighten under her hand just before he veered sharply to the left. She stumbled and peered questioningly at him.

"I think we're being followed."

Venice, 1485

Early spring rain overflowed the city's already full cisterns, made the streets slippery with mud, and turned the canals brown, but nothing could dampen Nino's spirits.

In the ten days since their first chance encounter on the cemetery isle, he and Serafina had found a way to see each other every day. At the fish market, a book-seller's stall, before or after mass, they managed to share a few words, a touch, longing glances. Nino's days revolved around those meetings with Serafina, and during his mostly sleepless nights, he worked by candle-light sculpting clay likenesses of her.

Though he managed to sleep through most of Nino's late night sculpting, Fredo had noticed his roommate's preoccupation and teased, though he had not discouraged his hopeless pursuit. Nino didn't deny that his feelings were indeed hopeless, but he refused to let it spoil his momentary happiness. Serafina was all his mind, body, and spirit craved. Deep down, he knew himself to be a fool, but he didn't care.

This morning Serafina had accompanied her brother Antonio to the quays near St. Mark's Cathedral. While her brother inspected a shipment of marble, Serafina had stayed out of the rain under a canvas shelter. A shelter Nino easily found and shared. They had spent the better part of an hour talking and laughing before Antonio concluded his business.

Thoughts of their meeting and anticipation of their next one now kept Nino's heart light, in spite of the persistent drizzle. He loaded one of the brick kilns behind the *scuola* where itinerant artists like himself and Fredo lived and worked. He hoped he would not have too much trouble lighting the wood to fire up the kiln.

"Nino Andriotto?"

The sound of his name startled him. A brown-robed friar stood a few yards away.

"I am he." He extended his hand, but the priest kept his tucked inside the sleeves of his robe.

"The Signorina Lombardo bids you come as soon as you may to Santa Maria dei Miracoli."

That was the church Serafina's father and brothers had designed and recently built. Where the family, and now he, attended mass.

Cold fear grasped Nino by the throat. Something must be terribly wrong. Serafina had never before sent someone to seek him out.

"D-did she say why?"

"Only that she must speak with you."

A dozen clay pieces sat waiting outside the kiln. The fact that the rain would most likely ruin them never entered Nino's mind.

"I'll go now."

The friar nodded. "I trust you know the way." Before Nino could pull on his doublet, the man glided away.

Nino didn't pretend to walk. He dashed through the sodden courtyard and into the street as if Saracen mercenaries pursued him. Scant minutes later, he huffed inside the main door of Santa Maria dei Miracoli.

Removing his soggy cap, he dipped his fingers into the fount of holy water, touched his forehead, and scanned the interior of the church for signs of Serafina. In his agitated state, the beauty of the place was lost on him, but he was grateful for the scores of brightly burning candles and the weak afternoon sunlight diffusing through the high stained glass windows.

Nino slowed his pace when he passed the steps to the chancel. However, he still didn't see Serafina anywhere. He almost reached the altar when a stocky priest with a pointed black beard stepped from the apse and motioned for him to approach. Recognizing him from previous services, Nino followed the man behind the altar, where the priest opened the door to a small antechamber.

Serafina sat on a stool inside the room, dabbing her eyes with a linen kerchief. The moment she saw Nino, she launched herself into his arms and pressed her cheek against the rough, wet wool of his ragged doublet. Unable to stop himself, he caressed the damp strands of her hair.

"The Viscount insists we wed in a fortnight," she sobbed. "My father has agreed. Oh, Nino—" More sobs choked off her words.

All the air rushed from Nino's lungs, and a bitter taste rose into his mouth. His happiness, his dreams, shattered around him, exploding like wet clay fired too quickly.

How soon his happiness had all crashed to wreckage around him!

'Twas a foregone certainty that any man would jealously guard a wife as young and beautiful as Serafina. And even if the two of them could somehow manage to see each other, marriage was a holy sacrament, and Nino refused to endanger Serafina's immortal soul. No matter how he longed for reality to be different, he knew it could never be.

"Let us shut the door."

The low tones of the priest made Nino acutely aware of their surroundings and of how Serafina's honor might be compromised. He gazed frantically over his shoulder, then guided her back to the stool. When the priest closed the door, Nino shuffled to stand behind Serafina. The other man's appraising stare caused him great unease.

"The lady and I are not… This is not…"

The priest inclined his head. "I am Father Mateo, Serafina's confessor."

Nino sagged with relief. The man knew the truth.

"You know of the lady's desire to enter a holy order." Though it was not a question, Nino managed a slight nod.

Serafina gave another ragged sob. What felt like an iron vise tightened around Nino's heart. Her suffering pained him far more than his own.

"She has asked for my help to arrange such a thing." Father Mateo spoke as if Serafina were not in the cramped little room with them. "Though I have warned her 'twould not be possible here in Venice. Her family would not allow it." He paused and studied Nino again. "Such an undertaking would be risky as well as costly."

"I'll give you all I have, though it be very little." When the priest said nothing, suspicion prickled across the back of Nino's neck. He was obviously a struggling artist. The Lombardos, however, possessed great wealth.

Father Mateo's shrewd, dark eyes narrowed. He finally addressed Serafina, but his gaze never left Nino. "Is that still your wish, my child?"

"I don't... I mean, yes... I-I cannot marry the viscount!"

Sobs interrupted her words again, and she covered her face with her handkerchief. A rush of incoherent, muffled sounds tumbled out.

"There, there." The priest patted the top of her head. "Dry your tears, daughter. Since your heart is so set against it, I shall contrive of a way to prevent this marriage."

The possibility should have left Nino elated. Instead, he continued to feel apprehensive. At least Serafina had stopped crying. She blotted her eyes with her crumpled handkerchief and mumbled her thanks to the priest.

Unsteadily, she rose to her feet, reaching for Nino's arm for support. "Will you walk with me?"

"I do not think that would be wise." Father Mateo intervened before Nino could reply. "The two of you must meet me here the day after tomorrow before vespers. Then I will have a plan."

"I shall take my leave first." Nino lifted Serafina's hand from his sleeve, giving her fingers a reassuring squeeze. "All will be well."

When he released her hand, she raised it to cup his cheek. Tears glittered in her dark eyes, and her lower lip trembled. It took every bit of his self-control not to kiss her tear-stained face, cover her lips with his. Unable to trust himself a moment longer, Nino turned and strode away.

Chapter 4

"I THINK WE'RE BEING FOLLOWED."

Samantha cast a glance sideways but didn't turn her head. "Are you sure?" she whispered.

"Not certain, but we'll find out."

Keirnan angled across the stairs toward the back of the train station, away from the Grand Canal. His gait far from steady, he was actually grateful for her hand under his arm. But at the same time, he did not want whomever this might be connecting her with him. The last thing he needed was another damsel in distress, or worse. The idea that he might have placed Samantha in danger stung at his conscience most unpleasantly.

They reached the bottom of the steps, and he turned down a major thoroughfare that paralleled the canal. He didn't need to look behind him, the prickling on the back of his neck told him they were still being followed.

How the bloody hell could he get them out of this? In his weakened state, he wasn't capable of moving fast or far. In fact, he could feel himself tiring already.

Church bells rang nearby, the call to noon Mass. Several people walking in front of them picked up their pace. The looming bell tower fifty meters ahead gave him an idea.

"The church up there." He gritted his teeth and pushed himself to move faster.

Samantha nodded in understanding. They arrived at the massive wooden doors with a half-dozen other people and stepped into the cavernous, gloomy interior. Keirnan pulled her to the left as he scanned the place.

Not enough people in the pews to blend in.

Too much light in the side chapel to hide there.

On the far back wall, he spied the wooden confessional booths—their only option. He sidled over to the nearest one, and with a last glance to be sure no one saw, he pulled Samantha inside with him.

He sat down hard on the wooden seat. She nearly tumbled into his lap but managed to throw her hand up and brace herself against the wall over his head. With no room to maneuver, she was stuck in that position.

Just as well. He knew he was too exhausted to stand, even if he could trade places with her. However, her ungainly stance made it impossible for him to crack open the door and peek out. Worse, it left a very tempting part of her anatomy very near his face. Not that her bulky coat revealed any hint, but just the knowledge caused his libido to stir.

Great timing, boyo.

He started to silently recite the multiplication tables as a distraction, a tactic that only lasted through the middle of the sevens. Then the closeness inside the wooden booth brought a whiff of her peach scent into his nose and straight to his groin.

Why couldn't she have showered with the hotel soap?

His sweatpants were too tight under the best of circumstances. He switched to mentally calculating square roots.

Through the thick wood, Keirnan could hear the drone of the priest and the answering murmurs of the congregation. Minutes crawled by. With a stifled groan,

Samantha shifted awkwardly so that she leaned on her other hand. His concentration splintered in a wave of sweet peach fragrance, and he nearly groaned himself.

"Sorry," she whispered. "My hand went to sleep."

"Hang on a wee bit longer."

He hoped he could. Her slight shift had not improved the situation. His cheek now rested against the slick, waterproof fabric of her coat. He gave up on mathematics and silently repeated the familiar refrain of Hail Mary. Might as well get a head start on penance for his lustful thoughts.

After what felt like an eternity, Keirnan heard the sounds of people standing and walking. Mass must be over. Time to make their move.

"Can you open the door?"

Samantha turned her head to the side and groped with her free hand. The latch clicked.

"Go," he urged.

She bounded out. He hoisted himself to his feet and followed. Blending in with the crowd was their best chance. He grabbed her hand and shouldered his way past a pair of middle-aged women so that he could reach the door with a large group of other people. Back on the street, he turned in the direction of the *stazione*.

"Vaporetto," he murmured in answer to Samantha's questioning look.

He tried for what he hoped would look like a casual stroll, though in truth it was as fast as his aching legs and body would allow him to move. The tingling on the back of his neck was gone, but he glanced into every window they passed in an effort to recognize anyone behind them.

❖❖❖

Keirnan's fingers, interlaced with hers, were like a conduit channeling his pent-up tension and anxiety directly into Sam. She felt the vibration between them as they trudged back toward the Grand Canal. With it came the overwhelming urge to look behind, something she knew would draw attention, so she resisted.

By the time they reached the water, Keirnan's breathing was labored again. Sam almost cried in relief when she spied the launch gliding to a stop a few yards in front of them. Only one other couple got on with them. She felt the uneasiness drain out of Keirnan as he slumped into the first available seat.

He didn't release her hand.

The cold breeze blowing against her face was a welcome change from the stifling interior of the confessional. She had never considered herself claustrophobic, but after being shut inside there, she'd been ready to admit to just about anything in order to get out.

Being in those close confines with a certain Irish rogue appealed to her in a way she'd never experienced before. Or perhaps she was reacting to the exotic locale and the seriousness of the situation.

Yes. That had to be the reason, because practical, dependable Sam Lewis did not have sudden sexual attractions to men, much less act on them.

She quickly killed that train of thought by concentrating on their surroundings. It was a dreary day with very little light, even at this hour, and a murky dampness clung to everything.

The other passengers disembarked at the next stop, and

four more people got on. Keirnan rested his head against the wooden rail behind them, the picture of disheveled weariness. When the looming shape of the Rialto Bridge rose up in front of the vaporetto, he snapped his head up, confirming Sam's theory that he was not really as out of it as he appeared. Then the boat bumped against the dock next to the bridge, and he pulled Sam along after him. Without a backward glance or word, they hustled up the steps to the top of the tall structure. The shops lining both sides of the wide expanse were closed, and only a few people walked by them.

Keirnan's footsteps faltered again when they came within sight of the hotel. They slipped inconspicuously inside; however, before they reached the stairwell, Sam's stomach reminded her that it had been quite some time since her tea and toast.

"Can you make it the rest of the way alone? I'm going to pop into the café and get us some lunch," she explained.

He frowned, dark brows drawn together over his bright baby blues. "Of course I can. Just don't go wandering about."

She gave him an eye roll to let him know her opinion of his concern. "I'll be right up. Oh, and I guess you won't need my key?"

"No, I don't expect I will."

He turned for the stairs. His lopsided grin made a funny little flutter kick up in her stomach.

Another hunger pang, that's all.

Fifteen minutes later, Sam opened the door and entered her freshly made-up room. Maid service had to be the biggest perk of traveling. Also, Keirnan had obviously turned on the radiator.

She put the plate with the two hard rolls and thin slices of prosciutto on top of the bureau, then removed her coat. Keirnan's ripped leather jacket and new sweatshirt lay draped across the chair. Keirnan himself was in bed, covers pulled up to his chin, sound asleep.

At the moment, he undoubtedly needed rest more than food. Plus it might not be wise for him to put much in his stomach just yet. Hers was another story, however. She ripped open the roll, stuffed in half the slices of meat and devoured the entire thing without even bothering to sit down.

The clock next to the plate on the bureau top showed a few minutes before two. In five hours she had to be at the station to board the night train for Rome with the rest of her tour group. Her exciting adventure would be over.

And what about Keirnan Fitzgerald? Would he safely ransom his sister, Kathleen?

Guess I'll never know.

Why did that thought cause a dull aching pain in her temples? It must be lack of sleep, because she couldn't be deeply concerned about someone she'd only met yesterday morning.

Slowly, Sam edged her way to the bed and studied Keirnan's face. His long, dark lashes fanned under his closed eyes, and a tousled curl lay on his forehead, making him look younger than his thirty-two years.

Young and vulnerable.

But the dark stubble shadowing the lower half of his face was a stark reminder that he was indeed a grown man. A man whose touch carried a sensual jolt of electricity when he made contact with her. Or was that just her overactive imagination?

A huge yawn overpowered her. The growing warmth in the room and her now satisfied stomach made Sam acutely aware of her own fatigue. She doubted she'd get much sleep tonight on the noisy, jostling train. She glanced over at the armchair and shuddered at the thought of trying to rest in it again. As Keirnan had pointed out last night, there was plenty of room for her to stretch out on the bed next to him.

The old Sam would have never entertained such a thought.

An extra blanket lay folded neatly across the foot of the bed. She would only take a short nap. She wouldn't have to crawl under the covers. As soundly as he was sleeping, Keirnan wouldn't even know she was there.

One more glance at the chair cemented Sam's decision. Kicking off her shoes, she stretched out on the edge of the bed, pulled up the extra blanket and let blissful slumber claim her.

What was that sound?

Sam struggled against consciousness. She'd been dreaming she was in Renaissance Venice again. This time she felt safe and protected in her lover's arms. A lover whose dark curly hair and bright blue eyes bore more than a passing resemblance to a certain Irishman.

She longed to stay in the sheltered comfort of the dream, but something heavy lay across her shoulder. Reluctantly opening one eye, Sam recognized a very real and warm arm.

Keirnan's arm lay draped across her side. On top of

the blanket, thank goodness, since his fingers trailed alongside her left breast. Both her eyes popped open.

His even breathing puffed against her check. He was still sleeping. Careful not to wake him, Sam slid from his unconscious embrace.

Through her confused haze, she heard the noise again. This time she realized it was someone lightly rapping on the door. She stumbled across the room and looked through the peek hole. Paolo, the Venetian tour guide, stood outside. She opened the door a quarter of the way.

"So sorry to disturb you, Signorina," Paolo apologized. "But I needed to remind you that you must be at the train station in an hour."

How long had she been asleep?

Groggily, Sam swung around to look at the clock which read 6:05 p.m. She grasped the edge of the door, which had opened most of the way, and her glance snagged on Keirnan.

He still slumbered peacefully, his arm lying protectively across the spot she'd just vacated. The soothing security of her dream hovered on the edges of her consciousness while warmth spiraled through her heavy limbs. She turned back and saw the guide peering over her shoulder at the sleeping man in her bed.

Her head suddenly felt as if it were underwater. She couldn't breathe, couldn't think.

The languid comfort of the dream dissolved. Images of Keirnan floated through her muddled mind—the seeping knife wound across his ribs, his anguished admission that his sister had been kidnapped, his struggle to reach the train station, and his fear-laced whisper that they were being followed.

"My husband," she heard herself saying sotto voce. "He's joined me after all, but he... uh, he has the flu."

Paolo looked unsure, as if he didn't know whether he believed her story or not. "Do you want me to call a doctor?"

"No! I mean, I'll take him tomorrow if he's not better."

"Then you are not going to Rome?"

Sam glanced back over her shoulder. Keirnan's words at the train station echoed inside her head. "*They gave me a twenty-four-hour reprieve.*"

Such a short time, and obviously, he was still ill. He had no one else to help him.

"Not tonight. We'll catch up with the group later. Can you arrange with the hotel for us to stay one more night?"

Keirnan awoke with the tantalizing feel of a woman curled against him, her head pillowed under his chin. It had been a while since he'd engaged in that aspect of a relationship, and certain parts of him were very pleased. He breathed in the enticing fragrance of peaches.

Ah, Samantha...

However, with the recognition, his bleary brain also registered the darkness. He glanced across at the bureau and saw the red digits of the clock: 3:19 a.m.

That couldn't be right.

For one brief, crazy moment he thought the past twenty-four hours might have been a dream, but even as he thought it, he tried to move. His muscles cried out like he'd just gone ten rounds with a world champion heavyweight. Plus, now that he was fully awake, his mouth tasted like something had crawled inside and died.

What the bloody hell was going on?

He wasn't supposed to be here, and neither was she. He distinctly remembered her mentioning the night train to Rome. He'd been exhausted but only intended to take a short rest.

Well, first things first, and nature called. Very gently, so he wouldn't awaken Samantha just yet, he scooted away and crawled out of bed.

Once in the bathroom with nature satisfied, Keirnan splashed cold water on his face and ran his damp hands through his tangled hair. The toothbrush she'd bought for him lay on the edge of the sink. He loaded it with toothpaste and scrubbed out the foul taste, then popped some aspirin.

Saints in heaven, he looked a fright! And he was starving. Since the idea of food didn't double him over the loo, the bug, or whatever it had been, must have run its course.

Well, food would have to wait a bit.

Still peacefully sleeping, Samantha hadn't moved. Keirnan sat on the edge of the bed next to her and switched on the bedside lamp. She looked otherworldly and beautiful enough to make his pulse quicken. However, the light shining on her face made her stir. Her lashes fluttered for a half-second, then her arm came up reflexively to cover her eyes.

She groaned. "What time is it?"

"Three-thirty."

She groaned louder, no longer the slumbering innocent, and rolled away from him. "Turn off the light."

"Samantha, luv." He reached over, grasped her shoulder, and gently shook. "It's three-thirty in the morning. What are you doing here?"

She batted at his hand. "I'm sleeping. Leave me alone."

"Why aren't you on the train to Rome?"

She rolled back, her face scrunched up against the light, her bottom lip stuck out in a childish, sleepy pout. "You were asleep, sick. I'll go tomorrow. Turn off the light."

Heaven help him! She'd stayed because of him.

The twin urges to kiss or throttle her sprang into battle. He let go of her shoulder, but his fingers brushed the softness of her cheek. "Samantha, luv…"

Her eyes snapped open wide.

Oh, now you've done it, boyo!

He jerked his hand away, turned off the lamp, then got up and put some space between them.

She turned the light back on and sat up, fully awake now. He noticed she was also fully dressed except for her shoes. That was a relief, though her sleep-mussed hair made his fingers twitch for want of smoothing it away from her flushed face. He ran his hands through his own tousled mop instead.

"Th-there's a roll on the bureau, if you're hungry."

"Thanks. I'm starving." *In more ways than one.*

Keirnan broke the piece of bread in half and gnawed, not daring to look in her direction.

"The prosciutto's been sitting out all night, but I think I have some crackers in my luggage."

He listened to her rummage about for a few moments as he devoured the rest of the stale roll. A clear plastic package of crackers with peanut butter filling dangled in front of him.

"Leftovers from my flight."

Why was she so bloody considerate, not to mention appealing?

What the hell was wrong with him?

The last thing in the world he needed right now was this kind of distraction. He took the crackers, being careful not to touch her fingers. Still, he couldn't stop himself from looking at her. Her beautiful, golden green eyes held trust, compassion, and something else. He turned aside fast.

Back off, boyo! Focus on the task at hand.

"Shall we split them? You must be hungry too."

"No, I'm okay."

He bit back the temptation to tell her she looked far better than okay. So much for focus.

"Well, maybe just one."

Keirnan handed her two then wolfed the rest down before she'd finished murmuring her thanks. He snagged his sweatshirt off the chair and slipped it over his head. He didn't dare tuck the T-shirt in, so he left the end hanging out with the fervent hope that it concealed enough of the obvious, plainly visible through the tight sweatpants. He sat in the chair and pulled on his— make that *her*—socks. His aching muscles grumbled in protest.

"What are you doing?" she asked.

Besides totally humiliating myself? Keirnan shoved on his shoes. "I have a wee errand to run."

"At three-thirty in the morning?"

"Safest time."

He straightened up and shrugged on his coat, willing himself to ignore the aches and pains. The three butterfly bandages he'd fastened to the jacket lining kept the knife hole from gaping quite so badly.

"Nobody will expect me out and about now, will they?" God, he hoped that was true.

To his dismay, Samantha grabbed her own shoes. "Then I'm going with you."

"Absolutely not!"

Without realizing he'd moved, Keirnan found himself grasping her arm. Her face hovered a hand's breadth beneath his. The twin urges fought another round. He had no time to give in to either.

"Why not?" She pulled out of his grasp. "If it's so safe, why can't I go? Besides, I have a flashlight."

He floundered about searching for some of his scattered logic. *Stay cool. Get some distance.*

"This is none of your affair, Samantha, and I'm sorry I got you involved. Now go back to bed, and in a few hours, pack your bags, go to the *stazione*, and get on the first train to Rome."

"No. We've already been through this." She smoothed her hair and fastened it behind her head with an elastic band. "I'm already involved. Your sister's life could be at stake. Besides, you still have a fever." She snatched up her coat. "And there's nobody else to help you."

Keirnan's façade of control shattered. "I don't care! You can't—"

"Well, I do care!" She interrupted, shoving her arms into the coat sleeves. "And I'll follow you if I have to."

He knew by the set of her jaw and the glare in her eyes that the little chit would make good on her threat. *Bloody hell!* He was losing time and this battle. He needed to do this under cover of darkness.

"All right then." He turned and shook a finger in her triumphant face. "But don't you ever call *me* pigheaded again."

It was eerily dark out on the street, but when Sam pulled the flashlight, really just an oversized penlight, out of her pocket, Keirnan shook his head. Mist hung in wet, wispy spirals over the water, and deeper shadows pooled in the darkness beside buildings. The chilly dampness distorted sounds so that the creaking of wood and slapping of water seemed to come from living entities.

Shivering, she pulled up the hood of her parka and hastened to keep pace with Keirnan, who moved silently through the spooky landscape. He looked neither right nor left and didn't vary his pace as they moved away from the familiar, well-traversed area near her hotel.

"Where are we going?" She finally dared to whisper as they crossed a narrow wooden bridge.

"My sister's lodgings in the Sistiere di San Polo."

Sam followed as he snaked his way down a tight path right next to the water. The four- and five-story buildings on either side of the minor canal blotted out all light. If not for the white letters on the leg of his sweatpants, she wouldn't have been able to see him at all.

Another diminutive bridge, this one with iron railings, arched up next to them where another canal intersected the one they followed. Instead of crossing, Keirnan crawled down next to the footings, then motioned her to join him.

As Sam carefully picked her way, she heard the grind

of wood on stone. When she got closer, Keirnan held out his hand. He stood with one foot resting on the prow of a wooden rowboat, and clearly he wanted her to get in.

"This isn't your boat!" She hissed as he grasped her upper arm.

"Well, the owner's hardly using it right now." His tone was clipped with impatience. "And if we're quick, he'll never know we borrowed it for a bit."

She stiffened and refused to budge. It was bad enough that she'd lied to help him, but she wasn't ready to steal. Larceny seemed to come effortlessly to him, which gave her pause.

"Samantha, please." Keirnan blew out a frustrated breath. "We'll bring it back soon. I promise."

She remained unconvinced. "Why can't we walk?"

His grip on her arm tightened ever so slightly. "My sister's flat has two entrances, one from the street and one from the water."

"Don't tell me the water is easier."

"Let's just say, last time I tried the street entrance I encountered a bit of resistance." His free hand strayed to his ribs.

A whimper of fright bubbled out of Sam's lips. Keirnan used her momentary hesitation to pull her toward him. "Step carefully now. That's it."

"Borrowing" suddenly didn't seem so bad. She did as he instructed and plopped down on a rough board nailed across the tapered front end of the rickety boat.

It was four in the morning; surely bad guys slept sometime. Her jangled nerves settled a bit. Keirnan was right. They wouldn't expect someone sneaking around at this hour, especially not on the water.

Keirnan shoved the bow with his foot and hopped in next to her. The boat bobbed unsteadily as he untied it from the piece of metal protruding from the base of the bridge. Seating himself on an up-ended rusty bucket in the center of the craft, he twisted the oars around in the locks, dipped them into the water, and pulled.

Sam jumped at the loud rasp of dry wood and rusted metal. So much for calming her nerves. At the moment she wasn't sure which scared her most, this decrepit boat or two thugs with knives. Thank goodness the canal wasn't very wide, but a dip into the icy water was far from appealing.

Leaning on one oar, Keirnan guided them under the bridge. Then he sat back and pulled, grunting with obvious discomfort. Considering he'd barely been able to walk eighteen hours ago, she knew he must be in pain.

She bent toward him. "Can I help you row?"

Predictably, he waved her off. "No need." He strained against the oars again. "It's not far. Mind your head."

They both ducked as the creaky vessel slid under another low bridge. A pale light filtered down from a second-story window to reveal a profusion of orange peels and cigarette butts floating in the nearly motionless canal. She also saw a growing puddle around her feet.

Why hadn't they borrowed a gondola?

Sam scooted slightly to one side and noticed the building had a yawning mouth of black water where the first floor would have been. Keirnan shifted the boat toward the canal bank opposite the light.

They passed three more buildings with spooky water entrances. Thugs with knives started to seem not so bad, especially when Keirnan stopped their forward progress and pointed Leaky Lena toward a cavernous opening under the next building.

Venice, 1485

Wearing his knee-length cloak, Nino lingered in the early morning shadows outside the garden gate of the Lombardos' palazzo. In spite of hardly sleeping at all, his mind continued to tumble over and over the events of yesterday. Every fiber within him longed with desire for Serafina and hummed with dislike for Father Mateo.

Though he had no logical reason, he did not trust the priest. Having survived largely by his wits for the past two years since leaving Florence, Nino did not try to second-guess his instincts. He'd encountered unscrupulous clergymen before.

A movement from the direction of the palazzo caught his attention. A familiar golden-haired figure closed the door and glided down the path to the bench they'd shared less than a fortnight ago. Dressed in a pale robe with her hair hanging loose down her back, she looked more angelic than human as she paused and ran her hand along the side of the bench.

"Serafina," he called softly through the gap between the stone wall and the metal gate.

He could scarcely believe his good fortune that it was she who appeared so early in the morning. She turned her head in his direction as if not trusting what she heard.

"Here, at the gate."

She grabbed two fists full of material, hitched up her dressing gown, and ran to him.

"Nino, I knew you'd be here!" Her voice a breathless whisper, she slid back the bolt and swung the gate inward. "My heart told me you would be."

When he stepped inside, she pulled him toward a gnarled pear tree with branches starting to bud. In spite of the lack of foliage, the trunk and tangled framework of branches easily concealed them from the view of anyone inside the palazzo.

"And my heart told me I must speak with you alone." He couldn't look into her beautiful dark velvet eyes or he would be lost. "Even though it's not right."

"I-I know, but I—" She raised his hands to her cheek, but he quickly pulled them away.

"Shush, we must be brief." He hadn't been fast enough to escape the sensual bolt of awareness that leaped from her to him and made his desire roar to life in his veins. He willed it down. "Serafina, I must hear it from you, because what you propose is not only dangerous but will tear you away from your family and everything you've ever known."

Even after nine years, Nino still remembered the forlorn homesickness that had reduced him to secret tears when he'd first gone to Florence as an apprentice to the great della Robbia.

The velvet in her gaze suddenly went as unyielding as ebony. "The Viscount is a harsh man. My sister died trying to bear his child, and I believe the same fate will be mine. I shall never willingly become his wife."

The thought of her being misused by another man filled him with anger. For a long moment Nino had to look up into the twisted branches of the tree, dark smudges against the pallid sky, before he dared to speak again.

"Then you mean to enter the cloistered life." Swallowing the bitterness that had risen in his throat, he looked back down at her. "When Father Mateo asked you yesterday, you seemed unsure."

"I was… I am…" She twisted and intertwined her fingers into a painful knot, her eyes now moist with tears. "Oh Nino, ever since that first day I saw you on the cemetery isle, all I can think about is seeing you again."

Her fingers fluttered free and reached for his face.

Before she could touch him, his own hands tangled into the silken strands of her hair and pulled her to him. Unable to stop himself, his mouth slanted across hers.

This was no light, chaste kiss like they'd shared before. His tongue plunged into her mouth and loosed all the pent-up, hopeless desire and frustration he'd endured these past days as he claimed the one thing he knew he could never possess.

She tasted warm and sweet. He knew she would, but the lingering hint of salt from her unshed tears caused reason to flicker in the back of his lust-filled mind. Then she gave a breathy little moan, and her tongue tentatively caressed his.

He was lost.

The exquisite torture of wanting her and knowing she wanted him ripped away any remaining shards of logic. His hands left her hair and pulled her tightly against him as his tongue explored the wonders of her mouth.

Her body felt softly pliant under his questing hands. Nino could feel her passion stir at his touch, and her tongue grew more bold. Her fingers pushed aside his cloak and clutched at his doublet as if she wanted to crawl inside with him. He wanted very much to oblige her, but before he could, the faint ringing of church bells broke the sensual spell around them.

Cold, unjust reality slapped him sharply.

"Please, my love," she murmured when Nino reluctantly pulled his mouth away. Encircling her hands around his neck, she stood on tiptoe to plant a moist kiss below his jaw.

"Serafina, we must take care."

Her passion-darkened eyes encouraged him to throw away caution. He pulled her hands into his and raised them to his face, but reality's stinging slap would not be denied. Her warm, smooth palms reminded him again of the hopelessly wide gulf between their worlds, the impossibility of bridging it.

"No, I don't wish to." Her tone sounded fierce, as if she knew where his thoughts wandered. "I want to be with you, Nino." She rubbed her downy-soft cheek against his rough, callused hand. "Let's run away together."

Every part of him wanted to do just that, but his memories of the long road from Florence to Venice were too fresh and would not be ignored. The words pained him but must be said.

"My love, I can scarce support myself. I can't provide the proper food, clothes, or anything for you."

"I have plenty of clothes, and I don't care about food. I've fasted before, during Lent."

His heart felt as if it was being wrenched from his chest, but he had to make her understand.

"Being hungry when there's a full larder is altogether different than being hungry when there is nothing in the larder. I can't do that to you, Serafina. You don't know what it's like to be penniless."

She sniffed back a sob. "Being wealthy has a price too. Though it may provide for my physical self, it puts my spirit in a cage. A cage that separates me from you."

Her words defied what his logic told him to be true. Being poor could never be preferable to being rich.

Nevertheless, Serafina's lower lip quivered and tears glittered on her dark lashes. "And when I am not with you, I can't breathe, can't see. I'm not really alive."

She launched herself against him, pulled his head down to her trembling lips, and claimed his mouth.

Nino's battle of logic, reason, and understanding roared down in flaming defeat. As he abandoned himself in another soul-searing kiss, the only thing he knew for certain was that he would defy heaven itself for her.

Chapter 5

SAM FOUGHT THE URGE TO COVER HER EYES. A MOMENT later, she didn't need to. The boat slid into the inky maw, and darkness obliterated her vision. She yelped in alarm at the screech of wood scraping stone.

Noises echoed hollowly all around them, and a heavy, dank odor hung in the air. Keirnan's shoulder brushed against hers as he groped along the side of the boat. Fearing he might tip them over, she grabbed the penlight out of her pocket and squeezed it on.

The tiny shaft of light revealed the bow of the boat brushing against the bottom of a dozen steep concrete steps. Keirnan looped the rope over a wooden mooring pole sticking out of the water next to the stairs. Using the rope, he angled the boat next to the bottom step and sprang out.

"Kill the light," he muttered as he reached for her free hand.

Sam didn't obey until she had both feet planted on the cement. He obviously had better night vision than she did, for after only a moment, he started to climb.

"Come on," he encouraged.

She still couldn't see anything. Acutely aware of the lack of handrails, she fumbled until she felt his outstretched hand.

She clung to him like some useless ninny, certain each step would send her plunging into the murky water below. Sweaty and shaky when they reached the top, Sam salvaged what little remained of her self-respect and let go of him. After a brief moment, Keirnan worked his "magic" on the door, and they stepped into a tiled entry.

Add breaking and entering to their growing list of offenses.

Another staircase went up, and he motioned with a turn of his head for her to follow. At least this one had a wooden banister, which Sam gripped all the way.

By the time she reached the top, her eyes had grown accustomed to the gloom, and she could see two doors, one on either side of the landing. Keirnan stood in front of the door on the left side and shoved it open just as she reached him.

He snaked his arm around her and pulled her over the threshold, noiselessly closing the door behind them.

"Let's have that light now."

Sam obeyed his whispered command and switched on her penlight.

The slender beam illuminated chaos. The room's contents lay scattered across the floor: sofa pillows, pictures, books, even a small microwave oven.

Her breath hitched in her throat, and the light wobbled. Beside her, Keirnan swore under his breath. He grabbed the light from her unsteady hand and shone it on another partially open door.

Sam could see a four-poster bed against the far wall. She stepped carefully around the clutter and followed him for a closer look.

The bedroom was a bigger mess than the sitting room. Bureau drawers lay upended, their contents strewn everywhere. Bedclothes were heaped on the floor. Sam couldn't suppress a horrified shudder as she gazed at lacy camisoles and silky undies thrown haphazardly on a pile of bulky sweaters. A small file cabinet lay on its side, papers spewed around it.

Keirnan switched on the miraculously unbroken bedside lamp and thrust the penlight at her.

Feeling as helplessly violated as the woman whose trashed bedroom she surveyed, Sam choked back a lump in her throat. "Do you think this happened before or after she—they—"

"Hard to say," he murmured in a husky, strained voice. He stooped to finger the papers sticking out of the file cabinet.

"Wh-what exactly are we looking for?"

"My sister's working papers. They'd be on computer CDs." His voice dropped back to the hoarse tone. "And a leather-bound journal, she favors those." Without warning, he threw the file folder in his hand across the room. "So help me, if they hurt her…"

He sank to his knees and scrubbed his hand across his eyes.

Sam turned aside, battling the urge to drop down next to him, pull him into her arms, and comfort him like a small child. She'd performed the same ritual with her mother at least a dozen times over the years, every time Mom's latest "love" bowed out of the scene. Only Mom hadn't been there to return the favor when Michael dumped her, not that she'd wanted her to. Keirnan probably wouldn't welcome her sympathy either.

He was on his feet again, standing next to a wooden desk that held a printer and a laptop docking station, but no laptop. The electrical cord was still fastened into the wall but hung limply off the edge of the desk.

He kicked an empty, plastic CD holder.

Hesitantly, Sam voiced her concern. "Maybe whoever was here found it already."

Keirnan shook his head. "If they had it, they wouldn't need her, wouldn't be after me." He crossed the room, muttering.

Sam couldn't help herself. She righted the file cabinet and started putting papers back inside.

Keirnan prowled the room like a hound that had lost the scent, his fury and frustration barely contained. Then he stopped beside a large wooden armoire, which served as a closet. Clothes and shoes were heaped around it.

"*The Lion, the Witch and the Wardrobe*, that's it!" His sudden cry startled Sam. "Bring the light over here, will you?"

She picked her way through the disorder as he tossed things aside like a lunatic.

"She said 'remember Narnia' in her note," he explained as he grabbed the light and began a careful examination of the now empty interior.

"*The Chronicles of Narnia*?"

He nodded, running his hands over the smooth wood on the back of the armoire.

"We both loved those stories when we were young. The children had a magic wardrobe."

He finished running the light and his free hand over the sides and moved on to the bottom.

"Here it is!"

A board squeaked, then to Sam's amazement, Keirnan extracted a slim leather book from a space between the bottom of the main compartment and the drawer underneath.

"Thank all the bloody stars in heaven!"

Still clutching the journal, he turned and gave her a hug that nearly bowled her over into a heap of his sister's clothes. His bristly cheek rasped against hers, and the sudden press of his body sent a ten-thousand-volt shock of sensual awareness screaming through her.

Thugs with knives, leaky rowboats, and steep stairs in the dark all combined were not half as scary as that sudden primitive jolt of connection. She'd never felt anything like it before with anyone.

She could see it was the same for him. Surprise sparked in the depths of his sapphire eyes in the split second before he broke the embrace.

"I... uh, sorry, luv," he mumbled, stepping backward. "Didn't mean to get carried away." He stowed the journal in the inside pocket of his jacket. "Let's get that boat back before it sinks, shall we?"

Unable to trust her voice, Sam merely nodded.

The gray edges of dawn crept across the horizon as Keirnan juggled the lock on the hotel's front door. Their little nighttime escapade had taken only a couple of hours and had succeeded beyond his most hopeful expectations. At the moment he felt more positive about safely rescuing Kathleen than he had since this whole madness started. And he would never have made it this far without Samantha's help.

His elation almost overrode his guilt at involving her. After all, she was a grown woman, capable of deciding for herself whether to stay or go. He could almost make himself believe that, except for the weird feelings she stirred up inside him.

Physical attraction he knew all about, but this was something else. Something foreign, but at the same time familiar.

Well, whatever it was would have to wait. The journal and Kathleen were more pressing.

He held the door for Samantha then closed and relocked it behind them before following her to the stairwell and up.

"Allow me."

He grinned at her unmistakably facetious comment as she pulled a key from her jeans' pocket and fitted it into the door.

Once inside the room, they both shed their heavy jackets. A glance at the clock confirmed it was still too early for any businesses to be open. Keirnan's gaze skimmed over the bed before he settled deliberately into the armchair.

"Still tired?"

Her eyes flicked briefly over the bed also. "No, I think I'll take a shower and wash my hair."

"Good idea." He watched her rummage in her bag, pull out clothes, toiletries, and a pair of penny loafers. "Try and leave a bit of hot water for me?"

"Sure."

She disappeared into the bathroom. The distinct click of the lock made him smile. *Like that would make a difference.*

He opened the leather journal, and a shiny CD fell into his lap.

Ah, clever girl. Always have a backup.

Now all he needed was a computer. Slipping the CD into his jacket, Keirnan settled back to read through the journal.

Too clever by half, his sister—very few of the entries were written in English. Still, he was probably the only other person in Venice who could translate them.

He was only a quarter of the way through when Samantha finally emerged from the bathroom. Her shining hair framed her face and floated like polished bronze around her shoulders, while her dark green sweater molded enticingly against the curves of her breasts and emphasized the green in her eyes.

Raw desire kicked him hard in the solar plexus and settled like a stone somewhat lower in his anatomy. He nearly dropped the book.

"Did you find what you needed?"

When she crossed the room to deposit dirty clothes back into her suitcase, the snug fit of the jeans across her derriere made her look just as desirable walking away. He wouldn't be using any hot water after all.

"Not…" He cleared his throat as he fought to control his raging libido. "Not yet. I have to translate as I go along."

"From Italian?"

She moved to look over his shoulder and sent a sweet cloud of peach scent cascading around him.

"Ah, no." *Bloody hell!* He needed that cold shower in the worst way. "From Irish, that is, Irish Gaelic. They've taught it in schools in the Republic for over twenty years now. Kathleen was always much more proficient at it than I was."

"But you can do it."

"Yes, it's difficult though, especially on an empty stomach."

"Do you want me to go—?"

"No, I'll just shower and shave, then we'll see about some real breakfast and some new clothes too." *Like nice baggy trousers.*

As Keirnan dashed into the bathroom, Sam picked up the journal. It contained the same loopy feminine script in the same unusual language as the note she'd found in his wallet. Gaelic—that explained why she hadn't recognized it. She thumbed through a few pages before placing the book on the bureau.

The sound of running water told her Keirnan was in the shower. Naked. The image of his wet, gleaming muscles caused her mouth to go dry. Her face flushed.

Get a grip, Sam!

To distract her wayward mind, she heaved her suit-case onto the end of the bed and began rearranging and repacking. Before she finished, the water stopped. Good, at least that meant he was getting dressed. She squeezed her sneakers into the corner of her tightly stuffed case. No more being picked out as American because of those.

Then the unexpected memory of his lean, muscular body pressed against hers made her hands shake.

He's just a guy. Her old practical self tried to ratio-nalize, but the new Sam wasn't buying it for a second. Keirnan Fitzgerald could never be *just* anything.

The jangle of the telephone made her jump. It rang

again before she could coordinate her startled mind and body enough to answer.

"Signorina Lewis," the hotel clerk's heavily accented English reverberated from the handset. "A man from the tour company is here to speak with you."

Probably to tell her there'd be extra charges for not leaving last night.

"All right, tell him I'll be right down."

"No Signorina, he is on his way up."

"Oh, all right, *grazie*. Thank you."

As she replaced the receiver, Keirnan pushed the bathroom door open.

"Who was that?"

His face was half covered with shaving cream, and to her great relief he was dressed in the sweatpants and oversized T-shirt.

"The front desk. A person from the tour company is here."

Wariness melted from his beautiful azure eyes. "Don't worry, luv. I'll reimburse you for any extra costs."

Before she could reply, someone knocked.

"Signorina Lewis?"

She only opened the door a crack, but a tall man with short brown hair pulled it from her grasp and stepped inside.

"*Buon giorno*, Signorina. Good day, miss." His dark eyes swept her from top to toe, then his gaze moved to the bathroom. "*Buon giorno*, Keirnan."

Keirnan returned his measuring stare. "*Buon giorno*, Carlo."

Sam's mouth opened and closed like a beached trout, but no sound emerged.

Keirnan's penetrating cerulean gaze caught hers. "'Tis all right, luv. Carlo's not from the tour company. He's with Interpol. At least that's what his badge used to say." His voice dripped sarcasm.

Interpol?

Cops?

Spies?

Sam stumbled backward and plunked down on the edge of the bed, still unable to find her voice. Neither man noticed. They were exchanging lethal stares again.

"Why are you in Venice, Keirnan?" Carlo spoke with a clipped, frosty accent.

"'Tis a beautiful city." Keirnan folded his arms across his chest. "I happen to like it."

"And your sister, Signora DiLucca?" Something in his detached tone told Sam this was not about kidnapping.

"She likes it, too."

The Interpol agent's eyes narrowed, but his voice remained dispassionate. "Perhaps there are things in Venice the two of you like too much. Old, valuable things you want to keep for yourselves. Or sell to the highest bidder."

Keirnan wiped the lather off his face. "Prove it."

"Oh, I intend to, and when I do, I will see that you and your sister are put away for a very long time."

Carlo made a dismissing gesture then turned to look at Sam. For an instant she felt like a deer in a rifle's cross hairs, then the deadly gleam in the man's dark eyes softened.

"So sorry for the intrusion, Signorina." His voice grew solicitous. "But this man is not to be trusted. Five years ago, his sister and her husband were jailed for art forgery, and he was an accessory—"

"That's a bloody lie!"

"You are the expert at lies, are you not, Keirnan? Lies and half-truths. But you won't get away with them this time." He turned back to Sam, still unruffled. "Please, Signorina, stay as far away from this one as you can."

He pulled a hand from his pocket and extended it in her direction. Before she could blink, Keirnan leaped next to her.

"Don't touch her!"

Carlo patently ignored him as he offered her a card. "Call me at any time."

Only after her trembling hand closed over the small rectangle of paper did he turn once more to Keirnan.

"Forget about the jewels, Keirnan. Leave Venice. Go back to America, and take your sister with you."

In two long strides, the Interpol agent was at the door. He looked at both of them for a long moment, then without another word, he left.

Sam studied the white embossed card and tried not to hyperventilate. Engraved in black letters were "Carlo Bergamon" and a phone number. Apparently Interpol agents didn't always advertise the fact. She felt the mattress shift as Keirnan sat next to her.

"I'm sorry, luv."

"Is what he said true?"

Her head buzzed as she searched his handsome, half-shaved face for clues. Was this man she'd so blithely allied herself with a criminal after all?

Keirnan dropped his gaze and gave a slight nod. "Some of it is, I'm afraid. My sister's husband, now ex-husband, was an artist. Quite good too, but more than a little eccentric. Successful... I'm afraid was another story." He pressed his lips together as if the words were difficult.

She helped him. "So he forged paintings and sold them as genuine?"

"Yes." He raised his eyes, and Sam saw anger as well as pleading in their blue depths. "But my sister didn't know until it was too late. Neither did I. Hell, I wasn't even in Italy!" He stopped, sighed. "Even though the evidence against her was circumstantial, her attorney thought it best to plea-bargain. Her husband went to jail. She got time served and probation."

"It's okay. I believe you."

Though she couldn't explain why, she did. Gratitude flooded his face. Still she had to ask, "But why did that man—Carlo—tell you to forget about the jewels? What jewels?"

He rose to his feet and fingered the closed drapes at the window, not looking at her. "The Jewels of the Madonna."

Again, Sam's mouth gaped in surprise. "You mean they really exist?"

"Oh, they exist all right." He faced her, his expression fierce. "But in spite of what most everyone seems to think, I don't have them."

"Why in the world would you?" she blurted. "Have them, I mean."

He passed a hand across his eyes. "I suppose it's too late now to worry about how much I should tell you." He sat next to her and placed his hand over hers. "My sister is a scholar of history, Renaissance history."

"The painting you showed me…"

"Yes, that painting of Serafina Lombardo was part of her study and grew into her obsession. Kathleen did extensive research on the Lombardo family for her thesis. Then she discovered the possible link between the Lombardos and the story of *The Jewels of the Madonna.*"

As Keirnan spoke, a vague recollection stirred on the fringes of Sam's mind. Or maybe it was something she'd dreamed?

"She proved it was true," she murmured more to herself than to him.

He wasn't looking at her and continued as if he hadn't heard. "After the ugly business with her and her husband's arrest, the trial, and the divorce, she was in a very bad way for quite a while."

He pressed his lips into a tight line, then glanced down and intertwined his fingers with hers. Joining their hands seemed to strengthen his resolve.

"About a year ago, she told me she wanted to come back to Venice to take up 'the quest' again. I was so bloody happy to see her interested in anything that I gave her a couple grand to get established." His voice faltered while his eyes grew unfocused and far away. Then he swallowed hard as if he had something bitter in his mouth. "Three months ago, she emailed me in Gaelic, which was our private joke, and said the pieces were finally in place. She was closing in on the where-abouts of the jewels."

Sam gasped, not at his words, but because of the image forming in her mind of dark blue, unfaceted stones half the size of her palm. Her hand pulled free of his and went to the hollow of her throat where her breath seemed to be stuck.

"I didn't take her seriously until last week."

Keirnan rose and paced to the window, a bundle of raw, nervous energy.

"Then what happened?" Though she had spoken, her whispered tone sounded foreign, like it came from someone else.

His voice was husky, and he wasn't looking at her again. "I got a handwritten note from her in Gaelic. She said her 'discovery' had been noticed by certain people, and she was frightened. But she had things written down and 'remember Narnia.' Three days later, I got a phone call." He stopped abruptly and squeezed his eyes shut.

Heavy tension settled on Sam's shoulders. "Did you know who it was?" As if the question weren't odd enough, again she felt like someone else asked.

Keirnan looked at her as if he thought the same. "Maybe. The voice was distorted, but the bloody bastard told me he had my sister, and if I wanted her back, I'd better bring him the Jewels of the Madonna."

Venice, 1485

When Father Mateo emerged from the sacristy of Santa Maria dei Miracoli, Nino stepped from the nearby shadows. The priest's dark eyes narrowed in suspicion.

"You're early, boy." His tone and facial expression left no doubt that the good father didn't like him either.

"I wanted to speak with you alone before Serafina arrives."

The priest made a show of adjusting his vestments. "Very well, walk with me, then."

Nino kept pace with the shorter, heavier man as they

traversed the side aisle and approached the nave of the church. Several other people milled about, some with lighted tapers. The priest raised his hand in blessing to an old, richly dressed woman and at two lay brothers who dusted and polished the wood and marble of the twin pulpits.

"I presume you didn't come to make a confession."

"No." Nino pitched his voice low enough so that only Father Mateo could hear him. "I shall speak plainly. I must know why you want to help Serafina."

The priest paused in mid-stride and gave him an appraising glance. "Certainly not the same reason you do." He resumed walking. "She is deeply infatuated with you, boy, but I'm sure you know that very well. I just hope you have not acted on it."

Nino's step faltered, and he sucked in a breath. "I love her," he challenged. "I only want to see her happy."

"Which she never will be with you." Father Mateo's dark eyes bored into him with unspoken contempt. "Not for long anyway. A few weeks, a month or two. But a year from now, when she is wretched and hungry and your babe grows big in her belly, then she will hate you."

"I am not such a fool I don't realize that." Nino's fisted hands ached from the force of holding in his anger. The other man's eyebrow twitched, no doubt in surprise at his admission. "But I want to know what it is *you* want."

The priest broke eye contact with an exaggerated sigh. "Want? Ah, there are many things. So very many. But with regard to the Signorina Lombardo, only a little recompense."

"Money." Nino had suspected correctly. "How much?"

"More than you will ever have, boy. But the Lombardos have so much they will scarcely notice."

Nino followed the priest's gaze to the right side of the chancel. In the corner of the parapet rose a larger-than-life-sized statue of the Madonna. Serafina's older brothers Antonio and Tullio had sculpted it.

The stone sash of the Madonna's cloak ran from her right shoulder across and under her left breast. Seven egg-sized sapphires adorned the sash, and their indigo depths twinkled in the light shining through the stained glass windows.

Father Mateo sighed. "Venice has so much squandered wealth. I suppose Florence is the same."

"Yes." Was this man as completely false-hearted as Nino feared? "But stealing is a sin. How can you ask the lady to endanger her immortal soul?"

"There is always atonement for sin."

Even though it was the answer Nino expected, his veins thundered with a rage to commit a far more grievous offense than stealing. He had to fight for a long moment before daring to speak. "Then let the sin be mine."

"As you wish." The priest murmured then glanced over Nino's shoulder. "Ah, here comes your lady love now. Go and wait where we talked before. We will soon know what resolve both of you possess."

Flushed with anger and the sting of Father Mateo's dismissal, Nino complied nonetheless. The fewer people who saw him with Serafina, the better. While he waited inside the uncomfortably airless little room, he began to form a desperate plan.

The arrival of Serafina with the priest scattered his thoughts. Serafina's eyes were red-rimmed, her face pinched with worry. Father Mateo had no doubt questioned her intentions once more. Nino longed to pull her into his embrace but couldn't. She seemed equally restrained, not reaching for him, nor even speaking his name. They both stood rigidly side by side.

"Last night, a group of holy sisters arrived by ship from Ravenna," the priest began without preamble. Apparently he saw no further need to question their purposes, nor motives. "When they have rested, they will continue by land on their journey to Padua. One novitiate more or less will hardly be noticed."

"But Serafina's family will notice her missing," Nino argued. "They will search for her, even outside the city."

"Not if they believe she is dead."

The priest's tone was impassive, but Serafina's gasp was not. Her trembling hand secretly sought for Nino's, and she laced her fingers tightly with his.

Father Mateo addressed her in the same even tone. "First you must complain of not feeling well. Say your head and throat ache. Then you must take to your bed for an entire day and night. Eat nothing, and drink only when no one is looking. Swoon if anyone tries to make you get up. Everyone must believe you are gravely ill, that you have the plague."

Serafina automatically crossed herself with her free hand, but Nino was skeptical. "How will she convince them without the sores?"

The priest turned triumphant, glittering eyes on him. "Because you will paint them on her. You're an artist, are you not? You have seen the plague before."

His pronouncement left Nino thunderstruck. "Yes, but this is madness!"

"No, this is your most important commission. Fulfill it well, and no one will get close enough to see that they are not real. Once I am summoned, I shall announce that Serafina is dead. To spare the contagion, I will remove her body myself."

The man's ruthlessness truly knew no boundaries.

Serafina's quaking had spread from her hand to the rest of her body.

"There must be another way," Nino insisted.

"Then tell me what it is," the priest replied. "But be quick. The sisters will depart within the week, and the week after, the viscount will have his marriage."

"No!" Serafina spoke for the first time, her voice surprisingly strong in spite of her shaking limbs. "I will do as you say."

She loosened her grip on Nino's hand and pulled a large gold signet ring off her index finger. "The viscount gave me this. I wish for you to have it, Father." She dropped the ring into the priest's upturned palm. Then she pulled a long strand of pearls interspersed with heavy gold beads out of her bodice, over her head, and dropped that into his hand also. "And give these to the holy sisters to pay for my journey to Padua."

The necklace was probably worth as much as everything Nino owned.

"Thank you, my child." Father Mateo's eyes met Nino's, and they exchanged scathing glares as the priest's fingers closed around the jewelry. "And are you willing to play your part in this plan, my son?"

"Five days," Nino replied. "I'll need five days."

Chapter 6

"WELL, NOW YOU KNOW THE WHOLE, BLOODY AWFUL story." Keirnan rolled his shoulders to release his pent-up emotions. It actually felt good to tell someone. No, that wasn't quite true—it felt good to tell Samantha.

Best not to linger there, boyo.

He mentally forced himself to switch gears. "Let me finish shaving, then we'll get ourselves a decent breakfast and me some decent clothes. Not necessarily in that order."

Unfortunately, Samantha wasn't as ready as he was to let his confession go. "*Then* what are you going to do? About the jewels? When you find them, I mean."

Her faith in his abilities was gratifying, and he hoped not misplaced. And at this point, he wouldn't lie to her.

"Kathleen's all I have. Interpol and everyone else be damned, I'll do whatever it takes to see my sister safe."

Her green-gold gaze was soft with sympathy. "I understand. I'll help you."

"You already have." He beat another hasty retreat into the bathroom, not trusting himself to leave the door open.

Twenty minutes later, they tramped down the Strada Mercerie, the main thoroughfare between the Rialto and St. Mark's Square. Shops were opening, and Keirnan turned into the first one that sold men's clothing. He quickly snagged a package of boxers and another of plain white T-shirts.

As he thumbed through a rack of wool trousers for his size, Samantha held out a pair of dark socks and glanced meaningfully at the ones he wore. He grinned and headed toward the dressing room, grabbing a charcoal gray sweater on the way.

"This, too." Samantha shoved a pale blue oxford shirt at him just before he closed the dressing room door.

A few minutes later, he stood at the counter newly dressed, credit card in hand. In typical Italian fashion, the sales clerk rang up the loose price tags and placed the soiled sweats and extra underwear into a plastic bag, quirking an eyebrow but saying nothing.

Keirnan shrugged on his ripped leather jacket—a new one would have to wait a bit—put away his wallet, and captured Samantha's hand. For the next hour, he intended to act as if he really were on holiday with nothing else to do but entertain a pretty girl. It was the least he could do, even though he owed her so much more.

He took her to a place modeled after an American diner that served a fair imitation of American food. Over three-egg omelets and mounds of potatoes, he coaxed her into revealing a bit about herself. She reluctantly confessed that she'd grown up with no sisters, brothers, or father, though her mother was never without a "boyfriend" for more than a few months at a time.

She worked as a librarian at the University of Indiana in Bloomington, which explained why she was far from empty-headed. And some lout of an engineering professor had broken their engagement but definitely not her spirit.

The world was full of shortsighted fools it seemed, and the old "it takes one to know one" adage definitely applied. In another time and place…

Keirnan had no doubt he would have…

Uncomfortably heavy silence stretched between them. Keirnan hated what he must do now, but there was no help for it.

"Let's go get your bags and check you out of the hotel."

Surprise sparked in her lovely eyes. "What about the journal and the CD?"

"Later." She opened her mouth to protest, but he plunged on, his voice low. "Samantha, luv, please. With Interpol involved, you know you can't stay."

She dropped her gaze, twisted her napkin in her lap. "You're right."

Even though she'd agreed, he didn't like the way her lips pressed into a thin, determined line.

She remained tight-lipped for the next hour, which was a pity. He'd have far preferred to see her smiling during what was left of their time together.

Even the weather decided to cooperate. Though the air was still brisk, the oppressive fog had burned off, and sunlight skittered over the waves. This was more like the Serenissima he knew and loved. A place of dreams and possibilities, where two people from totally different circumstances could find happiness together.

Keirnan draped his arm across Samantha's shoulders as the vaporetto wound its way down the traffic-clogged Grand Canal. A sense of calm and familiarity settled over him. For the first time in five days, he actually believed things were going to be all right. He could do this!

The boat pulled into the dock at the foot of the Santa Lucia Stazione, and reality reared its ugly head.

Samantha's mouth dropped open in surprise as he

stood and wrestled her heavy, wheeled suitcase out onto the steps. But she hitched her carry-on onto her shoulder and followed him off the vaporetto. He'd never met a woman so gutsy and spirited, not to mention appealing.

Wordlessly, they climbed the wide fan of steps and entered the bustling, noisy, smoke-filled lobby. The times and destinations on the departure board flipped, and Keirnan scanned the newly formed list.

"We're in luck. An Inter-City leaves for Rome in fifteen minutes."

"I… I didn't think you meant—"

"Shush." He placed two fingertips lightly against her lips, stopping her words. "We don't have time for this." *More's the pity.*

Keirnan hurried to the nearest automatic ticket machine before he changed his mind. Before he put his mouth instead of his fingers against her lips.

He shoved the first-class, one-way ticket into her hand without meeting her gaze. His throat felt as if someone had him in a choke hold. He coughed to pull in enough air to speak.

"Platform four. We have to hurry." However, as they approached the archway leading to the trains, a wild, unreasoning inspiration made him stop and snatch a printed advertisement off a wire rack. "Do you have a pen?"

Samantha groped in her bag and pulled out a ballpoint. Confusion and something else swam in the depths of her expressive eyes.

Damn, he was a weak, selfish fool!

But he just couldn't help himself. He scribbled on the back of the ad, then thrust the paper and pen into her hands.

"This is the name and address of a hotel in Rome, the Locanda Stella. 'Tis near the Spanish steps." He grabbed the handle of her suitcase and hustled her onto the platform. "Wait for me there. I'll call you tomorrow night."

Dozens of people jostled around them, hurrying to board the idling train.

She hesitated. "But what if—"

"I promise I'll call you." Keirnan grabbed her shoulder, intending to kiss her cheeks in farewell, then thought better of it. Too close to her tempting mouth.

"Don't make a promise you can't keep." The catch in her voice shot an arrow of pain straight into his chest.

"I never do." He cupped his palm around her smooth cheek. "Now you really need to go."

Still she hesitated in front of the open door of the first-class car. A man in an overcoat rushed up and ducked around her to climb aboard.

"Please go," he repeated.

With a shaky breath, Samantha pulled herself up the two steps and stood inside the compartment. He pushed in the long handle and reached the heavy suitcase to her. She swiped at one eye with the back of her hand.

"*Ciao*! *Ciao*! *Arrivederci*! Good-bye! Good-bye!" A dozen feet away, a group of teen girls shouted and waved at two other girls seated inside the train.

"*Ciao*, luv." His own voice came out a hoarse whisper, and he turned quickly away.

When he reached the end of the platform, the conductor called out and the train rumbled. Keirnan stopped and turned to watch. Amid grinding, clanking, and more shouted farewells, the train pulled away.

Of all the shortsighted, ill-advised things he'd done in the past few days, why did this feel the worst? And what the devil had possessed him to ask her to wait for him in Rome? He had absolutely no right.

The group of giggling girls brushed past him and revealed Samantha standing in the middle of the platform. Her suitcase and carry-on were stacked on the ground at her feet.

When had he started running?

The distance between them disappeared.

"I... I'm s-s..." Her voice wavered. "I'm sorry. I just couldn't..."

He grabbed her shoulders and pulled her against him. "Don't be sorry."

Then he stopped her silly apology with his mouth. He felt her melt against him as his tongue parted her soft, yielding lips and tasted the sweetness inside. Her hands looped around his neck as she angled her head and took a taste of him also.

The silky feel of her tongue elicited a low, animal growl from someplace deep within him. Blood and desire roared through his veins. He cupped the back of her head with his left hand while his right circled her waist and pulled her possessively close. Scorching hot need engulfed him. Their tongues danced in a sensual rhythm as familiar and ancient as this city and the lagoon surrounding it.

His heart thundered against his chest, or maybe it was her heart hammering against him. He couldn't distinguish where one of them stopped and the other started, and God knew he didn't care. He only knew she was his and he was hers, and in spite of everything, or maybe because of it, their destiny was sealed.

"*Bravissimo*! *Amore*! *Bravo*! Love!"

Keirnan felt Samantha stiffen at the shouts. Panting, he broke their kiss and looked across at the next platform. A dozen people stood watching and making catcalls.

"Take a bow, luv," he murmured, tipping an imaginary hat to the onlookers. Face flushing scarlet, Samantha bobbed in a half-curtsey, and applause and laughter broke out from their unwanted audience. He couldn't help but laugh as well. "Congratulations, we've now made a public spectacle of ourselves."

And it felt bloody wonderful.

Sam settled her carry-on on top of her suitcase and closed the door of the locker. Securing the lock, she slipped the key inside her fanny pack. "All set. Now what?"

Keirnan's bright azure gaze took on a steely cast. "It's been twenty-four hours, time to contact the kidnapper."

A wave of anxiety broke over Sam, temporarily closed up her throat, and clawed its way into the pit of her stomach. Unable to speak, she glanced at the row of pay phones against the wall, but Keirnan shook his head. "I had a face-to-face confrontation in mind."

Sam sputtered incoherently for a moment. "But how… where…?"

"Remember earlier? You asked me if I knew who might have abducted my sister, and the more I've thought on it the more certain I am." He seemed unnaturally calm as he placed her hand in the crook of his arm and turned toward the doors.

"So tell me," she prompted.

Her impatience brought a hint of a smile that flashed

briefly before his alluring mouth went grim. "He's a professor here at the university named Roberto Spinelli. Ten years ago, he and my sister were lovers."

The word caused the old Sam to squirm with discomfort. *Was that what she and Keirnan were soon to be? Could she do that?*

The new Sam gave a shiver of anticipation. She certainly wanted to try. "Has your sister seen him since she came back to Venice?"

"Not intentionally. But he certainly knows all about her fascination with the jewels, her research…" He paused to hold open the door for her. "And Spinelli always loved to gamble."

Sam chewed her lip as she processed this information. She, of all people, knew that university professors possessed a host of shortcomings. "Is he dangerous?"

"Not as much as I can be." Keirnan's glib reply contained a definite edge, and the solid muscles in his arm testified to the probable truth in the statement. It struck her again that she had no rational reason to trust this man. "Before we go to his flat there is one thing I need."

Sam's thoughts whirled. *A gun? A knife? A tazer?*

Panic must have showed on her face, because he smiled again. "A cell phone. Mine doesn't work in Europe."

An hour later, phone purchased and their plan formulated, Sam stood, hand interlaced with Keirnan's, outside an elegant four-story building not far from the university. He rubbed his unencumbered thumb over the engraved brass nameplate next to the bottom button in a row of six.

"I knew the old windbag would still live here,"

he muttered. He gave her fingers a gentle squeeze. "Ready then?"

She nodded, even though she felt anything but ready. What had sounded simple when they'd talked didn't seem that way now. Taking a deep breath, she released Keirnan's hand and pressed the buzzer to the intercom. After a full minute, she was ready to give up and retreat when a tinny voice barked through the speaker. "*Prego*? If you please?"

"Professor Spinelli, I'm Sam Lewis from the University of Indiana, and I need to speak with you." Her voice came out amazingly calm.

She scarcely got the words out before he replied in accented English. "No. I… I am sorry. Call my office for an appointment."

"Please Professor, this is urgent. I must speak with you now."

This time there was a brief pause. "Do I know you?"

"This isn't about me. I must speak to you about my friend, Kathleen DiLucca."

As soon as Sam said the name, she heard an audible gasp, and the door lock buzzed. With lightning speed, Keirnan shoved it open.

She followed him into the tiled foyer to an elevator, a luxury not found in most buildings in Venice, and she'd bet even more rare for a professor's residence. As the elevator moved upward, she lurched with dizzy nervousness. Beside her, Keirnan looked grimly determined.

They got off on the top floor, and Sam waited until Keirnan scooted to the side and out of the line of vision of the peek hole, before she lifted the heavy brass knocker.

"Who—" Before the man could say two words,

Keirnan crashed against the door and grabbed him by the collar.

"Where the hell is my sister?"

Several inches shorter than Keirnan and at least twenty years older with a definite paunch, the professor reeled backward with the force of Keirnan's onslaught. The two of them crashed against an ornate brass coat rack that stood just inside the door. Miraculously, they remained upright. The coat rack didn't.

"Where is she, Spinelli?" Keirnan twisted the collar of the man's shirt and nearly lifted him off the ground, but his voice remained deadly calm. "Don't bother lying. I know you took her."

Sam stepped inside and discreetly closed the door. She glanced quickly into the room for signs of other occupants then she looked in the other direction. Nothing.

"*P-per favore*. Please." Spinelli gasped, his face rapidly turning purple from lack of oxygen.

Sam sucked in a shaky breath in sympathy as she sidled around the two men and the fallen rack. Earlier, Keirnan had made some vague comment to her about falling in with a gang of "street toughs" in his early teens. Obviously he'd never forgotten what he'd learned.

Keirnan loosened his grip on the professor's shirt a fraction. "Talk fast," he commanded.

The hapless man wheezed in air then let loose with a spate of Italian. Whatever he said did not please Keirnan, who snarled back an answer in Italian punctuated with a rough shake that rattled Spinelli's teeth.

Cringing inwardly, Sam hurried through the sitting room and into the kitchen beyond. No signs of anyone else there either, nor in the formal dining room on the other side of the kitchen. Her fingers slipped into her pocket and touched the edge of the Interpol agent's card. Why hadn't she argued to call the authorities? She could still faintly hear Spinelli whining in Italian.

She saw neither sharp nor blunt instruments anywhere in the tidy, ultramodern kitchen. Still, given what she'd just witnessed of Keirnan's temper, she hoped he didn't decide to drag Spinelli in here. There was no doubt in her mind now that he could indeed be dangerous. But given the circumstances, could she honestly blame him?

She re-entered the sitting room, where the interrogation continued in English.

"You'd better pray like hell they haven't hurt her." Keirnan's voice remained eerily composed and lethal sounding.

"You must believe me, Keirnan." Spinelli's eyes rolled in fear, and his voice sounded raspy. "I never meant for it to go this way."

"Call them." The implied threat of "or else" hung in the air for a moment before Keirnan let go of the other man's shirt. "Now."

Spinelli's shaking legs almost gave way. He gripped the edge of the wall to keep from falling. "B-b-but they will call me—"

"I said now."

"The ph-phone is in m-my study."

Keirnan's eyes flicked in her direction; the deadly cold glinting in them chilled straight to her bones, but his tone softened. "Fetch it for us, will you, luv?"

Sam bit her lower lip and gave a small nod. As she turned toward the hallway, she saw Keirnan grab Spinelli's shirt again and shove him roughly into the sitting room. Still gnawing her lip, she darted down the hall.

When she re-emerged with the cell phone, Spinelli was seated in a straight-backed, Queen Anne–style chair, his wrists and ankles bound with electrical cords. Mouth dry and her eyes undoubtedly bulging, she handed the phone to Keirnan, who in turn thrust it at the other man.

Spinelli raised his tied hands, which noticeably trembled, as he awkwardly punched in the number. Keirnan immediately clasped the phone to his ear, but after a moment, he flipped it closed.

Spinelli sagged in visible relief. "See? I said th—"

Keirnan silenced him with a glance, but his voice remained matter-of-fact. "We'll just keep trying until they do answer."

"Uh, Keirnan?" Sam hated when her voice squeaked. She cleared her throat. "There's a laptop in his office."

"Good."

An ornate millefiori vase sat on the windowsill. Keirnan picked it up and handed it to her. It was so heavy she had to grab it with both hands.

"If he moves, bash him."

Shifting the heavy vase in her hands, Sam watched him stride down the hall. She'd known this would not be a pleasant scene. Keirnan had even warned her that she might not want to go inside since he intended to "rough Spinelli up" if his sister wasn't there. That was unsettling enough, but it was really difficult for her to reconcile the exuberant, passionate kiss they'd shared in the train station with this calculated ruthlessness.

"That one never liked me."

Sam snapped her gaze back to the professor. He looked and sounded pathetic, not like a man who would callously kidnap a woman he'd once loved. But that's what he had done.

That reminder kept her voice steady. "Looks like he had good reasons not to."

"Not until now." Raising his bound fingers toward his throat, Spinelli studied her for a moment and narrowed his dark eyes speculatively.

"Sometimes I think he and his sister like each other a little too much… like the brother and sister in *The Jewels of the Madonna*, eh?"

Then, in response to her obviously puzzled look, he added, "You don't know the story?" Sam shook her head, and Spinelli continued. "The blacksmith, Gennaro, he wants to save his sister Maliella from Rafaele, who is… I think you say a 'bad boy.' So Gennaro steals the Jewels of the Madonna—"

"Shut your mouth." Keirnan ordered as he re-entered the room carrying the laptop.

Spinelli instantly obeyed, but his gaze stayed on her.

"It's okay." Sam carefully moved to the opposite side of the room and set the vase on a side table. "He was telling me the story of the opera *The Jewels of the Madonna*."

Keirnan seated himself in a chair that matched the one Spinelli sat in. Then he pulled up another side table, placed the laptop on it, and booted it up.

"Don't believe anything he says."

For several agonizing moments, the only sound was the faint hum of the computer and the click as Keirnan slid the round CD from his pocket into the drive.

Finally Sam dared to break the oppressive silence. "So what happens after Gennaro steals the jewels?"

Spinelli looked from her to Keirnan, who was bent intently over the laptop, then back to her again before he spoke. "He gives them to his sister, and then he seduces her."

Revulsion knotted in Sam's throat as his heavily accented voice dropped to a venomous whisper. "Maybe like Antonio and Serafina Lombardo, eh? Maybe even like…" His voice trailed off when Keirnan scowled at him over the top of the computer screen.

"Shut your filthy, lying mouth, or I'll gag you." His gaze moved to her and softened once more. "He forgot to mention that Maliella was Gennaro's adopted sister. And as for Antonio and Serafina…"

A sudden spark of knowledge blazed from Sam's subconscious to her conscious mind.

"It wasn't Antonio Lombardo," she blurted. She had no idea where the notion came from, but she was certain it was true. "There was someone else. Someone with… with a similar name."

Both men stared at her as if she'd sprouted a second head. Maybe she had, or at least a second brain, because her old brain had certainly never functioned like this.

"That's what my sister believed as well," Keirnan acknowledged quietly. "And she's spent years trying to prove it."

"So Keirnan…" Spinelli's tone had changed to goading. "Your girlfriend is—how you say? A psychic?"

"I'm not his girlfriend," Sam quickly denied.

"She's not my girlfriend," Keirnan asserted at the same time.

"No?" Spinelli raised one eyebrow in that most annoying of Italian habits.

"No," Sam declared. "I'm his... his..."

Exactly what the hell was she? Accomplice? Accessory?

"Friend," she finished a bit lamely.

Spinelli's eyes gleamed knowingly.

"Speaking of friends—" Keirnan speared him with another deadly glare. "Time to phone yours again." He flipped open the cell phone and punched the redial button.

Venice, 1485

The residual heat emanating from the open door of the kiln warmed the predawn air enough so that Nino's shirt-sleeves were rolled up to his elbows. The pottery pieces within the chest-high earthen oven still glowed, but he had no time to wait for them to cool.

Using a pair of long-handled tongs, he pulled out an oval lump the size of a hen's egg and dropped it into a wooden bucket of water. Steam hissed and belched over the rim, twice, thrice, four times as he deposited each successive matching knob. Then he picked up the bucket and carried it toward the privacy of his room.

All was quiet and dark within the *scuola* as he stealthily climbed the stairs, but when he reached his room, a glow of candlelight shone in a small arc in the hallway. His door was ajar. Unease prickled down his spine; he always made sure it was closed. He cautiously edged his way inside, but the door squeaked as he crossed the threshold.

Fredo whirled to face him, a small bowl of red powdered substance in his hand. His sudden movement made the flame of the stubby candle on the worktable behind him flicker erratically.

"There you are! Why the devil are you skulking around in the middle of the night?"

Nino closed the door and carefully set the bucket behind him.

"Why are you?" he countered. "I thought you were in Burano."

His lanky friend sighed heavily. "I've only just returned. Mariana and I had another disagreement, and I thought it best not to wait until morning."

"She threw you out, you mean?"

Of all the times for Fredo and his mistress to have a falling out, which they did frequently, this was the worst.

"Don't tell me it was over Giacomo again." The widowed Mariana's six-year-old son hated Fredo on sight, if his friend was to be believed.

"That boy is demon spawn, a changeling. I'm sure of it! But enough about that, I know why I haven't slept tonight." He waggled his eyebrows salaciously. "What about you?"

The painter cocked his head and studied him for a moment. "You look terrible. Have you slept at all since I've been gone? Did the beautiful Serafina break your heart so quickly?"

Nino didn't have time to waste talking, nor did he have any intention of revealing the truth to his friend, better to say as little as possible. "Just go to bed, Fredo."

"Not until you tell me what all this is about." He motioned to the worktable behind him where a few moldy crusts of bread lay scattered among bowls and jars of various pigments, tools, brushes, and several half-formed lumps of clay.

"I've a new commission and not much time to finish it."

"Maybe I can help—"

"No." Nino reached for the bowl Fredo held in his hand and realized too late that he'd exposed the bare skin of his forearm.

His friend sucked in a sharp breath. "Holy Blessed Mother…"

He grabbed Nino's arm and held it close to the candle. The light played across a large reddish brown and yellow splotch. Fredo looked again before he touched an inquisitive finger to the bumpy stain. "For a moment there I almost thought…"

Nino jerked his arm away and shoved down his sleeve. "Just trying out some colors."

"And I'm the Doge's chief arse wiper! Nino, what is going on?"

"Nothing of concern to you." He turned away and set the bowl on the table. "Just go to sleep. I'll be quiet and not disturb you."

But the other man would not be persuaded. He planted his hands on his hips in a belligerent stance.

"I'll not do a thing until you explain to me why someone would try to look like they have the plague."

"I can't explain." Nino's temples throbbed. His entire body felt leaden with fatigue. "Please, Fredo…"

He had only two more days and the night between them before his time was gone, and his latest effort still was not good enough. It hadn't sufficiently fooled Fredo for an instant.

He sank onto the stool beside the worktable. "I just can't."

"I thought we were the best of friends, Nino. More like brothers." His friend clapped his shoulder. "Your secrets are safe with me."

Nino stared into the candle flame as the silence stretched uncomfortably long between them. Finally, Fredo gave another heavy sigh. "This is about Serafina Lombardo, isn't it?"

A wave of despair washed over Nino. He covered his face with his hands. No matter what the cost, he could not afford to fail.

"Florentine jackass," Fredo muttered. "Fine, you don't have to tell me, but you still need my help."

Nino raised his head and saw his friend examining the contents of one of the bowls, rubbing the sticky substance between his fingers.

"You're obviously no painter, but luckily I am." Fredo stuck his fingers into several other bowls and made a derisive sound. "This is the wrong medium. We need to make up some tempera. As soon as it's light, we'll go rob a henhouse, mix up a fresh batch. Plus, the eggs will draw up the skin when they dry, make it look more like a real wound…"

"Fredo, I…"

His friend was right. He needed help. And not only that, Fredo was a gifted painter. He'd probably be as celebrated as one of the Bellinis someday.

Nino gave a resigned sigh. "I can't thank you enough."

"No, you probably can't," the other man retorted. He set down the bowl in his hand. "I think we may be able to use a couple of these, but we certainly don't need

this pot of blue glaze." He gave Nino a knowing stare.
"Unless of course, it has something to do with that
bucket you left by the door."

Chapter 7

THEY'D BEEN AT PROFESSOR SPINELLI'S FOR OVER AN hour, and the tension had frazzled Sam's nerves to the breaking point. Keirnan had tried twice more to phone the people who now supposedly held his sister, but with no success. However, he seemed to have better luck with the files on the CD. Though he said nothing, she saw unmistakable excitement flicker across his face several times.

Once, he'd sent her into the kitchen for something to eat. Still hesitant to look for a knife, she'd brought back some apples she found in a bowl on the dining room table. Hers sat half-eaten on the arm of the brocade settee while she paced to the window and back.

Spinelli sat rigidly in his chair, staring at a black silk Armani tie that hung ominously over the arm of Keirnan's chair. When he'd mentioned something about past lives, Keirnan vowed to gag him if he spoke again.

The cell phone, which sat next to the laptop, suddenly chirped out the chorus to "Santa Lucia," and Sam nearly leaped out of her skin. Keirnan looked momentarily startled too, but he recovered quickly.

Rising to his feet, he flipped the phone open and held it to Spinelli's ear. The professor obediently answered, and after a sentence, Keirnan took over, speaking in Italian in his low and deadly tone.

Though Sam could understand no more than a word or two of what he said, Keirnan's expression did not bode well. Spinelli didn't seem very pleased with what he heard either. His jaw worked in growing agitation, and he started to rise to his feet.

With his free hand, Keirnan shoved him roughly back into the chair and lapsed into English. "I don't care what becomes of him. You're dealing with me now." He cast a murderous glance at Spinelli. "You'll get nothing from me until I've seen her."

Sam's pulse kicked into triple time, her breath hanging in her throat. This was it! The real deal…

"No, I must see her, *capisce*? Understand?"

After what felt like an eternally long silence, Keirnan spoke a few more sentences in Italian ending with *va bene*, the Italian equivalent of okay, then he flipped the phone shut.

Sam's breath whooshed out, and she sagged against the arm of the settee. Spinelli started to rise again, but Keirnan shoved him back down.

"I could kill you with my bare hands," he growled, "except you're not worth the effort."

He grabbed the black silk tie, secured it to the chair leg, then wrapped it around the electrical cord binding the other man's wrists. "Bring me some more of these," he ordered.

Sam scurried down the hall to the sound of Spinelli's protests. When she reappeared, Keirnan sent her off once more to find the carrying case for the laptop. "Our friend here won't be using it, and I'm sure he won't mind if we do."

She didn't wait for Spinelli's reply.

When she came back to the living room, Keirnan had trussed the other man's arms and legs together with neckties, securing them to the legs of the chair as well. He'd silenced Spinelli by shoving her half-eaten apple into his mouth and securing it in place with another tie.

She looked away quickly and fought a wave of revulsion washing over her.

Keirnan gave the knot around the gag one last tug. "*Ciao*, Roberto. When you get free, I'd strongly suggest you get as far away from Venice as possible. Though if anything happens to Kathleen, be very sure I will find you."

Sam couldn't get to the cool outdoor air fast enough. Not waiting for the elevator, she hurried down the three flights of stairs as quickly as her unsteady legs would carry her.

"Don't worry, luv," Keirnan reassured. He shut the security gate behind them. "His cleaning lady will find him in a day or two if he doesn't work himself loose before then."

Samantha continued to gasp for air and did not reply. He reached for her hand, and she shied away like a spooked filly. He should never have allowed her go into Spinelli's apartment with him. Even he felt a wee bit sickened by what he'd had to do. Anger and desperation were powerful forces, and his had been simmering overlong. Just like when he was a lad.

Unfortunately, this business would likely get worse before it was over. He had a very bad feeling about Spinelli's creditors.

They trudged along in silence for several blocks before he spoke again. "I'm truly sorry you had to see that, luv. I'm not normally the kind of guy who likes to bully and bash people around, but I had to."

"I know." Her reply was a low whisper. She stopped and looked into his face as if she were searching for something. "But you were really, really good at it."

"Desperate times, desperate measures and too much American TV." His flippant remark garnered him a hint of a smile, and he reached for her hand again. This time she didn't pull it away. "Are you hungry?"

She shook her head.

"Then let's go to the *stazione*, fetch our stuff, and find a hotel, shall we?"

She hesitated. "We... I mean, uh, I..." Her cheeks flushed a pretty rosy pink. "I'm not usually the kind of girl who uh..."

He gave her hand a reassuring squeeze. "I know."

After scanning the listings at the tourist information office in the crowded, noisy stazione, Keirnan located a hotel not far from Saint Mark's with a room that met all his requirements—a lift, Internet access, room service, and two beds.

He wasn't about to make Samantha do anything she didn't feel comfortable doing. No matter what he might feel.

Check in proved a bit trickier, however. He'd forgotten that his passport was still at his hotel at the airport. After some circuitous explanations, phone calls to the other hotel, and his promise of extra cash compensation all around, they agreed to send everything over by messenger. Finally, the clerk handed over two room keys.

"Do you think it was Spinelli's... um, friends, who trashed your room and your sister's apartment?" Samantha asked when they were in the lift together.

"Must've been."

His hand inadvertently brushed his ribs. She saw the movement, and her eyes went round with fear. The elevator stopped, and the door slid open.

"He must be really afraid of them to do what he did."

Keirnan's grip on the handle of her suitcase tightened as he walked briskly down the hallway. "That scumbag brought all his problems on himself." He opened the door and took a deep breath to control his roiling anger. "Sorry, luv, but when I think about what he did, and the things he implied to you—"

He shut the door with a bang and a muttered curse.

Samantha paused and looked at the two beds, then glanced hesitantly at him before setting her carry-on bag on the nightstand nearest the window. "It's all right. I didn't believe him."

He slid the laptop case to the floor and heaved her suitcase onto a bench at the foot of the closest bed.

"My sister raised me from the time I was eleven. No easy task since she was only sixteen herself, but our mother died and—"

"You don't have to explain."

"No, I want you to know." It was suddenly important that she knew, which was odd, considering he seldom told anyone about his family. But with Samantha it was different somehow. "My father always drank, but once my mum was gone there was no reason for him to ever sober up. If it hadn't been for Kathleen…"

Samantha sat perched on the edge of the bed, staring out the window. Good, he didn't want to see any pity in her eyes. He sat on the bed across from her and studied his hands.

"She was always there for me, and God knows I needed her. She even put off her university studies for a year because she was afraid I couldn't sufficiently care for myself." Couldn't adequately defend himself from their drunken lout of a father. That was the truth of it. He raised his head and met her gaze. "Though any faults I have are my own doing, not hers."

"Please, Keirnan," Samantha's voice was soft with compassion, as were her lovely golden green eyes. "You don't need to confess to me." Then a wave seemed to pass across her face, a shutter closed off her expression, and she rose to her feet. "It's not like we're involved or anything."

Her prickly comment gouged like a thorn.

"Oh no?" He stood also, and before he actually knew what he was about, he pulled her face to his. Then his lips crashed into hers, and his tongue plunged inside her mouth for a fast, urgent kiss. "Does that feel uninvolved to you?"

Damn! He shouldn't have…

The half-formed thought vanished under the sudden press of Samantha's lips against his. Desire erupted everywhere inside him. Need and longing that had been denied for far too long. Somehow, his coat landed on the floor, and he slid hers off her shoulders.

Keirnan broke the kiss long enough to pull his sweater over his head and push her onto the nearest bed. Her fingers grasped his shirt, pulled it out of his pants, worked at the buttons. White-hot flames blazed at her touch, igniting the simmering passion he'd felt since that first morning in the Doge's Palace.

The mattress sank under his knees. He nuzzled the tender spot behind her ear as he rolled her beneath him.

His hand shoved inside her sweater and undershirt, cupped her breast through the lace of her bra. She gave a breathy little gasp then claimed his mouth again. Searing heat burned away all his senses except need.

Her fingers moved from his shirt to fumble with the button on his fly. Keirnan was far more adept with the hook on her bra. With one deft movement he undid it, while his other hand pushed the lace aside to cradle her smooth breast, the nipple tantalizingly hard against his palm. He rolled his thumb across it, and she moaned into his mouth.

The fingers of her other hand had worked their way inside his T-shirt, and one lightly grazed the scab across his ribs. The sudden twinge of pain jogged his wits.

Saints in heaven!

He had to stop—*now*! He pulled his mouth from hers. "D-did I hurt you?"

God help him, she was so sweet, caring, beautiful. The kind of woman he scarcely let himself dream about. He'd give anything to make her his. He couldn't remember ever wanting a woman quite like this.

"No." The voice rasping from his dry throat belonged to someone else, someone with far more scruples and standards than he would ever possess. "No, but we…"

He let go of her breast—it fit so perfectly in his palm, as though it was made for him—pulled his hands away, and rested on his elbows.

"We have to stop, luv."

She looked dazed, her lips swollen and dark pink from his kisses. It took every ounce of will power in him, and then some, to roll away and sit up.

"I've no protection."

"Oh." She pulled her knees up to her chest and steadied her rapid breathing. "But I'm on birth control…"

Oh trespass sweetly urged… But he wouldn't. She deserved so much more than he had to offer right now.

"No." He stood up and shoved his T-shirt back into his waistband. "I just—" *Have no control when it comes to you.* "—don't think we should do that."

That wary, shuttered look washed over her eyes again. "You're right."

He reached down and cupped his palm around her soft cheek. Maybe when all this was over…

"Please don't look at me like that, *grá mo chroí*."

"What?"

"Oh, uh… just a little Gaelic term of endearment, which reminds me…" He grabbed the laptop and crossed to the desk in the corner of the room, a nice safe distance from either bed. "I need to access an Irish-Gaelic dictionary. My brilliant sister's vocabulary has outdistanced mine in a few crucial spots."

From the edge of his field of vision, he saw that she'd righted her own clothes and scooted to the edge of the bed. "Anything I can do to help?"

"Call room service? Order us up some coffee and a snack."

Sam's caffè latte had long since grown cold, but she finally managed to finish her tramezzini sandwich. Keirnan had wolfed down both of his without moving from the laptop. From time to time, he'd given her a sketchy update on his progress, but his intensity was so obvious that she'd been reluctant to speak to him too much.

Instead she watched him and kept feeling his hands glide across her skin, his lips press into hers, the weight of his body on top of hers. The way she'd thrown herself at him was thoroughly embarrassing, but not enough to make her stop wishing she could do it again—right now.

Unfortunately, he didn't seem to be in the same frame of mind. Was it the circumstances or her?

What was it about him that made her feel things she had never felt? Do things she would never even consider doing?

She had dated Michael for four months before she'd finally let him coax her into bed. She hadn't even known Keirnan for four days. And yet being with him felt familiar. As if they'd always been together.

"Care to go for a stroll?" His question jerked her out of her reverie.

"Okay." She grabbed her coat, happy to distract her mind. "Where to?"

He closed the laptop and pulled on his jacket. "Santa Maria dei Miracoli, to check out the Lombardos' tomb."

Twenty minutes later, they stood in front of the lovely, white marble front of the church, which was actually small by Italian standards.

The late afternoon sun twinkled in the round stained glass window over the front double doors. The relatively clean façade and the sparkling interior were testament to a fairly recent refurbishing. At the far end of the church, Sam could see the painting of the Madonna and child that was said to perform miracles and gave the church its name.

Keirnan strode purposefully down the aisle toward

a robed man polishing the wooden newel post on one of the twin pulpits in front of the high altar, and she followed. While he spoke to the priest in Italian, Sam turned and looked at the beautiful stained glass windows on the side walls. Sunlight diffused through them and spread soft motes of color on everything.

Something drew her eyes toward the chancel. At the top of the raised marble platform, a large sculpture of the Archangel Gabriel silently blew a long slim trumpet. Opposite him stood a similar sized statue of the Madonna, her arms spread, palms out. Sam's breath abruptly hitched in her throat. Across the sash of the Madonna's cloak, large blue jewels gleamed in the muted light.

"K-Keirnan?" She clutched at his sleeve, heart racing.

He turned to her, and his questioning eyes were the same dark glistening blue. Her tongue stuck to the roof of her suddenly dry mouth. She raised a shaky finger to point, but when she looked back at the statue, the jewels were gone.

Keirnan asked a question in Italian.

The priest nodded and answered. "Si, Tullio Lombardo."

Keirnan asked something else. Sam squeezed her eyes shut and rubbed the bridge of her nose, then looked at the Madonna again. She was losing it! The sash was still plain, unadorned.

The priest motioned for them to follow, and Keirnan laced his fingers with hers.

"Are you all right, luv?" He murmured as they crossed to a small side chapel. "You look as if you've seen a ghost."

"Maybe for a second there I did." She tried to make her tone light, but it came out a bit too strained.

The priest gestured at the alcove, said something, and then raised his hand in a brief blessing before he walked away. Keirnan pulled her toward the back wall where a large marble rectangle protruded, a sarcophagus with the image of a man sculpted onto the lid.

"This is the tomb of Pietro Lombardo and presumably his family as well." He ran his hands lightly across the stone likeness, then along the edges of the lid.

"Serafina's father?"

Keirnan nodded as he examined the carvings across the front. "Can you hold one of those candles a bit closer over here, luv?"

She plucked a taper off the altar in the center of the chapel and did as he asked. His long, nimble fingers explored the corners and sides of the marble tomb for several minutes before he stood with a sigh.

"According to Father Benedetto, this place was renovated and refurbished inside and out four years ago."

However, Keirnan scooted to the other end and started the same exploration there also.

A heavy disappointment settled over Sam, making her arms and legs feel leaden. "So if the jewels were here, then they'd have probably been discovered."

"Yes, I expect they would. And my sister would have known that also." His fingers played along the seam on the lid again. "But it's possible that something was missed, a clue of some sort." When he raised his eyes to look at her, his handsome face was hard with determination. "I'll come back later when no one's about."

His words made a chill crawl down her spine. She saw another early morning escapade in her near future, and this time the agenda might include tomb raiding.

He took the candle from her and made a thorough inspection of the walls of the chapel before he replaced it in its holder.

"Now what was it about the Madonna that spooked you?"

"It must have been some trick of the light through the stained glass." She pressed her lips together in hesitation, unsure if she'd actually seen anything at all.

His questioning azure gaze demanded full disclosure.

She reluctantly complied. "For a second, it looked like there were jewels on the sash, big blue jewels. Only when I looked again, they were gone."

Keirnan tapped his lips with his forefinger for a moment; his eyes had shifted far away in thought. "Let's have a closer look at her."

They left the chapel, crossed the church, and mounted the steps of the chancel. The sunlight outside was obviously fading because the interior of the church had grown considerably darker.

The gleaming marble Madonna was mounted in the right-hand corner on top of the stone balustrade. She loomed over both their heads. Keirnan reached up to finger the carved sash running diagonally across the statue's chest.

"I can feel some slight indentations in the stone," he murmured, stretching to reach higher. "Like something might have once been attached there." He pulled his arm back with a grunt. "A pity she can't talk."

Sam stared at the serene white features, not altogether sure she wanted to hear what the statue might have to say. "Did your sister mention her?"

"Not specifically… that I could decipher." Keirnan was doing another of his slow visual scans, moving around the statue. "However, the fact that she was carved by Serafina's brother Tullio makes her worth further study."

Keirnan started to run his fingers along the statue's base when a sudden chirping from inside his jacket broke the stillness. Sam gasped as her heart jumped into her throat. She recognized the sound—the chorus from "Santa Lucia."

Keirnan jerked Spinelli's cell phone from his pocket and double-timed it down the chancel steps and the side aisle of the church. She sprinted to catch up with him, but he beat her out the door.

Outside, the twilight was disintegrating rapidly into night, and it took her a moment to see him leaning against the corner of the church. His expression grim, he flipped the phone shut. Before she could utter a sound, he gripped her arm and pulled her along at a rapid clip.

"I have to hurry. They've only given me an hour to get to the Lido."

She hustled to keep pace with his long strides. Not wasting her breath with questions, she searched her whirling brain to recall what she'd read about the Lido. The guidebook had pictured a narrow strip of beach, the last barrier between Venice proper and the Adriatic. Crowded during the summer, few tourists ventured there in winter.

A lump of cold dread struck her stomach at the thought of confronting the kidnappers there, but it quickly disappeared as an even colder shock of certainty slammed into her.

He intended to go alone.

She stumbled, pulling them both to an abrupt halt. "Wh-what are you—"

"Samantha, luv, please." Keirnan rested his hands on her shoulders, his beseeching tone contrasted sharply with his fiercely determined face. "We've no time to argue. You must wait for me at the hotel. You must!"

He grabbed her hand and resumed his rapid pace. She battled against the stranglehold of panic.

"But they might—"

"I'll be ready this time."

She bit back the impulse to shout "How?" and tried to picture him when he'd confronted Spinelli, in control, deadly calm. But all her mind kept flashing was a knife. A whimper slid past her paralyzed lips.

He stopped again. His expression softened, and his fingers lightly caressed her cheek. "Samantha, luv, I can do this, but not if I have to worry about you."

"But I won't—"

"Shush." He placed two fingers across her lips in what was becoming a familiar gesture. "Promise me you'll stay in the room until I come back."

Hot tears prickled at the back of her throat. She took a shaky breath. "What if you don't… can't…?"

In the darkness, his eyes were smoldering indigo. "They don't want me. They want the jewels."

He reached inside his jacket and pressed his newly purchased cell phone into her hand. "I'll call you as soon as I can. I promise. Now promise me."

Clutching the cell phone in a death grip, Sam swallowed hard to gulp back the knot of terror-laced tears.

Though her mind balked, she forced out the words he demanded. "I promise."

He pulled her against his chest, whispered something into her hair, those Gaelic words again. Then he quickly shoved himself away and went back to his swift march down the street. Sam stumbled along behind him, their intertwined fingers her lifeline.

Hold it together! Don't be a bigger liability to him than you already are.

The lights of their hotel suddenly loomed in front of them. He opened the door with his free hand and held it for her. Determined not to be a sniveling ninny, she took a deep breath and walked over the threshold. He squeezed her fingers in the second before he released them, then melted into the darkness.

The air exploded out of her lungs as she stumbled for the elevator. He was right. She couldn't do a damn thing to help him. In fact, her very presence might spook the kidnappers. Do more harm than good. But it still took all her willpower to keep from sobbing.

They don't want him. They want the jewels. Each time she repeated the mantra, a nagging voice in the back of her mind kept reminding her… *but he doesn't have them.*

Sam's hands shook so badly that it took three tries before she could get the card key into the door. She hung her coat in the closet and checked the cell phone to make sure it was working. The ringer was off, and when she punched it on, there was a message. While they'd been in the church, the hotel had called to tell Signor Fitzgerald that his passport and other belongings were at the front desk. She used the room telephone to call and ask for someone to bring them up.

She could have gone down to get them, but she'd
promised to wait in the room, and she took her prom-
ises very seriously, always had. Besides, up here away
from the street, she wouldn't be so tempted to try and
follow him.

She worried her bottom lip with her teeth. That
morning at the train station, she'd admonished Keirnan
about making a promise he couldn't keep, and he said
he never did. Never was a long time.

Picking up the phone again, she called room service
for a pot of herbal tea. Maybe it would sooth her jangled
nerves. Spinelli's laptop sat on the desk next to the
phone. If she didn't find some way to occupy herself,
she'd be climbing the walls in no time, so she opened it
and booted up. Once she was online, she went to the last
page Keirnan had accessed, an Irish Gaelic dictionary.

What was it he'd called her? She pulled up a list of
common phrases and scanned down until she found
it. *Grá mo chroí*. A pair of sobs wrenched their way
out of her constricted throat. He'd called her love of
his heart.

Venice, 1485

Clouds obscured the moon and made the night unearthly
dark. Nino used his step stool to heave himself to the
top of the Lombardos' garden wall. His fatigue, coupled
with the heavy knapsack strapped to his back, made his
movements awkward. Even though all his preparations
were complete, anxiety had rendered him incapable of
more than a short nap since he'd consumed an evening

meal he hadn't tasted. His mind churned with all the things that might go wrong and what he could do to avoid them, but far too many had no solutions.

He hauled the step stool up by the rope tied around his waist, dropped it, and followed it to the ground on the other side of the wall. He left the wooden stool next to the pear tree to use when he returned, then crossed the shadowy garden to the dim monolith of the palazzo.

Feeling his way carefully along the wall, he came to a shuttered window, then another. The second shutter was unlatched, as Fredo had prearranged. His friend had visited Serafina the day before yesterday on the pretense of using her likeness in another of his paintings. He swung one side of the shutter open and carefully raised the sash of the inner wood and glass window, which was also unlatched. Then he boosted himself over the sill and landed as soundlessly as possible on the stone floor inside.

Pulling the outside shutter closed, Nino glimpsed a figure detach itself from beside a large cabinet on the opposite wall. As the room plunged into total darkness, he felt Serafina's delicate fingers clasp his arms. Then her body pressed against him, and burning need erased all weariness and apprehension.

He crushed her against him, wanting to imprint the soft feel and scent of her permanently into his soul. Her arms were around him too, but neither of them dared speak, scarcely dared to breathe.

After several long moments, Serafina placed a kiss beneath his jaw that set his heart pounding. Breaking their embrace, she gripped his hand tightly in hers and led the way to a staircase.

With silent stealth, they mounted the stairs. Thankfully,

Nino's eyes had adjusted to the darkness, and his steps did not falter when she had to release his hand to hold up her long robe, which hindered her ability to climb. They reached the first landing, and she continued to lead the way down the dim hallway. A sliver of light glowed from under a door. Serafina glided noiselessly to it and slipped inside, pulling him after her.

The lone candle inside its brass holder shed no more than a faint blush of light across the chamber. But compared to the darkness everywhere else, it could have been the summer sun at noon. Nino slid his knapsack from his shoulders, hastily removed his wool cloak, and shoved it against the crack at the bottom of the door to blot the offending illumination from the hallway.

He turned and retrieved his pack. His pulse still beat too rapidly in spite of his efforts to maintain calm. Serafina stood next to her ornately carved and canopied bed, her expression unreadable in the muted light.

"It's" —his whisper rasped harshly in the stillness— "not too late to change your mind."

She shook her head. The candlelight shimmered across the golden curtain of her waist- length hair.

"No, my love, I'm ready."

Her hands undid the fastenings of her robe. She shrugged it off her shoulders onto the floor and stood before him naked.

A gasp commingled with a moan ripped out of his throat. Nino's suddenly paralyzed fingers let go of the knapsack, but he managed to grasp it again before it hit the floor. Passion roaring in his ears, he sank to his knees and willed himself to look away. His breathing sounded coarse and rapid. He opened his mouth but could force out no words.

She stepped closer.

He could see bare feet, slender ankles, and the curve of her calf muscle. His blood still thundering in his veins, he squeezed his eyes shut and forced his numb fingers to unfasten his doublet.

"P-please, my love…" He finally managed to croak as he pulled the doublet off and held it in front of him.

Peeking through one eye, he rose unsteadily to his feet and pressed the padded fabric against the hollow of her throat. The sight of her creamy bare shoulders almost overwhelmed him with desire. How would he ever be able to paint when his hands couldn't stop trembling?

"Put your robe back on before I—we—"

"But I want you to." She reached for him.

"Serafina, no!" He flinched away, fearing her touch would shatter his tightly held control. "I can't send you unchaste to the holy sisters."

"I wouldn't be the first."

So she too knew that families sent their women with sullied reputations into cloisters. He hadn't expected that—not that it changed anything. He clenched his fists tighter to help strengthen his resolve.

"I won't risk…" He still had to pry the words out. "… leaving you with… with child."

He thought that would end her words, but her velvety eyes took on a defiant gleam. "There are other ways a man and woman can pleasure one another. My sister told me the viscount—"

Nino's choked cough stopped more details. "You… must not… say…"

Her revelation left him too stunned to avoid her soft hand as she ran her fingertips down his cheek. Of all the things he'd worried might go wrong tonight, this had never occurred to him. He'd vowed to control his own lust, but hers was altogether unforeseen.

"Nino, please." She stood on tiptoe and tilted her beautiful face up to his. "I want to belong to you always, and I want you to belong to me."

His will was not made of iron after all. More like Chinese porcelain. It slipped and shattered into countless shards as he let go of his doublet and wrapped his arms around her cool, silky flesh.

"I will, Serafina. I'll always be yours."

She claimed his mouth, her hot, honey-sweet tongue colliding with his in a sensual possession almost too tempting to bear. Pulling away, he scooped her into his arms and stumbled over his knapsack, doublet, and her robe to the bed. She sprinkled heated little kisses down his neck as she untied the fastenings of his shirt, pulled the fabric aside, and kissed his chest.

"No, my love." He scarcely recognized the passion-thickened whisper as his own. "The pleasure will be for you tonight."

But when he deposited her on top of the coverlet, the candlelight played across her flawless ivory breasts, the dusty rose halos of her nipples, the burnished curls at the juncture of her thighs. His need throbbed so hard within him that he teetered on the brink of total abandon.

He forced himself to back away, take a half-dozen long, shuddering breaths before he obeyed the insistent beckoning of her slender arms.

His work-roughened hands worshipped her soft, unblemished flesh, moving from her throat to her shoulder to claim her breast. He had to capture her wrist with one hand to prevent her from performing the same wondrous explorations on him.

As his hand moved lower, sliding over her satiny belly, he made sure his mouth was over hers to stifle any sounds. When his fingers gently nudged between her thighs and touched the most sensitive part of her, she jerked and nipped his bottom lip.

The salty taste of his own blood coupled with the heat of her desire almost sent him over the brink. Somehow, he reined himself back, steadied his shaky breathing.

Her free hand was tangled in his hair, her breathy little moans panted in his ear. She was as tightly strung as he was. He could feel her release tantalizingly close and reclaimed her mouth, plunging his tongue inside while his fingers thrust into the hot moist center of her.

A moment later her breath caught, and she arched against him, shattering in his arms. His own release was so dangerously near that he could see stars flashing against his tightly closed eyelids.

He didn't dare move as she broke the kiss, fell back against the fluffy coverlet, trembling, then exhaled a long, ragged sigh. Finally, his own breathing evened out enough so that he heaved himself over and collapsed beside her. She curled languidly against him and nestled her head in the space between his neck and shoulder.

"Oh, Nino," she whispered against the side of this throat. "For a moment, I thought I almost touched heaven."

"So did I, my love." He reached across and tugged

the edge of the coverlet up so that it partially covered her. "So did I."

After tonight, this was undoubtedly the closest he'd ever be to paradise, but it no longer mattered.

Chapter 8

KEIRNAN PRESSED A FISTFUL OF EUROS INTO THE TAXI driver's hand and slid out of the vehicle into the chilly air. Five hundred meters ahead, the towering white bulk of the San Nicolo lighthouse stood out in stark relief against the darkness of the sky and the choppy Adriatic. The bright beam at its top cut through the inky stillness with regular searing flashes, an impossible beacon to miss on such a cold, clear night.

Unlike Venice proper, automobiles were allowed on the Lido, but he hadn't dared ask the driver to bring him any closer in case the kidnappers were already waiting for him. Tires crunched on gravel, and the vehicle's retreating taillights bathed the roadway in front of him in an ominous red glow. Shoving his hands into his jacket pockets, he jogged toward the massive white spire and his dicey rendezvous.

Frigid fear had rendered his guts into a knot of Gordian proportions and complexity the moment he'd answered the cell phone. Now it gave a vicious twist.

What would he do if they didn't bring Kathleen?

For that matter, what would he do if they did?

His mind simply would not allow for the fact that they might already have hurt her, or worse. That possibility was not an option.

That way lay madness.

He forced his churning thoughts to focus on Samantha,

a far more pleasant topic, though still unsettling in an entirely different way. Every instinct he'd felt about her so far had proven correct. Plus, the immediate, intense connection between them was like nothing he'd experienced before, and he was certain it was the same for her.

His conscience, however, screamed that he could not allow her to be involved further on any level. The risks were too great and not entirely physical. One bloody fool had already broken her heart. He refused to be the second.

Even though he'd had no choice, leaving her at the hotel had been one of the most difficult things he'd ever done. But she'd promised to stay put, and he knew she would—knew it as surely as he knew his own name.

Something moved on the surface of the sea. Keirnan strained his eyes to see across the murky roiling water. It wasn't his imagination; a small light bobbled on top of the waves. The faint whir of an outboard motor carried on the cold wind.

Ignoring fear and rational thought, he hurtled the remaining way down the road. His feet sank into the deep sand of the beach surrounding the lighthouse as its beam sliced the air and outlined the oncoming craft.

Panting, Keirnan slowed to a more cautious pace. The engine choked into silence, the running lights on its side winked out, and the boat bumped alongside the rock jetty that curved out from the end of the shore.

When San Nicolo's beam passed again, he could see a man standing in the bow of the boat, a curved metal hook in his hand. Two other figures crouched in the stern, one slumped against the other. Keirnan's racing pulse kicked up a notch faster. The two men who had jumped him outside Kathleen's flat had worn white Carnevale masks, but none were in evidence on the boat's occupants.

"No closer, little brother," the standing man warned in Italian. His accent sounded Sicilian just as it had on the phone.

Keirnan obeyed and stood immobile near the edge of the rocks, his open palms held out to his sides.

"*Mi sorello*," he demanded, as the rotating beam threw its blinding light across the landscape. "Show me my sister."

"Patience, bambino." The man wore a heavy, yellow rain slicker over his clothes, the hood pulled low to obscure his features. "We wouldn't want her to fall overboard."

He reached across to the rocks and dug the metal hook into them, securing the boat.

Keirnan's fingers flexed with edginess, and he bit back a pithy retort.

Steady, boyo. Focus.

The man muttered something too low for Keirnan to hear, but the figure in the stern stood. Taller than the man in the slicker, the second one wore a dark, heavy coat, and a Greek fisherman's hat cast a shadow across his face. He hauled his much smaller seatmate up by the arm and jerked what looked like a pillowcase off the third figure's head.

A shout exploded from Keirnan's mouth as Kathleen's flaming red curls whipped in a chilly gust of wind.

"*Sionnach*!" She yelled her Gaelic nickname for him— fox—as the white beam slashed across them again. Her hands were bound in front of her, but she tried to wrestle away from her much larger captive nonetheless.

"*Deirfiu'r*! Sister." He called back at her in the old tongue. "Are you hurt?"

"No."

A surge of relief pumped through Keirnan at her answer. She looked small in the tall man's grip, but she was far from helpless.

Still struggling, she thrust her elbow into the ribs of the thug holding her. The boat tilted as she lunged for the side, but her captor jerked her backward with a curse and slapped her across the face.

With a howl of rage, Keirnan sprang forward as the lighthouse beam raked over them again.

"Stop!" Yellow-slicker bellowed in English. "No closer!"

The light flashed on the silver gleam of a knife in his fist. Keirnan instantly froze. His breath, even his heart seemed to stop in the grip of pure terror.

"The jewels—"

"Don't give them anything!" Kathleen shouted. The brute holding her raised his hand again.

"No!" The hand dropped at Keirnan's command. He wrenched in his anger, his fear, and addressed Yellow-slicker in as close to a normal, reasonable tone as he could muster. "Let her go. Take me instead."

"No!" Kathleen shrieked.

"Tempting, but no," Yellow-slicker replied, stepping to the back of the boat where Kathleen continued to writhe and curse.

He grabbed her bound hands and slammed them onto the metal rail that ran down both sides of the vessel. The knife blade glinted as it flew downward.

Keirnan's cry of anguish lodged in his horror-paralyzed throat.

Kathleen screamed the brief, piercing wail of a banshee that ended abruptly with the sound of metal hitting bone. The lighthouse beam pulsed across the narrow, crimson ribbon flowing down the side of the boat.

As his sister's limp body slumped into her tall captor's arms, Keirnan fell to his knees with a choked sob. "God in heaven…"

"Now you know we are serious, little brother." The Sicilian picked up the bloody lump of flesh and tossed it into his lap. "You want the rest of her, bring us the jewels."

Clutching what had once been his sister's finger, Keirnan doubled over in the sand and retched.

Sam glanced at the clock on the nightstand for the fifth time in as many minutes. She had been alone in the room for almost four hours.

Where was he?

Half expecting to see a trail worn in the carpet, she paced across the room and picked up her cup, but put it down without drinking.

The tea was tepid. Two partial pots of it sat on a tray along with a half-eaten plate of pasta and an untouched bowl of fruit salad. So much for her attempt at dinner.

She'd also taken a long, hot shower, put on her pajamas, and tried to lull herself to sleep by turning on the TV. None of it had worked. In spite of being awake for over eighteen stressful hours, her adrenaline-laced psyche would not rest. Thoughts tumbled around and around her mind, along with disjointed images and errant feelings.

Keirnan.

Michael.

Kathleen's trashed apartment.

Spinelli's beady eyes.

The serene stone face of the Madonna.

Fear.

Doubt.

Desire.

Her finger traced the crisp edge of the Interpol agent's card, which lay face down next to the hotel telephone. She'd dug the card out and put it there a half hour ago, but a voice inside her head that sounded suspiciously like Keirnan's kept her from dialing the number.

Not yet.

Wait a bit longer.

If something didn't happen soon, she'd be a raving lunatic.

She sat in front of the laptop again, pinched the bridge of her nose, and forced her exhausted eyes to focus on the screen. This was the only distraction that worked for more than a few minutes at a time. Research was something she knew how to do.

She'd managed to access the university library database back in Bloomington, and she'd done some cross-referencing of information in Kathleen's files. Most of the information she'd laboriously translated word by word from Gaelic.

Serafina Lombardo and her sister Simonetta appeared to have died in the same year, 1485. Long before their father Pietro, who lived until 1515, and their two older brothers, who died after he did. Presumably long before the Lombardos' tomb was constructed inside Santa Maria dei Miracoli.

The sisters must be buried elsewhere. And wherever Serafina was, Sam knew with eerie certainty the Jewels of the Madonna would be there also.

She'd just figured out Simonetta was married to a nobleman named Treviso and was trying to determine where he might be buried when the phone rang. Not the phone on the desk, but Keirnan's cell phone, which chimed like Big Ben.

Heart in her throat, she lunged to answer. "K-Keirnan?" When nobody replied, her heart threatened to pound its way up into her mouth. "H-hello? Keirnan?"

Finally in what sounded like a strangled whisper, he answered her. "S-Samantha, luv…"

"Oh my God! Keirnan!" Fear ripped through her, and she sat down hard on the bed. "Are… are you okay?"

Oh God, please let him say yes!

"Y-yes."

Thank-you-thank-you-thank-you!

But his unsteady voice must mean—Oh God! Cold, paralyzing dread almost made her drop the phone.

"Your sister—"

What sounded like a sob spluttered in her ear. "Sh-she—" Another very definite sob choked off his words.

The metal phone bit into her palm as her fingers tightened in terror. Battling back hysteria, she forced herself to ask, "Is she… alive?"

"Yes," said on a breath of relief that Sam immediately echoed.

"But they—" He inhaled sharply. "They hurt her."

A thousand gruesome images flashed in front of her, making her gasp again.

"Not badly." His voice almost sounded normal for a moment, but went strangled again. "Her hand…"

Sam took a deep breath, held it. She had to find him. Help him.

In spite of her thumping heart, she forced herself to speak calmly. "Keirnan, where are you?"

"Santa Maria dei Miracoli."

"Good!" She was pretty sure she could find it, even in the dark. "Stay there. I'll be right there."

"No, don't." His voice took on an odd tone. "I intend to find those bloody jewels if I have to rip this place apart one stone at a time."

He sounded desperate enough to do just that. Anxiety blazed through her fear-frozen veins.

"No! Keirnan, please, listen to me. The jewels aren't there."

"How do you know?"

How indeed? But she did know, and she had to make him believe her.

"They aren't there because Serafina's not there. She died almost thirty years before that tomb was built."

Silence on his end of the line, heavy with uncertainty. Beads of perspiration broke out on her forehead as a terrible feeling washed over her.

He was going to do something foolish.

"Wait in front of the church. I'm on my way."

"No, I'll be right there."

Sam stared at the suddenly dead phone. He was the most infuriatingly contrary man she'd ever met, and he'd better walk through that door within the next fifteen minutes.

Still trembling, she put the phone on the nightstand and walked unsteadily to the bathroom. The cool water splashing over her face revived her somewhat, but she felt in need of something more to fortify her. Something stronger than tepid herbal tea.

While most of the other passengers had slept, one of the flight attendants had slipped her a tiny bottle of Amaretto to celebrate her first trip to Italy. Since she hadn't felt in a celebratory mood, she'd stashed it in her carry-on. That now felt like it had happened in another lifetime, or maybe to someone else entirely. Drying her face, she went out and rummaged in her bag to find out if it had.

"Good-bye ten thousand brain cells," Sam muttered as she raised the miniature bottle of liqueur to her lips.

The strongly sweet liquid flowed over her tongue and nearly gagged her. Before she finished coughing, the door rattled and Keirnan stepped inside.

She flew across the room to him. He looked worse than he had after being stabbed and falling in the canal, after going five rounds with the stomach "bug."

Defeat seemed to have overpowered him, and his entire body sagged under its crushing weight. She closed the door behind him and grasped the collar of his jacket as he slid it from his sloping shoulders. His blue eyes looked lifeless, annihilated by sorrow.

"K-Keirnan?" She hesitated, unsure what to say as she dropped his jacket on top of her open suitcase.

Flecks of dirty gray sand clung to the black leather. She looked back into his face, so careworn, haunted.

"Oh, luv…" With an anguished sigh, he pulled her into his arms, laid his head against her neck, and sobbed. "Oh, luv."

Sam wrapped her arms around him. Her hands on his back patted, soothed, tried to impart comfort. She'd never felt a man cry before, and it touched her in a way nothing else ever had.

"Shhh," she murmured. "It's all right now. It's all right."

"I'm so afraid," he whispered into her hair. "So afraid they're going to—"

"Shhh, don't worry."

Carefully she guided him to the edge of the bed and pulled him down. He broke the embrace and scrubbed his sweater sleeve across his eyes.

"It was so… horrible." His voice was still thick with tears. He stared down at his tightly clenched fists, and then the words began to tumble out. "Two of them had her in a boat. Her hands were tied, but she fought them anyway."

He raised his eyes to hers, and the raw agony tore at Sam's heart. "I tried to exchange myself for her, but they—"

He stopped, covered his face with his hands, and shuddered. Icy horror overrode her pain. She knew even as he spoke the words, "The Sicilian had a knife."

She could see it. Light glinted along the steel blade as it slashed downward. A whimper of fright escaped from her frozen throat. She hugged him against her as he whispered hoarsely, "He threw her severed finger into my lap."

Bile rushed into her mouth, and she fought the urge to vomit. His arms around her waist tightened as if he couldn't get her close enough.

His voice shook. "They're going to kill her, and I can't stop them."

Unable to speak, she held him, pressed herself to him as tightly as he gripped her. Two insignificant scraps in the midst of a sea of aching fear, they clung together. The moisture from his tears dampened the side of her throat.

After a hundred ragged heartbeats, she finally managed to murmur, "We'll find the jewels." She swallowed and took a steadying breath. "I know we will."

He didn't answer, just clutched her like a drowning man caught in an undertow. She could feel his heart pounding against her, uneven and erratic at first, but gradually, after long minutes of silence, it became more regular, as did his breathing. The tightness in his grip grew a little less frantic.

Sam shifted one of her arms so that her fingers could reach the back of his head. She ran them through the tangles of his hair, smoothing the silky strands.

Such beautiful hair for a man, thick and rich like espresso…

She pushed a wayward lock behind his ear, and he turned so that her hand rested on his cheek. The stubble on his face tickled her fingertips. After another long moment, his lips feathered across her palm.

Her own heartbeat stuttered. He pulled away enough so that he could meet her gaze. His extraordinary sapphire eyes were red-rimmed but no longer flat and full of despair. They pulsed with a low blue flame.

He loosened his own grip enough to run his fingers down the length of her hair from her forehead to her shoulder. The touch of his hand on her bare flesh startled Sam. Looking down, she saw that the tie on her pajamas had come undone, and the wide neck hung loose across the top of her breast and shoulder.

He bent his head and exchanged his fingers for his mouth. Her breath caught in her throat, then escaped in a long sigh as his lips moved from her shoulder across her collarbone.

"*Grá mo chroí*," he groaned in the instant before he claimed her mouth.

Heat washed over her, but not the instant scorching flamethrower that had engulfed her earlier in the day. This was a slower sweep of liquid warmth that chased out the chilling dread and uncertainty. Every swirl of his tongue spread the warmness further through her veins. She absorbed the life-giving warmth and gave it back to him.

Then, his hands were no longer around her. They cupped her breasts, molding the smooth satin of her pajama top against her erect nipples. It was him she wanted to feel. She broke the kiss long enough to shrug the top off over her head.

"So beautiful," he murmured as he tipped her back against the padded headboard.

He worshipped her breasts with his hands, then his mouth. She moaned and arched against him as the heat inside her intensified. His lips left a trail of liquid fire as they moved from one breast to the other. His thumb hooked the elastic waistband of her pajama bottoms and eased them over her hips, down her legs.

Sam grabbed a handful of his sweater and the shirt underneath it, wanting no more barriers between them.

"You're wearing too many clothes," she panted.

He pulled back and stared, first at her mouth, then his azure gaze moved down her body as if he just realized she was naked.

Please don't stop this time. She was afraid to say it aloud.

A flush crept across her face, but before it could spread to her throat, Keirnan flung his sweater over his head and onto the floor.

In a dreamlike haze, she watched the rest of his clothes peel away. As physically sublime as any Renaissance sculpture, his abs were chiseled, his gluts perfectly defined. But unlike a statue, he was fully aroused. And breathtaking. The flamethrower roared away the soothing, comfortable warmth.

"Please…" Sam whispered.

It was all the entreaty he needed.

The sensual feel of bare skin rubbing on bare skin engulfed her in an inferno of need like she'd never felt before. His lips played over her shoulders, neck, breasts, while his knee nudged between her thighs, and his hands found her hot, liquid center. Just when she thought she would die from the exquisite torture, he replaced his fingers with the silken steel of his erection.

Engulfed by the blaze searing right through to her soul, she dug her fingers into the hard muscles of his back and forgot to think, breathe. Nothing else existed as the two of them melded into one, moved and felt as one. Exploded over the edge of oblivion as one.

When she floated back to earth, Sam never wanted to move again. If only she could prolong this intimate, heretofore unknown, feeling of completion forever. She hugged the waves of warmth and connectivity to her even as they receded away.

"Samantha, luv…" Keirnan murmured, levering himself up onto his elbows, bringing cold reality back into focus.

"Don't you dare say you're sorry!"

He kissed the end of her nose. "I was only going to suggest we get under the covers."

"Oh." She looked self-consciously away as he rolled over and tugged at the tangled mass of bedding. "Maybe the other bed would be easier."

"Good idea."

The mattress squeaked as he heaved himself up. Had it made any noise a little while ago? She was rather embarrassingly sure she had made more.

"Come on, crawl in." He twitched the covers back and patted the space beside him.

Feeling vulnerable and exposed, she grabbed her pajama bottoms and hugged them against her suddenly chilly flesh.

Where was the blasted top?

"Don't worry, luv." His voice was husky. "You won't be needing those."

The high-pitched keening of his sister's scream jolted Keirnan awake. The scene on the beach dissolved in front of his sleep-blurred eyes. Only a dream, thank all the saints in heaven!

His relieved sigh stirred the silky strands of Samantha's hair resting under his cheek. For once reality was far more pleasant. The fingers of his right hand closed possessively around the smooth globe of her breast.

Unlike him, she slept soundly, her naked body curled trustingly into his. The delicious feel of her derriere curved against him made his groin stir with desire all over again.

Would he never get enough of her? The first time

had been born from a raw, aching need that threatened to tear him apart, only she had healed him. But the cure had left him immediately wanting more.

The second time had been pure incredible pleasure, so intense it shook him to his very core. He'd called her his beloved in at least three languages, possibly more. He wasn't sure. But he was very sure that making love with Samantha was unlike any other thing he'd ever experienced before, and that bothered him. Another tangle in this mess that he had thus far failed miserably at unraveling.

He glanced at the clock on the nightstand and groaned in disbelief. It was scarcely two hours later, and he wanted her now more than he'd ever wanted any woman. He battled down the urge to awaken her for a third round.

As much as he longed to stay in the blissful sanctuary Samantha offered, the image from the dream would not be denied. He dropped a light kiss on her shoulder and carefully crawled out of bed.

Venice, 1485

Passing for a beggar was not difficult, probably because it wasn't very far removed from his actual circumstances. Nino's mouth quirked with the irony as he gripped the tattered edges of the dirty cloak he'd purchased for a few pennies from an old ragman in the Guidecca.

The faded and patched garment was large enough to easily conceal him and his bulging pack, which now held all the belongings he could stuff into it. He'd had to leave some things behind, but he didn't dare risk returning to his room in the *scuola*. Once he was safely on the road to Padua, then he could abandon his rather odorous disguise.

No one in Venice would ever guess that a bent-back beggar carried the Jewels of the Madonna in his knapsack.

Nino wasn't sure if it was confidence in his disguise or sheer desperation that drove him, but he hadn't been able to stay away from Santa Maria dei Miracoli. After a fretful day of lurking and hiding, then another almost sleepless night, he'd spent the long hours of the morning prowling in the shadows near the church.

In spite of his stealthy watchfulness, he couldn't tell if the comings and goings were normal or not, and the church's cool white marble façade gave away nothing. Finally, he dared approach a brown-robed friar who emerged from the garden behind the church.

"I'm sorry, my son. I've no food to give you." The small man pulled his arm away from Nino's grasp. He looked nervous. "And the poor box was distributed last week."

"I only seek to ask about the Holy Sisters from Ravenna." Nino kept his eyes averted and his voice pitched low. "Are they still here?"

"How very strange." The friar's puzzled tone made him risk a glance at his face. The man met Nino's gaze with a questioning one of his own. "You are the second man to ask me this question in as many days." Nino felt his throat go dry as the friar continued. "As I told the other fellow, the sisters left for Padua three days ago."

"Th-three days?" A cartload of bricks crashed inside his chest. He staggered. "Are you sure?"

"Yes, of course." The friar reached out a hand to steady him. "Are you ill, my son?"

Nino shook his head and forced his voice out of his tightly constricted throat. "Fa-father Mateo... I must see him."

"I haven't seen him since matins. You look most unwell. Shall I take you to Father Giancarlo instead?"

"No."

Matins was hours ago. Desperation and rage battled inside Nino's shocked soul, but he didn't dare give in to either. Not just yet.

"Thank you, but no."

The friar looked even more puzzled but Nino didn't care. He had to get to the docks as quickly as possible, in case by some miracle, the treacherous priest was still there. He turned and ran before the friar could raise his hand in blessing.

The quays at the foot of Piazza San Marco teemed with vessels of every shape and size, including several sailing ships large enough to brave the open waters of the sea. Nino knew instinctively that Father Mateo would take one of those. Abandoning all pretense of being an infirm beggar, he asked every likely passerby if they'd seen a priest.

He couldn't believe that God might have already forgiven him for his grievous sin of stealing the jewels, not to mention the worse sin he might shortly commit. More likely, Father Mateo's sins were far more terrible. Serafina's beauty would fetch a high price in an Ottoman slave market.

Whatever the reason, scarcely an hour later, Nino slipped aboard the vessel on which the perfidious priest had booked passage to Constantinople.

Careful to avoid most of the bustling crew, he spied an open hatch and darted down the ladder. He nearly

collided with a young cabin boy obviously on his way
to the deck.

"Is the priest in one of these cabins?" He demanded
in a low growl.

The lad stared at his patched cloak and wrinkled his
nose. "Are you his travelling companion?"

"No, I... have something for him."

Nino fingered the dagger concealed in the pocket of
his doublet. He used the knife mostly for eating, and it
wasn't particularly sharp, but it would suffice.

The boy pointed at the narrow passage behind him.
"Third door starboard. Don't linger. We sail with the tide."

Nino waited until the boy disappeared up the
ladder before he rapped on the cabin door with the
hilt of his dagger.

"What is it now?"

As soon as Nino heard the door catch move, he shoved
roughly inside, knocking the priest against the bunk on
the side wall. Before Father Mateo could regain his feet,
the point of Nino's dagger rested against his throat.

"Where is she?"

He grabbed the front of the priest's robe, hauled him
upright, and pushed him against the doorjamb.

Father Mateo matched his deadly glare. "Not here, as
you can plainly see."

A quick glance confirmed they were indeed alone in
the confined space.

"Well, she's certainly not with the holy sisters either."

Nino pressed the dagger into the flesh at the base of
the priest's throat until a few drops of blood reddened
the blade. "What have you done with her?"

"I—can't tell you if you cut my throat." In spite

of his bold tone, the other man's Adam's apple bobbed convulsively.

Nino shoved his free hand under Father Mateo's chin, then dropped his blade low and pointed it up into the priest's belly.

"Then perhaps you'd prefer to talk with your guts dripping onto the floor." He worked the dagger tip through the fabric of the priest's robe. "I left you the two jewels in the chapel of St. Anne on the cemetery isle, just as we arranged—"

"Someone took them before I arrived!" Father Mateo interrupted with a venomous hiss.

"Liar!" Nino felt his blade pricking flesh, saw the priest's nostrils flare with fright, and prepared to slide the dagger hilt deep.

"When I got to the alcove inside the church, the medallion you hid the jewels inside was lying shattered on the floor." The dagger point seemed to have loosened Father Mateo's tongue, for his words tumbled out quickly. "I sifted through the broken pieces just to be sure, but there were no jewels. Whoever took them was gone as well."

Nino couldn't believe what he was hearing. He held the dagger steady. "And Serafina?"

"I left your precious Serafina bound and gagged in the bottom of my gondola. When I saw for certain that the jewels were gone, I ran back to the dock. My gondola and Serafina were both gone as well. Someone has betrayed us both, it seems."

Chapter 9

KEIRNAN RUBBED THE BACK OF HIS NECK AND GLANCED away from the glowing screen of the laptop. In spite of his fatigue, his tightly coiled nerves cried out that he needed to do something. Anything besides stare endlessly at a blinking computer monitor.

Every time he closed his weary eyes, he saw the Jewels of the Madonna, glittering provocatively just beyond his reach. Instead, he looked at the bed where Samantha continued to slumber curled in the same position he'd left her in more than an hour ago.

An unaccustomed sensation flooded through him that he didn't want to identify just now, very definitely desire, but so much more complicated. Again, he was sorely tempted to take off his clothes and rejoin her, find comfort, maybe rest. But if their two bouts of love-making in very rapid succession hadn't brought him much sleep, he knew rest would continue to elude him now. Not that his libido wasn't still urging him to test the theory just to be sure.

He forced his gaze back to the open, leather-bound book beside the laptop. His sister's large, looping script brought the harsh reality of her doom crashing over him. His inability to protect her and secure her safety was a jagged, gaping wound he couldn't staunch. The idea that at any moment the two thugs who held her could mangle the rest of her body the same way they had her hand made him shake with anger and terror-laced frustration.

Beneath the journal lay two pages of hotel stationery covered with Samantha's neatly printed notes. Everything about her astonished him. Starting with basically nothing, she'd made remarkable progress. He'd spent the last hour tracking down the link she'd uncovered to the Viscount Treviso, husband of Simonetta Lombardo, Serafina's sister.

The Lombardo brothers, Tullio and Antonio, must have been close. Historical proof showed they'd worked together, and with their father, their entire lives. It seemed likely that the sisters would be equally close.

Close enough to be buried together? And if they were, Samantha was right. They wouldn't have been buried in Santa Maria dei Miracoli, but the tomb of the Trevisos on San Michele en Isola, the cemetery isle.

He hadn't discovered anything to prove or disprove this theory, but at the moment it was the only thing he had. One fragile gossamer connection to the jewels, to his sister's life.

He hadn't been able to pinpoint the location of the Trevisos' tomb either, but having visited San Michele on several occasions, he knew where the majority of the Renaissance era monuments were.

His gaze slid to the clock. 'Twas the middle of the bloody night, of course. This could be another wild goose chase. But his sister might not have until morning.

This time when he kissed Samantha's shoulder she stirred. "Mmmph… I'm cold," she complained in a drowsy mumble. His libido very definitely disputed that statement.

He snagged her pajama top off the floor and sat on the edge of the bed next to her. "Put this on then." He pulled the loose satin shirt over her tousled head.

"No," her protest was that of a sleep-fogged child, for she clumsily shoved her arms into the sleeves even while she quarreled. "You come back to bed."

"I will in a bit," he lied. Then he eased her head back down onto the pillow. Her eyes shut before her cheek touched it.

An incessant noise dragged Sam from the deep reaches of sleep. How could Big Ben be chiming? She was in Venice, and it was 1485. She was wearing a doublet and hose.

The chiming persisted, dissolved the last remnants of the dream. As she struggled to sit up, a shiver raced over her. Where was Keirnan?

She peered across the room at the desk and could just make out the low rectangle of the closed laptop in the gloom. The chair sat half pulled out and empty. She seemed to recall him sitting in it, facing away from her. Then he had kissed her on the shoulder, and she told him to come back to bed.

"Keirnan?"

Only a tinny rendition of Big Ben's chime responded—the cell phone. *Why didn't he answer it?*

She stumbled out of bed and groped her way to the desk. She had to switch on the reading lamp before she could locate the phone.

Still in a groggy haze, she flipped it open. "Keirnan?"

"No, Signorina," said a low accented voice. "But Signor Fitzgerald, he needs you."

She jerked instantly to hyperawareness. "What? Who is this?"

Her eyes frantically scanned the top of the desk. Scrawled across her notes on Simonetta and Serafina were the words: "Gone to the tomb. Stay put!"

Panic roared in her ears and drowned out the man's muffled words. "Wh-what did you say?"

"He is hurt—needs your help."

Was his accent Sicilian? She had no idea, but the image of a blood-smeared knife danced in her horror-stricken mind.

"Wh-where" —her shaking hands nearly dropped the phone— "is he?"

"Come to Piazza San Marco, the Procuratie behind the Campanile. Hurry." The line went suddenly dead.

"Wait!" Sam stared at the lifeless piece of plastic, her pulse pounding in her throat.

Calm down! Think!

The Campanile was the tall, brick bell tower that stood on the opposite side of the square from St. Mark's Cathedral. The Procuratie were the portico-covered shops and restaurants that lined the piazza on three sides. Whatever tomb Keirnan had gone to, she knew it wasn't there. But nobody had this cell number except him.

He had Spinelli's cell phone with him and had used it to call her a few hours ago. Someone must have taken the phone and punched redial. Ice rocketed through her veins.

How had that someone taken it?

With a ragged gasp, she threw down the phone and snatched underwear, socks, and jeans out of her suitcase. She yanked her green sweater on over her pajama top and shoved on her jacket.

Where were her shoes?

What had they done to him?

What was she going to do?

Love of my heart. He was that and so much more.

Panting, she grabbed an elastic band off the night-stand and secured her tangled hair behind her head, then thrust the plastic card key to the room into her jeans pocket.

Please God, don't let me be too late!

She had to calm down.

She finally saw her shoes over near the desk. As she pulled them on, she picked up the cell phone again. The letters on the clock glowed: 3:23 a.m. Her finger hovered over the redial button. What would she say if they answered? What if they didn't?

The white rectangle of the Interpol agent's card caught her frenzied gaze. "Call me anytime," he had said, but he also believed Keirnan and Kathleen were criminals.

Were kidnappings even in Interpol's jurisdiction?

Her trembling finger pressed the last number as she eased the door shut behind her. She punched the button to summon the elevator. While in her ear, a voice mail message came on in Italian.

So much for his help.

It repeated in German as the door slid open, then in English, though the reception crackled inside the moving elevator so badly that she couldn't really understand it.

"Th-this is Sam Lewis." Her voice came out a croaking mumble, and she sagged against the elevator wall at a total loss where to begin. "P-professor Roberto Spinelli kidnapped Kathleen DiLucca, but someone else took her. They… want the jewels. They—they've hurt Keirnan—" A sob stopped her jumbled words.

The elevator door opened. She flipped the phone closed and sprinted across the lobby, stuffing the cell into her jacket pocket.

Outside, the frigid, crystalline air burned her lungs and reemerged as a pallid halo in front of her lips. Starlight glittered on the surface of the canal where the shadowy hulks of moored boats bobbed with the lapping of the waves.

Nothing else moved. Pulling the hood of her jacket over her hair, Sam forced her unsteady legs toward the pale streetlights that marked the perimeter of St. Mark's Square.

On her right, the tall, white-topped spire of the Campanile pointed heavenward in the dark sky, while on her left, the five rounded domes of the cathedral looked like alien vessels about to take flight. Carefully, she picked her way across the damp cobblestones. The deserted piazza felt miles wide, and the dark overhang in front of the shops seemed threatening.

Every cell in her body screamed a warning against moving closer—except her heart. It cried out for Keirnan. Inside her pocket, her hand clutched the plastic cover of the phone, but her nearly hysterical brain could not dredge up the Italian equivalent of 9-1-1.

She sidled over to a stack of metal tables and chairs chained together outside a café. The same café where, just a few mornings ago, she'd sipped a latte and watched a handsome stranger cross the square. But he was no stranger. He was the man she loved… had always loved, more than anything.

Trembling, she pulled the phone from her pocket and wiped the back of her free hand across her blurry eyes. She punched the redial button, laid the phone on the edge of the nearest table, then turned toward the dark column of the Campanile.

Pull yourself together!

You're no good to him this way.

The bricks of the bell tower were the color of dried blood in the wan light. Just beyond loomed the gaping black tunnel of the Procuratie, the perfect place for a trap. She stood, hesitant to abandon the dim light in the piazza, and peered into the darkness, straining her eyes to detect movement in the shadowy passageway.

About a third of the way down, she could just make out a darker blur. Something seemed to be propped against the wall, something large and unmoving. She took two cautious steps forward.

"K-Keirnan?"

No answer, no movement. She took another step, looked behind her before she took another. The dark shape moved and made a low muffled sound that could have been a moan. Even though her subconscious screamed against it, Sam's feet leaped forward.

She stopped herself two yards from the form, which was definitely human. Before she could squeeze out a word, it turned and revealed a blank white oval instead of a face. Two dark holes for eyes and a slit for a mouth split the pale, smooth surface.

With a startled gasp, Sam whirled away, but another dark figure blocked her escape—her worst fear realized!

This one's face was half white and ended with a large grotesquely hooked nose. It reached for her, and she shrieked as loud as she could. The sound momentarily stunned her assailant, and Sam darted around him, but not quite fast enough. He caught the edge of her jacket and pulled her off balance.

As she stumbled, she started to let out another blood-curdling screech, but her opponent shoved a gloved hand over her mouth. Anger quickly overcoming her fright, she clamped down with her teeth, but got only a mouthful of knitted fabric.

"Hellcat," muttered her foe. He pulled her against him with his free arm.

Sam twisted and jabbed her elbow into his ribs. Noise would arouse attention, and she was determined to make more. He swore in Italian while she clawed at his hand and managed to dislodge his fingers enough to get out another brief scream.

He wasn't that much larger than she was, and he didn't have a weapon. The realization made her fight harder, shoving with her hands and lashing out with her feet, all the while yelling against the gloved hand over her face.

But by now, his cohort on the ground had joined in the fracas. He hissed something in Italian as he circled around the two of them.

She landed a kick squarely on the second man's knee that sent him staggering, but the man holding her managed to capture one of her flailing arms and twist it behind her back. Pain shot from her wrist to her shoulder.

"You've been a very bad girl," her captor jeered in English. "Behave now, before I hurt you."

Sam stamped down on his foot as hard as she could in answer, then dug her nails into the exposed skin of his wrist hovering next to her jaw.

He grunted something, and the second man lunged at her with a smelly rag in his hand. She held her breath and thrust her knee toward his groin.

Unfortunately, she hit his thigh, and the noxious cloth settled over her nose and mouth, the fumes stinging her eyes. Still holding her breath, she tried to jerk her head aside, but the goon holding her gave her arm another vicious twist. She sucked in her breath with the stab of pain.

Fetid vapor seared her sinus cavities. She coughed, pulling the foul odor down her throat into her lungs. It made her gag.

Tears streamed out of her eyes, but she continued to blindly claw at the hands holding her. Another wrench on her arm made her gasp again. This time the fumes made her upchuck right onto her captor's shoes.

"*Merda*! Shit!" he swore.

With grim satisfaction, Sam felt his grip loosen. The rag dropped away, but whatever she had been forced to breathe was making her head spin. She managed to jerk her arm free, but tumbled headfirst into the grasp of the second man.

The bones in her legs seemed to have disappeared, so she threw her arms around his neck to keep from falling. His white, masked face swirled out of focus as she made a last ditch effort to battle back the unconsciousness hovering on the edges of her mind.

"I told you to behave," the first man scolded.

She felt his shoulder shove under her arm as he pulled her away from his companion. Still coughing and gasping for air, she was vaguely aware of the second man supporting her other side with his shoulder before total darkness claimed her.

How long she floated on the sea of blackness, Sam couldn't tell. Once it seemed she saw pinpricks of starlight far away over her head, but a whiff of the horrible odor had obliterated them before she could be sure.

Finally, something reached her through the formless, freezing dark. Fingers patted her lifeless cheeks. She could hear them smacking against her flesh before she could feel them.

Her eyes refused to focus on anything, but she could hear a man's voice somewhere in the swirling gloom around her. She couldn't understand his words. Then the fingers left her face and grasped her arms.

The murky world tilted unexpectedly, and nausea churned into a greasy mass in the pit of her stomach. The whimpering of a frightened puppy replaced the man's voice. Except the pathetic sound wasn't a puppy, it was her.

She was being dragged down some stairs. She could feel her shoes scraping across stone, thumping down onto the next riser then scraping again.

Her arms ached. They were draped across someone's shoulder; whoever was dragging her had lashed her wrists together. They reached the bottom of the stairs at last, and after hauling her a short distance more, her transporter dumped her onto a lumpy couch.

Her stomach gave a sickening lurch, and she felt the urge to vomit again, but the feeling slowly subsided along with the whirling inside her skull. She became aware of her own breathing and concentrated on filling and emptying her lungs, which still burned with the aftereffects of the toxic inhalant.

The chilly air felt damp and smelled of mold. Bit by bit, her surroundings came into focus—a dim room with unpainted brick walls and open beams over her head.

The grotesque hooked nose hovered above her face. She gave a startled gasp.

"Easy, *cara*."

The man shoved off the mask and revealed a normal, straight nose and large, liquid-chocolate eyes. Sam would have thought him handsome, if not for a scraggly moustache bristling atop his perfectly sculpted lip and oily dark locks straggling across his forehead. His fingertips glided lightly down her cheek.

"Ah, you are so much nicer when you cooperate." His voice was as soft as his touch, but neither eased the terror strangling her.

She tried to shrink away, but there was nowhere to go. He reached behind her head and pulled off the elastic band holding her hair.

"*Bella*, beautiful," he murmured as he threaded his fingers in the tousled strands and pulled them over her shoulder. "My little brother the fox still has the eye for beauty."

She shivered at his touch, then noticed her jacket was missing. A thousand scary questions crowded into her foggy brain, but she was afraid to voice any of them.

"Who… who are you?" She forced her frozen lips to form the query.

"You don't know me?" A note of disappointment sounded in his voice. "We share a bond, you and I. We have for a very long time. But in this life at least, we've both lost our hearts to Fitzgeralds." His languorous brown eyes moved down the length of her, then back to her face. "Only yours hasn't been broken yet. Whereas mine, alas, has been cast aside."

"D-DiLucca?" she whispered as she struggled to make sense of this revelation. "You're Kathleen's ex-husband?"

A spark of indignation snapped across his velvety gaze. "I am her only husband. And whether she wants it or no, I will have recompense for what she has done to me."

"But you—" Sam clamped her mouth shut so she wouldn't give voice to the thought.

He couldn't be Spinelli's creditor, but he could be working with them. She took a shaky breath as she surveyed the almost empty room. No sign of the other man or anyone else.

"I… I had nothing to do with that." She swallowed hard, then added. "And neither did Keirnan."

Saying his name made a terrible flood of despair wash over her. She'd been so stupid to fall for the trick. She'd failed him utterly.

DiLucca's teeth gleamed even and white in the dismal surroundings. "Don't you understand, *cara*? We are all a part of this, just as we were long, long ago. I exchanged you for the jewels once before."

"What?"

His words made no sense. Was he crazy?

Clattering on the stairs and the appearance of a second man interrupted their bizarre tête-à-tête. Sam guessed, by his size, he was the same man who had been in the Procuratie, though his mask was also missing.

"Angelo," he called softly, inclining his head toward DiLucca.

Kathleen's self-proclaimed husband sidled toward the stairs, never taking his gaze off Sam for more than a moment. She thought of Keirnan's words when he'd made her promise to stay in the hotel—

"...*I can do this, but not if I have to worry about you.*"

She wanted to die of shame and guilt.

The second man muttered in Italian, gesturing toward her, then toward the door at the top of the stairs.

Though she couldn't make out any words, Angelo appeared unruffled. However, his eyes darted restlessly from his compatriot back to her. The other man sighed heavily, shook his head, and walked to the other side of the room out of her line of vision.

Angelo came back and squatted beside her, his expressive dark eyes soulful. "That was very naughty of you to call Interpol."

He ran his fingers through her hair again.

Fighting revulsion, she tossed her head and struggled to sit up, but he held her down with a firm but gentle hand on her shoulder.

"People might get hurt if Carlo interferes." His eyes bored into hers. "And Keirnan won't be pleased."

Love of my heart.

She couldn't allow herself to go there.

"How do you know who I called?" she asked instead, trying to sound belligerent rather than scared.

Angelo cocked his head in the direction the other man had disappeared. "Manny is very talented with telephones, especially cell phones. That's how we called you. He also went back to the piazza and found your phone, so we know you dialed Carlo Bergamon's number before we grabbed you in the Procuratie." He lightly rubbed the back of his fingers across her cheek. "I'm sorry we had to hurt you, but you left us no choice, *cara*. Just as Kathleen and Keirnan left me no choice."

So far tonight, her choices seemed extraordinarily bad, but sometimes honesty really was the best policy. She gave it a try. "You're making a big mistake."

"I've made many mistakes."

His dark eyes ran the length of her again, and her spine prickled under his appraisal. She wanted to keep him talking, occupied, but couldn't think of anything to say. She tried to move, and his hand pressed her shoulder again.

"It's their eyes, Kathleen and Keirnan," he mused. His index finger stroked his moustache as he contemplated. "So blue you lose yourself in them. Blue like a della Robbia."

Just what she'd thought the first time she met Keirnan's gaze. Sam raised her bound hands and rubbed her suddenly moist eyes.

"Keirnan doesn't have the jewels," she blurted.

Angelo smiled again, not in amusement, but an indulgent, patient smile one might give a child. He pushed her hands away from her face.

"No? Then soon he will have an even better reason to find them—and quickly."

With his free hand, he reached into his pocket and withdrew a slim piece of metal. He touched a button on the side, and to Sam's horror, a wicked stiletto blade popped out.

She gasped and tried to jerk away, but in one fluid movement, Angelo was on top of her, his knees on either side of her hips, the point of the knife blade a hair's breadth from her throat.

Would he really kill her?

Had he already killed his ex-wife?

She heard an echoing gasp from across the room, then the other man's voice. "*Jacopo no piace*, Angelo."

Angelo hissed something in Italian that was undoubtedly a curse, but the blade moved backward a couple of inches.

"What have you done to Kathleen?" Sam whispered, then squeezed her eyes tightly shut in anticipation of the knifepoint.

"That old fool Spinelli has her, you know that." Angelo's low, calm tone made Sam ease her eyes open. "That is why *we* have you."

His answer made her mind race in spite of her peril.

So they weren't helping Spinelli's creditors after all. This was even worse. Theirs was a whole new bid to possess the jewels.

"You—you've made a big mistake."

Might as well tell him and spare the intolerable suspense. Then maybe he would kill her. Fast, she hoped.

"Keirnan will ransom his sister with the jewels, not me."

"You don't believe that."

The stiletto's tip came closer once more. Sam winced. Her breath jammed for a moment in spite of her best effort, and a tear leaked out of one eye as she closed them again.

God, she was such a useless ninny!

"It's true," she answered with absolute honesty, but admitting the whole truth was untenable. So she added a half-truth. "We're only business associates."

Angelo gave a derisive snort. "I know my little brother the fox better than that." She felt him twist a lock of her hair. "There is far more than business between the two of you, Serafina."

Sam's eyes jolted open. "Wh—what did you call me?"

"Stop pretending you don't know." Angelo gave her a narrow-eyed glare as he inserted the tip of the knife under the neckband of her sweater and cut through the fabric to her skin. "He stole the jewels for you once, and he'll do it again."

He *was* crazy!

A stark-raving lunatic.

If he wasn't going to kill her, what was he going to do?

Almost as if he'd heard her mental question, Angelo smiled, a predatory gleam this time. He grabbed her sweater in his fist and slashed through it twice with the stiletto, then tossed the chunk of green knitted fabric to the floor.

Sam stared in mute horror at the gaping hole.

Amazingly, the creamy satin of her pajama top still lay intact against her skin, but not for long. Angelo cut the tie at her throat with one deft flick of the knife.

Too petrified to breathe, much less shut her eyes, she watched as he ever so carefully guided the tip of the blade through the thin, silken material, parting it neatly down the center.

He pulled the intact portion of the sweater and pajamas from beneath her bound wrists and sawed through them.

"Stop it!" Sam hardly recognized the shriek as her own. "Stop!"

Instinctively, she jerked her tied hands up to cover her bare breasts. "Stop!"

Let him stab her. She didn't care!

"Angelo!" A strangled cry from Manny on the other side of the room echoed Sam's own yell.

But Angelo didn't pay either of them any heed. A wide roll of silver duct tape appeared in one of his hands. Awkwardly, he peeled back a short length of it and severed it from the roll.

"No!" Sam shouted.

Determined not to make the assault easy for him, she thrashed under his weight, tossing her head from side to side and kicking her legs. All in vain, for Angelo slapped the piece of tape over her mouth, stifling her cries of protest.

Maybe not in vain! Heavy footsteps sounded on the stairs.

"*Silenzio*! Silence!" a deep voice commanded.

Sam twisted her head, as did her assailant, and watched a short, rotund man descend into the room.

"Jacopo," Manny rushed up to him babbling a string of apologetic sounding Italian.

However, Angelo took advantage of the momentary distraction to capture her motionless legs. Grasping her jean-clad ankles, he deftly wound three layers of duct tape around them then sliced the remaining roll free with the knife. His weight pressed against her rib cage and made it impossible for Sam to catch a breath. Still, she tried to shove at him with her bound hands.

"Angelo, what is all this noise?" the heavyset man demanded in oddly accented English as he brushed the obsequious Manny aside.

Still holding her taped ankles, Angelo stood. Sam thankfully drew in a long draught of air while he casually knocked off one of her shoes with the handle of the knife.

"My little brother's beloved," he drawled as her other shoe clattered to the concrete floor, "is very spirited."

Jacopo sighed. "If you're going to rape her, do it, and be done. Don't toy with her."

Venice, 1485

Betrayed by his best friend!

Nino's mind still balked at the horrible truth.

When the enormity of Father Mateo's words had finally sunk in, he'd run from the ship, though not before he'd done a bit of carving on the false-hearted priest's soft belly just to be sure this was not another lie. Mateo had wept and swore that Serafina was gone, and Nino knew with dread certainty that Fredo Rosso had taken her.

"I thought we were the best of friends… more like brothers. Your secrets are safe with me."

Fredo's words kept echoing inside his head, and every time they did, Nino's gut churned.

Unable to accept the reality of his friend's deceit, he rashly returned to the *scuola*, burst into the room they'd shared for nearly a year. It was empty of all personal possessions. Even the things he'd left behind were gone, along with everything that belonged to Fredo.

Nino fell to his knees in the middle of the bare room and cursed. He cursed long and vehemently. Cursed Fredo, Father Mateo, Pietro Lombardo, the Viscount Treviso, but mostly he cursed himself. He cursed himself for being every kind of fool, for letting himself love so rashly, so completely. Then somewhere in the midst of his self-flagellation it occurred to him that perhaps love had driven Fredo too.

Though he knew his friend had opportunities to have other love affairs, as long as Nino had known him, the painter had been faithful to his mistress, Mariana. In spite of their often turbulent relationship, Fredo and Mariana always ended up professing their love for one another. But even though Mariana's circumstances were relatively humble, Fredo still did not earn enough with his painting to support himself, her, and her son.

The temptation of the jewels had proven too great for his friend to resist. If that were the case, why had he also taken Serafina, and what had he done with her?

Only Fredo could answer those questions. Or maybe Mariana.

Near exhaustion, Nino hauled himself to his feet and haltingly retraced his steps to the quays. The weak sun had already reached its full height, as had the tide. The large sailing vessels were gone, the devious Father Mateo with them.

Nino couldn't stop himself from hoping that the priest's belly wounds, no matter how shallow, would fester. And if Fredo had caused harm to come to Serafina, then friend or not, Nino would hunt him down and kill him.

What was one more sin on top of the multitude he'd already committed?

Within a surprisingly short time, he found a vessel embarking for the island of Burano. The barge-master was pleased to earn a few extra coins by taking on a passenger.

Nino stepped carefully through the piles of grain sacks and sat with his back resting on a fragrant rack of hay while the man and his two helpers pushed the loaded barge into the lagoon.

Once they were in open water and the small sail was set, one of the men came and lounged beside him. He took a long drink from a leather flask he unhooked from his belt.

"What business takes you to Burano?" he asked, offering the flask to Nino.

"I seek a lace maker named Mariana." Nino took a gulp of the strong red wine and passed the flask back to its owner. "Do you know her?"

"I know of no woman in Burano who doesn't make lace, my friend." The man chuckled as he took another generous swallow and offered the flask again.

"This woman is a widow of twenty-two or twenty-three years with a young son." Nino refused the offer of more wine, knowing it would only increase his fatigue. "His name is Giacomo, and he's very mischievous."

"You must mean Giacomo Sortello." The barge-master intervened with a broad, gap-toothed smile. "That little devil spreads trouble all over the island. His mother's shop isn't far from the harbor."

In the time it took to complete their short voyage from Venice to Burano, Nino pulled the hood of his cloak low over his face and napped fitfully, trying not to allow himself to hope.

The barge scarcely nudged against the dock when he thanked the three crewmen and bid them a hasty farewell.

"Don't turn your back on that imp, Giacomo!" The barge-master called after him with a laugh.

Brushing aside his fatigue, Nino strode purposefully toward where the island's main canal dumped into the harbor. The narrow stream smelled strongly of sewage. Small two- and three-story houses crowded tightly along both banks. He found the footpath between the houses that the barge-master described and followed it to a piazzetta with a covered cistern in its center.

A trio of small boys cavorted on one side, dueling with sticks. A slightly older boy in a floppy hat hauled up a bucket of water. One of the smaller boys was so intent on chasing after the others with his stick that he jostled the older boy and upset the bucket.

"Sorry Simeon!" the smaller boy called out. The larger boy seemed more intent on righting his hat than the bucket.

"Let's play a different game," another of the trio suggested.

"No," the first boy insisted. "I need to keep practicing so that when I'm bigger I can buy a real sword and kill Fredo Rosso!" Then he saw Nino, a cloaked and hooded shadow, and covered his mouth with alarm.

"Why do you want to kill this Fredo Rosso?" Nino asked in a low, menacing voice that made all four boys stand still and stare wide-eyed. "Is he a very bad man?"

The boy looked down and shuffled his feet, his mouth twitched before he answered. "Y-yes, I guess so."

"Then take me to him." Nino grabbed the boy's shirtsleeve, making him gasp. "Perhaps I will kill him for you."

Squawking like a flock of disturbed ducks, the boy's goggle-eyed companions all took flight in several directions. The older one even forgot his bucket.

"B-but Fredo is in Venice." The boy's voice shook with fear, and his bottom lip quivered.

Nino tightened his grip on the boy's arm. "Then take me to your house so we can wait for him. You are Giacomo Sortello, are you not? And your mother is Mariana?"

Tears welled in the boy's wide dark eyes as he nodded. "P-please s-sir, don't kill my mother too."

Chapter 10

"IF YOU'RE GOING TO RAPE HER, DO IT AND BE DONE. Don't toy with her."

Sam shuddered in abhorrence at the man's matter-of-fact words. She hugged her arms tightly against her chest. She would die first.

"I don't have to force a woman." Angelo's tone was contemptuous. He dropped her legs, sheathed the knife, and shoved it back into his pocket.

Jacopo lumbered closer and studied her. Sam defiantly stared back into his eyes, which looked like raisins in his pasty, fleshy face. His hand grasped her wrists and forced them down, exposing her bare breasts.

"Very lovely," he stated neutrally.

Face blazing, Sam turned aside, unable to stomach the open scrutiny of both men.

"Any man would gladly trade jewels for that." Angelo's pronouncement made her skin crawl.

"As long as your brother-in-law does."

Sam knew he wouldn't... couldn't.

What would they do when they learned it too?

Jacopo let go of her wrists, and she hugged her arms back against her chest. Tears of shame and frustration burned in the back of her throat. She doubted ten thousand showers would make her feel clean again. If she survived to take them.

The fat man squinted at her speculatively. "I don't

suppose you would tell us how to contact him? Save us all a little time?"

She willed all the loathing she felt into her gaze and shook her head.

Jacopo sighed again, then his eyes shifted to Angelo, who'd stepped away. "Where do you think you're going?"

"Serafina's beauty has inspired me. I need my palette."

Jacopo rolled his eyes and muttered so that only she could hear. "Crazy fool thinks he's a reincarnated Renaissance painter. Thinks this is all some past life repeating itself."

He gave Sam another calculating appraisal. "As long as we get those jewels, I really don't care." Then he wound a knitted scarf around his jowly throat and shivered. "It's so cold in this subterranean hole. I don't blame Angelo for wanting you to warm him up a little. Perhaps if I watched, it would warm me up as well."

Sam tried to tell him exactly what she thought of him, but the tape attached to her lips prevented any intelligible sounds from emerging. If only looks *could* kill, the fat jerk would be writhing in agony instead of snorting with amusement.

At least he'd never get his paws on the Jewels of the Madonna. She took some small consolation in that.

Angelo sauntered back over, his left thumb thrust through the center of an oval piece of wood and a long-handled paintbrush in his right hand. "And I don't suppose you'll cooperate and put your arms down."

He just chuckled at her venomous glare. Holding the paintbrush in his teeth, he yanked her bound hands up over her head. Against her squirming and muffled protests, he held them in place against the arm of the couch with his knee. Then he took the brush into his hand and swirled it through the blue paint smeared on the wooden oval.

"Now hold still," he ordered, and with a smirking Jacopo looking on, he began to paint directly on her bare skin.

Keirnan stumbled over a stray chunk of marble on the weed-choked gravel path. The moon had long since disappeared and left only a dark, starless sky. Finding his way had proven more difficult than he thought, and he'd lost track of how long he'd wandered through the eerie silent landscape of graves and monuments.

He ran the tiny beam of Samantha's penlight over the stained marble husks towering up all around him. At least he was in the right vicinity. Majestic winged seraphim, their faces blurred by the ravages of time and weather, guarded columned tombs the size of small houses. Vandals had broken into many of them, maybe last year, or a hundred years ago.

But if anyone had stumbled upon the Jewels of the Madonna, then surely his sister would have uncovered some evidence of the find. He wouldn't let himself believe differently.

The names carved across the front of the tombs had fared little better than the faces of the angels. He prayed that the battery in the penlight wouldn't fail, while he forced his weary eyes to study each one carefully until he was sure it could not have once read "Treviso."

Too many letters.
Not enough letters.

Definitely a "CH"...

The proverbial needle in the haystack seemed easier. And all the while the image of his sister's severed finger hovered on the fringes of his mind.

The stillness of the deserted cemetery was abruptly broken by a muffled tune from inside his jacket— Spinelli's cell phone. Keirnan's heart lurched from his chest to his throat.

Dropping the light, his hand jerked convulsively for the chiming phone. It too almost slipped from his unsteady grasp. He held onto it with both hands.

"*P-pronto,*" he answered in Italian, his heart pounding in his ears like a dozen timpani drums gone wild.

"*Ciao, Sionnach,*" said a silky voice he didn't recognize at first. But only one other person besides Kathleen used his Gaelic nickname.

"A-Angelo?" Keirnan's dazed mind couldn't process what he was hearing. His sister's crackpot ex-husband had called Spinelli's number.

How?

"Surprised to hear from me, I see. So tell me, little brother, do you have the jewels yet?"

"Wh-what?" His pulse continued to pound in triple time.

"The Jewels of the Madonna. Your *ragazza* claims you don't have them."

"My…" Girlfriend? Keirnan choked on the realization. *He couldn't mean Samantha.*

Oh God, don't let him mean her!

"Serafina," Angelo purred as Keirnan continued to sputter. "Or whatever she's called in this life."

Stay calm.

Focus, boyo!

"Samantha." Keirnan forced the name from his tightly constricted throat. "But she's not—"

"Don't waste my time claiming she's nothing to you," Angelo interrupted. "I know better." Then his voice dropped to a sinister tone that made Keirnan's gut twist. "Hair like bronzed silk, golden green eyes." He inhaled deeply. "And she smells like a sweet, ripe peach."

God in heaven, no!

He had let her get involved, and now she was in danger!

Calm and focus crashed and burned. Raw anguish imploded inside Keirnan, and a strangled noise escaped from his horror-parched mouth.

The other man continued to gloat. "That little pink spot on the top of her right breast, it begs to be kissed, doesn't it?"

Samantha had a tiny strawberry birthmark on the top of one breast. He had kissed it, more than once, just a few hours ago. White-hot fury seared through the iron vise gripping his chest. A nameless, faceless kidnapper was one thing. This was something else entirely.

"So help me, Angelo," he snarled with tightly controlled rage. "If you've laid a finger on her, I'll make sure you never lay a finger on any other woman again."

The crazy bastard just laughed at his threat.

"I knew she was special, worth any price. I'd let you talk to her." He gave another snort of laughter. "But she's a bit tied up."

Silently, Keirnan fought the overwhelming urge to kill. Every word was a battle. "Let—her—go!"

"As soon as we make a simple exchange, the same as long ago. Your beloved for the Jewels of the Madonna."

Angelo sounded sane, but he wasn't. Prison must

have completely unhinged him, not that Keirnan cared. If he'd harmed Samantha, he was a dead man.

"Do you have them, little brother?"

The burning anger inside Keirnan solidified to steely resolve. The past few days had been living hell. He'd only survived this long because Samantha had helped him. God knew Angelo had caused enough suffering for him and Kathleen. Keirnan would not allow him to harm Samantha too.

He was done with being led around, letting madmen call the shots. Saving Kathleen might prove beyond him, but this was not. *He* was taking control this time. Angelo could come to him.

He would be ready.

"They're on San Michele en Isola, the cemetery isle. I'll have them by the time you arrive. Bring Samantha and come alone."

"I'm afraid I can't quite do that. My two friends will insist on coming along. You know how it is."

"They don't trust you. Wise fellows."

Three against one, not exactly great odds, but as long as they didn't have guns he could still pull it off. Not that he had a choice. He had caused all this, and only he could put it right.

Angelo gave another throaty chuckle. "They're just anxious to have the jewels, *Sionnach*. We'll be there by dawn. Don't keep us waiting."

"I'll be there."

The words no sooner passed his lips than the phone went dead. Keirnan shoved it back into his jacket pocket then bent to retrieve the flickering penlight. He clicked that off too and studied the inky sky. Dawn must not be more than an hour or so away. He couldn't let himself think about what Angelo and his compatriots might do to Samantha between now and then… what they might have already done to her. He had to concentrate on what he had to do now.

An isolated island in the middle of the Venetian lagoon, San Michele was easy enough to reach by boat. However, a solid, two-meter high wall completely encircled it with only a single boat dock and one way in and out. The place was actually ideal for his purposes.

Everything that mattered, his sister and Samantha's safety, now depended on his ability to out-maneuver his foes. His search for the jewels would have to wait awhile longer. He had a "welcoming" party to prepare. Angelo and his two friends would soon discover that running a fox to earth could be a dangerous gambit.

Red streaks of light stained the eastern sky and made it easy for Keirnan to recognize the distinctive shape moving across the lagoon toward San Michele. A low-lying vessel with both ends curved upward, a single figure stood on the back.

Angelo and company were arriving by gondola, a nice, quiet conveyance and unlikely to draw attention. If anyone did notice it, they'd simply shrug it off as eccentric tourists.

Crouched in the dark shadows of the entry, Keirnan watched the narrow boat negotiate around the glowing wooden channel markers that blemished the flat surface of the calm water. From this distance he couldn't tell if the gondolier was Angelo, nor could he make out any seated figures, but he knew they were there. No more than three, he hoped, and Samantha had better be one of them.

For the thousandth time since Angelo's unexpected phone call, he prayed she was all right. He hadn't had time to consider what he might do if she weren't. Truth be told, he hadn't taken time to think about much of anything or worry if his crazy, half-formed plan would succeed.

First he'd jammed the throttle of the small skiff he'd used to get to San Michele with a rock and a piece of wire, sending it puttering off in the direction of Murano. When this was over, he and Samantha or Angelo and his friends would be stuck on the island.

The rest he'd been improvising as he went along. He knew he would have to strike quickly and fiercely. Just like his old days in the Dublin street gang—no finesse and no second chances. He intended to grab Samantha and get the hell out.

And no better place to do it than the entrance to the cemetery isle, which featured three tall doors set into the brick outer wall, then an enclosed chamber a dozen meters square with an iron-gated archway leading to the island's interior. Truly a fox's lair.

With one last glance at the approaching boat, he withdrew back inside to finish preparing his arsenal of broken glass and rusted hunks of metal.

Sam huddled on the edge of the double seat next to Angelo, who twirled a lock of her hair over and around his fingers, his knife held loosely in his right hand.

Manny stood on the gondolier's platform behind them, skillfully stroking the single, long oar through the water. Jacopo filled most of the double seat across from them.

Angelo had cut the duct tape around her ankles so that she could walk, but had not given back her shoes nor removed the tape from her mouth. As if to prove his words to Jacopo, he hadn't forced her to do anything except submit to being painted. He did cut her sweater and pajama top the rest of the way off to admire his own handiwork, but he hadn't undressed her any further.

He had painted large blue jewels diagonally across her chest, just like the ones she'd momentarily glimpsed on the statue of the Madonna in Santa Maria dei Miracoli. He'd finished four before Manny's excited exclamation and proffering of the cell phone had stopped him.

She heard every word of Angelo's call to Keirnan. In fact, she was sure he'd spoken in English just so he could take perverted pleasure in letting her understand what was being said. The degradation and shame she had suffered while they mocked and ogled her was nothing compared to the misery she experienced knowing she had caused Keirnan to play precisely into their hands.

Maybe not precisely. Sam knew he wasn't going to give them the jewels, not at the risk of his sister's life. Instead he would risk his own trying to save her. And he was going to get himself killed, because Jacopo had a gun.

Unwilling to unbind her hands, Jacopo had wound and tied his knitted scarf around her breasts. It reeked of his cheap aftershave. Her missing jacket had reappeared, and he'd tied that around her neck by the sleeves. When he and Angelo forced her up the stairs, he'd pulled the pistol from the pocket of his overcoat and admonished her not to do anything stupid.

Too late!

Everything she'd done in the past few hours was stupid. She was responsible for sealing all of their dooms—Keirnan's, Kathleen's, and her own.

The certainty of it made her ill, numb, and drove her tortured mind into an unfeeling oblivion beyond fear and hopelessness. Though a fair amount of her torso remained bare and exposed, she was so far past caring that not even the frigid air got through her deadened senses.

This was what the condemned must feel like.

"Ah, there it is, San Michele en Isola," Angelo breathed, when a dark, fortress-looking structure loomed out of the water ahead of them.

Jacopo twisted around to glimpse their destination with a grumbled, "At last!"

"What a shame I have to let you go, *cara*." Angelo ran a lock of her hair across his lips. "But alas, you were never meant for me. I must content myself with the jewels."

"I don't see another boat." Jacopo turned an accusing glower toward Angelo. "He'd better be here. It's getting light."

Angelo gave her hair another caress. "Don't worry. He's here. I know it."

Sam knew it too. Pain she didn't think she could feel suddenly lanced into her chest.

"I don't like this," Jacopo muttered as the gondola moved briskly over the dark water toward the brick and marble portico.

"Then call it off," Angelo stated simply.

"Too late for that."

Too late for everything. Especially this huge lump of dread in the pit of her stomach.

The wood and metal bow of the gondola bumped into the corner of the marble-clad dock, jarring Sam from her misery. She watched Manny heave on the oar to turn the vessel around so that it sat beside the short pier facing out. Then he secured his end by looping a piece of rope around a jutting marble knob.

The gondola swayed precipitously as Jacopo heaved his bulk up and out.

"Stay here," he ordered Manny, then he turned to help Angelo pull her out of the boat and onto the damp platform.

It was almost over. Very soon now, Keirnan would appear, then they would both probably die.

But not without a fight.

Hope had not completely abandoned her after all. Some tiny spark still remained, stubbornly insisting she must fight.

"I told you he was here." Angelo inclined his head toward the three massive doors at the back of the dock. The one on the left stood open, revealing a gaping black-ness beyond it. "He's always had a way with doors."

Doors and who knew what else? The thought made Sam stagger, her socks slipping on the damp stone surface.

Angelo gripped her upper arm and brought the knife blade up close to her throat. "Easy, *cara*. Nice and slow."

Jacopo moved to her other side, but the three of them couldn't fit through the door together, so he had to step behind them. With Angelo still holding her arm, they walked over the threshold into Stygian darkness.

Keirnan was here.

Even though she couldn't see or hear him, Sam could feel his eyes on her. She could also feel Jacopo's raspy breath panting on the back of her neck scant inches behind her.

A half-dozen yards to the right, a pale gray archway, wider than the doorway, beckoned. Jacopo huffed up beside her as they shuffled toward it, his movements jumpy, agitated.

Angelo too seemed nervous. His fingers tightened around her arm when his shoes crunched on the gravel path beyond the archway.

The small rocks poked through Sam's socks and into the tender soles of her feet, forcing her to go even more slowly. Gingerly, she walked a half-dozen halting steps. Angelo tugged impatiently; the hand holding his knife now dangled at his side. Jacopo was two full strides ahead of them. She took two more careful steps, then another.

"*Ciao*, Angelo."

Even though she'd been expecting him, Keirnan's sudden greeting made her jump. Angelo and Jacopo did the same as Keirnan materialized behind them, a darker shadow against the blackness beyond the archway.

Angelo released her arm as they turned, but quickly shifted the knife to his other hand so that the blade was still pointed at her neck. His teeth gleamed in the gray half-light.

"*Ciao, Sionnach.*"

"The jewels," Jacopo hissed over Sam's shoulder.

Even as he said the words, Keirnan tilted his hand to reveal a rounded blue object resting in his palm.

No! It couldn't be!

As the frenzied thought slashed across Sam's disbelieving brain, Keirnan's dark azure eyes met hers. Then everything happened at once.

Angelo reached out with his free hand, moved a half step away from her, and lowered the knife. Keirnan rushed at him, raking his open palm across Angelo's arm.

Sam saw shock flicker across his face in the split second before Keirnan's other hand came up. He held a chunk of broken brick, which he bashed into the side of Angelo's head.

But Sam didn't see Angelo fall. She twisted toward Jacopo, who was leveling his pistol at Keirnan. Using her bound hands as a club, she swung them down with all her strength on the stout man's elbow.

As Jacopo cried out, the gun flew from his grasp.

"The dock! Run!" Keirnan shouted at her.

He now clutched a four-foot length of rusty pipe in both hands. The last thing Sam saw before she fled was him swinging it low and underhanded like a cricket bat in the direction of Jacopo's knees.

A howl of anguish reverberated through the air as she sprinted through the archway into the dark enclosure. Keirnan was only two steps behind her.

She rushed for the open doorway illuminated ahead of her. From the far corner of her field of vision, she saw Keirnan shove an iron gate across the opening. She heard metal and glass crash onto the floor and block the gate from swinging back. Then she was out the door, nearly colliding with Manny who'd apparently left the gondola to investigate the noise.

Sam's feet slipped on the wet stone of the dock, and she went down hard onto one knee. Swearing, Manny leaped into the boat and scrambled up onto the gondolier's platform. As he jerked the rope free, Sam glimpsed Keirnan hurling past her. He hit Manny with a flying tackle that knocked them both down.

For a brief moment they dangled off the edge of the narrow gondolier's perch, and Sam thought for sure they'd go over into the water. But before she could reach the gondola, Keirnan grasped the ornately carved oarlock and heaved himself backward and onto his knees. Manny thrashed with his arms and tried to regain his balance, but a single push from Keirnan propelled him into the lagoon.

"Hurry, luv!" Keirnan urged as he pulled himself to his feet and smacked the oar down into the water in the vicinity of Manny's head.

Still hampered by her bound hands and now a throbbing knee, Sam scuttled crablike to the dock's edge then heaved herself toward the front seat of the wildly bobbing gondola. She landed sprawling, facedown across the vinyl cushions as the boat surged forward. She couldn't seem to get enough air into her lungs, and fear continued to thunder through her veins as she struggled to turn around.

Keirnan stood on the gondolier's platform, a dark silhouette against the reddening dawn sky. He hauled on the single oar in swift, choppy strokes. They pulled away from San Michele at a fairly rapid clip, but he was a far too vulnerable target.

Sam clawed at the duct tape still firmly covering her mouth, but her tied hands trembled too hard for her to get a grip on it.

"Hang on just a wee bit longer, luv." Keirnan's voice soothed, but his rowing remained frenetic. Though she couldn't make out his features, he could obviously see her distress. "See those lights up ahead? That's Murano, and we'll be there in—"

The cracking retort of a gun interrupted his words.

Sam gave a muffled scream against her gag. Keirnan dove for the bottom of the gondola and pulled her off the seat as two more shots rang out.

The boat bobbed drunkenly, and Sam attempted to cry out again as they rolled together on the rough floorboards. Then Keirnan's arms were around her, pulling her close. The supple leather of his jacket glided over her bare skin. Her own coat had fallen off somewhere back on the dock, but that wasn't the only reason she couldn't stop shaking.

The enormity of the past few minutes—the past few days—hit her with full impact.

Kill or be killed.

Keirnan may have killed Angelo, maybe Manny too. At the very least, he had been forced to fight off two armed men with only a brick and a rusty pipe. He might still get shot. And all because of her.

"Are you all right?" His voice didn't sound very steady as he pulled back, and his sapphire gaze roamed worriedly across her face.

She tried to nod, but she just seemed to tremble harder. She couldn't even cry.

"Oh God, luv!"

He lifted one corner of the duct tape and carefully peeled it away from her mouth. Sam gulped in a draught of cold air in the split second before his lips replaced the tape. She exhaled on a long, shuddering sigh and fingered his cheek with her bound hands.

Thank God she hadn't lost him!

Not yet anyway.

His lips slid gently away, and he levered himself into a low crouch. Then he extracted a piece of jagged blue glass from his jacket pocket and began to carefully saw through the twine binding her wrists together. His breath came out quick and raspy in the abrupt, eerie silence.

Why had the shooting stopped?

Even though her gag was gone, Sam still couldn't force words out of her quivering lips.

"They may be out of bullets," Keirnan answered her unasked question while he worked the edge of the glass through the last piece of binding. "But I expect they're waiting to get a clearer shot."

The severed ties fell off, but her hands continued to shake so hard she couldn't reach for him. Keirnan's questioning gaze suddenly snagged on the jewels—one painted just below her shoulder, the next at the top of her breast, a third peeking above the knitted scarf wound around her torso. He made a strangled sound and reached for her shoulder, his fingertips tracing the edges of the egg tempera.

"Did Angelo... did they... Oh God!" His voice broke, and he hugged her tightly to him. Each word seemed to cost him a supreme effort. "What—did—they—do?"

Sam could feel his heart pounding against her, so solid, so alive.

She found her voice at last. "Nothing." She sucked in a ragged breath. "Th-they didn't hurt me."

He broke his embrace and searched her face. "Are you sure?"

"Y-yes, I'm okay."

She saw relief flood his beautiful cerulean eyes, then they immediately clouded with concern. "No, you're not. You're freezing!"

He removed his jacket and draped it over her, then he peeled off his sweater and pulled it over her head. Both were warm from the heat of his body.

Warm and safe.

Like sanctuary.

Sam plunged her arms through the sweater sleeves and wrapped them around her chest. That's when she noticed the streaks of red on one cuff.

"You're bleeding!" she gasped. Then she burst into tears.

Venice, 1485

In spite of Nino's reassurance that he had no intentions of killing Giacomo's mother, the boy continued to whimper all the way down the path to the canal. He still sniffled when they reached the pink stucco structure that housed both his home and his mother's shop.

Nino released Giacomo's arm when they entered the sparsely furnished front room.

"Mama! Mama! Mama!" the boy wailed, dashing for a short, plump woman who stepped through an ornate lace curtain at the back of the room. "This man wants to kill Fredo!"

Nino watched first surprise then alarm chase across

the woman's softly rounded features. Then she thrust the boy behind her and faced Nino with the same fierce expression he was sure a mother wolf wore when defending her cubs.

"Who are you?" she demanded, eyes flashing fire.

He threw back the hood of his cloak. "Nino Andriotto."

Disbelief extinguished the ferocity in her gaze. "But Fredo left for Venice at dawn to find you." She faltered for a moment. "He… he loves you like a brother…"

"So it was brotherly love that made him steal the jewels and my beloved?" Nino interrupted in a harsh tone. "If you want me to spare his life, you'll need to do better than that."

Mariana's face flushed dark pink, but she turned imperiously to her son. "Giacomo, go upstairs."

"But Mama, he might kill you too! He looks very mean."

"Nobody is killing anyone. Go upstairs now, and don't come down until I call you."

The sobbing boy retreated through the curtain, and his footsteps clumped on the stairs.

Nino looked around the room, his tone accusatory. "Your shop looks nearly empty, almost as if you were leaving."

Mariana glanced nervously through the curtain, then she moved closer to Nino. "My son talks too much, so it's better he doesn't know—"

"That you and Fredo are taking the stolen Jewels of the Madonna and moving someplace far away?"

Face flaming crimson, Mariana nodded, her voice scarcely above a whisper. "Once he found you, we planned to sail for Ravenna." She took a deep breath and shot him a challenging look. "Far better for us to have those two jewels than that monster Father Mateo!"

Nino gripped her arm, bent his face close to hers, and hissed, "The jewels be damned! Where is Serafina? If any harm has come to her…"

"Thanks to Fredo, she is safe enough." Mariana jerked her arm free and gave Nino another scathing look. "She's hidden somewhere no one would think to look for her."

"Here on Burano?"

"How do I know I can trust you?" Mariana asked, eyes narrowed in appraisal. "How do I even know you are who you say?"

"Of course I—" Nino was interrupted by the sudden opening of the door.

The youth who'd been at the well rushed inside, slamming the door behind him. The empty wooden bucket slipped from his grasp and clattered to the floor the instant before he launched himself at Nino.

"My love! Oh my love, you're safe!"

Soft hands cupped Nino's startled face. He pulled back enough to stare at the dirt-smudged features. Serafina's radiant smile overwhelmed him.

A thousand trumpeting angels could not have astonished him more. Before he could utter a sound, her lips closed over his. A thunderbolt of rapture exploded inside him at her touch, obliterating the agony and desperation of the past hours. His arms moved of their own accord, encircled her slim body, and crushed her against him.

"Well, I see you're Nino Andriotto after all," Mariana murmured sardonically. "Have a care now. People passing on the street might see you." She tugged them apart and shooed them toward the back room.

Too overcome to speak, Nino obeyed, but plucked the floppy hat from Serafina's head.

"Your hair…" he choked out as he ran his hand over her sheared, darkened locks.

"It will grow back and be golden again before you know it." Mariana quickly reassured. "I knew a beautiful, golden-haired woman would never go unnoticed. But few would remark if I took an awkward youth into my household. Or if they did, I'd merely explain he was the orphaned cousin of my intended, Fredo Rosso."

Serafina gave him another exuberant hug. "So we cut off my hair, darkened it with some henna, then bound up my breasts and dressed me in doublet and hose." She giggled. "You never even gave me a second look back at the well, my love."

"Oh nooo!" A long moan sounded from the top of the stairs.

"Giacomo!" Mariana cried sharply.

The boy slunk down the stairs, his lip jutting in an angry pout. "Please Simeon, don't tell me you're really a *girl*."

"I should thrash you for eavesdropping," his mother threatened.

"But Mama, I had to," Giacomo protested. "In case the mean man tried to kill you." He glanced at Nino then quickly averted his gaze. "Only I guess he's not so mean because Simeon… I mean *she* loves him."

"Go back upstairs, Giacomo," Mariana ordered sternly. "And if I catch you listening again, you'll have no supper."

"Oh Mama!" The boy groaned, but turned and trudged back up the stairs anyway.

"I may have to tie him in his bed to keep him quiet."

Mariana's tone was purposefully loud. Somewhere overhead, a door slammed. She turned to Serafina, her voice now low. "You need to continue in this disguise until you reach Padua."

Nino's brain was finally starting to function again. "I thought you said you were sailing to Ravenna."

"We are, but the two of you are not."

He nodded his understanding at Mariana's reply. The five of them together might draw undue attention.

Serafina squeezed his hands. "Mariana is teaching me to sew and cook so that I can be a proper wife for you."

His heart threatened to pound out of his chest at the joyful thought. He lifted her hands to his face. Two red blisters already marred one of her pristine palms.

"There'll be no need for you to do those chores, my love, now that we have the jewels."

He started to caress her palms with his lips, but she jerked her hands away. "What do you mean? I thought you only took two as payment to Father Mateo. That was bad enough, but now you tell me you took them all?"

The look of distress on her face startled Nino. "You know I'll be hung and sent to hell for stealing them, whether it's two or all."

Serafina bit her lip and crossed her arms tightly across her chest. Nino reached for her, but she turned away. "I want no part of them."

Mariana gave a snort of disgust. "Foolish girl! Don't be so impossibly noble."

"Please my love." Serafina faced him once more. Her velvety eyes glittered with tears. "You must give the jewels back."

Chapter 11

KEIRNAN GLANCED AT THE OOZING RED GASH ON THE side of his hand then scrubbed it against the leg of his jeans. "Cut myself on a piece of glass. 'Tis nothing."

But Samantha continued to sob incoherently. She must be in shock—small wonder, after what she'd been through in the past few hours. The idea that Angelo or one of his sleazy friends had put their hands on her sent a white-hot bolt of rage rampaging through his body. He fought to maintain some semblance of control.

All that mattered was that she was safe. For now… but for how long?

He scooted so that his back rested against the bottom of the seat in front of the gondolier's platform. He took care to ensure that his head was still below the top of the gondola's side, then he pulled her into his arms.

"It's all right now, luv," he murmured as she wept quietly against his shirt. "It's all right."

He sincerely hoped he was telling the truth, but in his current state, he couldn't tell if they were drifting away from San Michele or back toward it. Either way, in another minute or two he must climb back up and start rowing.

Samantha needed to be examined by a doctor. He'd seen her fall on the dock and feared her knee might be broken. And then there was the matter of what to do about the three ruffians left behind on the cemetery isle.

He would lose it completely if he thought about his sister right now. His frayed nerves were too close to the breaking point.

At the moment, all he wanted was to hold Samantha. He stroked her hair and tried to relax. Her sobs seemed to subside a little. Keirnan wanted to ask her what the hell happened and how his crazy ex-brother-in-law fit into this mess. However, that might not be a wise topic to discuss with her just yet.

From far away the singsong wail of police sirens drifted on the chilly dawn air and made the back of Keirnan's neck prickle with unease. Venice was certainly not living up to her serene nickname this morning. He kissed the top of Samantha's head and crawled onto the seat behind her. She clutched at his leg and whimpered.

"It's all right, luv." He patted her icy fingers. "We're going to get you someplace safe."

She withdrew her hand. "B-be careful."

He poked his head over the top of the seat. The sky was now magenta, the water dark indigo, and San Michele was a foreboding dark blotch behind them. Too dark to distinguish the dock, much less anyone standing on it. He scrambled up onto the gondolier's stand and grabbed the oar.

After two pulls, a gunshot rang out. Keirnan flinched, and Samantha yelped. Obviously they could see him. He dropped to his knees and kept rowing. The pop of another shot sounded, but it was almost drowned out by the wail of the approaching sirens. He could see the flashing red and blue lights skimming across the water. Three police boats were headed in their direction, motors roaring full throttle.

He scarcely had time to slide down into the seat and pull Samantha next to him when two of the boats, sirens screaming, careened around on either side of them. Their twin wakes tossed the gondola roughly and nearly capsized it. Keirnan hung onto the oarlock as water sloshed over the sides. Samantha had her arms in a death-grip around his neck, her face buried in his shoulder.

The third boat cut its engine to a fast idle directly in front of them. The siren stopped abruptly, but the blinding lights continued to flash as the boat came about. The gondola kept lurching crazily as a uniformed officer with a bullhorn shouted in Italian, and a thick length of rope sailed through the air.

Keirnan peeled Samantha's arms away. "It's all right, they're towing us back to Venice," he explained at her panicked expression.

He crawled across the seats to avoid getting his shoes full of water, then secured the rope to the metal *ferro* on the gondola's bow. A moment later, the rope jerked taut and almost sent him tumbling.

They whooshed off in the midst of flashing lights and renewed shrieking sirens. He had to wait until he'd regained his balance and they were moving smoothly before he edged back to the seat Samantha still occupied. One side of his shirt was soaked, and the wind whipping against it felt bloody damn freezing.

Samantha sat huddled under his jacket, trembling. He doubted it was from cold.

He pulled her against him, but her shivering went on unabated. His overburdened nervous system gave another lurch. He needed her to be all right. Really needed it.

"Talk to me, luv," he cajoled, rubbing his hands up and down her spine. "It's going to be all right."

"N-no." Even her voice quivered. She pulled away but wouldn't look at him. "It isn't." A lone tear leaked from the corner of her eye, followed by a single sob. "They're here because of me."

"I don't know what you mean?"

Her disjointed words, interspersed with the siren, made no sense to him. Fortunately they appeared to be heading straight for the docks at Fondamenta Nuove, not far from Venice's hospital. He'd get her there if he had to commandeer the police boat himself.

"The police," Samantha choked out. "They're here because… because…"

"Hush now, luv," he soothed, all the while willing the boat to move faster. "We're almost there."

"I called Interpol!" she blurted, then buried her face in her shaking hands.

A cold far more biting than the wind against his wet shirt slapped Keirnan in the face. "You what?"

The sharpness of his tone cracked the floodgates that had held back her words. "I'm sorry! Oh my God, I'm so sorry! I… I didn't know what to do. They said you were hurt. I thought… I thought you might be dead. So I… I called…"

Now it was his turn to go numb. Her babbling loosed a torrent of ice that rushed through his veins, left him too stunned to speak, move, or breathe. If the authorities stepped in, he would no longer be in control. His sister's life would depend on people he didn't know, didn't trust.

"I've killed her, haven't I?" Samantha sobbed, giving voice to his biggest fear. She doubled over with the painful realization. "Oh my God, Kathleen…"

Before Keirnan could form a thought, much less a reply, the police boat slid smoothly into the side of the dock. But the gondola banged roughly against the post on the end and knocked him back to reality. He snagged his leather jacket as it slid from Samantha's heaving shoulders and shrugged it on.

First things first…

"*Ospedale*! Hospital!" he shouted as he clambered onto the gondolier's platform, dragging the still hysterical Samantha with him. "*Dottore*! Doctor!"

In the distance he could hear the sirens of the other two boats heading back in their direction.

Two Venetian police officers materialized in front of him when he jumped onto the dock.

"Signor Keirnan Fitzgerald?" one of them asked.

"*Si*," he acknowledged briefly before he turned and lifted Samantha into his arms.

She continued weeping apologies against his neck as he shoved her into the startled grasp of the larger of the two policemen.

"Get this woman to hospital!" he ordered in Italian. "She needs a doctor."

"Signor Fitzgerald," the first policeman spoke in English. "We must ask you about an assault on Professor Roberto Spinelli…"

Bloody hell! Things were going downhill fast. Which meant he must think and act even faster.

The policeman who held Samantha tried to set her on her feet, but one of her legs gave way, the one she'd fallen on. Scooping her back up, the officer turned to carry her away.

"Keirnan! No!" she shrieked. One of her hands flailed helplessly in his direction.

Much as he might want to, he couldn't go with her. In fact, if things turned uglier, as well they might, distancing Samantha from him was definitely the best thing for her. She'd suffered enough because of him.

His heart sinking like a lead weight, he gave the English-speaking cop his most steely-eyed stare. "I'll talk only to Carlo Bergamon of Interpol."

Then right on cue, the muted strains of "Santa Lucia" chimed inside his jacket pocket.

The ride was short and swift and Sam tried to pull herself together, but now that the tears had started there seemed to be no stopping them. She scarcely noticed when the silent police officer draped a lightweight blanket over her shoulders.

All she could see was the look of betrayal on Keirnan's face, the horror in his beautiful sapphire eyes. She'd only wanted to help him, and now he would never forgive her.

The golden streaks of early morning sunlight sparkling on the surface of the water mocked her and her utter failure. Sobs continued to work their way up and out of her aching chest.

The police boat pulled up directly in front of a four-story building with a large red sign that read *Emergenza*. Two men rushed forward with a gurney, and before Sam had time to respond, they had her on it and shoved through the automatic doors.

She had never been in an emergency room before, but this was hardly the controlled chaos she'd seen on TV and the movies. A dozen or more people gestured wildly and demanded or cajoled in loud, forceful tones. A baby squalled, while a slightly older child blubbered.

The policeman walked beside the gurney and gave two and three word answers to the babbling stream of Italian coming from the man pushing at her head. The second man, who was pulling at her feet, barked a question at Sam.

"I only… speak English," she choked out between sobs.

He shook his head and guided the gurney to the far wall where white curtains strung on metal poles divided the area into partitioned cubicles. A middle-aged woman in a green scrub suit with a stethoscope around her neck hurried over and jerked the curtain closed with one hand while she shooed all three men away with the other. She fired a question in rapid Italian at Sam then grabbed her right arm, shoved up her sweater sleeve, and slapped on a blood pressure cuff.

The noise continued unabated on the other side of the curtain while the woman frowned at the dial on the cuff. She said something else in Italian, and any resemblance of control Sam had left shattered.

She clamped both hands over her ears and shrieked, "Get me someone who speaks English!"

With a haughty sniff, the woman spun on her heel and disappeared through the curtain. A moment later, a short, stocky man also wearing green scrubs and a stethoscope stepped hesitantly inside.

"Good morning, I am Doctor Coletti," he said in perfect, almost unaccented English. He squinted through his thick glasses at the clipboard in his hand. "And you are Miss Samantha Lewis?"

He raised his round, boyish face to meet her gaze.

Dry-eyed now, she nodded, and he consulted his clipboard again. "Which of your legs is hurt?"

"Th-the left." Her voice still sounded thick with tears.

He handed her a box of tissues as he peered myopically at her jean-clad legs. "I'm sorry, but you will need to remove your pants."

He turned discreetly aside and asked her age, height, weight, and address as Sam slid her jeans off. Having to talk and actually do something helped her keep crying and hysteria at bay. However, she winced with pain when she bent her left knee, and it was soon apparent why.

Dr. Coletti gave the purple and black bruise covering most of her kneecap a single glance before pronouncing, "We will need to take an X ray. Are you injured anywhere else?"

Sam tucked the blanket around her and shook her head, but the young doctor's eyes strayed to the raw red marks on her exposed right wrist. "Are you sure, Miss Lewis?"

She dabbed at her still leaking nose and nodded. He gave her a stiff, white hospital gown and a plastic bag for her clothes and disappeared.

The brusque woman in green reappeared as she untied Jacopo's woolen scarf. Sam snatched the gown closed but not fast enough. The sharp-eyed woman rushed to her side and poked at the edge of the jewel painted below Sam's shoulder. She fired off several phrases in Italian, then over Sam's protests, folded back the edge of the gown to reveal all four of Angelo's painted jewels.

The woman gasped then cried out some sharp orders. Blushing furiously, Sam clutched the gown closed as the waiting policeman hurried back around the curtain, followed a moment later by Dr. Coletti. They both stared at the painted jewel still visible at the neck of Sam's gown while the woman continued her rapid-fire spate of Italian. Both the doctor and the policeman nodded in agreement, and the woman bustled out.

Dr. Coletti moved closer, his eyes darting between the jewel and Sam's face. "Please Miss Lewis, you must tell me if you have been sexually assaulted."

She could feel the hysteria creeping back and a fresh mountain of tears growing in her throat. Refusing to give in to either, she gripped the neck of the gown tighter and shook her head.

"Are you sure?" The doctor's tone was skeptical. "Because we need to run tests, and Officer Ligure can take your statement. Please don't be afraid to tell me the truth."

"Nobody raped me."

Plainly they didn't believe her, but she was afraid if she said much more, she'd start crying again, so she pressed her lips tightly together and tried to take some deep, calming breaths. After a moment of conversation with the policeman, Dr. Coletti said something about a sedative.

She didn't want drugs. She wanted Keirnan, but just thinking about him made her breath catch, and she started to tremble again. The woman in green reappeared, and before Sam could stop her, she'd jabbed a hypodermic into her arm.

"Please relax now, Miss Lewis," Dr. Coletti soothed. "I'll go with you to take the X ray. Then, perhaps in a little while, you will feel more like talking."

Keirnan stabbed the off button on the cell phone just in time to see a familiar figure in a dark brown trench coat striding down the dock in his direction, Carlo Bergamon.

The two policemen he'd waved aside while he spoke to the kidnappers now hovered closer behind him. A third followed on the Interpol agent's heels.

He'd run out of options and time. Circumstances required him to do the one thing he had most wanted to avoid. But since he must enlist the aid of the authorities, he intended to make one last attempt to do it his way.

"*Buon giorno*, Keirnan." Bergamon's sarcasm made Keirnan's hands clench into fists and he seriously reconsidered the "better the devil you know" adage.

"Or perhaps not," Bergamon continued, sneering. "Problems with the Venetian police?"

"Like you don't know." Keirnan spat back, then reined himself in sharply. Without Carlo's intervention, he stood no chance at all with the police.

The same traits that made the Interpol agent a formidable enemy would also make him an excellent ally. The man could be relentless, and he seemed to have his own agenda.

Keirnan had no choice but to hope and bluff. Bluff for all he was worth. Appealing to the agent's interest in antiquities could well be his last and only chance of rescuing Kathleen.

"This is about the Jewels of the Madonna."

Carlo glared through narrowed eyes. "Did your pretty American convince you to cooperate?"

"Leave her out of this." Too bad he couldn't have done the same. Though God knew, if this mess finally sorted itself out decently, Keirnan intended to do everything in his power to make it up to Samantha. *If* she would let him. "'Tis my sister whose life is at stake."

"And what about Professor Roberto Spinelli?" The sarcasm, though toned down a notch, was still apparent. "He says you assaulted and threatened him."

Keirnan's frayed nerves were past the snapping point. The policeman who had followed the Interpol agent stepped forward at the mention of Spinelli's name.

Before he could speak, Keirnan plunged in. "Listen, Carlo, I've no time for this good-cop, bad-cop rubbish."

He swiveled to include all three policemen in his accusatory glare then fastened his attention back on Bergamon and went for broke.

"You're smart enough to fill in the blanks on Spinelli's story. He took my sister so he could exchange her for the jewels. Now his Sicilian friends have her, but the ransom is the same. So who's the best man on the Venetian police force for this sort of tricky situation?"

He had to admire Bergamon—not one muscle on his face twitched. If any of this was news to him, he certainly didn't show it.

His voice was totally bland. "Giuseppe Dario."

A fleeting expression crossed the cop's face who stood nearest to Bergamon.

Good, the name meant something. The Interpol agent wasn't just shining him on.

"Get him here. The three of us are going to rescue my sister."

Bergamon remained impassive, but the cop who'd spoken in English started to say something.

Keirnan held up his hand for silence. "If we succeed and Kathleen is all right, the Jewels of the Madonna will be turned over to you. Won't that be a nice feather in your cap?"

Keirnan saw the slightest hint of a gleam in Bergamon's eyes. "So you have them?"

"No."

Here's where the whole thing could fall to pieces. Apprehension stabbed deep into Keirnan's gut. If it hadn't been for his freezing wet shirt, he'd probably have broken out in a sweat. It took every ounce of self-control to keep his tone neutral.

"But I know where they are, and if anything happens to Kathleen, I'll take the secret to my grave. That's my offer. Take it, or leave it. And we have an hour and fifty-five minutes."

The Interpol agent's eyes went flat and emotionless once more. He stared silently at Keirnan for a score of agonizing heartbeats while the strident wail of the police boats returning from San Michele grew louder.

Finally, he flicked his eyes to the cop who spoke English. "Call Dario."

Keirnan wanted to shout in momentary relief, but he knew he didn't dare. Besides, everything was still a long way from a resolution, happy or otherwise.

Bergamon inclined his head in the direction of a small building on the end of the dock. "Shall we wait inside?"

A propane space heater blasted warmth into the windowless room. One of the cops produced a thermos from somewhere and offered both the Interpol agent and Keirnan paper cups filled with steaming espresso.

Carlo unbuttoned his trench coat and sat on a metal folding chair out of the direct path of the heater. "Fill me in."

Keirnan took a sip of the strong, hot brew. "You first. I'll wait for Dario."

To his great surprise, Bergamon complied. Samantha's first call had been garbled but led to Spinelli, who after immediately blaming Keirnan, had been forced to admit at least part of the truth.

The two goons who held Kathleen belonged to a much larger organization Interpol had been investigating for quite some time. Keirnan didn't need Carlo to tell him that capturing them might implicate others farther up the food chain.

Samantha's second attempted contact in the Piazza San Marco made Carlo call in the locals for reinforcements. They'd intercepted Angelo's cell phone transmission to Keirnan on San Michele and dispatched the three boats to the cemetery isle.

Kathleen's ex-husband had already violated the terms of his parole, and one of his associates Jacopo, alias Yacub Tolenka, was a Russian national with the familiar mile-long rap sheet.

Keirnan had just finished admitting he had no idea how Angelo and his buddies fit into this whole mess when a short man in a khaki hat and overcoat walked in and introduced himself as Captain Giuseppe Dario.

"Now then, Signor Fitzgerald," Captain Dario said after the brief introductions were over. "Tell me the details of the kidnap exchange."

Keirnan met the sharp gaze of the Venetian. A web of crisscrossed wrinkles ran from the corners of his dark eyes into the silver hair lying over his temples. The knowledge that this man held his sister's life in his square, blunt-fingered hands twisted the ever-present knife in Keirnan's gut.

"In a little over ninety minutes, I need to make the

drop in the Public Gardens at the foot of the bridge over the Rio dei Giardini. I don't know how much they've forced my sister to tell them…"

His voice trailed off, and he swallowed hard while trying to banish the image of Kathleen's severed finger. In spite of the heat blasting into the small, enclosed space, ice water washed through him.

"…But I don't think a broken bottle of *acquae minerale* is going to do the trick this time."

"The Jewels of the Madonna." Captain Dario removed his hat and raked his fingers through his closely cropped hair. "I'd never have believed your story." His thick black brows drew together as he slanted Carlo Bergamon a sidelong glance. "Except that Interpol apparently believes it."

The agent silently took another sip of his espresso.

Keirnan rubbed the cut on his palm, which burned now that his hands were warming up. "We'll need a half-dozen stones, or lumps of glass. Dark blue, not faceted, the size of small hen's eggs. And a clear plastic bag so they can see the jewels inside."

"The Public Gardens in such a short time, I don't like it."

Dario raked his fingers through his hair a second time, then turned and barked out orders to the two policemen, who hastily tossed away their coffee cups and jumped to do his bidding. He gave Keirnan an appraising once-over as he dialed his cell phone. "We'll need an officer your size and coloring."

"No!" Keirnan's declaration stopped the other man in mid punch. "They've seen me before, so I have to do it. I won't take the chance with someone else."

"I agree." Carlo Bergamon finally spoke, and

his unexpected support stunned Keirnan into momentary silence.

Dario was also startled, for he turned and scowled openly at the other man. "I don't want to argue with you about jurisdiction, Agent Bergamon."

"Then don't." The Interpol agent rose to his feet, but his face and voice remained impassive. "And if Signor Fitzgerald wants to risk his neck, far better him than one of your own. Don't you agree?"

Dario muttered something under his breath, then went back to dialing his cell phone.

Venice, 1485

"Give them back?" The look of incredulity in Nino's beautiful eyes jammed the breath in Serafina's lungs and made the back of her throat burn with forming tears. She nodded.

From behind her, Mariana gave a loud, disparaging sigh. "She's been trying to convince me to do the same thing." The older woman crossed to the staircase and shot Serafina a long-suffering look reminiscent of her mother. She addressed Nino. "Maybe you can talk some sense into her. I'm going to check on Giacomo."

Nino waited until Mariana's footsteps faded away at the top of the stairs, then he placed his hand on top of Serafina's shoulders.

"My love, even if I wanted to, I couldn't do such a thing. I can't just walk back into Santa Maria dei Miracoli, hand the jewels to a priest, and ask for penance."

Even though she longed to slide her arms back around him, Serafina kept them tightly folded across her chest and stared at the wall behind his left shoulder. Somehow she must make him understand how important this request was.

Nino dropped his hands back to his sides. "Unless, of course, you'd prefer I spend the remainder of my painfully short days in the deepest hole beneath the Doge's Palace."

"Do not jest about such a thing!"

"This is no jest." He gathered her hands and stacked them between his, then probed her face with his penetrating blue eyes. "If I set foot in Venice again, I'll be arrested."

As he spoke, love and desire, frustration and anxiety, all tumbled about inside her and made her tremble. She wanted him more than she wanted her next breath, but not under these circumstances.

"The false jewels have undoubtedly been discovered by now," Nino went on. "And it will be easy to tie them to me. You said yourself, my love, no one in Venice possesses my skill with blue glazes."

She raised their tightly clasped hands to her face and rubbed her cheek across his knuckles, fighting back the tears.

"Perhaps you can send them back," she stubbornly insisted.

"Who could I trust to take them? The one man I trusted most, Fredo, couldn't withstand the temptation to take two of them."

The catch in his voice told her that the knowledge of his friend's failing, though not as terrible as he may have at first believed, still pained him. "And anyone caught with the jewels would be arrested as a co-conspirator."

The truth of his statement caused the tears to rush

back up Serafina's throat and prick at the edges of her eyes. To make matters worse, Nino pulled her hand to his face and brushed his lips across her palm again.

"My fate is hopelessly sealed, but I knew that all along."

With a sob, she threw herself against his chest. Her need for him had driven her to act impetuously, selfishly, and the ramifications now crashed harshly upon her. Not only her family and friends had suffered, but she'd also harmed the one person she loved most.

"I know what you did was for love of me," she spoke thickly through the tears of guilt and despair. "But don't you believe I love you equally as well? I'm also willing to sacrifice—my life, if I must—for you."

She pulled away and swiped at her eyes with the padded sleeve of her doublet, determined to make him comply.

"The cost of these jewels is your immortal soul, Nino, and that price is too high. Please don't make me live with that. Please don't make me spend eternity with that."

In spite of her best efforts, she dissolved into weeping once more.

He pulled her into his arms and rested his cheek atop her newly shorn hair. "Please don't cry, Serafina. All I ever wanted was to love you, to see you happy. Beyond that, the consequences don't really matter to me."

"Well, they do to me. One lifetime will never be sufficient to expend my love for you!"

"Nor I for you," he whispered, his arms tightening possessively. Before her heart could lighten, he added, "But in this lifetime, I can't care for you, provide the things you need."

She refused to let the specter of her family's wealth continue to haunt her life, to stand between them.

"It won't always be so. You have a great talent, and someday it will be rewarded. Until then, we have each other, and that will be enough. We don't need the jewels."

"I know you believe that now, my love, but in a month or two, or a year, you'll feel differently."

"I won't." She pulled away from the protective warmth of his body and held herself at arm's length. "Tell me what to say or do to prove it. I beg you."

Nino stared at her for a long time without speaking. His bright blue eyes roved from her short hair and smudged face down the length of her over-large gray doublet to the tight brown hose clinging to her legs.

Serafina bit her bottom lip to stop it from quivering as his gaze made the slow journey back up. When his beautiful azure eyes finally returned to her face, she saw his need and love for her shining in their depths, and her own heart rejoiced in triumph.

"I suppose time will provide the only real proof," he murmured.

"We've plenty of that now, my love," she answered, stepping back into the circle of his arms. "If by this time next year we have not needed the jewels, can we then seek for a way to return them to Venice?"

His even, white teeth flashed in a brief, indulgent smile. "If that is your wish, Serafina."

She pulled his head down and claimed his mouth in answer.

Chapter 12

TEN MINUTES BEFORE THE APPOINTED RENDEZVOUS time, Keirnan stepped off the vaporetto at the Giardini stop. As prearranged, he'd been the only passenger, and no other people waited to board. Though Dario's team had been covertly clearing the area, the nasty drizzle that had started almost an hour ago had certainly helped. Nobody would willingly wander about in this miserable weather.

With his heart beating a rapid tattoo, Keirnan thrust both hands into his jacket pockets and struck out through the dead grass and skeletal trees toward the Rio dei Giardini Canal. He gripped Spinelli's cell phone with his left hand, while his right toyed with the clear plastic bag that held the fake jewels.

Dario had dispatched someone to Murano where a glassblower had produced the six identical pieces to his exact specifications in record time. His pocket sagged with their weight, and he prayed that the dark blue glass would be sufficiently convincing to secure his sister's release.

He skirted a children's play area, the seesaws and swings deserted and forlorn in an expanse of mud. He'd brought more than one girl to the Public Gardens on the numerous school holidays he'd spent here in Venice with his sister. He'd taken them walking along the path at the edge of the lagoon on balmy summer nights, or for impromptu picnics of cheese, fruit, and stolen kisses under the trees.

God willing, he wanted to bring Samantha back here someday. If she would go.

And if he could still stand the sight of the place.

He would know very soon. He glimpsed the stone bridge over the canal directly in front of him, and his grip tightened on the plastic. All he had to do was drop the bag next to the pillar at the foot, walk over the bridge, and wait.

Heart still pounding loud and fast, he paused and wiped his sleeve across his forehead to blot the moisture out of his eyes. Whether rain or sweat, he wasn't sure.

Off to his left, a tall figure in a dark trench coat glided through the trees—Carlo, signaling that he was in position. Dario had men in boats a short distance on either side of the bridge.

Keirnan chewed his lip and crossed the remaining patch of grass to the gravel path, praying harder than he ever had in his life.

The cold and quiet felt like a tomb. The world seemed to hold its collective breath with him as he stopped next to the white marble pillar. He rested his left arm on the top in what he hoped looked like a casual pose while his eyes darted fervently around the somber, sodden landscape.

No movements, no sounds.

Steady, boyo! Steady.

Slowly he drew the heavy plastic bag from his pocket, deliberately held it out at arm's length for a moment before easing it to the concrete at the pillar's base.

A white puff of steam billowed around his lips as he expelled his pent up breath and forced his feet to move. A half-dozen strides brought him to the apex of the bridge.

Halfway down the other side, the sputtering of an outboard motor from up the canal made him stumble. It was all he could do not to jerk his head in the direction of the sound.

Panting as if he'd sprinted five hundred meters, Keirnan stumbled again when his feet hit the gravel path on the other side of the bridge. Turning, he saw the boat approaching fast; dark water churned behind it. The same boat as last evening at the San Nicolo lighthouse.

In the next instant, he saw a figure on the bridge, plastic bag in hand. Where he'd come from, Keirnan wasn't sure. But the man halted at the top. The boat's engine cut back to an idle.

When it glided under, the man on top of the bridge threw one long leg over the balustrade, then the other, and landed squarely in the back of the vessel. The boat's engine roared back to life.

The man stooped and lifted a large squirming bundle, which he heaved over the side as the boat lurched forward.

Keirnan leaped toward the canal with a shout. He hesitated just long enough to rip off his jacket and shoes, then plunged headfirst into the oily gray water.

He reached his sister's bound body in less than a minute, hooked his arm around her, and shoved himself toward the surface. He knew immediately she was alive because she thrashed violently against him.

"Kathleen!" he shouted the moment his head broke through the waves.

He yanked her pillowcase-covered head up next to him, but she didn't seem to hear.

No wonder, the deathly stillness had exploded with sounds. Men shouted, engines screamed, sirens wailed. Keirnan fought to keep both their heads above water as chaos reigned, and his sister struggled in his grasp.

"*Deirfiu'r*, Sister, 'tis me!"

This time she heard because she instantly went still.

Fortunately the canal wasn't deep. A moment later, his feet touched the bottom, and he towed her speedily to the shore amid the continued noise and confusion.

Oblivious to everything around him, Keirnan heaved her onto the gravel path, his fingers clawing at the knot on the pillowcase tied around her head. Kathleen wheezed out a strangled cough. Her hands were lashed behind her back with yellow nylon rope, and more of the same was wound around her trouser-clad legs.

When the wet knot refused to budge, he jammed his fingers right through the material and ripped the pillow-case away.

Wet hair obscured his sister's features. A garish red and white scarf was tied over her mouth. He pulled it down to her chin. With his other hand, he smoothed aside the hair plastered over her eyes.

Without the gag, she coughed vigorously, then opened her mouth to speak. However, her words were drowned out by the loud cracking retort of a pistol, followed immediately by a succession of other shots.

Cringing, Keirnan pushed his sister down and shielded her with his own body. A bullet ricocheted off the stone balustrade and splashed into the water directly in front of him. Beneath him, Kathleen squirmed and gave a muffled cry.

Two more shots rang out.

He heard footsteps pounding on the gravel path behind him and jerked around to see who was coming. He recognized the brown trench coat of Carlo Bergamon in the split second before something slammed into the side of his head and threw him sprawling backward.

The force knocked away his breath and made him think of the time he'd been kicked by a horse. When he was ten, a foul-tempered stud had hit him a glancing blow through the paddock fence and cracked three of his ribs. This time the excruciating pain emanated from the left side of his skull.

Blinking hard to clear his blurry vision, Keirnan reached tentatively for his head. A burning red haze clouded the sight in his left eye, but he could make out the legs of the Interpol agent's trousers and the hem of his long coat.

Struggling to lift himself up on his right elbow, the fingers of his left hand encountered a warm sticky fluid in his hair. Keirnan pulled his hand down and stared stupefied at the bright red blood coating his fingertips and running into his palm.

Dark spots danced across his limited field of vision while Carlo barked out a command in Italian. He'd never heard the Interpol agent raise his voice before. He ordered something about waiting for help, but Keirnan couldn't really hear him because close by a woman screamed.

Confusion overwhelmed Keirnan. He swiped at his eye with the back of his hand, but he couldn't see any better. And an even more prodigious amount of blood dripped onto his wet sleeve.

He realized that the woman wailing and crying out his name must be Kathleen because Samantha didn't carry on so loudly. The dark spots whirled, blotting out the other colors and shapes.

Saints in heaven, he was cold!

And his head throbbed worse than the devil.

He felt someone's hands on him. He couldn't see who, couldn't understand what they were saying. He tried to speak but couldn't do that either. Then everything slipped away, casting him into fathomless, soundless oblivion.

Something terrible was happening to Keirnan. Blackness swirled around Sam, making it impossible for her to see, but she felt it, knew it with dread certainty. Malevolence spun in slow eddies like viscous canal water.

Through the inky darkness, something shook her. Gasping in fright, she tried to lash out against whatever had a hold on her, but her entire body felt weighed down with lead. Then dark began to fade, and a face coalesced in front of her.

"Keirnan?" she whispered, but the round worried face was not his.

"Wake up, Miss Lewis. It's Dr. Coletti."

Realization dawned slowly. She struggled to sit up, but her head felt full of cotton and her mouth parched.

"How long have I been asleep?" she croaked. Except it hadn't felt like sleep, more like unconsciousness.

"Nearly three hours." He offered a half-full water glass with a bent straw, and she sipped greedily. "The men who abducted you were treated and taken to police headquarters."

Sam coughed, spit out the straw, and pulled on the neck of her gown. The jewels were gone, only a slight blue stain remained on her skin with a lingering scent of acetone.

Dr. Coletti studied his clipboard. "Nurse Turnabuoni cleaned you up." He raised his gaze back to Sam's face, his expression unreadable. "Do you wish to talk about what happened?"

Sam fell back against the pillow with a sigh. "I told you before, nothing happened."

"That is also what one of the men told the police." Dr. Coletti searched her face for the truth. "He was most anxious to talk, to implicate his two friends in exchange for leniency."

She was pretty sure that would be Manny, which meant he was all right. Angelo and Jacopo must be too, since they'd been released into police custody.

But what about Keirnan?

Apprehension clawed at her, and she chewed her bottom lip. "Do you—" Her voice came out thin and strangled. "Do you know what happened to the man I…"

Love.

Betrayed.

May have destroyed.

"…I was with?"

When the doctor shook his head, tears welled up inside her again.

Get a grip, Sam!

She forced her voice to come out stronger. "Are any of the police still here?"

"They left when they took the three men away. However, Officer Ligure left a number if you wish to press charges."

"No."

Dr. Coletti gave her another of those probing looks that made her hesitate a long moment before asking, "Was there someone here from Interpol?"

Her question left the doctor predictably nonplussed. Tears still hovered dangerously close, and the ache in her chest spread rapidly into her skull. Groaning, Sam rubbed her fingertips against her temple.

"I don't know what to do."

Dr. Coletti cast a furtive glance toward the door, making Sam realize that she was no longer in the crowded, noisy emergency area but a private room.

"Miss Lewis, may I speak to you frankly?"

Taken aback by his low, guarded tone, Sam nodded, then forced herself to sit up.

"Have you been in Italy before?" he asked, and when she shook her head, he murmured almost inaudibly, "I thought not." He looked at the closed door again before he spoke. "Please believe me. You do not want to become embroiled in the Italian justice system."

His unexpected tone of bitterness startled her. "You sound like you speak from experience."

"I do." The doctor's boyish face took on a harsh set. "It took me over six years to exonerate myself. I have only been allowed to practice medicine again in the past year."

The hard expression in his eyes kept any questions Sam might have asked at bay.

With an edge of rancor still in his voice, he went on, "I know this is not my business, but the man you just asked about? If you truly care for him, the best thing you can do is go home and hire him the best attorney you can find. At the very least, go to Rome where there are many more English-speaking attorneys."

Rome.

Reality washed over her in a frigid blast, making her shiver. Everyone seemed determined that she should go to Rome—the tour company, Keirnan, and now Dr. Coletti.

Her flight home was scheduled to depart from Rome tomorrow afternoon. She would have to leave Venice tonight in order to catch it. That left only a few hours to find Keirnan.

"Am I free to go?" she asked tentatively.

"Of course, the hospital has no authority to hold you if you wish to leave, and medically there is no reason for you to stay." The doctor pulled back the blanket to reveal a thick elastic bandage wound around her left knee. "There was bad bruising, but no permanent damage. You may want to check with your own doctor in a few days."

Her own doctor.

A few days.

Sam's mind balked at both concepts. Still, she needed to think about them, about what she would do tomorrow, or tonight, if she couldn't locate Keirnan. Or if Kathleen were dead...

"I'd really like to leave now. Do you know where my clothes are?"

When Dr. Coletti motioned at a small bureau under the window, she remembered how little she'd actually been wearing. She bit her bottom lip, then asked, "Do you think you can find me some shoes?"

"I will see what I can do." He turned to go, then said over his shoulder, "And I will go with you to complete the discharge paperwork."

His kindness made the tears threaten to overwhelm her yet again, but she choked out, "Thank you, for everything."

Once the doctor left, Sam threw her legs over the side of the bed and winced with pain the moment her left foot touched the floor. Since she couldn't put much weight on her left leg, she had to sit on the bed to get dressed. With her leg almost immobile, the process proved to be tediously slow. Her jeans barely went on over the bulky bandage. Not only that, she seemed to have bruises and aching muscles virtually everywhere.

Stomach clenching in disgust, she threw Jacopo's stinky scarf into the trash. The neckline of Keirnan's sweater carried a trace of his scent, which she inhaled deeply before she pulled it on. Then she saw the blood stain still on the cuff, and the horrible rush of doom doubled her over with its force.

Gasping, Sam struggled to overcome the relentless grip of terror. He had to be all right.

He *had* to be.

A moment later, the phone on top of the bureau rang.

She snatched up the receiver, practically shouting, "Hello? Hello? I mean, *pronto*?"

Please be Keirnan! Please!

A nasally voice rattled off something in Italian ending with "'E Samantha Lewis?"

"Yes! I mean *si, sono* Samantha Lewis."

Then a familiar voice broke through. "Sam? Is that you, Sam?"

He sounded like he was at the bottom of a well.

"Michael?"

She nearly dropped the phone. Luckily the bed was behind her because she sat down hard.

"Yes. Are you all right?"

"Michael?" She asked again, sputtering. "How? Why?"

Her stunned mind simply could not accept that the last person in the world she expected to talk to was on the other end of the line, a continent-and-a-half, an ocean, and a lifetime away.

"I've been trying for almost two hours to find you." His voice still sounded hollow and far away, though decidedly upset. "Someone from the hospital called me. I guess I'm still listed on your passport to contact in an emergency."

Belatedly she remembered filling out the page when they'd received their passports back in December. Dr. Coletti had asked what hotel she was staying at, because they all kept foreign guests' passports at the front desk. Someone must have read the emergency information and contacted Michael.

"Sorry, I forgot to change that," she murmured, but he didn't seem to hear her.

"Are you all right?" he demanded. "They told me you were hurt, that you…" He broke off with a strangled sound.

Surely he couldn't still care, not after all that had happened. Two weeks ago, the thought would have left her elated. A week ago she would have felt smugly vindicated. Now all she felt was empty.

"I'm okay, Michael. Sorry for the mix-up."

"Dammit, Sam, it's two in the morning! How could you do this to me?"

"Me?" His self-centeredness stunned her. "I didn't do—"

"They told me you'd been raped!" he interrupted, the outrage in his tone unmistakable, accusing. "Then the tour company told me you'd stayed in Venice *with your husband*. What the hell is going on?"

Annoyance quickly overrode her surprise. "Nothing that concerns you," she snapped. "And I wasn't raped."

Dead air followed for a half-dozen heartbeats. Just when Sam suspected the connection had been broken, a strange sound somewhere between a snarl and a snort came from Michael's end.

"I get it. This is your idea of pay back, isn't it? Go to Italy, have a fling, and make damn sure I know about it."

"*Me* have a fling?" Indignation sharpened her tone.

Of all the hypocritical pronouncements. And to think she'd been ready to marry this jerk! So much for her long-term commitment criteria.

"I doubt you'll believe this Michael, but not everything is about you. I'm sorry the hospital called and disturbed you, but I am fine and there is absolutely nothing you can do for me."

She slammed the receiver back into the cradle without letting him say another word. She had utterly and completely had enough of Michael Atcheson!

Turning, she saw Dr. Coletti standing just inside the door staring intently at his clipboard.

"These are all I could find."

Not looking at her face, he held out a pair of plastic-soled clogs with fake leopard fur uppers. Sam took the proffered footwear, which appeared about two sizes larger than she usually wore. She could readily understand why nobody had claimed them. However, they were an improvement over her dirty, bedraggled socks.

"Thanks," she murmured and shoved her feet into them.

With Dr. Coletti's assistance, she answered questions and signed forms for the better part of an hour, though her mind was not truly engaged in the task. Lingering ire at Michael and continued anxiety about Keirnan kept her insides in turmoil and her mind scarcely coherent. Finally, the discharge clerk handed her a large envelope with all her copies of the myriad forms and bid her *arrivederci*. Good-bye.

Dr. Coletti walked with her to the hospital's main doors and pressed some coins in her hand for the vaporetto. Overcome once more by his kindness, all Sam could manage to say was thank you.

Her residual anger quickly dissipated in the drizzly rain. However, the heavy feeling of dread over Keirnan's whereabouts and safety intensified as the almost empty boat plowed through the murky, gray water toward the Rialto Bridge. She got off at the stop right before Saint Mark's and prayed he would be there as she limped in her awkward, oversized shoes to the hotel.

Unfortunately, when she opened the door to the room, everything was just as she'd left it some eight hours ago. The laptop. The half-eaten plate of pasta. The two disheveled beds.

Hands trembling, Sam picked up the room's phone. It took her two tries to get Carlo Bergamon's number dialed correctly, then the same annoying voice mail message in Italian, German, and English rattled off in her ear. In a tone growing increasingly thick with tears, Sam left her name, number, and said it was urgent she speak with someone about Keirnan Fitzgerald.

After a few moments of terrible, body-wracking sobs, she pulled herself together enough to unwind the elastic bandage on her knee and get into the shower. She turned the water as hot as she could stand it, then scrubbed at the traces of blue paint on her chest. The memory of the wet brush bristles stroking against her flesh and Angelo's leering face hovering inches away made her scrub until her skin was raw and chafed.

Thinking and feeling hurt too damn much. She let the hot water pound her until her aching knee wouldn't allow her to remain upright any longer.

She'd rewrapped the bandage around her knee and pulled on a pair of black wool slacks when the phone rang. She scrambled, sending up a fervent prayer that it was Keirnan.

"Ms. Lewis," said an unfamiliar, accented voice. "This is Lorenzo Righetti, an associate of Mr. Bergamon."

Interpol.

Oh God, let it be good news!

But it was no news at all.

While Sam wrestled to maintain a modicum of control over her rioting emotions, the man on the phone calmly explained that Carlo Bergamon was unavailable because he was in the field. The agent was sympathetic but firm in his insistence that there was no information he could give her at this time about anyone.

"Then Mr. Fitzgerald isn't being held or detained or whatever you call it?" Sam asked for the third time.

The man gave the same answer. "Not to my knowledge." Then he added in the same flat, detached tone. "I will leave Mr. Bergamon the message to call you at this number when he becomes available."

He'd already told her he had no idea of when that might be.

"Thank you," Sam sighed heavily and hung up the phone.

She absolutely could *not* stay in the room and wait, so she finished dressing and went downstairs to the hotel restaurant. Too numb to taste anything, she nonetheless forced down most of a bowl of minestrone soup and a thick slice of crusty bread. Even though she now had no coat, she'd layered on two heavy sweaters, so she went out without going back upstairs for her umbrella. Besides, the drizzle had almost stopped.

Hobbling along over the uneven pavement was painful, but the pain kept her mind occupied. Eventually, she found herself in front of Santa Maria dei Miracoli. Tired and hurting, she limped into the church.

The stained glass windows were muted from lack of sunlight, but scores of lighted candles made the interior glow with cheering warmth. No one else was inside. From her place in the chancel, the white marble Madonna greeted Sam with her outstretched hands and tranquil smile. The stone ribbon of her sash was conspicuous in its plainness.

A wave of bitter regret and longing broke inside Sam, and at that moment, she fervently wished she'd never heard of the Jewels of the Madonna. So many had gone through suffering, anguish, and betrayal, and for what?

Again, she saw in her mind's eye large, dark blue

stones with a cold fire shimmering in their smooth depths. If the Madonna could talk, as Keirnan had wished, she would undoubtedly scold everyone. The jewels were unimportant trifles after all.

The image in Sam's mind shifted. The fire in the stones changed, became warm, probing. The jewels transformed into eyes, a man's eyes, though whether Keirnan's or someone else's she couldn't be sure.

Or perhaps there were two pairs of eyes, one super-imposed over the other. And both could see into the very heart of her. A shiver raced down her spine.

Feeling anything but peaceful, Sam turned away from the chancel and made her way down the empty aisle to the front of the church. She settled into the front pew, extended her injured leg out on the wooden bench, and rested her back into the corner. Even sitting at an angle, she could clearly see the portrait of the Madonna and child hanging over the altar. The painting purported to perform miracles. A miracle would be very welcome about now.

Sam closed her eyes and began to pray. Not for herself. She prayed for Kathleen's safety, a woman she'd never even met. And she prayed for Keirnan, a man who stirred feelings within her that she'd never experienced before.

In the midst of her prayers, Michael's accusation slashed across her subconscious.

A fling.

What she felt couldn't possibly be a fling, though to someone else it certainly might appear that way. The unbidden thought stopped her prayers, and reality reared its ugly head.

She and Keirnan had never spoken about anything

beyond the immediate situation. Maybe because there was nothing to say.

Why would a man as handsome and charming as Keirnan Fitzgerald want her when he could have his pick of almost any woman?

Furthermore, what did she expect to happen once they left Italy? Especially if his sister was dead and Keirnan himself was in trouble with the authorities.

The past few days had been a crazy, adrenaline-surging thrill ride. Only now the ride had crashed to its inevitable, horrific end. Doubt, dread, pain, and fear smashed and slammed their way through Sam's tortured mind as she recalled for the hundredth time the look on Keirnan's face and the hulking figures of the police.

What was she supposed to do now?

The beautiful church held no answers, offered no comfort. Averting her gaze from the marble figure of the Madonna, she dragged herself back down the aisle, back to the empty hotel room and the too silent telephone.

Venice, 1486

The long shadows of the cypresses obscured the path and made Nino slow his pace. The warmth and humidity of the late summer day faded with the slanting rays of the sun, a welcome change. He'd been forced to wear his long, concealing, and decidedly stifling cloak, just in case.

The church of San Michele En Isola loomed in front of him like a great hulking beast, but not a dangerous one. A pair of robed figures labored in the nearby herb garden and did not raise their heads at his swift passing.

He slipped through the side door of the church. The wood and metal tools in his knapsack clanked together, the noise echoing hollowly. A cloaked and hooded figure glided to the entrance of the nearby chapel of St. Anne.

"Is it done?" queried the object of all his waking and sleeping desires.

She was dressed once more in her traveling clothes, an oversized doublet and plain brown hose. Her golden brown hair, which now brushed the tops of her shoulders, lay concealed beneath the hood of her cloak. Usually she wore it pulled into a black net fastened at the back of her head to disguise its unusual length. A sheen of perspiration glowed across her cheeks.

On the road these past days, the sun had left a tawny rose color on her face that, impossible as it seemed, made her more beautiful. Even more impossible was the fact that she was his.

Every morning when he awoke, and every night when he gazed at her lying beside him, Nino still had a hard time believing his good fortune. In the year and a half since they'd fled Venice, Serafina had exceeded his every expectation.

She had worked tirelessly to help him. Sometimes her clumsy efforts had resulted in tears of frustration, or, more often, dissolved them both into easy laughter. However, she had always tried again, refusing to give up. She'd also proven to have a keen business sense, earning him several lucrative commissions he would not otherwise have secured.

"One more thing to do."

He raised her palms to his lips. Her hands were no

longer soft and pristine as they had once been. Now they were the hands of a strong, capable woman.

His love for her knew no bounds.

"Have you the letter for your brother?"

Serafina pulled her hands away and reached inside her doublet to extract a folded and sealed square of parchment. She had printed her brother's name, Antonio Lombardo, in neat block letters on one side. She gave it to him then urged him a few steps forward.

"Look, your medallions are still here."

Three trumpeting angels on fields of shimmering blue danced in the chapel's flickering candlelight. The space, which had once held the fourth, was glaringly empty. Nino wouldn't let himself remember what had happened to the missing angel, of the two jewels he'd hidden inside it. Instead he thought about the day he'd first put the medallions in place. The day a beautiful vision stepped in and changed his world forever.

"It seems like another lifetime ago that I sculpted those pieces."

"That's because it was." Serafina raised his hand to her face and rubbed his knuckles against her cheek. "A life I've never regretted leaving."

She glanced quickly around the silent church then pulled his head down to her mouth and kissed him long and deep. As always, Nino was hard pressed to deny her every desire, but he broke the kiss after a dozen thundering heartbeats.

"We've time enough for this later, my lady wife," he teased.

Her dark eyes smoldered with a promise that made his footsteps light as they hurried out of the church and through the purple shadows of the vacant herb garden toward the rectory. Serafina purposely hung back in the twilight gloom while he rapped on the wooden door. One of the brown-robed friars answered.

"Please father, might someone be going into Venice who could carry a letter for me?"

The small man squinted up at Nino in the growing darkness. "Not before the morrow, my son."

"'Tis soon enough." Nino pressed the parchment and two silver coins into the friar's hand. "If you could see that this reaches Santa Maria dei Miracoli, they will know the man it is addressed to. 'Tis my final act of penance for a most grievous sin."

The man looked a bit taken aback, but he slipped the letter and the coins into the sleeve of his robe then raised his right hand in a blessing.

"It shall be delivered thus, my son. Go in peace."

In three long strides, Nino stood beside Serafina once more. Her lovely features were half-hidden by the folds of her hood, but his eyes sought and found hers.

"Now 'tis done, my love."

She gave his hand a gentle squeeze. "Then, my beloved husband, let us hurry home to Padua."

Chapter 13

A SLEDGEHAMMER WAS POUNDING INSIDE HIS SKULL. What else could account for the intense throbbing ache?

Dazed with the pain, Keirnan raised his left hand toward his head, only to have it snag halfway. He fought to focus his bleary vision. Clear plastic tubing taped to the back of his hand had stopped him from lifting it.

An I.V.

He must be in hospital. He dropped his hand back with a groan and struggled to remember what had happened before he got here. He seemed to recall gunshots and a lot of blood, but not much else. Reaching across with his right hand, Keirnan felt the soft cotton of a gauze pad near his left temple.

"*Sionnach*, you're awake," a familiar female voice exclaimed. "Saints be praised!"

But when he turned his head in her direction, his stomach gave a terrible lurch that threatened to disgorge everything from his toes upward. He had to squeeze his eyes closed against the pain and nausea. A dozen uneven heartbeats later, he eased one eye open and saw his sister's worried face hovering over him.

"Kathleen." He scarcely recognized the croaking whisper as his own. "Are you all right?"

"A mite better than you, 'twould seem. At least I wasn't shot." Her sassy tone did not reach the concern clouding her gaze.

"Your hand…"

"'Tis fine." She held up the heavily swathed appendage for his inspection. "Me pinky is only a stub, but the others still work."

Keirnan closed his eyes again and sighed raggedly. "Thank all the stars in heaven."

"And thank them even more that the bullet hit nothing vital on you, brother of mine. Only your wee thick skull, which we all know nothing penetrates."

In spite of the pain, Keirnan managed a smile. "Runs in the family, *Deirfiu'r*."

Her bright red curls were the only splash of color in the otherwise bland room. Kathleen cupped her good hand around his cheek. "I never claimed different, now did I?" Even with his blurry vision, her expression looked anxious. "Shall I call the nurse to give you something for the pain?"

"No." He knew pills would scramble his brain even worse and likely send him right back to dreamland. His gaze roamed the room for a clock or a window, some way to reckon the time. "How long have I been out?"

"I'm not exactly sure, but quite awhile. I've been here watching you sleep for over two hours."

His muddled brain still couldn't piece together the sequence of events, so he went back to the last thing he clearly remembered. *Samantha*. His heart knocked against the wall of his chest as he remembered the way she'd put herself in danger for him.

"Was anyone else here?"

Kathleen's hand moved to cover his, and she gave him a motherly pat. "Ah, well, our favorite Interpol agent, Carlo Bergamon, hung about until they finished stitching you back together. He and the local *polizia* both took my statement before they went off to interrogate the suspects." His sister's blue eyes narrowed knowingly. "But I'm thinking he's not who you're really asking about."

Keirnan attempted to shake his head, only to be hit by another spinning wave of nausea.

"No," he wheezed. Then, when the worst of the dizziness subsided, he added. "Have you seen a woman? American with dark blonde hair? Her name's Samantha Lewis."

For the first time, his sister's eyes twinkled. "Oh, you mean the one you've been calling for in your sleep?"

Bloody hell! Would he have to tape his mouth shut every time he dozed off?

Kathleen wore the satisfied, cat-in-the-cream gloat she'd perfected long ago in childhood. "Carlo mentioned seeing the two of you together. He said she was young and quite pretty."

"She's…" Words temporarily failed him, which proved he was indeed in a bad way. "I…"

How was he supposed to explain to anyone something he didn't understand himself? Their sudden and intense connection. Her beauty and brains. Her willingness to help him, even at risk to herself.

Stick to the facts, boyo.

"If not for her, I doubt either of us would be here."

"I see." His sister's expression changed rapidly to seriousness. Her hand tightened around his. "But 'tis more than that, I'm thinking."

"Much more," he admitted to himself as well as Kathleen.

A wave of pain splintered his vision and forced him to squeeze his eyes shut for a long moment. He finally slit one open and focused on Kathleen's pinched frown. "She was brought to this hospital earlier today."

Kathleen's palm rested lightly against his cheek again. "I'll see what I can find out." Her movements were a blur as her footsteps tapped across the tile floor.

Keirnan sighed and closed both eyes again. The knowledge that he'd hurt Samantha made more than his head ache. The idea of going back to his life without her in it was far more painful than his head wound. He had to do something.

But the headache wouldn't allow him to think clearly, so he centered his concentration on it and tried willing it to stop. Just when he seemed to be having some success at lessening the pain, the sound of footsteps interrupted him. His eyes flew open.

A stout nurse in a green scrub suit strode up to his bed and jabbed a thermometer under his tongue. He waited patiently while she fiddled with the bottle of fluid connected to his I.V. line. Then when she removed the thermometer, Keirnan asked politely in Italian if she'd take out the I.V. so he could get up.

She scolded him soundly and told him in no uncertain terms that he was not to attempt to get out of bed.

Piqued by her rebuke, he muttered a not-so-nice phrase in Italian and punched the button that raised his bed into a more upright position. Before it even stopped moving, he threw aside the blankets and started to swing his legs over the side.

He immediately regretted his rash movements. The room tilted at a crazy angle while the contents of his stomach launched into his throat. With a sardonic lift of her dark eyebrows, the nurse shoved a plastic tray under his chin, then expertly tipped his bare legs back under the covers.

Once he finally stopped retching, she took the tray and marched into the adjoining bathroom without a word. Groaning, Keirnan eased his bed back to a slightly more supine position as his sister reentered the room.

The nurse waylaid Kathleen within two steps. After a brief exchange, in which his sister tacitly agreed with the nurse's assessment of Keirnan's numerous character defects, the harpy in green stalked out.

"Amazing," Kathleen murmured, amusement dancing at the corners of her mouth. "A woman who's immune to your charm."

"Spare me." He tried to glare at her when she moved nearer, but the relentless pain wouldn't allow him to make any extra efforts. Just talking taxed his current capabilities. "Where's Samantha?"

His sister's quicksilver expression shifted. "'Tis sorry I am, darlin', but your pretty American checked herself out hours ago. I tried calling your hotel but got no answer, and no one at the front desk remembers seeing her."

Despair momentarily swamped even his pain, rendering him hopelessly mute. Not that his perceptive sister needed him to tell her anything.

"So that's how 'tis, then?" she murmured, but Keirnan scarcely heard. A heavy lump of dread had settled on his chest, nearly suffocating him.

Rome.

Her flight left tomorrow.

She was going to Rome.

Saints! He'd told her more than once to go. What ill luck for her to actually comply!

"I can't…" He fought to get the words out around the wad of tears suddenly clogging his throat. "…lose her now. Not after all this."

"No, you most certainly cannot, and you shall not."

He knew that tone in Kathleen's voice very well, and a tiny spark of hope flickered inside the dread.

"I'll find her. Just tell me again what she looks like. Since she's American I expect she'll be wearing blue jeans."

"Yes, I expect so. And sneakers, that is, trainers, white with pink trim."

The oppressive weight lightened considerably. His sister was nothing if not determined. Keirnan closed his eyes and visualized. Samantha's image seemed to quell the pain a little.

"She's a hand shorter than me. Slim. Straight hair just past her shoulders, that lovely golden color…"

"Like Serafina Lombardo's?"

His eyes snapped open at his sister's anything-but-innocent query. "Don't start, Kathleen."

"I was only asking as a point of reference."

And Venice isn't crumbling into the sea.

Her answering look spoke just as loudly as his: *This discussion is far from over, boyo.*

Incredible how everything fell so easily back into place, almost as if the past week had never happened.

Almost.

"Fine." Her chin jutting at a familiar angle, Kathleen brushed a bright red curl off her forehead. "I will find her, *Sionnach*. But whilst I'm about it, you must take your pain meds and stop antagonizing your nurse."

"Fine."

That bullet must have done more than graze his scalp. Why else would the bossy attitude she'd used on him for twenty odd years suddenly make him thick with emotion? She turned toward the door while he fought to regain some semblance of control.

"Kathleen, one more thing…" *No, he wouldn't start either.* "Try the *stazione* first."

"*Un biglietto per Roma.* One ticket for Rome."

Sam slid her credit card under the glass partition. She hadn't been able to figure out how to operate the automatic ticket machine.

The ticket agent didn't even look up. "*Ritorno?* Round trip?"

"No." She signed the charge slip and clutched her card with trembling fingers.

"*Binario sei, venticinque minutos.* Gate six, twenty-five minutes."

"*Grazie.*" Sam shoved the ticket into her jeans' pocket and pulled her suitcase to the nearest vacant bench so that she could put her credit card and receipt back into her neck pouch.

That accomplished, she propped her elbows on her legs and wearily rested her head in her hands. In twenty-five minutes she'd leave Venice, probably forever. She'd run out of time and options.

After three separate frustrating calls to the Venetian police, she would be lucky if they allowed her back in Italy again. Not that any of those calls had accomplished much, even with her phrase book in hand. Just the opposite, in fact. No one could tell her a thing. It almost seemed as if Keirnan Fitzgerald and his sister never existed, as much a dream as the phantom Renaissance lover who haunted her sleep.

Plus, between those calls, she'd contacted her tour group headquarters. They told her the only way to change her return home at this late date was to show up at the airport in Rome. She'd been forced to accept the reality of the situation. A one-way ticket from anywhere in Italy to anywhere near Bloomington would cost more than her entire vacation.

She really couldn't afford that extra expense, especially since she had made up her mind to quit her job and move elsewhere. She had toyed with the idea before she left for Italy, but now her decision was cemented. Even if the fates seemed determined to keep her and Keirnan apart, she simply could not stay at the university and face Michael and their friends. Not after all that had happened... might still happen.

She'd taken Dr. Coletti's advice to heart. Using Spinelli's laptop, she'd researched attorneys and had a list of three to contact in Rome. She'd also emailed the U.S. Embassy and asked for an appointment ASAP. Not much of a plan, but it was a start.

"Samantha Lewis?"

Sam jerked her head up at the sound of her name. "Yes—I mean *si*?"

A petite red-haired woman met her startled gaze, then quickly covered the short space between them, extending her right hand.

"I'm Kathleen Fitzgerald DiLucca, and I believe I

owe you my life." Her accent was more pronounced than Keirnan's with none of the flat American vowel sounds.

Agog, Sam stared open-mouthed as Keirnan's sister grabbed her hand and pumped vigorously. A flaming mass of red curls framed her translucent, milk-white face, but her eyes were the same startling blue as her younger sibling's.

"You don't… I didn't…" Sam spluttered, breaking contact with those too-familiar eyes. Then her own gaze snagged on the white gauze encasing Kathleen's left hand.

"He threw her severed finger into my lap."

Sam choked, remembering Keirnan's anguished words. Coughing, she tore her eyes away from the bandage and looked into the cerulean depths of Kathleen eyes for a heartbeat before she burst into tears of relief. Keirnan's sister slid down onto the bench next to her and pulled her into a motherly embrace.

"There, there luv," she crooned, patting Sam on the back.

"You're n-not d-dead?" Sam asked, wrapping her arms around the smaller woman as if she were a wisp of smoke that might disintegrate in the next instant. Sniffling loudly, she struggled to get a grip on her whirling thoughts and emotions.

Kathleen was here. She was all right. Could the waking nightmare be over?

"No indeed, I'm very much alive." Kathleen's thick brogue sounded a bit teary also. Pulling back, she produced a wad of tissues from her pocket and peeled one off for herself and another for Sam. "Thanks to you and my brother."

"Your brother—" Sam gasped out, then lapsed into another coughing fit before she could voice the thousand questions crowding her mind

Kathleen gave her several maternal thumps on the back. "Ah yes, 'twas himself sent me to find you."

Through the confusing miasma of cigarette smoke and disbelief, a voice came on the overhead speaker and announced which trains were now boarding. People around them began shuffling out of the waiting room.

"And not a minute too soon, 'twould seem. Surely you don't mean to be leaving now?"

Leaving. The word struck a chord in Sam's chaotic brain. Still in a daze, she stood and shifted the strap of her carry-on across her shoulder. "Sorry, but I have to. I have to be at the Rome airport tomorrow morning."

Kathleen rose and grabbed Sam's arm, clucking her tongue in dismissal. "Take a later train then. Keirnan will buy you a ticket." She waved her undamaged hand and added, "Trust me, he can well afford it. And 'tis the least he can do for the woman he loves."

"He—" Sam nearly choked again. Perhaps this mind-boggling passion wasn't one-sided as she had feared. "He said that?"

Bright blue eyes narrowed knowingly, Keirnan's sister resembled a satisfied feline. "He didn't need to, 'twas plain enough. Besides, I know the wee toad better than he knows himself."

"Then where—" A fresh burst of anxiety and confusion stopped Sam's question in midstream.

"Ah well, he's in hospital." In spite of her heart-stopping pronouncement, Kathleen's expression didn't change. "Not to worry, the bullet bounced right off his thick skull without damaging a thing."

"Oh my God! He's been shot?"

Her trembling legs ceased supporting her, and Sam

slid backward onto the wooden bench, heedless of the attention her outburst was attracting. Black spots danced at the edge of her vision.

"There now, luv," Kathleen soothed again. She picked up a section of discarded newspaper and fanned the air in front of Sam's face. "He'll be fine. 'Twas only a scalp wound."

Sam forced her spinning brain to concentrate on taking deep yoga breaths.

Keirnan would be fine.

His sister was fine.

Everything was fine.

She was only vaguely aware of Kathleen shooing away the onlookers with some tart phrases in Italian. Then in the background the overhead speaker announced the departure of the train to Rome on platform six.

"That's my train," she murmured, grasping at the only thing that was making any sense.

"Please, Miss Lewis." Kathleen dropped the newspaper and placed her hand on Sam's arm. "Don't leave without telling my brother good-bye. He deserves that much, surely."

He deserved that and so much more. Certainly more than ordinary Sam Lewis.

Now that he no longer needed her help, had he realized as much?

About time that she did, but heaven knew how badly she wanted to see him again.

"I… He…" Her suddenly parched lips refused to form words. Her whirling mind was no help at all. Her eyes darted across the waiting room to the crowded archways that led to the trains.

Breathe, damn it!

Then she sighed, and in a voice that seemed to come from someone else entirely, she said, "All right."

"Thank you." Kathleen's sapphire eyes sparkled with a mixture of triumph and something else. "Everything will work out, you'll see. 'All's Well That Ends Well,' even a bloody Englishman knows that."

Sam felt as though she had resurfaced from deep water. Keirnan's sister. The bustling train station. None of what was happening seemed real. "Did you just call Shakespeare a bloody Englishman?"

"Well, wasn't he then?" Kathleen grabbed the handle of Sam's suitcase with her good hand. "Shall we take your bags back to the hotel or go to the hospital straightaway?"

Still only half-coherent and not nearly so optimistic as her companion, Sam rose shakily to her feet. "The hospital."

"I expected as much."

Once more wearing her catlike smile, Kathleen tugged the heavy suitcase toward the exit. Feeling like she'd fallen down a rabbit hole, Sam followed. However, it took both of them, Kathleen with her bad hand and Sam with her gimpy leg, a dozen minutes or more to wrestle the unwieldy luggage down the steps to the Grand Canal.

Once they reached the bottom, Sam turned toward the vaporetti stand, but Kathleen stopped her.

"The vaporetto's too slow. Let's take a water taxi."

A dark specter of fear rose up in Sam's mind. "I thought you said Keirnan was fine."

Kathleen brushed an errant curl out of her bright eyes. "Unless he's come to blows with his nurse he will be, once he sees you haven't left him."

"Are you sure?" The specter split into the twin demons of doubt and uncertainty that had dogged Sam's subconscious since Michael had dropped his bombshell four weeks and a lifetime ago. "I mean, a man like your brother can have any woman he wants."

For such a small woman, Kathleen possessed an authoritative air any librarian would covet. Placing her unbandaged hand against her hip, she studied Sam in a long, top-to-toe appraisal before she spoke. "'Tis true. Women have thrown themselves at Keirnan since the day his voice changed. But 'tis an altogether different matter with the two of you."

Sam shifted uncomfortably under the scrutiny of her gaze. "I, uh, don't know what you mean."

Kathleen lifted one brow in that annoying Italian gesture she'd obviously acquired over years of living in Venice. "Yes, luv, I think you do. 'Twas clear to me the moment I laid eyes on you. You and my brother are meant to be together, just as you were in 1485."

Gasping, Sam clutched the handle of her suitcase with trembling fingers, unable to suppress a shudder. She could feel the hiss of Angelo's breath close to her ear… *Serafina*. Could Kathleen be as crazy as he was?

"You've heard this before." Kathleen cocked her head to one side in another familiar gesture. She didn't look insane. "Surely not from my brother…"

"No, your ex-husband."

A wave of sadness clouded Kathleen's beautiful eyes, and she sighed heavily. "Carlo Bergamon told me Angelo was involved in this mess."

Her sassy voice turned wistful. "For a time I believed Angelo and I were Nino and Serafina, but he never did. He insisted he was and always would be a painter."

A small, rueful smile twitched the corners of her mouth. "And he was truly gifted. Angelo's skill and talent matched Venice's best, Titian, Tintoretto, the Bellinis. Only he crossed over that line between genius and madness one too many times."

Sam bit her bottom lip while she pictured the liquid brown depths of Angelo DiLucca's haunting eyes. Then they abruptly changed to the beady gleam of Roberto Spinelli. Kathleen's choices in men were worse than Sam's mother's. Should she really be listening to her advice?

Too late for second thoughts now. Perhaps she was the crazy one.

A water taxi sputtered to a halt nearby, and the driver called out to them in Italian, snapping both Sam and her companion back to the present. Stepping forward, Kathleen answered back. After a brief exchange, the man helped them maneuver Sam's suitcase into the boat.

Hampered by her bandaged knee, Sam slid onto the seat next to Kathleen just as the driver gunned the engine. Then, in the midst of a cloud of smelly exhaust fumes, the taxi shot into the choppy water of the Grand Canal.

The noise of the boat's engine made talking impossible, leaving Sam to gloomily contemplate her imprudent behavior. She and Keirnan had shared something wonderful but transient. A fling that was now over. Their attraction may have been heightened by urgent circumstances, but not past lives. That just wasn't possible.

The chilly wind whipped into the partially open cabin when the driver gunned the motor and wheeled the vessel into the open waters of the lagoon. The taxi circled the familiar docks at the foot of St. Mark's Square. Sam's thoughts splintered, and she gripped the edge of the seat as the boat bucked and bounced over the wakes of the other numerous vessels crowding the popular area. All cab drivers, whether on land or water, seemed to be the same.

Several heart-pounding minutes later, the long, low shape of the hospital materialized in the fading twilight. Sam couldn't contain an audible sigh of relief when the taxi slid to an idling halt at the landing. She pulled her luggage onto terra firma, as Kathleen produced several bills from her pocket and passed them to the driver, who was off with a roar the moment his passengers disembarked.

Kathleen led the way inside and to the elevators along the side wall. Sam trailed hesitantly behind. The medicinal smell of alcohol and disinfectant made her stomach queasy, while a riot of conflicting emotions threatened to snap every nerve in her body.

What was she doing here?

What was he going to say?

Had she totally lost her mind?

"Don't worry, luv." Kathleen broke the deafening quiet inside the elevator. "I'll hire a private car to take you to Rome tonight if you still want to go."

Perhaps that decision wouldn't be up to her.

Before Sam could force a reply from her constricted throat, the elevator doors opened. She and Kathleen stepped out as several hospital staff members got on.

She followed Kathleen down the tiled corridor. The antiseptic aroma was stronger, and the incessant babble of Italian more subdued. Her luggage elicited more than a few stares. Near the end of the hallway, Kathleen halted at last.

This was it! Sam took a deep, cleansing breath and prepared for the end of all her angst. Though the door in front of them was closed, the sound of raised voices could be plainly heard arguing in Italian.

"He never listens to me!" Kathleen muttered, then gave a long-suffering sigh. "I shouldn't be surprised to find him sporting more than fourteen stitches from the sound of that row." She shoved open the door and strode into the room like a conquering general. "Is this any way to act, *Dearthai'r?* Brother? And after I went to such great pains to keep my promise to you."

She motioned Sam into the room.

The head of Keirnan's bed was raised just enough for her to see his face. Except for the dark stubble of his beard, he was almost as pale as the stark white pillow under his head. A plump nurse in a green scrub suit stood motionless beside a metal I.V. pole, a plastic bag of clear fluid in her hand. Both Keirnan and the nurse stared at Kathleen, momentarily speechless.

Numb with anticipation and worry, Sam edged her way into the room. The wheels of her suitcase made a small thump as they rolled over the threshold of the door, breaking the spell of silence.

"Samantha, luv?" Keirnan's sapphire eyes settled on her at last. His strained and scratchy tone was the sweetest sound she'd ever heard. "Thank all the stars in heaven! I was certain you'd gone to Rome."

"She very nearly did." Kathleen informed him, but Keirnan wasn't listening, or at least his gaze didn't shift away.

"Please…" He started to raise his hand, but the I.V. tube stopped him. His eyes did move then. He cast a baleful look at the nurse, who was taking advantage of the momentary distraction to switch pouches of fluid on the I.V. pole.

"Are you okay?" Sam couldn't hear her own voice over the roar of the blood pounding in her ears.

His eyes leaped back to hers, and a sudden urge to run across the room to him nearly overpowered her. She had dropped the handle of her suitcase and taken a half-dozen steps before she realized what she was doing and stopped.

Get a grip, Sam!

"Your sister said you were shot." Just saying the word nearly stopped her heart.

Keirnan raised tentative fingers to the white gauze on the left side of his head. "It's not as bad as it looks."

Fourteen stitches qualified as not bad?

"Don't tell me, just a scratch, right?"

"Exactly."

"I told you the bullet bounced off." Kathleen piped up. She'd scooted slightly behind Sam and proceeded to give her a not-so-subtle nudge in Keirnan's direction. Then she addressed the nurse, motioning broadly toward the door. "Signora, *per piacere.*"

The woman looked from Sam to Keirnan, then giving the pouch of I.V. fluid a triumphant pat, she strode out the door. Kathleen gave them an equally pointed stare and silently followed.

Still numb, and feeling as if she were moving in slow motion, Sam approached the side of the bed. "Your sister is…"

"A piece of work?" Keirnan filled in with mock naiveté. "That she most certainly is."

She found that quick and ready wit of his more appealing than ever.

Then his tone changed abruptly to seriousness. "I'm glad she found you. Glad you're all right."

"Me too." Sam swayed a little as the images washed over her, and she had to grip the edge of his bed to steady herself. "I was so afraid…" She squeezed her eyes shut, unable to finish.

"So was I."

The huskiness in his voice caused a warm, tingling sensation to invade Sam's senses. Still, "Glad you're all right" wasn't exactly the ringing endorsement Kathleen had touted. Maybe this was all about seeing she was recovered and sending her on her way. Better to keep the conversation light.

"What happened to your hair?"

She carefully avoided gazing into his eyes, lest she see something she would rather not. Instead, her fingers reached for the short spiky strands on the opposite side of the bandage.

Probably not a wise move either. She stopped herself just in time.

"They had to shave around the wound before they stitched it up, so I told them to cut all of it." He started to shrug then swallowed hard in obvious discomfort. "It was getting rather shaggy anyway."

"I liked shaggy." Her habit of speaking without thinking was still intact, unfortunately.

Her eyes collided unexpectedly with his, and the tingling warmth kicked up a notch. Tension all but crackled in the air between them.

"It'll grow back in no time." His voice radiated with heat too.

Fascinated, Sam watched his tongue flick across his lower lip. *Could he be as nervous as she was?* Silence reigned for a half-dozen heartbeats.

"I really want to kiss you, but when I move my head too suddenly…" He gave a small grimace.

Heart racing with the realization that he did indeed share some of her unease, she leaned toward him and feathered her fingertips down his cheek to his jaw. Heat sizzled like a live electrical wire all the way up her arm. Anxiety wasn't the only thing they were both feeling.

Her doubt and caution melted like snow in a warm spring downpour.

"Then I guess I'll have to kiss you."

"Good plan." His nervousness must have also vanished, for he flashed a hint of his familiar dazzling smile. "I'll just 'move not while my prayer's effect *you* take.'"

Sam started to pull back and ask if his sister knew he liked to quote bloody Englishmen, but her mouth had already settled on top of his. Then his tongue met hers, and she no longer cared if she ever saw Indiana, Illinois, or any other state again.

She broke the kiss just enough to lean her forehead against his and give him a quote from the same play. "'Forgetting any other home but this,'" she murmured and kissed him again.

Chapter 14

LOUD VOICES FROM THE CORRIDOR OUTSIDE INVADED the room, and Samantha hastily pulled her lips away. Before Keirnan had a chance to protest, the door flew open, and a small bundle of red-haired fury stormed into the room.

"Keirnan Sean Fitzgerald!" Kathleen's voice bordered on a shriek. "How could you do this? You've no right!"

Face blazing with color, Samantha attempted to back away, but Keirnan captured her hand. He wasn't letting her go anywhere just yet. There were things he needed to say, and he was hopeful she would do the same, but not with an audience.

Frowning, he remained calm in the face of his sister's wrath. "Precisely what is it I've done?"

"The Jewels of the Madonna!" Kathleen raged. "How could you promise them to… to… *him*!" She leveled an accusing finger as the tall figure of Carlo Bergamon stepped into the room.

"*Buon giorno*, Keirnan. I'm glad to see you well on your way to recovery," the Interpol agent said in a mild, measured tone while Kathleen did some colorful swearing in Gaelic.

Except that anyone could figure out her meaning based on her vehemence alone. Carlo patently ignored her.

"*Buon giorno*, Signorina Lewis. My apologies for being unable to return your calls."

Keirnan shot Kathleen a lethal glare. "Sorry, Carlo, my sister seems to have some objections about our recent business arrangements."

"You'd bloody well better believe I object!" Kathleen declared, ignoring his warning as always. She shook her finger at him. "You can't use the Jewels of the Madonna as some… some bargaining chip!"

Over the years, Keirnan had learned that the only effective method of dealing with Kathleen when she was totally unreasonable was to be unreasonable right back.

"Well, pardon me for saving your lily-white neck!" He laid sarcasm on thick. "I wasn't sure which part of you those thugs would carve off next, so I suppose I wasn't thinking too clearly."

As he'd hoped, that seemed to take a little of the wind out of her sails. She muttered a rude phrase in Italian, though she spared him the accompanying hand gesture. Her volume also decreased several decibels.

"You still had no right to promise the jewels to *him*." She tossed her red curls in Carlo's direction, refusing to look at him. "They're not yours to do with as you please."

"Nor are they yours, Signora DiLucca," the Interpol agent blandly reminded.

From the corner of his eye, Keirnan saw Samantha press her lips into a thin, tight line. Suppressing a smile, no doubt. His own lips twitched. Fortunately his sister didn't see. She rounded on Carlo, ready to give him a full blast of her ire.

"I know that," she snapped. "But they're the key to legitimizing my research, and I won't let you just waltz in here and take them away! Not after all these years of work, not after everything—"

She broke off abruptly and turned her back on all three of them, seeming to pull into herself.

"I won't." Her voice sounded choked, and she looked very small.

Samantha's grip on Kerinan's hand tightened. He met her golden green gaze and read sympathy for his sister swimming in its depth.

Shite! If there were anything more within his power, he would do it. Unfortunately, the Interpol agent now held all the cards. The final play was entirely up to him.

"You misunderstand, Signora." Carlo Bergamon's voice was suddenly quite soothing. "I have no intention of discrediting your work. My interest in the jewels is in preserving valuable objects from Venice's past."

Kathleen hesitated a moment, then turned, her sapphire eyes glittering with the moisture of unshed tears. "How can I believe you after what you did to me five years ago?"

"I can do nothing about what happened in the past." The man sounded surprisingly sincere. "But I can assure you, Signora, that as long as your actions are legitimate and above board, you have nothing to fear from me."

Kathleen raised her bandaged hand to her face and sniffled loudly. "I contacted the university and every historical society I could think of weeks ago. None of them took me seriously, except for one very low-level assistant at the Society for the Preservation of Venetian Antiquities."

Bergamon continued in his "good cop" persona. "I happen to know people connected with the Society. What is this assistant's name?"

Perhaps he too felt some genuine sympathy for Kathleen? Something in the medication must have put such a preposterous notion in Keirnan's head.

"Donatella Bottini." Kathleen sniffed. "I would give you her email address, but when I went to my apartment, it was ransacked and my laptop stolen.

"I can make inquiries at the Society immediately." The agent inclined his head in Keirnan and Samantha's direction before he addressed Kathleen once more. "If you truly do know the whereabouts of the Jewels of the Madonna, Signora, and I believe you do, then your Signorina Bottini should soon receive a very large promotion. Now, may we discuss the location of the jewels tomorrow morning?"

"Mr. Bergamon," Samantha quickly interceded, much to Keirnan's relief, before Kathleen could acquiesce. Or heaven forbid, raise more objections. "Since this is the culmination of years of study, would you allow Ms. DiLucca to accompany you when you retrieve the jewels?"

A surge of pride suffused Keirnan at Samantha's unexpected and rather audacious request. Now they'd see if the Interpol agent was strictly self-serving or not.

"And my brother!" Kathleen piped up. "And Ms. Lewis as well. 'Tis only right, after all they've been through."

Bergamon slanted a suspicious glance at her. "The three of you I may consider, but not the media."

"Sir, this is a scholarly endeavor," Kathleen replied with a haughty air of finality.

A smile quirked the corners of Carlo's mouth and made the dour agent look almost personable.

"In that case, let me see what arrangements can be made." With a nod that included all three of them, he turned for the door. "*Buona sera.* Good night."

"Don't be thinking you're off my 'S' list, *Sionnach*," Kathleen warned when the door clicked shut behind the Interpol agent. She waited a few seconds, obviously making sure he really was gone before she added, "Now, by some chance, did you find my journal and backup CD?"

"That we did, and more." Keirnan informed her, not trying to keep the smugness from his voice. "So if you are even entertaining some crazy notion about trying to fool Carlo…"

Kathleen pulled herself up to her full five-foot-two-inch height and mustered enough righteous indignation to make the Queen envious.

"Why, I never heard such foul slander, and from my own brother!"

"Samantha and I know the location of the jewels, Kathleen. They're on the cemetery isle in the tomb of the Viscount Treviso."

He had to hand it to his sister, even he almost missed the fleeting flash of astonishment that raced across her features.

"Of course you would know," she stated calmly. "After all, you're Nino, and she's Serafina."

Samantha made a choking sound, pulled away from him, and groped for the nearest chair. Her face looked drained of color, and he knew why. Angelo had told her the same bloody nonsense, and then he…

"No!" Both women jumped at his sudden harsh declaration. Keirnan reined himself in sharply. His sister didn't need to know all the details any more than Samantha needed to be reminded of them. "We figured it out from your notes."

He longed to pull Samantha into his arms and sooth away her fears. But just turning his head to look at her kicked up the infernal pounding inside his skull to an almost unbearable level.

It must have been the hammering that made him add, "Not some past lives rubbish."

"Fine." Kathleen crossed her arms over her chest and stared away from him. "Believe what you like, and I shall do the same."

Keirnan sighed. "Aren't there enough tragic figures in Irish history? Why would we be Italians?"

"I don't know. We just are." Kathleen stubbornly insisted. "And I refuse to quote that bloody Englishman about there being 'more things in heaven and earth,' however correct he may be."

Most of the color had returned to Samantha's face, and a small smile tugged at the corners of her mouth. His libido throbbed with the need to kiss her again. Or better yet, pull her onto the bed with him. If only a certain red-haired pest would leave them alone for awhile.

"Don't you have something else to do, *Deirfiu'r*?" he asked a bit more harshly than he'd meant to.

"Maybe I do." Kathleen's tone told him she was still peeved. "I promised Miss Lewis I would hire a car to take her to Rome tonight so she won't miss her plane."

A small flicker of panic skittered down Keirnan's spine. Pain be damned! He twisted his head so that he could look her fully in the face. "You don't want to go, do you?"

She stared at her suitcase, sitting against the wall near the door. "No, but I—"

"Please, don't go!" he interrupted, then abashed by his rashness, he added, "I… I really want you to stay." Samantha rewarded his outburst with a smile that made him thankful he wasn't connected to a heart monitor. He had to take a deep breath before he could say, "Besides, Kathleen is right. You deserve to be here when we unearth the jewels."

"Yes, indeed," his sister heartily agreed. Then, she made a regal sweep toward the door. "So now that we've settled that, I shall just have a word with the doctor to make sure he releases you tomorrow so you can go along as well. Oh, and I won't be gone long."

She shot them a meaningful glower and walked out.

"Finally!" Keirnan groaned with relief as the door swung shut with a click.

Samantha rose from her chair and moved closer, though her eyes were still on the door. "Do you and your sister always…" She turned to meet his gaze, her cheeks pink. "Um, you know…"

"Carry on like that?" He finished for her. "Actually yes, I'm afraid we do." He captured her hand and rubbed his thumb across her knuckles. "Don't worry. You'll get used to it. Now, where were we?"

Her flush deepened. "I think we're at the part where I go back to the hotel so we can both get some rest."

He knew she was right. They were both physically and emotionally exhausted from the past few days. However, even though his aching flesh was weak, his spirit was still willing, very willing. He rubbed her knuckles across his lips then murmured, "I can scoot over if you care to join me."

"And have your sister or that awful nurse come barging in? "

He mustered up his best martyr expression. "At least give me one more kiss, just to tide me over until tomorrow."

She smiled another heart-stopping smile before she carried her chair over and wedged it under the doorknob.

"That will give us some warning," she said, leaning over and enveloping him in her luscious peach scent.

He reached for her with his free hand and pulled her against him. She felt solid and warm, and the sheer joy of not losing her pounded fiercely through his veins. All his fears and uncertainty vanished. She belonged to him.

Now.

Always.

Forever.

As her sweet lips settled over his, and their tongues meshed, he worked his hand under her clothes to find the soft velvet of her breasts. She moaned her pleasure into his mouth, and a moment later her own fingers caressed the rigid length of him.

'Twas a feeling akin to heaven.

Even better.

Sam was savoring her second caffè latte in the hotel restaurant the next morning when Kathleen arrived. Burdened with several large shopping bags, the petite redhead dumped everything beside the table before she plopped into the vacant chair.

"Cappuccino, *per piacere*," she shouted, waving a ten-Euro note at the waiter. Then she turned her attention to Sam. "Sorry to keep you waiting, luv. I had some purchases to make after I finished up with Carlo and Signorina Bottini."

Considering the sparkle in Kathleen's bright blue eyes, the meeting must have gone well, but to be polite, Sam asked anyway. "So everything is all set?"

"Right as rain," she declared in her oh-so-Irish brogue. Then she flashed a dimple at the balding, middle-aged waiter who slid a frothy, steaming cup in front of her. "*Grazie mille*. A thousand thanks."

The man backed away murmuring some nicety that included *bella*. Beautiful. Charm had to be the chief component in Fitzgerald DNA.

Kathleen cradled the cup in her uninjured hand and took a sip before continuing. "Carlo is meeting us at hospital so we can collect Himself and go directly to San Michele."

Himself. Keirnan.

After their brief interlude, her dreams had been full of him all night. Since she'd arrived in Venice, her whole life seemed to have become a dream.

Sam's cup wobbled as some of the more pleasant images flashed across her mind. The knowing lift of Kathleen's dark auburn brow made her drop her gaze.

"That's his then?" Kathleen indicated a black duffel bag sitting beside Sam's chair.

"Yes, I thought he might need a change of clothes."

She'd buried her face in every item to catch any lingering traces of Keirnan's unique scent. She'd never been this completely enamored of anyone. She only hoped that hint of a smile at the corner of Kathleen's mouth didn't mean she suspected as much.

"Indeed he does, considering he jumped into the canal in the ones he was wearing yesterday."

"He does that a lot," Sam murmured, lifting her own cup.

She glanced at the shopping bags heaped on the floor, enough to outfit a football squad.

Eyebrow still arched, Kathleen took another sip of her cappuccino. "Does he, now? 'Tis probably good I bought him some extras then. I also got him a new coat, since his looked much the worse for wear." She bent over and fished inside the largest bag. "And I bought one for you as well."

Sam gasped as Keirnan's sister thrust a beautiful suede coat with fur collar and cuffs at her. "I... I can't accept this."

Kathleen made a clucking noise with her tongue. "Don't be daft. 'Tis much too chilly to go mucking about the cemetery isle without a jumper, and I noticed last night you didn't have one."

She looked questioningly at the pullover Sam had on. "Is it the fur, then?" She patted the collar of her own coat. "This is Europe, luv. Everybody wears it. And 'tis hardly mink, more's the pity."

"No, it's... it's just too much. I can't..." Sam tried to shove the jacket across the table, but the other woman insistently pressed it back into her hands.

"Miss Lewis, please, let me give you some token of gratitude. 'Tis the very least I can do after all you've done for me." She waved her gauze-wrapped hand in a sign of dismissal before Sam could protest further. "Besides, I've a feeling you and I are going to be very close, like family."

Don't worry. You'll get used to it.

She wasn't so sure anyone got used to a Fitzgerald, not that she wasn't willing to try. With a sigh of surrender, she pulled the gorgeous coat into her arms. "In that case, you better call me Sam."

"All right, Sam." Kathleen's dimple flashed again. She took a leisurely sip of her cappuccino. "What makes you think the jewels are in the tomb of the Viscount Treviso?"

Sam almost choked on her latte.

"Be—because Serafina and her sister are buried there?" She ventured at last.

Kathleen's shrewd sapphire eyes probed her face. "You're right about the sister, but I happen to believe Serafina didn't die anywhere near Venice, in spite of what records show."

A mixture of disbelief and disappointment washed over Sam. "Then the jewels aren't here after all?"

"Oh, they're here right enough, and most likely in the Treviso tomb."

"But how? Why?"

The satisfied feline smile tilted the corners of Kathleen's lips. "You remember the part of the story where the girl's lover steals the Jewels of the Madonna?"

Chewing her bottom lip in confusion, Sam nodded.

"That much of the story I believe is true. Serafina's lover, Nino, stole the jewels to finance their flight from Venice." She held up her hand to silence Sam's protest. "But Serafina wouldn't let him keep them because stealing meant the forfeit of his soul. Life expectancy was short in those days. Would you want to spend eternity without your beloved?"

Sam squirmed in her chair. "No."

Kathleen's words made sense even if she had no evidence that they were true.

"But your notes indicated Serafina and her sister Simonetta both died in 1485."

"Well, if she did, then Nino would have no reason to keep the jewels, would he? But he couldn't just give them back, since fifteenth-century justice was swift and more than a mite painful. In either case, he'd need to find a covert way."

She drained the last of the cappuccino from her cup and blotted her mouth on her napkin. "So put on your coat, and let's go find out if I'm right. Besides, I'll wager my brother doesn't fancy spending even another hour without you."

Sam pressed her lips together in a tight line. She wasn't sure what to believe about anything. This intense connection between Keirnan and her was wonderful but more than a little scary. Plus, the whole situation surrounding the Jewels of the Madonna, past and present, had her floundering so far out of her depth that she could scarcely walk and talk at the same time, much less make sense of any of it. She shoved her arms into the sleeves of the suede coat and zipped it up. It fit perfectly.

Kathleen nodded her head in approval. "'Whoever loved that loved not at first sight?'" she quoted then reached for her other bags.

"Christopher Marlowe," Sam muttered, following her to the door. "But wasn't he a bloody Englishman, too?"

Kathleen gave a jaunty toss of her red curls as they stepped into the chilly air. "Yes, but he was a spy."

They waited ten minutes for the correct vaporetto. Sam's knee had begun to throb, but she soon forgot to notice as the boat chugged its way down the Grand Canal in the midst of a score of powerboats and barges.

The sun shone directly overhead, and gulls called out while Kathleen regaled her with stories of Keirnan as a child. By the time they reached the hospital, Sam had heard how five-year-old Kathleen had lugged her six-month-old brother into the far pasture, intent on exchanging him for a fairy baby. Keirnan learned to pick locks before he could read when their mother shut them in various closets and cupboards to hide them from their drunken father. And at fifteen, he'd been in a street gang and quit school. Kathleen had hunted him down a year later and hauled him away to Italy with her.

The love and connection between the Fitzgerald siblings made Sam envious, while at the same time her heart ached a little for the two who'd had only each other for so long. Also, talking about Keirnan fueled her growing eagerness to see him. Whatever this was between them, it wouldn't be denied. In spite of her stiff, heavily bandaged knee, she hurried off the vaporetto and through the hospital's main entrance.

"You go ahead," Kathleen instructed, obviously aware of her impatience. "I'll make sure the paperwork is done and be right up."

Flushed with anticipation, Sam gathered the nylon duffel bag into her arms and squeezed onto the crowded elevator. Ignoring both the medicinal smells and the musical chatter of Italian, she walked as quickly as she could down the long hallway to Keirnan's room. She rapped lightly on the door before she pushed it open, in case he wasn't alone. To her chagrin, he wasn't.

"*Buon giorno*, Signorina Lewis," greeted Carlo Bergamon, straightening to his full height. "May I present Signorina Donatella Bottini from the Society for the Preservation of Venetian Antiquities?"

Sam scarcely saw the petite brunette standing next to the Interpol agent.

"*Buon giorno*," she muttered absently, her eyes riveted on Keirnan, who occupied a chair next to the window.

He rose to his feet. In addition to the bandage, he sported a bad case of bed-head, and his clothes couldn't have been more rumpled, but he still looked so good to her that the breath jammed in her throat.

"Samantha, luv."

Just the sound of his voice tripled her pulse rate. In the next instant, he closed the distance between them and pulled her against his chest.

"*Grá mo chroí*," he whispered against her hair.

His shirt was decidedly aromatic, but she didn't care. She threw her arms around him and thumped him with the duffel bag.

"Oh, sorry! I, uh…" She stepped away, face flaming at Signorina Bottini's muffled giggle. Brief as their embrace had been, Keirnan was unmistakably glad to see her. "I, uh, brought you a change of clothes."

"Ah, you're an angel, luv." His fingers squeezed hers as he grabbed the bag's strap. "I most definitely need them." He raised his sleeve and wrinkled his nose in mocking disgust. "I won't be a minute."

Keirnan had no sooner disappeared into the bathroom than Kathleen swept in, accompanied by a burly hospital attendant pushing a wheelchair. Even though they had met just a couple of hours ago, Signorina Bottini and Kathleen exuberantly greeted each other as if they were long lost friends.

The dour Interpol agent interrupted their gushing Italian by loudly clearing his throat. "I've made all the necessary arrangements with the administrator of San Michele. He even faxed me this map of the portion of the island that contains the Renaissance era tombs." He pulled a piece of paper from his coat pocket, unfolded it, and offered it to Kathleen. "Perhaps you would like to study the map over lunch?"

"No!" Sam surprised herself by speaking in unison with Kathleen, who flashed a dimpled thank you before she added, "I'll give it a look on the way over. You do have a boat waiting?"

Carlo nodded.

At that moment, Keirnan emerged from the bathroom wearing a dark blue sweater that turned his eyes indigo. A flare of heat singed its way from Sam's eyeballs to her toenails as she drank in the gorgeous sight of him, and she wasn't the only one.

In spite of a rather large diamond on her left hand, Signorina Bottini gave Keirnan a long, appreciative glance. Happily, incredulously, his attention was focused completely on Sam, which made her heart pound even faster.

"All set, then?" he asked.

"Ah, *Sionnach*," Kathleen acknowledged. "Glad to see you're up and about." She then asked Signorina Bottini something in Italian.

The petite brunette, who appeared to be around Sam's age, tore her dark eyes away from Keirnan and answered in the affirmative.

"We're in agreement," Kathleen explained to Sam. "Find the jewels first, then worry about a meal." She bent and rummaged in the largest of her shopping bags and pulled out a black leather jacket, which she shoved in Keirnan's direction. "Bundle up, brother of mine, then hop in." She indicated the wheelchair with a thrust of her chin.

Keirnan cast a disdainful glance at both the attendant and the chair as he shrugged on the new coat. "I won't be needing that."

"Well, the doctor says you do, or you'll likely be fainting in the middle of the cemetery isle." Kathleen's tart tone grew to a scold. "Now sit your wee arse down before I leave you here at the mercy of the nurses."

Grumbling under his breath, Keirnan did as he was told. *Here we go again.*

Sam pressed her lips tightly together to prevent herself from chuckling. A furtive glance at Carlo revealed he was doing the same, while Signorina Bottini giggled outright.

Ignoring them all, Kathleen pulled a bright red knitted cap from another of her shopping bags and plunked it on top of her brother's head.

"Wear this as well," she ordered, then deposited all the bags on his lap.

"I'm not a bloody shopping cart," Keirnan protested, but his eyes sparkled with mischief. "Samantha has an injured knee. Perhaps she should ride on my lap." He wiggled his eyebrows suggestively as he adjusted the cap over his ears.

Sam felt the blood rushing back to her face, but Kathleen merely rolled her eyes. "Save that for your hotel room."

Then like a drum majorette leading off the parade, she marched toward the door. "*Andiamo.* Let's go."

Chapter 15

WHILE CARLO MANEUVERED THE SMALL SPEEDBOAT across the lagoon, Kathleen and Donatella Bottini sat huddled over the map of San Michele en Isola and conversed in Italian. Keirnan's arm encircled Samantha's waist, keeping her close against his side to shelter her from the whipping wind. The wheelchair, which folded neatly in half, was wedged tightly in the back corner of the boat.

Keirnan would rather have a root canal without benefit of anesthetic than admit that his sister was wise to bring the blasted thing. But in truth he still felt light-headed when he walked, and the hint of an ache prickled over his left eye.

He only had to hang on a wee bit longer. Very soon now, they would find the jewels, and life would be… certainly not like it was before. He rested his cheek against Samantha's soft hair and breathed in the subtle fragrance of peaches.

Nothing in his past experiences had prepared him for the intensity of his feelings for her. Though God help him, he would endure any kind of torture rather than acknowledge that his sister's romantic notions about past lives and true love just might have some merit. One thing he was sure about, he had no intention of ever spending another night without Samantha.

The walled fortress of the cemetery isle suddenly loomed in front of the boat. Beside him, Samantha stiffened and sucked in a sharp breath.

"'Tis all right, luv," Keirnan murmured into her hair, pulling her closer.

She turned her face into the side of his neck and shivered. Her reaction made his gut clench. Carlo had assured him that the local authorities were dealing with Angelo and his two cronies, but the fact that they had laid their hands on Samantha still ate at him. She kept her face averted while Carlo guided the boat along the side of the stone dock jutting from the entrance.

The place looked far less forbidding in the light of day. The three tall doors stood open, and the cypresses beyond them waved dark green plumes against the pale winter sky. Carlo cut the motor and secured the boat under a large red and white sign listing the rules and regulations for visitors.

A short man with a bushy moustache hurried out and identified himself as Signor Favretto, an assistant to the administrator. Quick introductions in Italian were made all around, then Favretto engaged Carlo in a muffled conversation.

Keirnan put up no protest when Sam and Kathleen hauled the wheelchair out of the boat. He sat placidly and let the three women fuss over pushing him through the nearest open door and across the enclosed entry to the gravel pathway beyond.

No traces remained of the trap he'd laid here the night before last, but he could feel Samantha's discomfort rolling over him like a sudden wave. He clenched his hands with the overwhelming urge to comfort her. The sooner they were done here, the better.

A three-wheeled electric cart sat on the gravel path, and Favretto urged them to climb aboard. Kathleen and

Donatella squeezed into the front with Favretto. Keirnan, Carlo, and Samantha were obliged to wedge themselves into the back, facing in the opposite direction. Carlo held the folded wheelchair over the side of the cart, while a worn leather valise rested in his lap.

Samantha was forced to sit partially on the seat and more than halfway on Keirnan's lap. Though she looked uneasy with the arrangement, parts of him were quite pleased.

Saints! He'd had more control as a randy teenager. Fortunately, the bouncy ride soon made him disregard his libido.

Decidedly in her element, his sister directed Favretto past the round-domed, nineteenth-century brick church with the graves lined up right to its front door. They drove by multiple rows of tall marble crypts and neat rows of white crosses that marked the newest sections of the cemetery isle. A few people walked among the graves, and they passed a noisy white maintenance truck whose driver hailed Favretto.

Once they passed a dividing row of cypress trees, the graves were more overgrown and crowded haphazardly together. Only a solitary woman dressed in traditional black bent beside a white cross. The gravel road became more uneven, forcing the vehicle to a crawl.

Kathleen pointed the way beyond another line of cypresses. Tombs that looked like small buildings came into view. Keirnan recognized the area.

They were getting close now.

Unfortunately, the deeply rutted road rapidly became impassable. Favretto ground the lumbering vehicle to a stop, and everyone climbed out. Keirnan insisted the wheelchair stay in the cart, reasoning that it would be equally useless on the rough ground. His sister and Samantha were forced to agree.

Favretto handed Carlo a walkie-talkie and told the Interpol agent to call when they were ready to be picked up. He restarted the cart, which maneuvered much better without its five passengers, and with a jaunty wave, lurched back the way they'd come.

Stowing the walkie-talkie in his valise, Carlo took the map from Kathleen. Extracting a pen from his pocket, he leaned against a crumbling marble pillar and sketched a rudimentary grid.

"We should conduct the search methodically." He gestured at the paper. "I suggest we start at the lower end of the area and work upward, then over."

"'Twould be faster if we split up," Kathleen reasoned. She squinted at the map, then pointed to the square in the lower right-hand corner. "Donatella and I will start there." She quickly translated for the petite brunette who nodded in eager agreement.

Carlo looked ready to protest, but Samantha, who had been gazing distractedly into the distance, interrupted. "Good idea. Keirnan and I will start there." She waved her arm at a point over Carlo's left shoulder.

Keirnan looked in the direction she indicated, and some vague recollection stirred on the fringes of his memory. Had he searched that area the other night? Was there something Samantha wasn't telling him? She looked very much out of sorts, while Carlo still appeared less than pleased.

"All right." The Interpol agent sighed. Clearly outnumbered, he marked an "X" on two squares of the grid then indicated a point halfway between them. "I will start here." He turned on his heel and strode away.

"Sing out if you find it," Kathleen cried as she and Signorina Bottini eagerly tramped off in their chosen direction.

Keirnan interlaced his fingers with Samantha's. "Alone at last," he commented with a salacious lift of his brow.

However, Samantha remained pensive, her lips pressed together in a tight line. "I think Carlo still doesn't trust us very much."

"He's Interpol, luv. I doubt he trusts his own mother." He rubbed her knuckles against his cheek. "So is there a reason you think we should look for the Treviso tomb over there?"

"I don't know." She worried her bottom lip with her teeth. "I just felt like that's where it is."

He'd like to taste her lip himself, but first things first. "Then let's have a look, shall we?"

She was crazy. Stark-raving bonkers. Probably because this place totally creeped her out.

Sam had been in a few cemeteries before, but none affected her the way San Michele seemed to. Not even the elaborate, above-ground monuments in New Orleans' St. Louis Cemetery, where she had visited during a semester break, had given her such strange vibes. Here, something disturbing seemed to lie just beyond her range of vision, and the skin on her arms and the back of her neck crawled with anticipation.

Keirnan squeezed her fingers.

"You all right, luv?" Concern clouded both his

eyes and his voice. "Are you remembering the other night? Angelo?"

Sam shook her head. She actually hadn't thought of Angelo since they'd left the island's entrance. Whatever was distracting her was certainly effective.

"It's just this place, so still and so…" Logical explanations refused to form, but she knew his opinion of the supernatural. She even shared it, didn't she? "Otherworldly," she finished with a wince.

Keirnan didn't comment.

They made their way slowly over the uneven ground, the bright red of Keirnan's knitted cap the only splash of color in the otherwise stark landscape. Several of the tombs they passed had smashed doors and ruined walls. Sam couldn't tell whether vandals, time, the elements, or all three were responsible for the damage.

Then two large marble statues loomed in their path. Angels, though one was missing half a wing, and both faces were worn nearly featureless. Equally weathered tombs surrounded the statues.

Keirnan dropped her hand and leaned against the base of the half-winged angel. "I know for certain 'tis none of these."

"You were here the other night."

Even though it was not a question, he nodded, then ran his hand across his eyes. "How about we rest for a bit?"

He looked tired, and for all his false bravado, he was undoubtedly in pain too.

Sam fought down the urge to comfort him. "Okay."

She turned to look for some place to sit, but saw only tufts of dead grass, rocks, and some pieces of broken marble. That odd sensation of being on the verge of awareness made her whirl around.

The angels' rueful stone faces gleamed shiny white in front of her startled eyes. Cautiously, Sam shifted her gaze. All around her, colors were vivid and pristine as if someone had pulled away a grimy vinyl overlay to reveal the dazzling page underneath.

Trees filled with vibrant green leaves shaded vines redolent with pale pink blossoms. Just beyond the angels, she saw marble pillars shimmering in the light.

The Treviso tomb.

Careful not to blink or move her eyes from the shining apparition, she edged toward it.

"Samantha, luv?" Keirnan's questioning voice sounded miles away. She didn't dare turn to look at him and was almost afraid to answer.

"I'll be right back," she finally replied, and her own voice sounded hollow and far away, too.

Her feet seemed to glide over the ground. Even her bandaged knee, which minutes ago had throbbed with a dull ache, didn't hamper her forward progress.

The peaked roof of the monument came into view and carved just below it in thick block letters was the name "Treviso." Two low marble steps led to the columned portico, but as Sam approached them, something made her stumble.

Her knee almost buckled under her. She managed to brace it with both hands and stay upright. However, her concentration and unwavering gaze shattered, and with them went the clarity of five hundred years.

The dull winter afternoon washed back. Skeletal trees, blackened lichen, and the smell of decayed vegetation surrounded her. Before her stood the age-ravaged tomb, pillars veined with cracks, and steps broken into uneven chunks. The only distinguishable letters were the T, R, V, and the top half of the O. The carved marble handles on the double doors were wrapped with a rusty length of chain and secured with an enormous padlock the size of her fist.

The breath Sam hadn't realized she'd been holding wheezed noisily out of her mouth. She sucked in a couple more shaky draughts of air before she was able to cry out.

"Keirnan! Come quick!"

The words scarcely escaped her constricted throat when snapping twigs and rattling dried leaves sounded behind her.

"Samantha..." Keirnan's answering call died on his lips as he pulled up short beside her. He stared round-eyed and open-mouthed for a moment before he forced out a strangled oath.

"Saints in heaven!"

Then he drew in a deep breath and bellowed, "Kathleen!" Only to clutch at his head and stifle a moan, "Ow! Good God! That felt like my skull nearly split."

"Cover your ears," Sam ordered, then she threw her head back and yelled, "Carlo! Kathleen!"

"Ow! Ouch! Enough!" Keirnan protested.

Fortunately Sam didn't need to yell again, for an instant later the tall Interpol agent crashed through the bushes on the left side of the tomb.

"What...?" he began, only to fall silent when he saw the carved letters.

Before he could say anything else, Kathleen's

high-pitched voice called through the trees on the right. "Did you find it? Where are you?"

Her red curls bounced into view behind Keirnan's shoulder a moment before she and Donatella rushed onto the scene.

"Holy Blessed Mother!" Kathleen breathed.

"*Madre di Dio*," Donatella echoed in Italian, crossing herself.

Sam hung back while Keirnan and Carlo picked their way up to the door.

"Aren't any relatives of the Trevisos left?" she asked Kathleen, who was clasping and unclasping her hands in nervous excitement.

Donatella, meanwhile, pulled a small digital camera from her pocket and snapped several photos.

"No, the last of them died during the Second World War."

"And I'd say this chain and lock are at least that old," Keirnan confirmed, dropping the rusted object with a sigh. "I don't think even *I* can open this one."

"Then allow me." Carlo opened his battered valise and pulled out a short, metal pry-bar and a rubber mallet.

Everyone watched in silent anticipation as Carlo fingered the rusty links. Finally settling on one, he shoved the pry-bar into it, securing it against the face of the door before he struck the end of the bar with the mallet. Once, twice, and the rusted link broke, leaving the chain dangling in two. With a satisfied smile, the Interpol agent placed his tools back in the valise while Keirnan unwound and discarded the broken chain.

Grasping the left door handle in both his hands, Carlo braced himself and tugged. Nothing happened.

Keirnan reached to grip the right door, but Carlo

grabbed onto the bottom of the long carved handle also. That one didn't budge either.

"I'll help," Sam volunteered, stepping forward.

"No." Both men barked in unison.

Men! They really were all alike.

Sam gave them an eye roll as they both grabbed the left handle and gave one more equally unsuccessful attempt. She bit back a pithy retort as Carlo once again retrieved the pry-bar and mallet.

Kathleen was less restrained.

"What? No plastic explosives?· Not even a wee stick of dynamite?" the petite redhead chided. "I'd have thought an Interpol agent better prepared."

Keirnan shot his sister a lethal glare, but Carlo didn't acknowledge her jibe. He wedged the pry-bar into the seam between the doors and proceeded to whack it with the mallet, a process he repeated several times down the length of the doors.

The sound of metal grating against stone when Carlo inserted and removed the bar made Sam clench her teeth, while Keirnan covered his ears and cringed with each successive blow. Kathleen and Donatella flinched too.

After two more blows at the bottom of the left door, Carlo tossed the tools onto the ground and nodded at Keirnan. "Again?"

This time they were able to force the door open a couple of inches. Just wide enough for them to find finger holds on the door's side, Carlo high and Keirnan low, and wrench the protesting stone a few inches more.

"Other side?" Keirnan asked, his face fast approaching the color of his cap.

Carlo nodded, swiping his arm across his sweaty

brow, while they jostled into position on the other door. Fortunately this one proved more cooperative, though no less noisy. With a grinding screech of stone on stone, the two men muscled it open almost a meter.

Donatella gave a little cry of delight while Kathleen muttered, "About bloody time!"

"Are you all right?" Sam asked Keirnan, who was doubled over and panting from the effort.

"Fine," he replied predictably, though he looked far from it.

"A moment, please, ladies." Carlo raised his hand to stop the three of them.

Then he reached into the valise, pulled out two heavy flashlights, and passed one to Keirnan. The Interpol agent raked his light in a floor-to-ceiling 180-degree arc.

"All right," he said over his shoulder, stepping through the door. "But be careful."

Kathleen nearly trod on his heels. Donatella followed, equally eager. Sam stopped next to Keirnan, who was upright, but still breathing rapidly. A thread of worry pulled tight around her heart. She touched his sleeve.

"You don't look fine."

He brushed a stray lock of hair off her cheek. "Neither did you a few minutes ago. See another ghost?"

The tenderness in his touch unlaced the worry, but made her throat contract. She coughed to clear it.

"Not exactly."

She was saved from further explanations by a loud sneeze from Kathleen.

"*Salute*! Bless you," Keirnan chorused along with Carlo and Donatella as Kathleen sneezed again.

As she followed Keirnan over the threshold, Sam

almost sneezed herself. Decades of accumulated dust, which carpeted the floor, rose in clouds with every step.

The dry, musty smell of stale air overwhelmed her. The score of rectangular sarcophagi crowded in the gloomy interior looked draped in gray velvet. Thick ropes of shimmering cobwebs hung from the burial crypts built into the tomb walls. Thin streamers of pale light filtered in through a half-dozen niches high up near the ceiling of the west wall. The east wall held the same.

Donatella immediately started directing Carlo's flashlight beam so that she could continue snapping photos. Sam cautiously sidestepped around as the other two women and Carlo began a discussion in Italian.

The beam of Keirnan's flashlight played across the room. Some of the sarcophagi had bronze likenesses on their lids. Others had marble, and a few were devoid of decoration. The light stopped on what appeared to be the largest sarcophagus in the room.

"I'm betting that's our viscount," Keirnan murmured, still a little out of breath.

Every nerve in Sam's body felt like it was at attention, and the pervasive dust seemed to have deprived her mouth of all moisture.

"Me too," she managed in a faint whisper.

Keirnan wove his way toward the center of the room, and she limped after him.

The marble monument was topped with the full-body likeness of a large man. Though the facial features and lettering across the top were worn nearly indistinguishable, the clothing depicted was definitely Renaissance era nobility. Even without the flashlight, Sam could see that the sarcophagi on either side bore marble sculptures of women, probably the viscount's wives.

"Kathleen." All three of their companions responded to Keirnan's beckoning call.

While the other four clustered around the stone carving of the man, Sam turned to the woman's likeness on the left. Also sculpted in marble, it seemed to have fared better than the Viscount. Or perhaps the sculptor had been more gifted.

She had been young when she died, that much was still obvious. The carved sweep of her long gown looked almost like real cloth molded around her lithe body. Delicate hands lay folded across her chest.

Oblivious to the conversation going on behind her, Sam rubbed at the dirt and dust covering the letters carved above the woman's head. They looked like a Latin inscription, half worn away.

Below them were more letters, perhaps the name? She wiped her hand on her pants then rubbed vigorously, working the grime into her fingertips. The first two letters were gone. The third appeared to be an M, followed by an O. The next one was also gone, but the last four letters emerged starkly in the pale stone: ETTA.

"Simonetta." Sam startled herself by speaking aloud.

"Serafina's sister?" Kathleen gasped.

In an instant everyone crowded around her. Sam backed away as Donatella snapped more pictures.

Serafina's sister, but not Serafina.

Dust motes danced in the flashlights' glare. Sam retreated farther and looked away. Another marble sarcophagus sat behind and slightly to one side of Simonetta's, oddly isolated from all the others.

Sam's already overstretched nerves screamed as she approached it.

This one also bore the likeness of a young woman, carved by the same sculptor, for the dress was almost identical. Rosary beads looped around her clasped hands, and an ornate necklace with five large, oval stones hung around her slender neck.

Sam didn't need to rub the dust away from the name. She knew.

"K-Keirnan!" Her hands shook as badly as her voice, and her knee buckled under her.

He caught her before she fell, but his flashlight clattered to the floor. The beam flickered wildly across the walls and ceiling before it winked out.

"Samantha, luv!" Keirnan swayed a little himself before he shifted his grip on her. "Are you—" His gaze snagged on the marble likeness, and the same bolt of recognition flashed across his face. "Saints! It's her!"

Kathleen materialized next to them and, with a muttered oath in Gaelic, began rubbing furiously at the letters carved over the figure's head.

"*Che cosa*? What?" Carlo and Donatella demanded in unison.

By the time the Interpol agent had his light aimed at Kathleen's fingers, the readable letters left no mistake: F-I-N-A L-O-M.

"It's her! It's really her!" Kathleen squealed. She and Donatella jumped up and down, giggling like a pair of schoolgirls.

Carlo thrust his flashlight at Keirnan. "I'll get the tools." Even he sounded excited as he hurried toward the door.

Keirnan's left arm tightened around her. "Are you all right, luv?"

Sam turned her face into the smooth leather of his jacket and nodded. The solid feel of his chest under her cheek settled her overwrought nerves somewhat, even if his heart sounded like it was beating too rapidly. Then she heard Carlo's returning footsteps and reluctantly pulled away.

"I'm going to loosen the lid," the Interpol agent explained, holding up the pry-bar and mallet.

While Keirnan directed the light to the seam along the lid, Carlo hammered away just as he had on the doors. Sam backed up and stood with Kathleen and Donatella, leaning against Simonetta's monument to rest her knee.

The rhythmic scraping of metal on stone echoed off the walls and floor of the tomb and made Sam grind her teeth. Finally, after endlessly long minutes Carlo completed all four sides.

Laying his tools on the floor, he braced his shoulder against one corner and shoved. To everyone's surprise, the lid moved. Keirnan quickly passed the flashlight to Kathleen and leaped to the end opposite Carlo. Throwing his weight against the corner, he and the Interpol agent scooted the lid a few millimeters.

Ignoring her knee, Sam rushed to his side.

"I'm helping you. No arguments!" The words no sooner left Sam's mouth than Donatella stepped next to Carlo with a determined look on her face.

The two men exchanged glances but said nothing. The four of them shoved together, Keirnan and Sam at the head, Carlo and Donatella at the feet, while Kathleen held the light. The heavy lid scraped slowly, but enough for them to grip the edges and ease it down the side of the sarcophagus to the floor.

Even so, the weight was almost too much.

"Steady! Steady!" Kathleen cried as the monolithic piece of stone wobbled over the edge.

In spite of her best efforts, Sam's knee gave out about a foot above the floor. She crumpled down in a cloud of dust, and the heavy lid settled with a loud thump inches from her leg. The same instant, Keirnan was on the floor pulling her into his arms in a fierce embrace.

"It's okay. I'm okay," she reassured only to be interrupted by a loud exclamation from Donatella.

"*Vuoto!*"

"Empty?" Keirnan echoed in disbelief.

"Empty," Carlo confirmed, staring down into the marble box. "No one was ever interred inside here."

Chapter 16

"I KNEW IT!" KATHLEEN CRIED. "I KNEW SERAFINA didn't die in Venice. She and Nino fled to Padua."

For a stunned moment, everyone stared at Keirnan's sister. Finally Carlo broke the silence.

"That is a very romantic story, Signora DiLucca." His voice held a clipped edge of impatience. "But what about the Jewels of the Madonna?"

"Well, they must be here someplace," Kathleen answered blithely.

She ran the beam of the flashlight all around the interior of the sarcophagus.

The Interpol agent looked far from amused. "Since they are obviously not here, where do you suggest we look next?"

"They *are* here," Kathleen insisted. "Perhaps in Simonetta's sarcophagus?"

She looked toward her brother for support, but Keirnan seemed to be focused on something far away.

An icy fist of worry slammed into Sam's chest. "K-Keirnan?"

The instant her fingertips brushed his cheek, awareness snapped back into his eyes. He blinked, then swallowed hard. His fingers pressed against Sam's, flattening hers against his face.

"The jewels…" he murmured, his gaze moving to the carved marble features of Serafina Lombardo.

Rising to his knees, he let go of Sam's hand and fingered the necklace decorating the lid. Excitement and something else flared in the sapphire depths of his eyes, but his voice was quiet, as if he were speaking to himself.

"This isn't stone."

"Wh-what did you say?" Carlo's impatience had given way to confusion.

"Hand me the mallet," Keirnan ordered in the same soft tone.

Wordlessly, Carlo complied.

Without taking his eyes off the lid of the sarcophagus, Keirnan gripped the mallet handle. His fingers traced over the five smooth ovals of the necklace, lingering over the last one nearest the floor. Then, without warning, he jerked the mallet back and struck it.

The blow echoed hollowly, and the bottom half of the oval cracked and fell onto the dusty floor. On top of it dropped a dark blue object the size of a small hen's egg.

Sam sucked in a sharp breath and immediately sneezed. Muttering an oath, Carlo sank to his knees, stirring up dust and sneezing also.

"Holy blessed—" Kathleen began, then sneezed, too.

Donatella, who had not succumbed to the flying dust, cried out, "*Madre di Dio! Madre di Dio!*" Her camera was momentarily forgotten.

"Mind your fingers," Keirnan barked out the command. Then in rapid succession, he cracked open the four remaining ovals.

Three more identical jewels fell onto the dusty floor and into the eager clutches of Kathleen and Carlo. The last jewel hung up on a shard of the broken ceramic oval, and Keirnan was obliged to free it with his fingers. As it rolled onto his waiting palm, Donatella snapped a photo.

Much loud laughing, crying, and copious amounts of cheek kissing ensued. When the near hysteria calmed to ooing and aahing over the jewels, Carlo contacted Favretto to come and pick them up.

Since all the assistant and his boss were told was that a valuable Venetian artifact may have been located in the Renaissance era tomb of the Treviso family, the jewels were wrapped in Keirnan's knitted cap. Even in the afternoon sunlight, they looked nearly black against the bright red fabric with only a dark twinkle of indigo here and there in their smooth depths.

Carlo carefully placed the bundle inside his valise, then he and Keirnan shoved the doors of the tomb closed.

A ripple of relief played over Sam as she turned and walked back toward the gravel path where they would meet Favretto. If she never set foot on San Michele again, that would suit her just fine.

Keirnan fell into step beside her, and Kathleen's explanation of cabochon cut gems versus faceted blurred into an indistinguishable buzz. Warmth spiraled through her when he took her hand and placed it in the crook of his arm; however, his face looked drawn, undoubtedly from pain.

"How's your headache?"

He rubbed the bridge of his nose with his free hand. "Doesn't hurt half so bad as yesterday, but bad enough." He glanced briefly at her stiff knee. "We're quite a pair of walking wounded."

Their three companions were more than a dozen yards

ahead, but Sam didn't think it wise for either of them to quicken their pace.

"You've got to be running on pure adrenaline."

Keirnan gave a half-smile. "Yes, from about the time you stumbled across the Treviso tomb." His smile faded, and his sapphire gaze probed her face. "How did you know where 'twas?"

Sam worried her bottom lip before answering. "I don't know. It was almost like a dream. I just… all of a sudden I saw it." She took a deep, calming breath. "How did you know where the jewels were? Did you see them too?"

Now it was his turn to look uncomfortable. "Not exactly. Somehow I just *knew*. I don't know how or why…"

He looked at the three figures in front of them and dropped his tone to almost a whisper. "Don't tell Kathleen. 'Twill only encourage her."

Smiling, she followed his gaze. His sister and Donatella were exchanging a lively banter in Italian. Even the usually serious Carlo chimed in.

Sam rolled her eyes in mock dismay. "I think she's already getting plenty of encouragement."

"I'm afraid you're right." Keirnan sighed. Then he pointed at an object bobbing along the horizon. "Saints in heaven, let that be Favretto. 'Twill truly be a blessing to sit down."

Happily, it was Favretto. By the time Sam and Keirnan caught up to the other three, their jovial chauffeur had turned the little cart around and helped Kathleen and Donatella into the front seat. Keirnan's wheelchair was secured to the side with elastic straps.

Favretto asked Carlo something, and when the

Interpol agent answered *si*, the stocky man gestured broadly, kissing his pursed fingers.

"*Molto bene*! Very good!" he cried. "*Molto bene*!" He let go with another spate of Italian as he helped Sam climb onto the back seat.

"He asked if we found what we were looking for," Keirnan explained, pulling her onto his lap. "And when Carlo said yes, he said we need to have a celebration."

"And I agreed!" Carlo exclaimed, grinning broadly at Sam. He tapped Kathleen on the shoulder. "What do you say we all go for an early supper complete with champagne?"

"As long as *you* are buying the bubbly," she answered gaily.

The rest of the bumpy ride back to the entrance was filled with teasing repartee in both English and Italian about where they would celebrate and who would pay for what.

Favretto seemed determined to speed them on their way. He set the cart careening down the gravel paths at a pace that had Sam cringing and squeezing her eyes shut.

Once during the hair-raising trip back, Carlo's valise nearly bounced off his lap. When he and Keirnan both grabbed frantically to keep it from falling off the cart, reality slammed into Sam. She and Keirnan could only spend a couple more days together before she had to go back to Bloomington.

More than ever, she intended to break from her old life once and for all, quit her job, and leave as soon as possible.

She didn't think she would ever be glad to see the

island's fortresslike entrance, but by the time they arrived, miraculously unscathed, she was elated.

More cheek kissing, Italian salutations, and thanks were extended all around, then the assistant administrator left them. With exaggerated gallantry, Keirnan insisted Sam ride in the wheelchair. Since it was such a short distance, she agreed but only on the condition he did *not* drive like Favretto.

Though he pushed slowly, he made racing engine sounds all the way to the boat. Meanwhile, Donatella pulled out her cell phone and chattered away in Italian.

"Our table at the Poste Vecie will be ready in an hour," Kathleen informed them. "We'll drop the jewels off at the Society first for safekeeping. Donatella's talking to her boss right now."

By the Italian woman's tone and frequent exclamations, it was quite a spirited discourse. Sam seated herself in the back of the boat next to Keirnan, while Kathleen and Donatella, who were still talking, took the seats up front by Carlo.

From what Sam had gathered during the cart ride, the Poste Vecie was a charming restaurant in a building that dated back to the 1500s. The idea of food had definite appeal, and the setting sounded highly appropriate, but she would have preferred to be alone with Keirnan.

Past lives, predestination, or just plain crazy, she didn't care. Somehow, Keirnan Fitzgerald *would* be in her life, and she would do whatever was necessary to make sure he was. But in the meantime, she wanted to take advantage of every remaining moment they could spend together here and now.

Fighting the blush heating her cheeks, she snuggled

closer against Keirnan's side. "I know what I want for dessert," she murmured close to his ear. "Room service."

"Do you now?" Flashing his wicked, Irish rogue grin, he bent his head and nuzzled her neck.

A different kind of heat washed over Sam. Her bones began to liquefy.

"Did you hear that, brother of mine?" Kathleen suddenly demanded.

Keirnan jerked his lips away. "This better be good."

"Donatella says the Society will pay us a kind of finders' fee for the jewels," his sister gushed, perhaps not as totally oblivious of her poor timing as Sam wanted to believe. "Of several *thousand* Euros! I suppose that should help you and Sam get back to America."

"I suppose it will." Keirnan's tone was far less enthusiastic, but Kathleen didn't let that stop her from continuing.

"And the Society may be willing to help me finance further research. There were originally seven jewels after all, and I'm sure Serafina and Nino went to Padua—"

"Wonderful!" Keirnan interrupted with mock eagerness. "Do you think you might possibly leave tonight?"

From his place behind the wheel, Carlo snorted. Kathleen shot a disdainful glare at both men, and then turned back to her animated discussion with Donatella.

Sam couldn't suppress a chuckle. Then Keirnan draped his arm around her shoulders, and a warm, peaceful glow enveloped her. She settled back against him and watched the slender brick steeple of the Campanile and golden round domes of St. Mark's Cathedral draw closer.

Had she ever felt this happy before?

"Carlo, let us off near the gondolier stand, will you?"

Keirnan asked as they approached the entrance to the Grand Canal.

With a nod of his head, the taciturn Interpol agent cut the engine and pulled the boat to the edge of the piazza opposite the Doge's Palace. Kathleen and Donatella turned questioning gazes at Keirnan.

"'Tis Samantha's first time in Venice," he explained with a sardonic lift of his brow. "And she needs to take a proper gondola ride."

Kathleen raised her chin and gave a haughty sniff. "Fine, but we shan't wait for you if you arrive at the restaurant late."

He clambered out of the boat and offered Sam his hand. "I'd not expect you to do differently."

Sam seriously doubted she would ever get used to their verbal sparring, but she really didn't mind. Not as long as she could be with Keirnan.

She grasped his hand and heaved herself none too gracefully onto the pavement. She had no sooner steadied her wobbly knee than Carlo gunned the motor. Amid a cloud of diesel fumes and Donatella's cry of "*Ciao!*" the boat roared off down the Grand Canal, leaving the two of them alone at last.

Keirnan pulled her hand into the crook of his arm. "Don't worry luv, I promise we won't miss supper." He gave her a smoldering look that made her heart stutter. "Or dessert."

Anticipation sizzled through her veins as they threaded their way through the people and flocks of pigeons.

"Um… what if we have dessert first?"

"Now, now," he scolded, but his azure eyes sparkled with mischief. "First things first."

They strolled past the tall, round column with the majestic winged lion poised on top. In front of them at the edge of the piazza, a long line of shiny black gondolas bobbed on their moorings. Gondoliers in their traditional black-and-white striped shirts and flat straw hats called out to the crowds of tourists.

The scene was every cliché of Venice Sam had ever imagined. Sheer delight made her giddy.

"So is this gondola ride part of the exclusive Fitzgerald tour?"

"Indeed it is." His lopsided grin drove the air right out of her lungs.

"*Buon giorno,* Signor, Signorina." A brawny gondolier with a tanned, deeply etched face greeted them. "I am Ermanno. May I be of service?"

"Can you take us to the Poste Vecie? 'Tis by the Rialto Fish Market." Keirnan let go of her hand and extracted some bills from his wallet. "But we'd like to go slowly, *lento.* And can you take us under the Bridge of Sighs first?"

"*Si.*" The man's dark eyes gleamed knowingly as he pocketed the money. "The Bridge of Sighs on the way to the Pescheria. I know a very romantic way." He bowed and made a sweeping gesture toward his gondola. "*Prego.* If you please."

"*Va bene,* very good," Keirnan acknowledged, pulling another bill from his wallet. "And do you sing, Ermanno?"

"I will do my best, Signor." The money disappeared before he added, "But I am no Pavarotti."

"No problem. We don't want opera." Keirnan squeezed Sam's hand and winked as he helped her step into the narrow boat. "No tragic endings for us. Sing something happy when we get to the bridge."

"*Tutto va bene*. Everything is good," Ermanno replied.

Then placing his straw hat on his head, he climbed onto the back of the gondola and grasped the long oar.

The boat glided smoothly away from its mooring post and into the dark water of the lagoon. All around them other gondolas slid through the water, somehow managing not to hit each other.

"This is wonderful," Sam sighed.

She leaned against Keirnan's solid warmth and nestled her head on his shoulder. He rested his cheek against her hair for a long silent moment as they floated past the Doge's Palace.

Sunlight flashed on the ornate metal prow of the gondola while the water lapped rhythmically against the sides. This was better than the best dream she'd ever had.

"Wasn't your ex-fiancé's name Michael something?"

Sam jerked upright at Keirnan's unexpected question. "Michael Atcheson. Why?"

He ran his fingertips down the length of her hair, brushing his knuckles across her cheek. "When we get to Bloomington, I need to ring him up and thank him for breaking your engagement."

His tone was so matter-of-fact that he might have been discussing the weather, while utter shock coursed through Sam. "And I intend to make it very clear to him that I'll never be such a fool."

He tried to ease her head back against his shoulder, but Sam remained stiff with surprise. "'When we get to'—you're going to Bloomington?"

"Yes, if that's where you're going." His eyes still

held a hint of mischievous sparkle. "Surely they have commercial real estate there."

Sam tried to swallow, but the moisture had evaporated from her mouth. "I, uh... actually, I planned to relocate to Philadelphia. Surely they have libraries there."

His smile dazzled her. "Indeed they do." He laced his fingers with hers, then his expression suddenly turned serious. "I don't care where we are, as long as we're together." He took a shaky breath. "Samantha, luv, I—saying 'I love you' sounds so inadequate for what I feel for you."

Her heart pounded so loud in her ears that she couldn't think. "I know. I mean... me too. That is—"

Keirnan placed two fingers across her lips to stop her words. His forehead touched hers.

"There it is Signor, Signorina," the gondolier announced. "The Bridge of Sighs."

Sam looked up and gasped. The slanting rays of the late afternoon sun had turned the marble façade of the archway to a golden rose color. The curlicues across the top shone gilded with gold. Echoing gasps sounded from the tourists crowding the Ponte della Paglia Bridge behind them.

"I take it you're now more suitably impressed with this romantic Venetian landmark," Keirnan teased.

Temporarily robbed of her breath, Sam nodded. She stared into the sapphire depths of his eyes, and the words of Christopher Marlowe sprang into her mind.

"'Whoever loved that loved not at first sight?'" she quoted in a whisper.

"Who indeed?"

Keirnan's lips found hers.

"'Saaan-taaah Luuuu-chee-ah!'" The gondolier warbled. "Santa Lucia."

Three hours later, Keirnan easily finessed the lock on their hotel room and held the door open for Samantha. With a wry smile and a shake of her head, she walked past him.

While she set a Styrofoam container on the nearest nightstand, he shucked off his new leather jacket, and then helped her remove hers. Holding the coat in one hand, he pushed her hair aside so that he could kiss the side of her neck, but she scooted away.

"What a shame you were feeling too bad to finish dessert at the restaurant," she said, opening the container. "Looks like I'll have to eat this tiramisu all by myself."

Like that was the real reason he'd been anxious to leave.

Playing along, he replied, "What luck, I seem to have made a miraculous recovery on the vaporetto."

He stuck his finger into the edge of the icing, smeared the cream on her chin, and quickly licked it off. "Mmm, sweet."

She made a tsking sound. "How messy! I think I better feed you."

"Good plan!"

He wasted no time kicking off his shoes and crawling onto the closest bed, anxious to finish what they'd started last night in his hospital room.

Meanwhile, Samantha made quite a production of slowly chewing a forkful of the gooey cake, and then running her tongue across her lower lip. The surge of desire that raced through him effectively wiped out any residual aches and pains and made Keirnan groan aloud.

"Oh dear, I'm as messy as you," she murmured, sucking icing off her index finger. "You should probably take off your sweater to make sure I don't get anything on it."

Thinking he might die of the anticipation, he peeled the garment over his head, followed by his T-shirt. He heard her breath give a little catch and saw her eyes darken as they roamed over his bare torso. Twin spots of pink glowed on her cheeks.

"Why stop there? The first time I found you in my hotel room, you were naked."

How and why he'd managed to wind up there would always remain a mystery. Or maybe truly a miracle.

"Indeed I was, but you hardly seemed to notice."

She sat on the edge of the bed and carefully fed him a bite of cake. He barely tasted anything as he gulped it down. She took another forkful for herself and toed off her sneakers while she chewed.

"Believe me, I noticed." Her eyes never left his mouth while she speared another piece. "But I'd just had my heart broken, remember?"

Keirnan tasted no more of the second bite than he had the first. Instead, he swallowed it down then pulled her against him.

"Ah, yes, and has it healed?" he asked, just before he began an exploration of her throat with his lips.

Samantha gave a breathy little moan. "Just like you, I've made a miraculous recovery."

He stopped nibbling long enough to say, "Lovely miracles…"

Then they were interrupted by the crackling of the Styrofoam container crumpling between them.

"Saints in heaven, woman! Aren't you done with that bloody cake yet?"

With a knowing gleam of a smile, she scooped up the last of the tiramisu and smeared it down his bare chest.

"Almost."

She tossed the empty container on the floor and followed the trail of sweetness with her tongue.

The flaming roar of desire burned away Keirnan's last coherent thought. Her sweater quickly followed the container, along with her bra and both their jeans.

A moment later, her heated bare flesh melded against his as he sucked the sticky icing off her fingers, and then her breasts. Next, he peeled her knickers down her legs and shucked them onto the heap on the floor while she returned the favor.

Her hand caressing his hard length nearly sent him over the edge. He'd waited long enough. Entirely too long to take his time.

Tumbling her beneath him, he claimed first her mouth, then with a single thrust, her hot moist core. He wanted her, needed her more than his next breath. And as she met his next thrust, and they rushed together toward completion, he knew she felt the same.

Truly the greatest miracle of all.

A short while later, as they lay spooned together in the aftermath of climax, he whispered into the silky strands of her hair, "Grá mo chroí."

She was that and so much more, but he couldn't find adequate words in any language.

"You're the love of mine too," Samantha murmured

in a husky tone that stirred the heat in his veins all over again. But then she turned to face him, confusion clouding her golden green eyes.

"Do you think your sister was right? About the two of us being Nino and Serafina, I mean."

"I don't know," Keirnan answered honestly. "But she was right about one thing, I'll need more than one lifetime to finish loving you."

The End

A Few Facts about This Story

The story was inspired by the opera *The Jewels of the Madonna* written by Venetian composer Ermanno Wolf-Ferrari in 1911.

While Serafina, her sister Simonetta, and the other characters in the story are wholly fictitious, Pietro Lombardo really was a renowned fifteenth-century Venetian architect. He and his sons, Tullio and Antonio, designed and built the Santa Maria dei Miracoli church in 1485.

The famous Renaissance artist Luca della Robbia did produce a beautiful and distinctive blue glaze for his ceramic sculptures, many of which can still be seen in the Bargello Museum in Florence, Italy.

All the Venetian landmarks (the Doge's Palace, the Bridge of Sighs, the Rialto Bridge, and San Michele en Isola, to name a few) are real locales which the author tried to portray as accurately as possible.

Acknowledgments

For me, writing a book is my greatest joy and also a great challenge. That was certainly the case with this story, and as usual, I was fortunate to have the support and assistance of many friends and family. Since I don't have the space nor the brain capacity to thank everyone, I would like to give recognition and a special thank you to a few specific people:

First and foremost to Dave, my all time favorite ceramic sculptor, who took me to the number one place on my "bucket list," Venice, stopping off in Florence on the way to show me my very first della Robbia. I can never thank you enough for your love and support, and for enduring "fat cherub overload" just for me.

My editor, Deb Werksman, for giving this story a second look and deciding she loved it enough after all.

For my First Reader Extraordinaire, Marlyn A. Farley, who truly went above and beyond with her support and encouragement. Keirnan's middle name is just for you.

My critique partners, Aimee Carper, Cathy Decker, and Jo Lewis-Robertson, for all your insightful comments and for embracing my characters (especially Keirnan) as your own. I couldn't have done it without you!

My dear friend and writer-buddy Tina Ferraro for all the wonderful pictures and even a map of the Cemetery

Isle! And a very special thanks for giving me an authentic northern Italian name for Carlo.

My BFFs Whit and Shirl and all my many wonderful friends who cheered me on and believed so strongly in me and this story, most especially Sharen, who was so caught up that she kept reading right into the bathtub, and Donee Sue, who inspired me to create Donatella.

Writing sisters of my heart: Jeanne, Beth, FoAnna, Caren, Kate, KJ, Joanie, Christie, Jo (again!), Donna, Trish, Cassondra, Nancy, Kirsten, Susan, Vrai Anna, Tawny, Christine, and Suz, aka The Romance Bandits. It was because of this story that I met you, and I am so grateful for your continued love, good humor, and support. Banditas Rule!

About the Author

Blessed with the gift of "Irish Blarney," Loucinda McGary (everyone calls her Cindy) became a storyteller shortly after she learned to read. If she didn't like the way a story ended, she made up her own ending.

A longtime reader of romances, Cindy discovered and joined Romance Writers of America in 2001. At the end of 2003, she decided to leave her management career to pursue her twin passions of travel and writing. Cindy likes to set her novels of romance and suspense in some of the fascinating places she has visited.

Cindy loves to hear from readers, writers, and just about everybody! Please drop her an email:

cindy@loucindamcgary.com

Or send her a postcard for her ever-increasing collection:

P.O. Box 15492
Sacramento, CA 95813

For more from Loucinda McGary, read on for an
excerpt of

The WILD
SIGHT

Available from Sourcebooks Casablanca

Chapter 1

Donovan O'Shea strode across the dried grass behind the ramshackle cottage that had been in his family for at least five generations. The odor of freshly dug earth and the unique miasma arising from the nearby fens filled his nostrils. Nothing in America smelled remotely the same. And breathing it in evoked memories, none too pleasant.

The leaden October sky promised rain before the day was done, and Donovan picked up his pace, anxious to get this visit behind him. His light American running shoes made no noise, but he could hear the faint scraping sounds of a shovel in the otherwise still air. Up ahead of him heavy twine stretched between small wooden stakes, and two neat mounds of earth marked the area of activity.

"Hello? Professor McRory?" he called out to herald his own arrival. Nobody else would be out here. Heaven knew, he didn't want to be.

Aongus McRory's head and shoulders appeared above the lip of the trench he'd been digging. A half-second later, the head of his assistant, Sybil Gallagher, popped up beside him. The two reminded Donovan of a pair of prairie dogs he'd once seen on a holiday to Yellowstone Park.

"O'Shea!" McRory's deep baritone quavered with the same eagerness as it had on the phone twenty minutes ago. "Thank you for coming out here straight away." He pitched his small spade next to the mound of dirt and clambered out of the hole.

Reluctance took a firm grip of Donovan's subconscious, and he slowed his approach. "So you've found another pit?"

The professor wiped his hand on the leg of his canvas trousers then extended it to help his assistant. "Indeed we have! And this one, ah, this one is a beauty!"

"No more dog bones?"

The hair on the back of Donovan's neck prickled, as he remembered how he'd stumbled on the first storage pit a fortnight ago. The air going into his lungs felt inexplicably heavy, and he stopped walking.

The other man rushed on, "Much more exciting! Wait 'til you see."

Shoving his fair hair from his eyes with the back of his hand, McRory rummaged in a box on the ground with the other.

"Have a look." He thrust a dark, metal object in Donovan's direction. "'Tis a torc, late Bronze Age, I'm almost certain."

Donovan stared at the circular neck ornament in the professor's hand and the breath caught in his throat. A loud noise buzzed inside his head, a sound he recognized though he'd not experienced it for many years. He knew what was about to happen, but was helpless to stop it.

A moment later, his vision blurred into a spiraling mass of green, brown, and gray. The buzz faded, and in its place arose a harsh cacophony, the guttural blast of a war trumpet, the pounding of sword hilts against shields, and the strident shouts of men. Then the stench of the battlefield enveloped him.

Sweat, blood, and trampled earth.

The whirling shapes coalesced into men, bearded warriors with long, flowing hair. They brandished broadswords and carried oblong shields, but wore nothing except close-fitting helmets on their heads, torcs around their necks, and leather sword belts encircling their hips.

Donovan stared at the heavy sword clenched in his right hand and the shield in his left and realized he was part of this battle too. Splotches of red and ochre paint swirled down his arms and across his bare chest.

The blaring of more war trumpets set his teeth on edge, while the men around him surged forward. He jostled the man next to him, a hulking giant, even taller than Donovan and half again as broad, though not an ounce was fat. Dark, tangled hair streamed from beneath the warrior's helmet past his heavily muscled shoulders, and a bristly black beard obscured the lower half of his face. Still, something in the depths of his bright blue eyes and in the tilt of his head sparked a long-ago memory in the back of Donovan's disoriented mind.

"Ro?" His own voice sounded strange inside his head.

Somehow, through the din, the warrior heard him. His eyes skimmed Donovan's features. Then his black eyebrows lifted in surprise. "Dony?"

The pet name his mother, Moira, had given him. In her soft countrified accent, it rhymed with Tony. No one had called Donovan that since he was seven years old.

"Dony," the enormous man repeated in the same accent. "So you're all grown-up as well."

Donovan had no time to answer or voice the thousand questions that leapt into his mind, for the enemy was upon them. A half-dozen similarly armed men

charged at him. Ro and the other warrior beside him
lunged forward and Donovan felt his own sword rise
as he blocked first one blow then another. The shock
of metal crashing against metal coursed down his arm,
while more warriors from both factions joined in the
fray. Screams of pain and rage rang in his ears.

The man battling Ro crumpled in wordless agony,
bright red blood gushing onto the ground under him,
even as another sprang to take his place. The enormous
warrior dispatched his second opponent with even greater
speed, blood spattering his shield and helmet. Donovan
was not so skilled. Sweat stung his eyes as he struggled
to block and parry the blows his adversary rained down
upon him, and he was forced to give ground. But when
the man advanced to renew his attack, his foot slipped
on the blood-soaked grass, and he staggered. Donovan
lunged, and pulled his sword back. Gore dripped from
the blade.

As the man fell to his knees with a shuddering groan,
Donovan realized that Ro and his companions had turned
the attack into a rout. Their enemy fled toward the fens,
defenders roaring in victory on their heels. Then the man
in front of Donovan fell over, writhing in agony.

"Take his head!" Ro shouted.

Donovan jerked his gaze up and saw two severed
heads tied by their hair at his friend's sword belt. Bile
rushed from Donovan's stomach to his throat.

"'Tis your war prize, man!" Ro shouted again. Blood
glistened on his forearms and thighs. He reached down
and grabbed the man's hair, pulling his exposed throat
toward Donovan. "Take it!"

The stench of death and the overwhelming urge to

vomit swamped Donovan. Swaying, he squeezed his eyes shut, and drew in a deep breath of fetid air. A flash of white light exploded behind his eyelids and his pulse pounded loud in his ears. The smell receded.

From a great distance, he could just make out a woman's voice calling, "Mr. O'Shea? Mr. O'Shea!"

Then a man's voice, more distinctive, cried, "Donovan!" Fingers gripped his arm and shook. "Jaysus, man! Are you all right?"

Donovan opened his eyes into the worried gaze of Professor McRory. The noise, the stench, the battlefield had disappeared. But not his urge to vomit. He flung off McRory's hand, stumbled a few steps away, then doubled over and retched into a clump of weeds. Coughing, he gripped his jean-clad thighs to steady himself.

"Sybil, get that stool!" McRory barked out the command, and rested his hand on Donovan's shoulder. "All right, then?"

Awash in humiliation, he straightened and wiped his mouth across his sleeve. The professor guided him backward to a three-legged canvas stool and Donovan sunk down onto it, consciously steadying his breathing.

"Here's water, Mr. O'Shea." Pale blue eyes completely round with alarm, McRory's assistant handed Donovan a clear plastic bottle.

"Thanks." He swirled the first gulp around inside his mouth and spat it out. The second swallow felt cool and fortifying as it slid down his throat. The third was almost as good.

Taking a deep breath, he stood, his mother's long ago admonition ringing inside his head, "Never talk about your gift, Dony. People don't understand."

Some gift. Curse, more like.

He gave McRory and Sybil a wan smile. "So sorry. Must have been bad pub grub. But I'm all right now."

Though Sybil's expression remained uneasy, McRory clapped him on the shoulder. "Ah, right nasty stuff it must have been. I thought you were falling over there for a moment."

Still feeling self-conscious, Donovan switched subjects. "About the new pit . . ."

A spark of excitement ignited in the professor's eyes. "I've already contacted my department chair at Queen's. If this Bronze Age site follows true to form, there are more storage pits. The Celts laid them out in semi-circles."

"This could be the find of a career!" Sybil broke in, enthusiasm turning her mousy features almost attractive.

"Certainly significant enough to send a proper team out here to the site, not just Syb and me." McRory clapped Donovan on the shoulder like his new comrade-in-arms. "And maybe enough to convince the government to buy your family's property. Exactly how far into the fens does it go?"

"I don't know," Donovan admitted. "The fens have shifted even since I lived here as a child. And my mother's family has been here at least since the Hunger."

The professor warmed to his subject, all but rubbing his hands together in anticipatory glee. "You'll need to search the property records then." Sybil nodded in eager agreement, while McRory continued, "And with your consent, I'll contact a journalist friend of mine in Belfast. A blurb on one of the wire services might give just the extra nudge some official needs to expedite purchase."

An expedited purchase was exactly what Donovan wanted, and he didn't particularly care by whom. The sooner he left County Armagh and all of Ireland, the better. "All right, if you think that's the best course. You're far more familiar with this sort of thing than I'll ever be."

The pair seemed to have forgotten his momentary "illness," but for how long?

Donovan intended to avoid the dig site as much as possible, avoid contact with anything that might trigger his "gift" again. Just get himself back to America, where he never experienced anything remotely like visions.

Until his father's stroke four months ago, he'd come home exactly once since he emigrated at age seventeen. That had been nine years ago for his sister's wedding, and he stayed far away from the deserted homestead. Too bad he couldn't do the same this time. The physicians seemed pleased with his father's progress, and with the proceeds from the sale of the pub and the property, Donovan and his sister could get the old man into the best private rehab program in Northern Ireland.

He drained the remaining water in one long guzzle, and handed the empty bottle to Sybil Gallagher. "Thanks, I'll be in touch."

"Likewise," McRory affirmed.

Rylie Powell parked her rented car in front of a store with a chipped sign that proclaimed "Dry Goods and Hardware."

She stared across the street at the window illuminated by two neon signs. The yellow one featured a stylized Irish harp with the word "Harp" written below. The dark blue one simply said "Guinness." No other distinguishing signs hung on the door or window, but none was needed.

The manager of her B&B in Dungannon hadn't been kidding when she said the village of Ballyneagh was small. The long wooden structures on either side of the badly paved road were divided into four businesses. The pub was one of the center stores across the street, situated between a nameless barbershop and Brigit's Bakery. She had passed a scattering of a dozen stone cottages right before the line of shops, and through the growing twilight, she could see four more houses beyond the bakery.

Snagging her purse off the floor in front of the passenger's seat, Rylie shoved the car key into one purse pocket and pulled her lipstick from another. Three weeks ago, she'd never heard of this place, never guessed that it existed. Two days ago, she'd flown across an entire continent and an ocean to get here. Yesterday, she'd struggled to drive on the wrong side of the roadway over endless wet miles of country lanes in search of this little scrap of a burg and its no-name pub. All this effort so she could confront the man who had walked away from her and her mother almost twenty-five years ago. The owner of the pub, her father, Dermot O'Shea.

She peered into the rearview mirror to apply her lipstick and gave an inward sigh. Why the hell was she worried about how she looked? She wasn't here to seek his approval. More like, to rub his nose in the fact that by shirking his responsibilities as a father, he'd missed out. But that wasn't really the reason either.

For as long as Rylie could remember, there had been a gap in her identity that went far beyond using her stepfather's last name. In the six months since losing her mother to cancer, she had become consumed with unraveling the riddles of who she really was and where her roots lay. Riddles, she grew convinced, only her biological father could answer. Ghosts only he could put to rest.

At least the rain had dissipated to a drizzle. She flipped up the hood of her neon yellow windbreaker, the one she wore when jogging, and got out of the car. Dashing across the two-lane road, she pulled open the heavy door and stepped inside the pub. She folded back her hood and pulled her long hair free while her eyes adjusted to the dim interior.

Slowly, the large room came into focus. A long, gleaming, wooden bar hugged the wall closest to the front door and a dartboard hung in the far corner. The opposite wall had four high-backed booths built into it, three of them currently occupied. A half-dozen round tables were arranged in the center of the room, all empty. Unlike the bars Rylie had ventured into in California, this place had a surprisingly homey atmosphere in spite of a lingering odor of cigarette smoke.

Eyes now accustomed to the gloom, she consciously straightened into her "walking tall" posture, though at five-foot two-and-a-half inches tall was a relative term. She approached the bar. The two elderly men lounging against the polished wood, glasses of dark brew in hand, gave her openly appreciative looks, which she patently ignored.

The bartender bustled over, a gap-toothed grin on his ruddy face. "What'll it be, darlin'?"

Rylie studied his middle-aged countenance for a moment before she answered, "A Coke." Then, when he picked up a glass she added, "With ice."

"To be sure," the man said in the musical brogue that Rylie's ears were still not quite attuned to. "'Tis how all you Yanks like it. Right enough?" He didn't wait for her reply, but continued with a steady stream of talk that most everyone she had encountered in the past two days seemed adept at doing. "So what part of the States are you from, luv?"

Rylie could feel every eye in the place staring as the bartender plunked the fizzy beverage in front of her.

"And what would bring a pretty wan such as you to the middle of bloody nowhere such as this?"

The bartender chuckled at his own wit while Rylie sipped through the thin red straw and studied him. Short and paunchy, with thinning red hair faded to gray around his temples, he looked nothing like the few aged snap-shots she had of her father.

"I'm from California," she said, taking another sip of soda. "And I'm looking for someone."

The WILD SIGHT

by Loucinda McGary

"A magical tale of romance and intrigue. I couldn't put it down!" —Pamela Palmer, author of *Dark Deceiver* and *The Dark Gate*

◇◇◇◇◇

He was cursed with a "gift"

Born with the clairvoyance known to the Irish as "The Sight," Donovan O'Shea fled to America to escape his visions. On a return trip to Ireland to see his ailing father, staggering family secrets threaten to turn his world upside down. And then beautiful, sensual Rylie Powell shows up, claiming to be his half-sister...

She's looking for the family she never knew...

After her mother's death, Rylie journeys to Ireland to find her mysterious father. She needs the truth—but how can she and Donovan be brother and sister when the chemistry between them is nearly irresistible?

Uncovering the past leads them dangerously close to madness...

◇◇◇◇◇

"A richly drawn love story and riveting romantic suspense!" —Karin Tabke, author of *What You Can't See*

978-1-4022-1394-6 • $6.99 U.S. / $8.99 CAN

IN OVER HER HEAD

by Judi Fennell

"Holy mackerel! *In Over Her Head* is a
fantastically fun romantic catch!"

—Michelle Rowen, author of *Bitten & Smitten*

○ ○ ○ ○ ○ ○ **HE LIVES UNDER THE SEA** ○ ○ ○ ○ ○ ○

Reel Tritone is the rebellious royal second son of the ruler
of a vast undersea kingdom. A Merman, born with legs
instead of a tail, he's always been fascinated by humans,
especially one young woman he once saw swimming near
his family's reef...

○ ○ ○ ○ ○ **SHE'S TERRIFIED OF THE OCEAN** ○ ○ ○ ○ ○

Ever since the day she swam out too far and heard voices
in the water, marina owner Erica Peck won't go swimming
for anything—until she's forced into the water by a shady
ex-boyfriend searching for stolen diamonds, and is nearly
eaten by a shark...luckily Reel is nearby to save her, and
discovers she's the woman he's been searching for...

978-1-4022-2001-2 • $6.99 U.S. / $7.99 CAN

call of the highland moon

BY KENDRA LEIGH CASTLE

A Highlands werewolf fleeing his destiny, and the warm-hearted woman who takes him in…

Not ready for the responsibilities of an alpha wolf, Gideon MacInnes leaves Scotland and seeks the quiet hills of upstate New York. When he is attacked by rogue wolves and collapses on Carly Silver's doorstep, she thinks she's rescuing a wounded animal. But she awakens to find that the beast has turned into a devastatingly handsome, naked man.

With a supernatural enemy stalking them, their only hope is to get back to Scotland, where Carly has to risk becoming a werewolf herself, or give up the one man she's ever truly loved.

"Call of the Highland Moon **thrills with seductive romance and breathtaking suspense."** —Alyssa Day, *USA Today* **bestselling author of** *Atlantis Awakening*

978-1-4022-1158-4 • $6.99 U.S. / $8.99 CAN

DARK
HIGHLAND
FIRE

BY KENDRA LEIGH CASTLE

A werewolf from the Scottish Highlands and a fiery
demi-goddess fleeing for her life…

Desired by women, kissed by luck, Gabriel MacInnes has
always been able to put pleasure ahead of duty. But with
the MacInnes wolves now squarely in the sights of an
ancient enemy, everything is about to change…

Rowan *an* Morgaine, on the run from a dragon prince who
will stop at nothing to have her as his own, must accept
the protection of Gabriel and his clan. By force or by
guile, Rowan and Gabriel must uncover the secrets of their
intertwining fate and stop their common enemy.

**"This fresh and exciting take on the werewolf
legend held me captive."**

—NINA BANGS, AUTHOR OF *ONE BITE STAND*

978-1-4022-1159-1 • $6.99 U.S. / $8.99 CAN

WILD HIGHLAND MAGIC

BY KENDRA LEIGH CASTLE

She's a Scottish Highlands werewolf

Growing up in America, Catrionna MacInnes always tried desperately to control her powers and pretend to be normal…

He's a wizard prince with a devastating secret

The minute Cat lays eyes on Bastian, she knows she's met her destiny. In their first encounter, she unwittingly binds him to her for life, and now they're both targets for the evil enemies out to destroy their very souls.

Praise for Kendra Leigh Castle:

"Fans of straight up romance looking for a little extra something will be bitten." —*Publishers Weekly*

978-1-4022-1856-9 • $7.99 U.S. / $8.99 CAN

Romeo, Romeo

— BY ROBIN KAYE —

Rosalie Ronaldi doesn't have a domestic bone in her body...

All she cares about is her career, so she survives on take-out and dirty martinis, keeps her shoes under the dining room table, her bras on the shower curtain rod, and her clothes on the couch.

Nick Romeo is every woman's fantasy— tall, dark, handsome, rich, really good in bed, AND he loves to cook and clean...

He says he wants an independent woman, but when he meets Rosalie, all he wants to do is take care of her. Before long, he's cleaned up her apartment, stocked her refrigerator, and adopted her dog.

So what's the problem? Just a little matter of mistaken identity, corporate theft, a hidden past in juvenile detention, and one big nosy Italian family too close for comfort...

"Kaye's debut is a delightfully fun, witty romance, making her a writer to watch." —*Booklist*

978-1-4022-1339-7 • $6.99 U.S. / $8.99 CAN

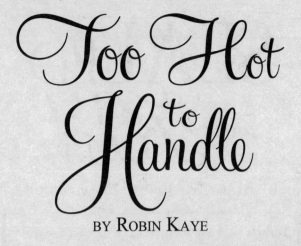

Too Hot to Handle

by Robin Kaye

He sure would love to have a woman to take care of...

To Dr. Mike Flynn, there's nothing like housework to help a guy relax, while artist Annabelle Ronaldi doesn't have a domestic bone in her body.

When they meet at her sister's wedding, Mike is sure this is the woman he wants to take care of forever. While Mike sets to work wooing Annabelle, she becomes determined to sniff out the truth of the convoluted family secret that's threatening to turn both their lives upside down.

PRAISE FOR *ROMEO, ROMEO*:

"Robin Kaye is sure to leave readers looking for a good Italian meal and a man as delicious as the hero." —*BookPage*

"Robin Kaye strikes gold... and deserves to have her name added to your favorite new author list." —*Book Loons*

978-1-4022-1766-1 • $6.99 U.S. / $7.99 CAN

SEALED
with a *Kiss*

BY MARY MARGRET DAUGHTRIDGE

THERE'S ONLY ONE THING HE CAN'T HANDLE, AND ONE WOMAN WHO CAN HELP HIM...

Jax Graham is a rough, tough Navy SEAL, but when it comes to taking care of his four-year-old son after his ex-wife dies, he's completely clueless. Family therapist Pickett Sessoms can help, but only if he'll let her.

When Jax and his little boy get trapped by a hurricane, Picket takes them in against her better judgment. When the situation turns deadly, Pickett discovers what it means to be a SEAL, and Jax discovers that even a hero needs help sometimes.

"A heart-touching story that will keep you smiling and cheering for the characters clear through to the happy ending." —Romantic Times

"A well-written romance... simultaneously tender and sensuous." —Booklist

978-1-4022-1118-8 • $6.99 U.S. / $8.99 CAN

SEALed

with a

Promise

BY MARY MARGRET DAUGHTRIDGE

NAVY SEAL CALEB DELAUDE IS AS DEADLY AS HE IS CHARMING.

Professor Emmie Caddington's quiet intelligence and quirky personality intrigue him. When he discovers that her personal connections can get him close to the man he's vowed to kill, will their budding relationship be nothing more than a means to revenge...or is she the key to his salvation?

Praise for *SEALed with a Kiss*:

"This story delivers in a huge way." —Romantic Times

"A wonderful story that will have readers experiencing a whirlwind of emotions and culminating with an awesome scene that will have your pulse pounding." —Romance Junkies

"What an incredibly powerful book! I laughed and sniffled, was turned on and turned inside out." —Queue My Review

978-1-4022-1763-0 • $6.99 U.S. / $7.99 CAN

Line of
SCRIMMAGE

BY MARIE FORCE

SHE'S GIVEN UP ON HIM AND MOVED ON...

Susannah finally has peace, calm, a sedate life, and a no-surprises man. Marriage to football superstar Ryan Sanderson was a whirlwind, but Susanna got sick of playing second fiddle to his team. With their divorce just a few weeks away, she's already planning her wedding with her new fiancé.

HE'S FINALLY FIGURED OUT WHAT'S REALLY IMPORTANT TO HIM. IF ONLY IT'S NOT TOO LATE...

Ryan has just ten days to convince his soon-to-be-ex-wife to give him a second chance. His career is at its pinnacle, but in the year of their separation, Ryan's come to realize it doesn't mean anything without Susannah...

978-1-4022-1424-0 • $6.99 U.S. / $8.99 CAN

THE
PRINCE
OF
MIDNIGHT

BY LAURA KINSALE
New York Times bestselling author

"Readers should be enchanted."
—*Publishers Weekly*

INTENT ON REVENGE, ALL SHE WANTS FROM
HIM IS TO LEARN HOW TO KILL

Lady Leigh Strachan has crossed all of France in search
of S.T. Maitland, nobleman, highwayman, and legendary
swordsman, once known as the Prince of Midnight. Now
he's hiding out in a crumbling castle with a tame wolf as his
only companion, trying to conceal his deafness and desperation. Leigh is terribly disappointed to find the man behind
the legend doesn't meet her expectations. But when they're
forced on a quest together, she discovers the dangerous and
vital man behind the mask, and he finds a way to touch her
ice cold heart.

"No one—repeat, no one—writes historical
romance better." —Mary Jo Putney

978-1-4022-1397-7 • $7.99 U.S./$8.99 CAN

MIDSUMMER MOON

BY LAURA KINSALE
New York Times bestselling author

> "The acknowledged master."
> —*Albany Times-Union*

**IF HE REALLY LOVED HER,
WOULDN'T HE HELP HER REALIZE HER DREAM?**

When inventor Merlin Lambourne is endangered by Napoleon's advancing forces, Lord Ransom Falconer, in service of his government, comes to her rescue and falls under the spell of her beauty and absent-minded brilliance. But he is horrified by her dream of building a flying machine—and not only because he is determined to keep her safe.

> "Laura Kinsale writes the kind of works that live in your heart." —Elizabeth Grayson

> "A true storyteller, Laura Kinsale has managed to break all the rules of standard romance writing and come away shining."
> —*San Diego Union-Tribune*

978-1-4022-1398-4 • $7.99 U.S./$8.99 CAN

SEIZE THE FIRE

BY LAURA KINSALE
New York Times bestselling author

"Magic and beauty flow from
Laura Kinsale's pen." —*Romantic Times*

AN UNLIKELY PRINCESS SHIPWRECKED
WITH A WAR HERO WHO'S GOT HELL TO PAY

Her Serene Highness Olympia of Oriens—plump, demure, and idealistic—longs to return to her tiny, embattled land and lead her people to justice and freedom. Famous hero Captain Sheridan Drake, destitute and tormented by nightmares of the carnage he's seen, means only to rob and abandon her. What is Olympia to do with the tortured man behind the hero's façade? And how will they cope when their very survival depends on each other?

"One of the best writers in the history of the
romance genre." —*All About Romance*

978-1-4022-1396-0 • $7.99 U.S./$8.99 CAN